Edge of Hope

The Edge Series: Book One

Lennan Daniels

Because consent matters…

While far darker works exist, The Edge Series may be too intense for some readers. We use p-words and c-words here. Every character has a backstory, and the sex leaves marks.

Please visit LennanDaniels.com for a list of content warnings specific to each installment in The Edge Series.

For specific questions or to recommend additions to the list of content warnings, reach out via social media or the author's website.

For those with cracked foundations and battered hearts.
The ones shamed for how they love or who they are.
For the Not-Good-Enoughs and the Too-Muches.

For us.

And for my person.
You know who you are.

HOPE

Bad for you is a potent aphrodisiac. Hope Lawson knew this with absolute certainty, as she sipped her Cab Sauv. Some things, not unlike the wine in her glass, were so wickedly seductive that, even when painted poison-apple-red, a small voice whispered that a little taste never hurt anyone. At least, it felt that way tonight. Maybe this was a rebound effect.

Hope's ex was the proverbial boy-scout-all-grown-up, and look how that turned out. But a guy with ink crawling up his forearms, standing under a hand-painted sign that read *You won't like him when he's Irish*, and surrounded by copious amounts of liquor? Tantalizing, if only because he inhabited the opposite end of the spectrum.

Devon Cleary looked nothing like a boy scout.

Devon Cleary looked like something to taste.

Add in the stress of the last three months, and a... What was it? Nine, ten-month dry spell? It explained Hope's current dilemma. Namely, crossing her legs tightly, unreasonably distracted by the dexterity with which the man in front of her poured Patrón. His knuckles went white on that bottle sending a shiver down her spine.

Hope looked back to her wine. Nope. Not going there. Not doing it.

"Hope?" Chloe, Hope's friend and across-the-hall neighbor said her name with the inflection of someone who'd tried more than once to get her attention.

"Yeah, sorry. What were you saying?"

Chloe flashed a dazzling smile. "I'm glad you came out tonight. Hanging out at your place isn't the same. I missed this. We need this." Being in her fourth or fifth appletini, Chloe dragged out the *neeeeed* as she squeezed Hope's hand. Hope smiled.

"I missed it too."

As her friend launched into a tangent on the perils of night-shift in the I.C.U. loud enough that the writers of HIPAA laws cringed somewhere, Hope's attention found its way back to her bartender—who was currently working shoulder to shoulder with a guy she didn't recognize. New Guy knew his way around, though, which made Hope wonder how long he'd worked here. Three months was plenty of time for a new hire to get comfortable in a job, and that's how long it had been since Hope had last set foot in Cleary's. Three, long months.

Yet, when she and Chloe sat down at the bar, Devon looked at her in a way that made her cheeks flush. He slid a glass of wine in front of her without bothering to ask for her order. Didn't that make a girl feel special.

Devon had that effect on people though. She'd noticed it the first time she and Chloe wandered into Cleary's. When he looked at you, he saw you. Not like he glanced at you long enough to remember which drink order went where—though he always did—or to appreciate the way your top displayed your cleavage—though his eyes skimmed that direction from time to time. This was different.

She'd once thought that Aaron *saw* her when he looked at her. Unfortunately, it turned out that Aaron's gaze was more scrutinizing than seeing—endlessly so. And when he wasn't happy with what he found, he made sure you knew it.

When Aaron was pleased, his affection swallowed you; drowned you. It was in your mouth, and up your nose, and all you could hear or see. But as their relationship progressed, he grew increasingly difficult to satisfy. She couldn't get anything right. Nothing was *enough*. Hope didn't claim to be perfect by any stretch of the imagination, but it grew tedious having every inadequacy noted and sports casted in his disapproving tone the moment they were out of earshot of others. Then when she neared a breaking point, he flooded her in affection again.

Hope found herself growing clumsier, more scattered by the day. She cried for every reason and none at all. Chocolate stopped tasting like luscious, melty goodness that should be sucked off fingertips and started tasting like *Are you really going to eat that?* She was slipping away from herself, and all Aaron noticed when he looked at her was that her hair was in a bun...*again*.

Hope started to wonder if she was crazy, and given that she only lacked a few thousand hours in the field to secure her spot as a fully licensed counselor, that said a lot.

But back to Devon. He saw *you*, or Hope liked to imagine he did. He was the freaking bartender, after all. He wasn't going to point out that she wore the same ankle boots every time she came in. Hell, her feet were under the bar; he wouldn't even know.

Staring over the rim of her glass, Hope watched him reach for a bottle on the top shelf. The movement pulled the black fabric of his button-down taught across his back and shoulders. She wet her lips and blinked back a visceral fantasy of yanking his shirttails free from his jeans. Pulling in a sharp breath through her nose, she closed her eyes.

Luckily for Hope, this harmless delusion—the effect of a light dinner, three glasses of wine, and her first night out in nearly three months—would wear off as soon as she stopped being tipsy. Devon Cleary might have the kind of hips that she periodically imagined wrapping her legs around, but he was nothing more than her bartender for the evening; she, a random customer. All Hope needed from Devon was the tab and judging by the increasing voracity of the thoughts circling her mind, she should get on that ASAP.

"Can I get you ladies anything else?" Hazel eyes flicked politely over Chloe, before landing squarely on Hope—who promptly forgot to ask for the check. She sank into his gaze, and Devon didn't look away. In fact, he rested his forearms on the bar in front of her and settled in.

He smelled *male*. Cedar and sandalwood, but beneath it, that musky scent that you immediately identify as masculine. The ghost of a smile played at the corners of his mouth, and with the wine humming in her brain, it took Hope longer than it should have to figure out why; she looked down like she'd been caught doing something she shouldn't—which she had.

No, Hope. Bad, Hope. Clean up your last mess before you play with something else.

This left her staring directly at his dexterous hands and tattooed forearms, while considering the merits of banging her forehead on the bar for clarity. Hope resisted the urge. Nothing would clear her head of Devon Cleary until the wine wore off and he wasn't around to look at.

"I think we're going to tab out, Dev." Hallelujah. Chloe's brain was still functioning enough for the both of them. "Put it on one, please," she added.

"Oh Chloe... No..." Hope protested, grateful for the excuse to turn away from him.

"My treat." As Chloe smiled like sunshine, guilt blossomed in Hope. She had barely heard a word Chloe said in the last fifteen-minutes because she'd been distracted by the rolled shirtsleeves, inked forearms, and... other parts of a certain bar owner who liked to play bartender. "I haven't had a real girls' night since Devon had to throw that guy out." She giggled in her drunken state, as Hope blushed hard. Chloe did not practice a three-beverage limit, even though the last of her filter evaporated around drink three. "It's been too long."

"Hey, I remember that." Devon jumped in as if he'd been waiting for his cue. "What was it, August? Last time I saw you. Is that why you haven't been in? I've seen Chloe some, but—"

"Oh, no." Hope took a deep breath and thought very sober thoughts. "This place is great," she said. "Only place I come. Ask Chloe."

Raging hormones aside, she liked Devon, and anyone could see that the level of safety at Cleary's was a point of pride for him. He put his name on the place. The bar's reputation was an extension of his own. The concern didn't leave his face, but he squared his shoulders and forced a smile.

"Helps that it's three blocks from home too..." Chloe snickered into the last of her appletini. "I'm gonna go pee before we leave." She kissed Hope on the cheek, as she handed over her debit card. "Is Nix still around?"

"Somewhere out there." Devon gestured to the tables.

"I'll say bye to her too. I'll take my time so you two can chat." She winked twice and wiggled away. While Chloe's sweater dress covered her delicate arms, it did nothing to protect her legs from November's chill. It barely cleared her ass. Wink and wiggle. Good grief.

Hope shook her head and looked back to Devon. The mask of a smile he'd donned earlier had slipped. He mechanically ran Chloe's card, face tight, brows bunched. *Not* happy.

"It's impossible to keep them all out, but I make sure they don't come back," he said, without looking up at her. Devon always looked you in the eye when he spoke. It's what made him so disarming. That hazel gaze was relentless.

He tore the receipt paper from the register and frowned harder, gearing up for a deeper dive into his despair over a crappy situation that Hope thought he'd handled impeccably if not a bit...aggressively. It wasn't his fault some idiot couldn't keep his hands to himself.

"If someone doesn't behave—"

"Devon," she said, and watched it pull his attention from everything else in the room. Whatever she'd planned to say went out the window when he looked at her like that. "Sorry I caused a scene that night," she stammered. This whole thing would go smoother if she'd stopped at two glasses.

"You didn't," he insisted.

Hope bit back a laugh. "I knee'ed a guy in the crotch on your dance floor. Caused such a scene that the owner himself tossed him." Winking playfully, she realized in horror that Chloe was rubbing off on her.

The look Devon leveled snatched the playfulness right out of her. "You defended yourself from a person who assaulted you. Here." He jabbed a finger into the glossy wood in front of her. "In *my* bar."

Hope blinked at him, distracted by the tingle at the top of her spine. *Definitely tipsy.*

"Still..." She hauled herself back to the thing that had kicked off this entire conversation in the first place. "It's not the reason I didn't come back. I haven't been much of anywhere since that night, but not because of what happened here." *Not exactly*, she thought. Devon nearly calling the cops hit too close to home when she didn't want Officer Ex-Boyfriend butting into her life. "Besides," she said, smiling up at him, "shit happens when people are drunk. What happened that night wasn't unusual."

"I don't want it to be *normal* for someone to grope my patrons." A muscle feathered in his jaw. "That isn't acceptable."

"That's not what I meant. You own a bar." Hope gestured widely. "It's the safest bar I've been in, but—come nighttime anyway—it's still a bar. If I want to go drinking and dancing..." Something flashed in his features, and he opened his mouth, but Hope put her hand up to stop his interruption. "This is the safest place I've found to do it."

"Except for that time a drunk guy put his hand—"

Hope looked at him sternly. Devon pressed his mouth shut and gave a single swift shake of his head.

"Yes, that happened," she agreed. "And you got me an apology. You wanted to call the cops." Not that Hope was ever, *ever* letting that happen. "You dragged him out. It wasn't even that guy." She nodded to the closest of the bouncers. Alan, maybe? Something like that. "You put up pictures of all three of them."

"All the creeps go on the wall of shame," Devon said, with a nod toward the extensive collection of photos plastered by the door. "It's how Mark and Alex keep track of who's banned."

Alex, Hope noted.

"You offered to keep a copy of his ID and the security footage in case I changed my mind about calling the police."

"We only had the one camera at the time. You could barely see anything," Devon said, frustration bleeding into the words.

"You drove us home," Hope countered.

"It was a really short drive," he replied, not giving her an inch.

Hope huffed. "Fine, but I don't know many people who would go so far out of their way for near strangers, especially in the middle of a work shift. You did all that because it matters to you that people are safe here." She slurred a little during that last dramatic declaration and watched him try valiantly to suppress a smile. Finding that she preferred him amused at her expense to brooding, Hope considered it a win.

"Thank you," he said, resting splayed hands on the wide bar in front of her once more. "I'll always be sorry it happened, but you saying that means more than you know." He drummed his fingers; pressing them flat again, he continued, "I still wish I could make it up to you."

"You gave us a free appetizer tonight." She chuckled. "We're even."

"I think you're owed more than an appetizer," Devon said, cocking his head. "Would you like his hand?"

A bright peal of laughter burst from Hope. "Are you offering to fetch it?" she asked, raising a brow. "No, don't answer that." She put up both hands in mock defense. "Just so you know, potato skins are my fave, so we're good."

Devon smiled down at the bar, glanced back up. "Yeah, well, they would have gone to waste if someone didn't eat them."

"Aw, look at you two." Chloe said, as she skipped up. She grabbed her card from Devon, before hooking an arm through Hope's. "You all should go out. See if you hit it off out in the real world," Filter-less Chloe declared.

"Oh... Chloe... I don't..." Hope felt her face flush hot with a blush that only got deeper when she looked to Devon. He stood with his arms crossing his chest and sported a mischievous smile. She would've appreciated some chivalrous feigned interest in anything other than her, but he didn't look away. The new bartender worked his ass off at the other end of the bar, while Devon stared at her like she was the only thing on his to-do list.

"Yes," Chloe insisted. She dug through bits of paper and tubes of lip gloss in her bag until she found her phone. After signing the appropriate receipt, she copied Hope's full name and number from her contact list onto the duplicate. Chloe drew a heart around the entire thing. A freaking heart. Then she slid it toward Devon. "You can both thank me later."

"That's really not..." Hope trailed off as he carefully pulled the slip of paper from the bar, folded it, and slid it into a wallet, before bringing that *I see you* gaze back to her face.

"May I?" he asked.

Hope's stomach landed somewhere near her toes. "May you?" she said nervously.

"Call? Or text? You can always say no." He leaned forward and lowered his voice conspiratorially. "I want you to say yes."

It must be nice to have the confidence this guy had. Hope's heartbeat would soon drown out the music, but he looked as grounded as a freaking boulder.

"What if I did say no?"

His brow furrowed; he laughed uncomfortably. "I wouldn't bother you."

She'd expected to trigger a bunch of game with that one. For him to mutter a string of playful protests. Maybe a hand over his heart for dramatic effect. She didn't expect him to give up. Often in life, Hope had wished a guy would take the hint and leave her alone. This was not one of those times.

"Well," she hedged, "what if I say nothing?"

Devon's lips moved—a slow, wicked grin that made her wine-flushed cheeks warmer and the nape of her neck prickle. "I would ignore the number in my wallet." He glanced toward the ceiling and bobbed his head a few times as if juggling information. "I'd probably make it a week before curiosity won out, and I sent a text to see if you'd respond," he said, looking back to Hope. "But nothing inappropriate, and only the one."

They were talking about a phone number, something innocuous. But something in his eyes, in the controlled, calculating expression on his face made her want to know what it would be like to be against him. Which was inadvisable.

She opened her mouth to make a joke about unsolicited dick pics, but "Don't wait a week," came out instead.

Damn.

"Yes, ma'am," Devon Cleary said. He beamed with satisfaction, and Hope knew she was in trouble.

DEVON

*T**hree months prior:*

"You'll take off the finish if you don't ease up," Nix said from a foot behind him, amusement saturating her words.

Devon swore under his breath, popping the end of the cloth against the bar with an audible snap. A blond leaning several feet down jumped and turned her head at the sound. Annoyed at Devon's disruption, the guy hitting on her responded to the disturbance with a glare. Devon glared right back, but kept his *You got a problem, asshole?* to himself. He wasn't in a customer-service mood tonight, but that didn't mean he was about to start accosting the patrons. Not the best business strategy.

"Has it been a bad bar?" Nix asked, her timbre deliberately sultry. Devon scowled down at her because it was his only option unless he sat, or she climbed onto the stool they stored under the bar for her.

Nix was a tiny thing, with a cap of short black hair, hard eyes, and a sugary-sweet center. For all her smartass comebacks and black eyeliner, she had a kind heart. She could also throw a punch with as much gusto as Alex or Mark, the two heavyweights who handled security during the rambunctious hours. Men especially tended to underestimate Nix, and she repaid their miscalculations by eating them alive. Devon enjoyed watching.

Tonight, she was waiting tables; tomorrow, she would bartend. Neither of them liked to be stuck in one restrictive role, so their owner/manager/friend/work relationship was as fluid as Nix's sexuality. Devon—who was usually hyper-aware of his surroundings— hadn't noticed her slip behind the bar for another tray of drinks. It said a lot about his current headspace.

"You should've asked her out months ago," Nix said.

"Not my type."

Screw the finish. He recommenced the vicious scrubbing. Nix barked out a short, incredulous laugh.

"Oh, really?" she asked. "How so?"

Devon shot her an irritated glare. Did he really need to spell this out for her? "Whoever takes that girl out needs to do it right."

"So, do it right," Nix said, meeting his gaze.

Devon opened his mouth, snapped it shut again. More scrubbing...

"Look," Nix reasoned, "I don't know what's holding you back. She likes you; you like her."

"Even if that were true, it's not that simple, and you know it," he groused, as Brandy, their newest server walked up with a string of requests.

What Cleary's needed was another manager, a third bartender who could close. But Devon had a hard time handing over those reins to anyone but Nix. He had to get on it though. If they were ever down for the count on the same day, the bar wouldn't open. Shelving that thought for later, he beamed at Brandy for her timing. Devon muddled mint, juggled jiggers, and strained martinis for several minutes, hopeful that Nix would wander off. All the while, he kept one eye on the dancefloor.

"It's only hard because you're ridiculously dramatic," Nix said, still waiting when he sent Brandy on her way with a tray of libations.

"Thank you for the unsolicited advice. Now, isn't there a customer somewhere you could check on?" he all but growled.

"*Somebody's moody...*" Nix sang under her breath, as she balanced about a dozen fresh glasses and went to make the rounds. She'd bring it up again. She brought it up every week.

Because she was right, he thought as he dug out another white towel.

If he weren't such a coward, this shit show of an evening would be different. He had certain tendencies that would see to that. The problem was those same tendencies amped up in unfamiliar ways when he looked at the woman on the dancefloor. Devon didn't like *unfamiliar*. It felt dangerously close to *uncontrolled*. Hard limit.

When they started coming in about six months prior, he tagged Hope—you learn names when you see people every week—as the responsible one. Warm and friendly, but also cautious. You could see it in the way her eyes scanned the room, the way she measured people up. And if someone didn't take the hint when she politely declined their offers for drinks or a dance, she got this look on her face that had them tucking tail fast. His darker side found it adorable—soft little kitten...with teeth. Hope didn't need his help, but tonight and for the first time since he'd met her, Devon worried she did.

The tiny black skirt, silver crop-top, and purple heels she had on were *not* Hope. The entire outfit screamed *I'm pretending to be someone else*. Which was fine. She could wear anything she pleased. It was just challenging for Dem...Devon to resist throttling every guy that looked at her like she was on the goddamn menu.

Hope's fifth glass of Cab Sauv sat half-empty and unattended in front of him, and she'd had at least one cocktail if you added up all the sips she'd stolen from Chloe when Devon delayed refilling her glass. He'd never served her more than three glasses of wine; she rarely made it past one or two.

Again, *not normal*.

Hope wasn't doing anything that would get her cut off if she were any other patron, though. She and Chloe always walked to Cleary's from...wherever, so it wasn't like he thought they'd be driving. If he stopped serving her, it would be solely from a desire to control her behavior. So as bad as he wanted to... Not his place. Plus, they'd probably be so pissed that they'd never come in again, which bothered him more than he cared to analyze.

He redoubled his bar-scrubbing efforts.

More than getting control of her situation, Devon wanted to know what triggered it. Something happened, and he had a consuming desire to haul her to his office, sit her on the desk, and scowl at her until she started talking. That also wasn't his place, he reminded himself for the nine-millionth time since they'd walked in.

Currently, both women were dancing barefoot on his dancefloor—a gorgeous tangle of brunette, blond, and a million miles of bare leg—while half of the male population of Asheville circled them like prey. Okay, not *half*, but it felt like a solid third from where Devon stood.

He stiffened as a blond guy seated near the dancefloor got up and moved closer to the two women, relaxing slightly when the man started talking to a quartet of giggling co-eds dancing a few feet from Chloe and Hope.

"Calm down," he mumbled, running a hand up his face and through his hair.

Here he stood, comparing every other guy in the place to a predator, while he scrubbed a hole through his bar fantasizing about turning her over his knee and wearing her ass out—with a flogger. Yeah... a flogger. He'd never choose a flogger without being asked, but watching her on the dancefloor, not a care in the world despite the risk, Devon saw the merits of something you could swing hard without ending the scene.

Black leather. Heavy in his hand. Over the knee wouldn't work. He'd put her over the side of the bed... No, have her grab the top bar and break out the restraints when she couldn't comply. Better angle that way. Easier to see. Watch her skin go pink, then red, then purple while she squealed and squirmed and promised to never, *ever*—

No.

Stop.

His internal dialogue was devolving faster than a newbie rope scene where the shears went missing, and now he had a hard-on. Fucking great.

Devon didn't do relationships, and Hope was a relationship kind of girl if he ever saw one. He didn't do punishment spankings outside of negotiated scenes with negotiated rules either. So, who was the predator now?

Hypocrite.

Scrub the bar, watch the drink, keep an eye on the dancefloor like any other night, but this was nothing like any other night.

Her glass had been sitting there for ten-fucking-minutes. Every time he looked at it, orders bubbled up the back of his throat, held down through sheer effort and a clenched jaw. His teeth hurt. What in the hell was she thinking? Sure, he had an eye on her drink, but that was because he paid attention, not because she'd asked. And even if she had thought to ask... Why him? What made him safe or trustworthy? In Hope's world, Devon was the random guy who poured. He could be some sort of freak. He *was* some sort of freak.

Devon swallowed hard, as he watched Chloe slide in close to Hope and bring their mouths together, a gentle melding of lips, breath and tongues that made his blood sing in his veins.

Good. Maybe they'd leave, and he could stop obsessing over this thing he couldn't change.

"Dev…" Nix said as she reappeared, her voice softer this time, but he flinched all the same. "Mark has the door and Alex is keeping an eye on things on the dancefloor. Take a break."

Things on the dancefloor… He swallowed the desire to snap at her, knowing he'd regret it before the words left his mouth. This problem was Devon's. Nix was nice, Hope was normal even if she was having a rough day, and Devon was a little twisted in the head—something all well and good in small doses between consenting adults, but it didn't fit into polite society, or relationships. Not that Devon was into relationships… Shit. Why did he keep thinking about relationships?

"Yeah… You're right," he said. "Take the bar?"

With his back to the dancefloor, he didn't see what happened next.

The music came to an abrupt halt—an agreed upon call-to-arms when Mark or Alex saw trouble. They used it about once a year, and Devon usually had a hand in instigating its need. Muffled sounds of pain and outrage took the place of the latest pop trend, as Devon spun back around. He caught the briefest glimpse of Hope's silver top before half of the place came to their feet looking for the source of the commotion. Drunk folks *love* a good commotion. Devon flushed with agitation at losing sight of her, but there was no chance of regaining a clear line from where he stood before the excitement faded.

You can't wait that long.

"Devon," Nix snapped.

It wasn't a conscious decision. One second, Devon was behind his beloved bar. The next, he was scrambling over it, sending Hope's drink plummeting. His boots crunched through wine and broken glass as he began pushing his way past patrons on the other side.

"Dev, wait!" Nix shouted behind him.

You knew she was in trouble, and you didn't do a fucking thing.

Devon shook off the intrusive voice in his head, shoving through the Friday-night-busy crowd. Alex, standing a head above the throng, had a harder go of it. Having eyes on the dancefloor didn't guarantee easy access.

By the time Devon broke into the small circle of open space surrounding a huddled Hope and Chloe and three guys who looked like they'd skipped away from college to party on daddy's money for the night, he was ready to put his fist through someone's face. The feeling didn't go away as he analyzed the situation. He *needed* to be a responsible, level-headed business owner. He *wanted* to be a territorial top—which was insane because, for the last time, that was not his place.

Both women were shaking mad. Two of the guys shouted a barrage of garbage excuses and accusations. Then, Devon zeroed in on the third. The blond. He gasped for air between spurts of misogynistic profanity, the way he clutched his crotch making the reason for his distress clear enough.

It also made him the first contestant.

"Devon!" Alex shouted, shoving his way into the ring of clear floor.

"He's mine," Devon said, stalking toward the offender. Familiar with the look on his boss's face, the bouncer didn't argue.

"Hey, bro," Frat boy whined as Devon reached him. "This cunt over here—"

Devon snatched him so quickly that he didn't have time to resist. He yanked an arm up behind blondie's back with one hand, while twisting the other into the nape of his collar.

"Wait, wait, wait, wait, wait!"

"Quiet!" Devon bellowed. The way he issued commands would make your average drill Sargent wet with envy. Everyone in the building obeyed.

"What happened?" he demanded.

Frat Boy opened his face to answer, still not figuring out the bit where Devon didn't want to hear a thing he had to say.

"That bitch—"

Devon shoved his arm higher.

"Stop! Stop! *Argh*!"

The guttural shout, triggered by pain inflicted by Devon's own hand, echoed through the space bringing a sudden crystalline clarity to everything around him. His rage hushed, and focus returned, as he settled into the familiar state of *control*.

Ah…see. That's all you needed.

"Not. You." Devon bit out. "You don't speak until I *let* you." He looked to Hope and Chloe and waited.

"We were dancing," Chloe supplied unhelpfully. "Me and Hope…" She pulled Hope closer, seeking security in proximity.

"Hope," he said, concentrating on the woman who made it hard for him to think. Devon instinctively skimmed a glance down her body—quick as a heartbeat— before bringing his focus back to her face. She was pale, except for the patches of color at her cheeks, but not particularly disheveled for someone too drunk to drive, who had been making out with her girlfriend a few minutes prior. "What happened?" he asked.

He watched her gaze drift to the guy in his grip, as she mutely opened her mouth.

"Don't look at him," Devon said, eliciting another yelp from the now shaking pervert as he pivoted him around to the side. Her eyes flicked back and forth between them. "Me. Look at me," Devon ordered. Uncertainty clouded her face, but she complied. "What happened?" he asked again.

Hope's brow creased, and she bit her lower lip. "He..." She swallowed hard and trailed off. Out of the bottom of his periphery, Devon saw the movement of her hands as she tugged the hem of her skirt, pressing those creamy thighs together. Something hot as fire and cold as ice replaced the blood in his veins.

You know what happened.

"Hope?"

It wasn't the single word question, but the way he'd delivered it. Question, command, and insistent expectation that left no room for denial. Devon watched it have the intended effect, even as he kicked himself for the card he'd played. It was a reaction to the situation, to his desire to get her talking, because maybe, somehow, her story wouldn't match his suspicions.

"We were dancing, but not with them." She gestured to the men, her cheeks growing pinker as she spoke. Her eyes met Devon's for a split second before focusing on his shoes. Devon seethed. "And then he came up behind me and...I didn't mean to knee him, but he..."

There she went again, tugging down that skirt, rolling the hem between her delicate fingers.

"It's fine," he managed, even though it wasn't. "I get it," he said, and he did. He got it, and he felt like he might be sick.

Devon leaned close to Frat Boy's ear, shaking him to get his full attention. "You fucked up. You're going to apologize."

"If she didn't want—"

Devon didn't shout. He simply turned up the volume on a chillingly even voice, as he hitched the guy's arm higher for a soprano-worthy squeal.

"Do not make me tell you again."

"Ah! You're going to break my—"

Devon canted his head, tightened his grip.

"I'm sorry!" Frat boy wailed.

"To her," Devon ordered. "Politely."

"M...ma'am," the sniveling little weasel began, "I'm so sorry. I never should have touched you. Pl...please! Please forgive me. I'm drunk, and you're hot. That skirt is... Ah! Fuck! Okay, sorry. Sorry."

"You can shut the fuck up, now," Devon said.

"I don't want you to go through it more than necessary," he told Hope. "We'll call the non-emergency line and—"

"No!" She cut him off, eyes wide and palms up. Everything in her body language repeated her refusal, and Devon froze for a second on instinct. "I...I don't want any more trouble," she stammered.

"Hope," he said, with a gentility that surprised him, given the circumstances, "we have to—"

"I want to go home," she said. "Please, let me go home." Something in her voice made his thoughts toward Frat Boy darker. "Please..."

HOPE

Hope sat at her dining table in flannel pants and a faded Linkin Park shirt, her dark brown hair tied up in a messy bun. She sported smudged eye makeup from the night before, but having chugged a glass of water before bed, she felt great. Hydration wasn't the only favor she had done herself before crashing, but Hope found it best not to dwell on one's deviant sexual behaviors in the harsh light of morning. Especially when you were expecting company.

Two plates of eggs and toast—one already half-finished—and two glasses of orange juice sat on the table in front of her. A cup of hot coffee was tucked snuggly between her palms, its color an opaque beige from all the cream and sugar she'd added. Dessert coffee? Yes, please.

She'd slept hard until after 9 a.m. and expected Chloe to knock on her door at any moment. Chloe dragged them out; Hope got them functional the next morning. It was tradition. At least, Hope assumed it was still tradition. Hope had spent most of the last three months ruthlessly murdering her few new traditions, so maybe things had changed.

She had stopped going to Cleary's after Aaron moved to town. She'd also dropped the yoga class she was starting to love. If it wasn't work, home, Chloe's place, or her brother's, it didn't happen. And the last two entries on that list only made the cut because Chloe and JJ wouldn't let her disappear.

As if on cue, there came a knock at the door.

"Come in," Hope called, but Chloe was already working through the locks. Giving someone a spare key, it turned out, made them significantly harder to ghost. Especially when they could see your door from their peephole. Hope felt gratitude, as she looked at her sleep-rumpled friend. They had known each other less than a year, but Chloe was loyal to a fault.

"Breakfast is served." Hope gestured magnanimously to the meager feast she'd prepared, as her guest flopped into her usual seat.

"You're a saint," Chloe said, shoving her blond ponytail over her shoulder and tucking into her toast.

When Hope moved in, Chloe had expected her to fill the vacant friend role as readily as the vacant apartment. The previous tenant moved back home after flunking out midway through her sophomore year and left a gaping dancing-buddy-sized hole in Chloe's world.

Chloe was a nurse, and her shifts were often up in the air. But she always managed to get a weekend night or two off, and she wasn't one to sit at home alone. Despite her gratitude for the friendship and distraction, Hope soon realized that Chloe partied a little harder than she did.

It worked out, though. Hope's more reserved idea of a fun time rubbed off on Chloe, once the memory of her sorority-sister-esque former neighbor faded, and Chloe made sure Hope ventured out into the world—at least until a few months ago.

The pair had given Cleary's a shot a couple of weeks after Hope moved in. It was a perfect compromise. Good atmosphere, better than average food, and the staff kept it clean and safe. During the day, the bar felt like a restaurant, but evening brought music loud enough for dancing on the small dancefloor—a mix of rock, pop, rap, Latin; whatever vibe the crowd or staff seemed in to at the moment. The place was as unique as it was eclectic. Also, Hope wasn't usually picky about her wine, but the house Cab Sauv was freaking amazing.

You could also drool into your drink over the owner and namesake, Devon Cleary, if that was your thing. Given the fantasies running through her head as she'd rubbed a vibrator on her clit the night before, or the way she hadn't managed to get off until she slipped it deep into her pussy while whispering his name, it definitely seemed to be Hope's thing.

"Of course, being a saint has its disadvantages," Chloe went on, placing the rest of her toast back on the plate with a smirk.

"You trying to say something, 3F?" Hope asked with mock hostility.

Chloe laughed. "Big attitude from somebody who's going to be Team 3F when her lease is up."

Hope winced. "Maybe. I don't know."

Hope was running out of time on that one. By February, she'd need to either sign another lease or make a different plan, but her incoming and outgoing cash flow complicated things. Actually... it wasn't complicated at all. She needed more dollars or fewer bills. Pretty simple really. Splitting an apartment with Chloe or moving in with her brother would work on paper, but Hope, like everyone else on the planet, preferred to make choices out of preference rather than necessity. She also hadn't had a roommate since college and didn't love it then.

Because Chloe was Chloe, she shifted the topic back to sex.

"It's none of my business," she said, as if she hadn't brought this up dozens of times, "but I can't help knowing when we live in a building with paper-thin walls. I know all of your comings and goings...and your *not*-comings. You haven't gotten laid since you moved in." She sipped her juice delicately. "I want coffee too." Pushing to her feet, Chloe crossed to the galley kitchen for a mug. Not bothering with cream or sugar, she was back across the table a moment later.

"Okay, first of all, that isn't even true," Hope began, although she wasn't sure her single sexual escapade with a partner since moving in should count. That was more of a relapse than a hookup. A highly regrettable relapse... "And secondly, you seemed to be doing a pretty good job of making it your business last night," she added, shifting the topic to something less likely to kick her right in the self-esteem.

"Yeah, well, it's the only time I've convinced you to go out in months. It might be your last opportunity to find a lover before retirement, so you're welcome."

Hope rolled her eyes. So much for the feel good. "I'm thirty-one, Chloe, and I don't need someone. I'm fine on my own."

Chloe pursed her lips, as she speared a bite of eggs. "That's all well and good," she said, bringing the fork to her mouth, "but you want him."

"Stop it." Hope threw her napkin across the table. "Maybe... But that's beside the point." She found herself blathering. "It's...complicated."

"I'm pretty sure he's single, and I know you are. How complicated can it be? You two start staring at each other, and the whole place reeks of pheromones." Chloe scrunched her nose like a bunny. She folded her legs up and leaned in, waiting.

What was Hope supposed to say? *I made the monumental mistake of dating the cop assigned to my last school. I moved two hours away to put distance between us, and even that didn't help because three months ago, he got a job with local P.D. and moved here. I'm kind of overwhelmed with all that, and I'm in the middle of a self-imposed hiatus from the world...except for you, and my brother...and maybe staring at Devon Cleary when I'm tipsy, so I can recall the way his muscles shift when he reaches for the top shelf, while I shove a fake cock in my pussy later?* Nope, nope, nope.

Hope chewed her lip. "It just...is." Chloe huffed, and Hope knew she had to do better. "Okay, fine," Hope continued, "You know how I told you that I saw my ex back in August?"

"We had to go out drinking over it. *Big drinking*. You never initiate the big drinking." Chloe nodded and settled in for the juicy stuff, as she ticked off what she already knew or assumed. "Worked with him before. Shitty breakup. He probably cheated. Blah blah blah."

Hope raised her brows. "*He probably cheated?*"

Chloe shrugged.

"Why do you want to hear it from me? You already know the story," Hope said sarcastically, reaching for her drink.

"Was he married?"

Chloe nearly got a shower. Hope put her mug down, sloshing coffee onto the table.

"No! Oh God..." Hope shook her head, as she mopped up the mess with Chloe's napkin; her own still somewhere on the floor behind her friend.

"I was kidding. Come on Hope, gimme." Chloe held her own mug between her palms and stared over the top with greed in her eyes.

Hope sighed, putting the soggy napkin on her plate. "Cheating wasn't the issue," she said. "We dated for about a year and a half. Longest grownup relationship I've ever had, but it ended badly. That's when I moved here." Technically, it was the other way around. The move triggered the breakup—because her accepting an offer for a counseling job in an Asheville private school triggered the crap out of Aaron. Violently. But Hope didn't want to say that part. "I needed a clean break," she went on, "but I screwed that up about two months later."

"So, you slept with him." The way Chloe said it— without a hint of judgment— helped the next words come easier.

"We were sitting on the couch talking," Hope said, skipping the part about how he got in in the first place. "He brought wine. One thing led to another. The next day, I told him it was a mistake." She twisted the hem of her shirt beneath the table. "Then he got a position with Asheville's finest," she added bitterly.

Chloe's brow bunched. "He became a cop?" Hope shook her head.

"He was a cop when we met. *Officer* Aaron Marden... He was assigned to my last school." Hope waited for the man in uniform jokes, but they didn't come. Another reason to love her neighbor.

"So, your ex has a badge and a gun, and he followed you to a city two hours away?"

Hope began blinking far too quickly. Her face twisted into a grinning mask. She couldn't make it stop.

"I know that sounds crazy," she said, the words tumbling out, "That's not what I'm trying to say. I broke up with him, but it was obvious that we weren't working out. He has family here. If anything, I moved to a place he was bound to end up."

Chloe pursed her lips. "That sounds an awful lot like you making excuses for things he should be making excuses for."

"It's fine." Hope waved it aside. "I see him around sometimes, and that's it." Mostly... She looked back to her friend and smiled. "I thought he was the one for a minute, and it hurt to realize that I was wrong. That's all."

Chloe lifted her coffee. "Fair enough, but why haven't you gone out with anyone else? You moved here in February, and you had already broken up with him before you did. Are you open to getting back together with him? Like do you think the two of you could figure things out or—"

"Oh, God no," Hope blurted, shaking her head before trying to temper the rest of her response. "The idea of dating anyone... Too stressful. I need to figure out the career thing, get myself settled."

"I know something that's great for stress." Chloe sipped coffee the same color as the eyes she currently had locked on Hope.

"You mean *someone*," Hope retorted.

Chloe gave an elegant shrug. "Semantics. That boy looks like sin...but the safe kind."

The laugh that rumbled out of Hope surprised her. Aaron looked like the safe kind of sin if there was such a thing. Devon looked like he would cut you for scuffing his bar—or lay you out on it like an all-you-can-eat buffet. Okay, that last bit was not helpful.

Still, Aaron's dark side caught her off-guard. It took her four months to get a glimpse of it and another six to admit to herself that it was a problem. By that point, Hope couldn't figure out how to extricate herself or if she really wanted to. Talk about stinging her pride. She had a master's in social work, an education certificate, and was nearly finished earning her counseling license, at the time. If anyone should have dodged Aaron, it was her. Hope had no interest in screwing up like that again. And Devon Cleary? She'd be more surprised if he *didn't* have a dark side.

Hope's phone buzzed from the tabletop; both women homed in on the source of the sound.

"Speak of the devil," Chloe said.

"I don't have the energy for a relationship," Hope repeated, even as she itched to pick up her phone. "I'm still trying to figure out how I misread the last one so badly."

No one in the world knew what had gone on between Hope and Aaron, and no one knew how she struggled to navigate the fallout. Even her brother, Hope's only close family member, had suspicions but no details. Hope broke out in a cold sweat if a cruiser appeared behind her in the dark. She heard Aaron's texts in his voice—that cocky tone that assumed that at some point she would give in; because why wouldn't she want to? She heard their subtext as well, up until she'd blocked him. Aaron had only really screwed up that one time, but it was enough to put her in a perpetual state of unease when dealing with him.

"Look, girl," Chloe said, pulling Hope out of her own thoughts, "I'm not telling you what to do, but I'm about to tell you what to do." Hope couldn't help but smile. "That sparkly thing in your nightstand can only get you so far. When Devon texts you, read it. Maybe respond to it. *Maybe* go out with him, or have sex with him, or...who knows...have a relationship with him." She lifted a shoulder as if any of these options were as valid as the next. "Do any or none of those things," she said, with fire in her eyes, "but don't let some asshole you aren't with anymore stop you."

"That's a whole lot of *maybe,*" Hope replied.

Chloe sipped her coffee, unbothered. "So, what did he say?" she asked.

Before she processed the question, Hope grabbed her phone, causing a flush of embarrassment. "It's probably not him," she said.

"Mmm hmm," Chloe said, as if she didn't believe that for a second. "But what did he say?"

Hope opened the text from a number she didn't recognize and grinned. "He, uh, asked if we made it home safely."

"I knew it was him," Chloe said, sitting up straighter. "What else?"

"He wants to know if I have plans for dinner."

"You do now." Chloe clinked her mug against Hope's on the table.

"I don't know. We went out last night."

"You need to make up for your three-month hiatus from society—then make up for your near year of celibacy."

Hope rolled her eyes, but she smiled.

HOPE

As it turned out, the text from Devon was a trap. Oh, that wasn't his intent of course, but that didn't change the fact that it led directly to Hope's ensnarement. A mouse to cheese, or peanut butter; whatever people use to lure rodents to their deaths. His text was cheesy peanut butter. She erased that terrible analogy from her mind before the gagging commenced.

Hope's phone had buzzed again, as Chloe headed back to her side of the hall, and because...Devon...she opened the text without hesitation. Unfortunately, it was from her mother. The third in a row to which she had yet to reply. Hope had gotten behind on her end of the superficial relationship lately.

I know you're off, today. Call me when you get this. It is an emergency.

Great. It was not an emergency, of course. Her mother would call in the case of an actual emergency. This was likely some social hoop that her mother expected her to jump through. Deciding to get the unpleasantness out of the way quickly, Hope brought the phone to her ear and waited three rings for her mother to answer.

"Hello? Beth Barrow speaking." The artificially refined voice poured over the line. Her mother used the same saccharine tone in all social interactions but did not maintain the act in private. She ripped the gentile façade off like a bra two sizes too small, at the first opportunity.

"Hey, mom," Hope said.

"Why haven't you replied to my texts?" she demanded, not wasting time. Fine with Hope.

"Sorry, I've been busy. What's the emergency?"

Reference to being busy, check. Generic interest question, check. Now, she could sit through the droning for a few minutes before making an excuse to hang up.

Because as Hope suspected, there was no emergency, her mother rambled on for fifteen minutes about Ashley, Hope's stepsister who was in law school and engaged to marry *The Doctor*. Aside from Hope and Ashley, the family rarely said his name—which was Greg. *Gregory Nice*, to be more specific. His last name was literally Nice, and he lived up to it.

Greg was kind and funny, and Ashley would have a wonderful life with him. Ten bucks said she didn't even use her law degree for more than a couple of years. They would pop out a kid, and Ashley would be home because that was going to be the plan. With the whole setting-the-wedding for Ashley's last spring break thing, maybe getting pregnant before graduation was also part of the plan. Take a year off after college... She might never start her professional career.

Twenty-six, with a degree, a house, a spouse, and a *baby*? Quite the over achiever, her stepsister was; no wonder that, at thirty-one and single, Hope's mom suspected that the fruit of her own loins might be a dud. Good on Ashley for doing the law thing though. Even as Hope sat on her own degrees and licensures for the time being, she knew their value. In a world where women still made less on the hour than men, those papers were power. A safety net, if you had the drive to use them. Sometimes partners let you down, after all, and you couldn't always judge a relationship from the outside looking in.

Her mother droned on, "... So, I told her we could always ask Aaron."

Hope's brain came back online at the mention of her ex. "I'm sorry, what?"

"To escort you... You can't be the only bridesmaid without a groomsman."

In the wedding. The fucking wedding. Hope cringed.

"The wedding isn't until March."

"Yes, but as I *just said* the fitting is the last week of December." Exasperation twisted her mother's voice into an admonishment. "The groomsmen will be gifted their suits for the ceremony, Hope. The appointments have already been made." Her mother said this with ever-increasing intensity, that stoked Hope's irritation further. Aaron? She couldn't be serious.

"Mom, I'm not walking down an aisle with Aaron. You cannot be suggesting that."

"He was a part of this family for nearly two years, Hope," her mother bit out.

"Eighteen months," she corrected.

Her mother made a sound of annoyance. "Even if you started seeing someone today, the wedding is in March. We can't have a stranger in the photos, and we need someone chosen before the fitting."

"You already asked him," Hope exclaimed, her cheeks burning as the realization landed. Her mother wasn't looking for input; she was explaining the choice she had already made. It shouldn't surprise her. The woman invited him to Christmas a few weeks after they broke up... And Aaron came. Her mother had been trying to revive their failed relationship, since the moment she found out it was dead in the water.

"I mentioned it to him, yes," her mother shot back haughtily. "And because Aaron is an adult," she added in a tone that dripped implications about Hope's maturity, "he said that he would be delighted to step in. Good Lord, Hope. He's given you all this time to get this out of your system. He's willing to request time off, give up his weekend to walk you in this wedding, while you won't even speak to him."

"Did Aaron tell you that?" Hope asked. "Do you all have lovely little chats about what a bitch I am?"

"I don't know why you're being so—"

"Stop it," she snapped. "Stop trying to make us a thing. I broke up with him, and I'm not going to walk down an aisle with him, so stop."

So much for keeping it light. Maybe her mother would be less inclined to push her down an aisle with her ex if Hope told her everything that led to their breakup, but their mother-daughter relationship didn't support that level of vulnerability. The woman used every scrap of information she scrounged together in whatever manner best served her, and Hope didn't want everyone knowing her mother's version of her life story.

"If not Aaron, then who?" her mother asked.

"I have to go."

"It's the weekend, Hope," her mother said, as if she were addressing a petulant child. "You do not. Who in the world are you—"

She wanted to say, *fuck you*, but it came out as, "Yeah, actually I do. I'll talk to you later," and she hung up.

The audacity of that woman to suggest that she be paired off with Aaron...*Fucking Aaron*... in her stepsister's wedding. It would serve her right if Hope brought home Devon Cleary. With ink peeking out of shirtsleeves and a perpetual five o'clock shadow... They would find her on the entryway floor, pearls still clutched in her cold, stiff hand. Not that Hope needed the promise of her mother's disapproval to make this connection worthwhile.

Truthfully, she liked him, or was infatuated with the idea of him, at least. She had to get back on the horse sometime, right? The fact that she'd popped a dress into one of the basement dryers long enough to get rid of the wrinkles before hanging it on the back of her bedroom door told her that she was considering getting on *this* horse. Maybe.

Hope pulled up the screen with his message again and reread the words. She wasn't ready to commit to dinner, but he would make an excellent distraction from her rage.

We lived, and I see you survived closing, she typed. Her finger hovered over the screen before she sucked in a bracing breath and hit send.

I won't lie. It got iffy around 2:30. Till didn't balance again, came the reply.

Her lips lifted into a smile as she responded. *That sounds annoying.*

Eh... Recounted twice, then pulled the missing $ from my tips. Probably my fault anyway. Kind of a joke on the nights I work the bar.

You're the boss, right? Have someone else work it.

She strode aimlessly through her apartment. Into the kitchen, down the hall; she stole a glance at her flushed cheeks in the bathroom vanity. They were pink from her conversation with her mother, but that wasn't what was keeping them that color. Something giddy and light replaced her agitation; a pleasant flurry of energy thrumming through her. Thrilling, but also kind of— Her phone buzzed again.

But then I wouldn't have an excuse to talk to you.

Hope stared at the words on the screen but saw his dark lashes and hazel eyes. Devon had no business being so disarming. He wasn't even in the room with her.

Surely you could come up with something, she responded, pacing like a zoo cat.

Dinner would make a decent excuse tonight if you're free. People talk over dinner, right?

Was she really going to go out with him? A niggling voice in the back of her brain said that she had no right if she couldn't sort out the Aaron situation. Her mother was trying to include him in a family wedding for crying out loud… But going out with Devon didn't have to be serious. Like Chloe said, it could be superficial, fun even. It didn't have to *mean* anything.

I'd hate to put you out, especially after you were forced to balance the register with your own tips… she sent back, slapping a playful mask over her inner turmoil.

You caught me. I'm flat broke after last night. I was going to pretend I lost my wallet to get a meal out of you.

Hope chuckled aloud, as another text followed swiftly on its heels.

Kidding. I can afford to lose $17 out of the tip jar, and still feed you dinner. I want to feed you dinner.

Hope chewed her lower lip and considered. It didn't have to be serious. It didn't have to be anything. They could go on one date and then pretend like it was a two-friends-grabbing-food thing, after. Or maybe a friends-with-benefits thing. Given that he'd starred in many of her self-pleasure fantasies over the last year, that thought sent an instantaneous swell of heat through her.

I suppose I could let you, she sent back.

HOPE

She needed shoes.

Her classic little black dress—snug, halter, with a keyhole slit down the front and a silver zipper up the back—clung to her curves. The hem sat far enough above her knees to be date material, but low enough that she didn't fear flashing her knickers climbing out of the car. She had worked her hair into a twisty updo she'd never be able to recreate, and stuck sparkly pins throughout. Hope had never worn them, but she loved them when she saw them at the store. They had lived in her bathroom drawer since the week she moved into her apartment.

The overall look meant that she needed little in the way of jewelry. For her ears, she opted for pearl teardrops, paired with a second set of studs. The pearls were a Christmas gift from her mother and stepfather several years prior. The diamonds came from Aaron—a birthday gift. Hope decided not to hold it against them. It wasn't the earrings' fault.

Her only clutch was solid black, so that was a non-decision. Her makeup was an evening version of what she wore most days—more liner, more mascara, and a matte lip color in a dark mauve that promised to stay on her mouth through flood, famine, or nuclear fallout. Only the shoes remained, and she had nine minutes to decide what to do about that.

Red was date color, but she felt like she should probably match something so bold to her bag or lip color. Her purple heels were adorable, but she had the feeling they were cursed after the last time she wore them. Hope wasn't exactly superstitious, but that was a bad night and not one she wanted to remind Devon of. But again...her bartender probably didn't spend a lot of time studying her footwear.

That left her black heels, which looked like she had exactly one thing on her mind, and it wasn't innocent. She could only walk in them for approximately three feet before hobbling like a newborn calf, but they made her ass look incredible. At least there was that.

Seven minutes. He would arrive in seven minutes, assuming he was on time.

Hope swore under her breath and texted Chloe a *Quick! S.O.S. Red heels or purple?* along with a picture of herself in the living room wall mirror. Chloe banged on her door five seconds later, having skipped grabbing her keys in favor of a faster trip across the hall.

"You're going out with him," Chloe accused, albeit gleefully, as she shot past. "You told him yes and didn't tell me. Holy shit, you look fantastic."

"Chloe, focus. He's going to be here any minute."

"Right. Are you eating, dancing, what?"

"Just dinner."

"Oh, that's easy. There's only one answer. Obviously." Chloe crossed her arms and jerked her chin toward the hallway that led to Hope's bedroom in silent command.

"Well, tell me what it is because it isn't obvious to me."

"The *Fuck Me* heels," Chloe said, as if the statement should be followed with a loud *Duh.*

Hope cringed. "Those weren't on the list."

"Get. Them." Chloe glared.

Hope looked reluctantly down the hallway. "I also have my boots..." Chloe scowled harder. "I can barely walk in those heels," Hope whined.

"He isn't going to let you fall on your face."

"What if he does?"

"Don't go out with him again." Chloe raised a slender shoulder. "Look, the purple heels have bad vibes. Last time you wore them, your date had to restrain a guy."

"He wasn't my date then."

"But tonight, he is, so they're a hard no. The red pair doesn't work with this perfection," Chloe added, with a sweeping gesture. "Why do you own shoes that you refuse to wear?"

"Because they're so pretty." Hope sighed, walking toward her bedroom, and returning with the heels in question. She perched on the sofa and began strapping them on.

"Yeah well, they deserve to be worn, just like you deserve to be—"

Hope put up a hand to stop Chloe's commentary, as she rose to her feet and got her balance. She did yoga twice a week. Well...

not for the last three months, but she did a month of twice-weekly yoga classes with Chloe before dropping out. That had to count for something. Surely, she could walk gracefully in these heels.

Chloe, oblivious to her struggle, clapped her hands and bounced. Hope's neighbor could walk over a sheet of greased glass in stilettos. It probably wouldn't even impede her wiggle. "Our little girl, all grown up and going on a date," she gushed.

"This morning, you said I was old." Hope reminded her, as she began shooing Chloe out the door. "Now get out of here before—"

It was the kind of thing that ends up filed in your *I should've known it would go badly* folder or your *What an adorable start* folder. Unfortunately, there is never a label on those moments when they happen, so you can only wait for hindsight to kick in. Hope yanked open her door and pushed Chloe out into the hallway—at the exact instant Devon knocked. To Devon's credit, he did catch her best friend when Hope sent her stumbling into his arms. It gave weight to Chloe's earlier supposition that he wasn't going to let Hope fall on her face.

There he stood, charcoal grey slacks, crisp white button-down, dark hair a little tamer than usual, but the same hazel eyes—and his arms wrapped snuggly around Chloe, still in her pajamas and lopsided ponytail. Devon got her solid on her feet, then stepped back a fraction.

"You look gorgeous," he said to Hope. "And, uh... hey Chloe." He grinned.

"I'm so sorry," Hope shot back.

"In case it wasn't already clear, we're a package deal," Chloe said between giggles.

Devon's gaze didn't leave Hope. "I suspected as much."

"I'm so sorry," she repeated, like a broken record.

Devon cocked his head to the side. "I can handle anything you throw at me. Clear?"

Surely, he hadn't anticipated her throwing Chloe, though. Surely. Hope blushed and nodded.

"Right, so... I'll let you kids do your thing," Chloe said, as she made her way to her own door. "Have fun, you two." She was shaking her head and laughing as she vanished.

Hope looked to Devon. "I'm—"

"Going to need a coat," he said. "You look amazing, but it's chilly."

"Right," she said, with a fresh flush of embarrassment. Hope reached into the closet by her apartment door. Devon pulled the black woolen peacoat from her hands and held it out for her. "But really... I'm—"

"Starving?" he said, with a grin.

Hope turned to face him. "You're doing that on purpose," she said.

Devon shrugged. "You keep trying to apologize."

Hope narrowed her eyes. "I'm—"

"Gorgeous." He kept grinning.

"You already said that."

"I'll probably say it again." He held out an arm. "Ready?"

***

Ciccio offered a wide variety of mostly Italian options, and the atmosphere to merit its price point.

To the immense pleasure of her feet, they valeted the car—which, Hope remembered from her last ride. A glossy black beast of a thing that probably came off the line in the sixties...seventies...? Okay, she didn't know enough about cars to comment, but apparently, it was the sort of ride some people got in a tizzy over. The kid working the kiosk lit up like Christmas when Devon handed him the keys and asked if he could drive a stick. Hope expected him to have a harder time releasing those keys, but he tossed them over without a second thought. He seemed far more focused on other things.

Devon's eyes lingered on her feet as often as her face, but she didn't miss the flash of desire each time his gaze skimmed between the two. It caused a flush of...pride? Hope had spent nearly a year being all but repulsed by most male attention, but she liked that he wanted her. It made the game more fun and the walking in heels more rewarding.

Devon steered them toward the bar—an expanse of pearlescent acrylic with silver accents. It lacked the warmth of Cleary's, but the sparkling shelves didn't disappoint. He perched her on a stool, before slipping onto the one beside her.

"They'll have a table soon," he promised, resting one foot on the lower rung of her chair. "We have a reservation for seven; it shouldn't be long." His eyes skimmed the room.

"Don't want to sit at the bar?" she asked wryly.

"I might be tempted to get behind it." He chuckled, signaling the bartender, who came over promptly and asked for their order. "Crown and Coke for me and..." He raised a brow at Hope as he added, "Cabernet Sauvignon for the lady?"

Hope nodded.

"The Alderlings or the Saldeva?" the bartender asked.

"Saldeva, please," Devon replied. He shifted to face Hope, as the man behind the bar gathered supplies.

"You know what I like," she said. Hope had never heard the names before, but he had her at *Cab Sauv.*

"I know what you drink." Devon shrugged. "Me, I'm a whatever I'm in the mood for or whatever the bartender won't screw up kind of guy. If the quality's good, I'm good. You drink the house red, which happens to be a Cab Sauv at Cleary's. I pay attention," he said, tapping his temple.

The bartender slid drinks in front of them, and both reached for their glasses with murmured thanks.

"To first dates and uncomfortable shoes. Slàinte," Devon said.

"To observant men... a species once thought extinct," she replied with a smirk, as they clinked glasses.

Hope sipped, notes of black cherry, warm cedar, and the pop of something acidic slipping over her palate and filling her nose with the most deliciously familiar bouquet. "Wait—this is... Is this...?" She watched Devon press his lips together, as realization washed over her. "You don't give me what I order."

"I don't know what you're talking about," he said, quickly pulling his glass to his mouth to hide the smile.

"You do too."

"Fine." As Devon returned his tumbler to the tiny white napkin on the bar, and turned toward her, his face took on the countenance of someone about to deliver terrible news. The worst kind of news... Death of a loved one... Eternal internet outages... Tragic, tragic news. He pulled in a deep breath and looked at her pleadingly. "I'm sorry to have to tell you this, but you order terrible wine."

Hope's mouth popped open. "*You're* terrible."

"Worst wine I stock..." He shook his head with regret.

"Devon."

"I only keep it in the bar because I'm too cheap to reprint the menus."

"I love it," she exclaimed, as she playfully swatted at his arm. He laughed, a warm, luscious sound that vibrated through her.

"You don't even know what it's called," he said.

"I do too. It starts with an A, I think." Devon cocked a brow at her, so Hope tried again. "Okay, maybe it's a C... I know it isn't Saldona."

"Saldeva," he corrected.

"That's what I meant... but I love it."

"You've never tasted it, at least not in my bar. Be grateful, it's awful. You," he gestured to her with his glass, "*love* Saldeva." Devon sipped.

"How dare you take it upon yourself to decide what I like," she said, with mock agitation.

There was a slight shift in his posture, a subtle straightening of his spine that caused an unexpected shiver to crawl from the base of her skull to the small of her back in a tingling line of sensation. Devon's gaze caught hers, stayed there, and when he spoke again, his tone was something akin to a dare. "Would you prefer a different wine, darling, or shall we stick with what I've ordered for you?"

Hope stared into his hazel eyes, mesmerized by the way the tiny slivers of gold caught the light. She didn't know if it was the unexpected endearment or the way that everything in her body sparked to life when he shifted on his barstool, but her brain went fuzzy. "I...like this one," she said.

Devon's brow furrowed; he blinked twice and glanced down to the bar. When he looked back up, it was as if he had returned to original programming. He smiled warmly and said, "Sorry for plying you with my best Cab Sauv at a bargain price. I wanted to keep you coming back."

"How did that plan work exactly?" Hope asked hesitantly.

She felt off kilter from whatever had passed between them, brief as it was. She needed to find her balance. Perhaps it was all in her head. Unsatisfied urges could do that to a girl. Things that go buzz are never quite the same as hot hands attached to someone who wants to get inside you; eventually, you went a bit punchy.

"You'd grow to love the Saldeva," Devon explained, "having no idea that was what you were drinking. You'd venture out into the world and continue to order it by *the A name*, or *the C name*, or whatever..." He winked, and she giggled. "Endless disappointment," he said dramatically. "That part didn't work out so well, once I realized that you were picking the house red, without reading the menu," he admitted. "But I was still hoping everyone else's house offerings would fall short. You'd come to believe that I was the only bartender in town who could satisfy your craving."

It was unfair for him to throw around words like *satisfy* and *craving* so flippantly. Both purred up out of him, stirring every hormone in her treacherous body. Hope swallowed hard and refocused.

"But now, I know your secret plot," she joked, swirling her glass for emphasis.

"True, but I'm also not planning to charge you seven bucks a glass tonight. Assuming you don't mind my company," he inclined his head, "I can make you a better deal than our previous arrangement."

"Now that I know that we had a previous arrangement," she replied.

HOPE

Hope was halfway through her first glass and giggling through a story about the first class she taught solo when a server appeared to relocate them to a quiet table in the back. Devon helped her into a seat that put her back to the wall and settled himself to her right, as Katie, their server, rearranged the table. She handed out menus and promised to return momentarily for their order.

As she walked away, Hope crossed her legs to guard against the chill, shifting uneasily as her ankle brushed down the side of Devon's calf beneath the table. "Oh, I'm sorry," she said, straightening.

"If I were afraid to touch you, I wouldn't have asked you out," he said easily, laying the menu on the tabletop. "What are you in the mood for?" Hope stared at him longer than she'd intended, before studiously leaning over the menu.

They ended up ordering a couple of appetizers and an entrée. Devon kept reaching for the stuffed mushrooms that had been Hope's suggestion, while she couldn't stop eating the bite-size caprese stacks he'd requested. The entrée was some sort of seafood pasta in a seven-billion calorie cream sauce. It was divine, and they frequently reached a fork toward the massive shallow bowl at the same time. It felt like a slow dance toward some deeper intimacy as they stopped retreating to allow the other to go first and instead twirled up pasta simultaneously.

Around the end of the stuffed mushrooms, Hope realized that she had wedged her crossed ankles behind his leg for warmth. While her dress was date-appropriate, it wasn't cozy, especially once she shed her coat. If Devon noticed, he didn't let on. Maybe this was what happened when you went out with someone that you had known casually for almost a year. The small talk came easily, and you could use them for body heat. At least until you became hyper-aware of every inch of contact between you.

"I can see you as a teacher," Devon said. "You're kind, but you don't take shit."

"You only ever see me out for drinks and dancing," Hope said. "Not in *Ms. Lawson mode*."

He skewered the last shrimp from the pasta on his fork and held it out to her. Hope leaned forward, opening her mouth.

"I didn't say I thought you'd like it, but you'd be good at it," he said.

She considered as she chewed. "Yeah, well," she said, dabbing her mouth with her napkin, "Maybe you're right. It's hard to imagine working in a school again."

The opportunity to be a counselor at Costings Academy had drawn Hope to Asheville, or that's what she had thought at the time... Maybe her entire life overhaul was more a matter of running *away* than running *to*. Regardless, when the time came, she hadn't signed the contract. After nearly a year of working outside of a school building, Hope did not want to go back. She missed the kids, but that was about it. Her internships outside of that environment, while often more challenging, were also more fulfilling. They stole her heart. Still had it, even as she'd come to discount her ability to perform the job she loved.

With her minor in education, master's in social work, and a counseling license waiting for her to finish logging post-grad hours, Hope currently possessed nearly every professional degree or licensure she'd wanted. And as soon as she'd *arrived*, she had lost sight of her long-term goals.

She impulsively took a job at Silver Sassafras, an odd little shop that sold a variety of New Age and metaphysical stuff, the week she declined Costings. The shop job utilized none of her education, and nearly a year later, Hope hadn't looked for a better fit. She couldn't stay at Silver Sassafras forever, though. Her bank account wouldn't support that much longer, unless she made cuts and gave up her own space. Hope was adrift. Rations were low. She had to set a course, and soon—but the Aaron factor complicated all that.

Hope had an irrational fear that if she were locked into a contract, he might end up locked in with her somehow. Which sounded silly, but she'd met him in her last school, and now he lived in her new town. The fear wouldn't go away. Hope thought back to that day when she had walked around the corner on the way to her car after work three months prior and plowed into her uniformed ex—an encounter that led to a rather ruckus night at Cleary's for her and Chloe...and Devon too.

Aaron would be livid if he saw her tonight. She frowned, scanning the room.

"Hey." Devon's voice cut through her thoughts, tinged with concern. "Where'd you go?"

Hope plastered on a smile. "Sorry. Wandering mind. I'm having a really good time, and this pasta is amazing."

He considered her for several seconds, then leaned closer. "Can I tell you a secret?" he said conspiratorially.

Hope nodded, warmth blossoming in her core as he leaned in close. God, he smelled good. The heat of his breath brushed her neck and ear when he whispered.

"I'm a bartender, and that makes me an excellent listener," he said, before straightening back up.

Hope giggled, sipping her third, and—what she was determined would be final—glass of wine for the evening. "That's not a secret."

"Something's bothering you," he said.

"It's nothing." She waved him off. "The fastest way to ruin a first date is to start talking about baggage, and like I said, I'm having a really good time."

The vague mention of baggage was more than Hope would have said to him without alcohol lubricating her system. She would probably regret it, but didn't people deserve to know that there *was* baggage? Even if you didn't open the whole suitcase and display each piece of dirty laundry, shouldn't they know the thing existed before they got too invested? And why was she suddenly concerned about people getting invested?

Hope ventured a guarded glance in Devon's direction and found him studying her. She never would have guessed what he was about to say next. Not in a million years.

"My sister died when I was fourteen." He paused, pulled in an audible breath, and let it out on a sigh. "It really fucked me up."

That suitcase weighed a ton.

"Devon—"

He pulled in another sharp breath—in through his nose, out through his lips—and kept going. "My dad took it hard. He wasn't great to begin with, but Kell's... My sister's name was Kelly," he explained. "Her death broke him. Eventually killed him. Unfortunately, he dragged out the dying part for another five years. Bastard that he was..." Devon grumbled to himself. "We used most of his policy to start a non-profit in Kelly's honor. We call it Redact and Recover, R&R for short. I'm there a lot when I'm not at the bar."

Hope blinked. She wanted to hug him but had the feeling that would come off as pity, and he might not appreciate it.

"Not enough?" Devon licked his lower lip, and before Hope knew what was happening, he began again. "Okay, I'll do the relationship stuff, I guess. Probably where I should've started... I suck at relationships." He went to drag his hands through his hair but thought better of it and changed course, swirling the ice in his glass with a finger instead. "No, that's not true. I have no idea how I would do in a romantic relationship. I *assume* I would suck at it. I've been so wrapped up in Cleary's and R&R that I've avoided anything serious." Devon paused long enough that she thought he might be finished. "When I'm around you, I kind of want to see if I could be good at it though."

Oh.

After a brief pause, he caught her gaze. "And did I mention that I'm a good listener?" he asked.

Hope nodded slowly.

"Your turn," he said. "If you want, I mean." He fidgeted with his napkin, twisting it into a tight knot—like *tight*—then putting it aside. Whoever bussed the table would trash it because getting that square of linen unknotted wouldn't be worth the effort.

"I..." Hope began, then reconsidered. "Isn't this a little heavy for a first date?"

"I don't know. I don't have a lot of experience with this kind of date," Devon admitted with a shrug, scrubbing his hands on his thighs under the table. "Is it too heavy for you?" His eyes found hers, anxious, but eager.

Hope shook her head, not wanting to send the message that hearing about something traumatic in his past would send her running for the hills—a weird place to be when she'd told herself that this date was just for fun. "So, what does the nonprofit do?" she asked.

"We... Actually, can we get into that another time? That conversation can turn complicated, and right now, I'm more interested in you." He lifted his drink, took a sip. "The way I see it, I've spent dozens of evenings staring across the bar at you. If we add up all the upgraded drinks, and the free appetizers—"

"You always say they made a mistake in the back," she said.

He laughed. "God, I am awful at it, aren't I?"

"At what?"

"Flirting with you." He shook his head. "You didn't even know."

Hope grinned. "I guess I knew that you look at me sometimes. I did worry your kitchen staff was a little unreliable with all the wrong orders," she admitted.

"Good thing they accidentally make what you like." Devon sipped his drink and went on. "I'm not trying to *you owe me* here, only to make a point. You already knew the superficial stuff about me, and I got your *I'm a retired teacher, who now sells candles and crystals* spiel earlier. I knew some of that because you and Chloe are always talking, but now I've got specifics. My point..." He sighed. "My point is that I'm pretty sure there's a natural progression when people are getting to know each other, and this isn't a first date with someone we met online two days ago. I've provided a streamlined account of some of the things in my head that are likely to pull me out of a conversation, and that opens the door for you." He gestured in her direction. "Up to you if you want to walk through it."

Hope studied him. "Is there a dating outline somewhere that I haven't read?"

Devon smiled. "I could use a resource like that. There are tons of *how-to's* for—" He stopped short. Cleared his throat. Was he *blushing*? "Um... anything else you'd ever want to learn, but I'm making this up as I go," he said.

"So, why now?" Hope asked.

"Excuse me?"

"If you've been flirting this whole time," she said, "what made you ask me out now?"

"Chloe gave me your number." He grinned; Hope laughed. "And, ah... yesterday was my birthday, so I guess I thought maybe it was a sign."

"You didn't say it was your birthday."

Devon shrugged. "I'd rather not have a woman agree to go out with me as an obligatory birthday gift. I kind of hoped you'd... you know... *want* to go."

"Well, did you have a good birthday? I mean, even though you had to work."

His smile was slow and satisfied. "I'm sitting with you now."

Hope took a breath, as her heart thudded hard in her chest. Sex she could do—fun, dinners out, but vulnerability was something that she might not have the fortitude for, at this point. If she said too much, she might end up pulling the plug on the whole thing. It was her typical defense mechanism, and she didn't want another relationship with substance to tank on the heels of what happened with Aaron. Better to not start at all.

"Don't you worry that you'll say something you'll regret?" she asked.

"Kind of," he admitted. "You haven't claimed to have a headache, so I'm still cautiously optimistic that I haven't completely screwed up. But you're lucky; you have nothing to worry about."

Hope arched a brow. "How so?"

"If I regret it, I'll still be at the bar. Completely at your mercy." He dipped his head in a mock bow.

"Unless you kick me out," Hope said. "You're good at that."

Devon nodded. "Yeah, but you aren't going to assault anyone. What are the odds that I would ever ban you from Cleary's?" He brushed past the rhetorical, with a wave of his hand. "If you regret it, you'll find a new hangout and pretend I don't exist. You'll pay more for the Saldeva, but that's the extent of it."

Hope took another sip of wine which slid over her tongue like a dark, velvety cherry, leaving an attention-grabbing pop of tang in its wake. She said nothing. Devon's expression shifted again. This time it wasn't vulnerable, like when he had blurted out a string of deeply personal insights, nor was it...whatever had happened as they sat at the bar earlier—when some unnamed energy inched its way down her spine. The look on his face was open, honest.

"You looked like you were somewhere else," he said. "I don't know what triggered it, but it was written on your face, plain as day. And you were upset."

"That's your go-to response when you see a problem, isn't it?" she said. "You need to fix it."

Devon nodded, and this time when his eyes met hers, they held the warmth of honey and the verdant green of a forest in summer.

"I can't always, but yeah, I tend to want to fix things quickly."

Hope thought of the seething anger that radiated off him the night a stranger groped her on his dancefloor.

"*Aggressively*," she corrected, before catching herself. She watched the faint hint of amusement flicker across his face.

"Occasionally," he conceded, "when it involves something I care about."

Hope rolled the hem of her dress between her fingers under the table. "I guess I'll do it how you did, so we're even."

His eyes widened. "Oh, you don't—"

"My big childhood trauma isn't very impressive," she said over him before she could change her mind. "My parents split when I was twelve. My dad remarried almost immediately, and that earned me a brother five years younger than me. We're close. He lives in town."

"Mom went through a second husband and then married a third time. I got a stepsister out of that, but I'd already moved out by then."

"I bounced back and forth, as an angsty preteen and teen, then made it a point to keep my distance from my college roommates. Got good at being an island, and it spills into my relationships." She sipped her wine.

"It doesn't matter if it's a month or a year, I keep it superficial enough to walk away. My last relationship lasted about a year and a half, so I'm probably due for a few quickies. I took a year off though, so who knows. New territory." Hope chuckled uncomfortably before realizing that Devon was blushing. No question about it this time. Full on, cherry-red from his cheeks to the roots of his dark hair. Above his crisp white collar, his neck turned a brilliant shade of crimson to match.

"So," he said slowly, "you're looking for fun, not really—"

"Oh no, I didn't mean..." Hope suddenly found it difficult to look at him. "I'd love to get, you know... the fairytale. I'm just not sure it exists."

When Devon stayed quiet, she went on. "He was the officer assigned to my school, the last guy. That's what I was thinking about when you noticed... *Who*, I mean."

He smiled awkwardly. "Not sure how to take that."

Hope again let her gaze drift around the room. "He wouldn't be happy if he caught me here. I still think about things like that sometimes. I guess it's habit." She snuck a glance at Devon.

Hope recognized her date's silence for what it was—a tension so dense you could stand on it.

"Sorry. Total buzz kill."

"A year and a half is a long time," Devon said.

Hope's mouth twisted into a small smile. "Yeah. Sometimes relationships are confusing. It started good, but it got..." She grasped for a way to end the sentence. "Weird," she finally supplied.

"Define *weird*." The ice in his tone sparked the same prickly sensation from the bar—an insistent tingle at the base of her skull—but their current topic of conversation was far from what triggered the response previously. This didn't feel flirtatious. This felt dangerously deep. "Please," he added.

Hope inhaled deeply, held it for a beat before releasing it again. "It wasn't a good fit, you know. Things started to fall apart, so I ended it." Her explanation shied away from everything that mattered. "He didn't take the breakup well, but I already had a job lined up. That was the final straw. I got an offer from Costings Academy. That's a private school here in town. It was a good offer, not that I ended up taking it. Anyway, I moved here." She tapped a nail on the bottom of her wine glass, absently thinking that she should have painted them. "We lived in Charlotte, so the drive kept him from coming around too often after that."

"You lived together?" Devon asked.

"Oh, no." Hope laughed. "He wanted to move in together, but that's always been a deal breaker for me. I like having my own space. Makes it easier when things go south." And in Hope's experience, things always went that direction eventually. "I was at his place more than my own for most of our relationship, but I kept my apartment. Being stuck in a house with him while lining things up here would have been a nightmare." Or worse, she thought, stuck with one of her parents... Her brother would have had mercy on her and taken her in, though. JJ was solid like that.

"So, you ended it when you got the job offer? Was that coincidence, or...?"

"It..." Hope stopped to think. His questions circled too close to things she didn't intend to tell. "I don't know. Things had been going badly for a while. They were never exactly *right*, even when they were good, if that makes sense. But the final straw happened the day after I got the job offer."

"What—"

"*And* that's my story for another time." She cut in, smiling stiffly.

Devon nodded, in deference. "That's how you met Chloe—when you moved here?"

"Yeah." Hope's smile widened. "Chloe's... Glitter. All sparkle and shine, you know? She gets on you, and you can't shake her off. She's amazing. She'll push your boundaries for your own good, but she'll never cross them. And she's always there if you need her."

"*Glitter.*" Devon shook his head, grinning. "I don't think a more accurate description of Chloe exists." He sipped his drink, as his smile faded. "So did it work?" he asked. "Moving here? The job change?"

"What do you mean?"

"Did he keep his ass in Charlotte?"

Hope shifted her gaze into her glass. "Mostly. For a while. He has family in Ashville. I knew it was a possibility, I guess, but he ended up getting hired on here."

"Three months ago," Devon said, features hard.

Hope's brow furrowed. "How did you know that?"

"I pay attention," he repeated, though it sounded far less playful than it had when they were discussing beverage preferences at the bar. "Call it an educated guess. You weren't yourself when you came into Cleary's, that last night. Then, there was what happened." The gravel in his voice would have had her scooting away from him if she were the target of his hostility. Instead, it made her feel oddly secure. "You didn't come back. After a while, I thought you wouldn't."

An astonished laugh popped out of her. "I'm surprised you noticed I was missing."

"I—"

"Pay attention?" Hope raised a brow and smiled. Hazel eyes found hers. "When it comes to you."

HOPE

Unlike the first night he had driven her home, there wasn't any discussion about whether Devon would walk her in. He helped her from the car, put her hand into the crook of his arm, and the pair slipped up the three flights of stairs. Hope's giddy anticipation drowned out her screaming feet.

"Do you think Chloe spotted us yet?" Devon stage-whispered with a grin.

"Probably," Hope replied. "I bet she's spying through the peephole. She lives for that sort of thing."

Hope glanced over at him; her keys already clutched in her hand. She wasn't sure if she wanted a decent goodbye or more than that, but she needed privacy. She turned the locks as stealthily as possible, and without hesitating for her nerves to get the better of her, she pulled him inside and shut the door.

"Well," she said, dropping her clutch and keys on the end table, "if she does know we're back, at least she won't be staring at us." The excitement and uncertainty coursing through her made her feel like she might come apart. Keeping it out of her voice proved challenging.

Reaching to pull off her coat, she found Devon's hands already at her lapels. With a smooth tug, it slid back and over her shoulders, his warm fingers skimming her arms as the coat fell away. Hope turned and found him standing closer than expected. She tilted up her chin to look at him.

"Ah… but now she'll invent all sorts of scandalous rumors," he said, dangling her coat from the same fingertips that he'd brushed over her skin. Hope took the garment, stowing it in the tiny closet by her apartment door.

"Let her." Her reply was sticky-sweet; flirtatious in her own ears. Hope's cheeks flushed.

"I had a great time tonight," Devon said, with a smile.

"Me too. This was…" She trailed off. Neither the way it stirred sleeping parts of her, nor the way that terrified her was open for discussion. "Thank you," she said when nothing else fit.

"I should be thanking you." He inched closer. Hope tilted her chin further and felt the most distracting thrum of sensation through her core. At least, that part wasn't scary. The physical part was the one thing she knew she could handle. "Engaging conversation, gorgeous woman on my arm." He raised a brow. "I'd love to spend time with you again."

"Are you sure? You already know all my deep, dark secrets. We might have nothing to talk about," she joked, trying to make light of the heavier parts of their date, while simultaneously kicking herself for bringing them up again.

"Ah... But you've only skimmed the surface of mine," he said, gliding the tip of one finger down the bare skin of her arm. "Can I take you—"

"Yes, please," she said softly. Staring up at him through her lashes, Hope watched as Devon's lips parted, and he pulled in a sharp breath.

"That look..." He canted his head, something changing in his tone. "You have no idea, do you?" Hope blinked up at him, a delicious tingle blooming at the top of her spine, and reaching down, down, down, as its twin reached up from her core. "Can I tell you a secret?" he asked again. Hope's blood heated, just as it had at the restaurant. She nodded. Devon leaned in close to her ear and whispered darkly, "I want to kiss you so badly that I can taste it."

He didn't move after he said it. Instead, he hovered there in the bend of her neck. His breath warm against her skin; his cedar and sandalwood and all-male scent in her nose. Hope's pulse spiked. She nervously wet her lips.

"I...I would like that," she finally managed, grateful that he couldn't see the blush coloring her cheeks from his current position.

"Would you, Hope?"

She nodded again and turned her face toward him seeking his mouth. To her surprise, a firm hand slipped up her throat, catching her chin and turning her head away in a gentle, but insistent move. With Devon close at her ear again, Hope's body temperature rose by the second. She wanted to pant. It was the most horrifying thought, but it popped into her head all the same. Pant for him when he hadn't so much as kissed her...

Devon clicked his tongue, sending a fresh shiver down her spine. "Impatient little thing," came his husky whisper. The sound of his voice turned her insides into something slick and aching. He slid his thumb along her jaw as he spoke. "If I kiss you, I'm going to have a hard time stopping."

Hope heard some small sound of frustration, and when a chuckle vibrated up from Devon, she realized that she had been the source. "Now, now..." he tutted. "I didn't say I wouldn't."

His free hand found the small of her back, while the other slid up into her hair, burrowing between the braids and twists that she'd pinned in place. This gave Devon the control he needed to put her exactly where he wanted, and Hope's body followed his unspoken commands without hesitation. He pulled her close, tilted her head back, and trailed his lips over the same path his thumb had traced moments earlier, stopping an inch from her mouth. "You can tell me to stop, darling."

That promise felt like an absurdity and a security blanket. There was no way in hell she was telling him to stop, but the fact that he would made him safe. Hope reached around his neck and skimmed her fingers through the short hair at the back of his skull. Another sound came out of her, this one unmistakably needy, as she arched toward him. At that invitation, Devon brought his mouth to hers, his lips soft, but unrelenting. Irresistible.

The intensity of his kiss defied her senses—swamped her in swirling, heady lust. The smell of his cologne twined together with the darker scent of a ravenous male. Between the taste of whiskey and coke sweet against her tongue and the heat of his body, everything in her longed to press closer until nothing separated them.

Devon's hand tightened possessively around her waist, while the one at the back of her head maintained its grip. It hurt, but she didn't care. His tongue plunged into her mouth over and over again, as Hope imagined him moving lower. Running his hands under her dress. Pulling her panties aside...

As if responding to her thoughts, Devon made a gruff sound. His mouth left hers, and somewhere in a flurry of movement and kisses trailing over her shoulder, Hope realized that he'd drastically changed their position. His hand now wrapped around her wrists at the small of her back, catching both of her arms behind her. His forearm and biceps created a steel cage for her body that didn't afford her a single inch of space to step away. She gasped and twisted, desperate for friction.

Devon answered by swiftly planting her shoulders against her apartment door with a thud and bringing his other hand back to her throat. One of his feet wedged between her heels, his thigh pressing into her until her little black dress hugged tight across her hips. Now her mouth did pop open with a breathless pant. Devon's eyes were dark and devious, as he looked down at her.

"Do you want me to let go, darling, or do you like the sensation of not being able to get away?" he purred.

In the span of a heartbeat, everything in Hope went quiet and still. Some nearly invisible wall materialized out of the ether to separate her from the rest of the room. Everything was muted, as she gazed out through it. The sounds. The colors. She wasn't there anymore. Not really. Her chest moved in a deliciously slow rise and fall, as energy pulsed in the air around her, against her, *through her*, like ripples in the fabric of her universe. All of creation was thick, and sweet, and the world was a million miles away, except for Devon.

Devon... Did she say his name, or think it?

Whether he heard her or not, his head tilted, and his brow furrowed, eyes darting in quick, precise movements as he studied her features. Hope watched as some sudden, disturbing realization washed over his face. Swearing under his breath, he took a step back. Hope's arms fell to her sides; her wrists cold where his hand had been a moment prior.

"I..." She looked around in confusion. "I'm sorry... Did I... Is something wrong?" she asked, panic seeping into her words as she reached for him. She felt untethered, far away, and ungrounded. She couldn't think of a single positive thing that could have triggered the shift in him.

Devon caught both of her hands, lacing their fingers together, while keeping several inches of space between their bodies. It wasn't much, but the connection pulled her back into reality, at least partially. He squeezed his eyes shut and let out a ragged breath that might have been a laugh.

"Not at all." His oddly lighthearted timbre rang in stark contrast to the visibly ruffled state of him.

"But...?" she prompted. Clearly there was more, or he wouldn't have stopped kissing her.

Devon swallowed hard. "But, I should go," he said, eyes still searching her face. "We need to—" He cut himself off, shook his head. "I want to see you again, okay? Monday. I'll be at R&R during the day, but I'm off Monday night."

Hope's lip trembled. She couldn't understand his sudden rush to leave. Things seemed good, right before he stopped. More than good. "Okay..." she said carefully.

He looked around aimlessly, released her hands, and ran his own through his hair, returning it to its normal state of acceptable disarray. "Are you alright?" he asked.

Hope looked down at herself. She should take off her heels soon, but nothing seemed to be amiss. "Yeah," she said, numbly. The numbness... The floaty feeling... That wasn't normal. But she hadn't drank that much. She'd eaten. It didn't make sense. "I'm sorry. I don't know what's wrong with me."

"There is nothing wrong with you. You did nothing wrong," he repeated. Devon framed her face between his palms and pressed a kiss to her forehead. Hope found herself leaning toward him, wanting to maintain the contact any way she could. He folded her into his chest, wrapping his arms around her snuggly and stroking one hand over her back. "It'll pass."

Hope breathed in the scent of him—*him*, not his cologne or the stuff in his hair, but the scent that peeked out from beneath the rest— and felt her whole body relax.

"I'm going to go, so you can get some sleep," Devon said, a bit stiffly. "But..." he added, hesitant at first, but with increasing resolve, "you can call me, or text. Anytime and for any reason, okay?"

"Alright." She wished she didn't sound so mousy.

"Promise."

"Okay," she squeaked.

He straightened a fraction, chin inching up and lids lowering, as he looked down at her. "Okay what, Hope?"

Hope sighed. "I'll call or text if I need to."

"Or if you want to," he corrected gently.

"Or if I want to," she agreed, feeling oddly comforted by the idea.

"Get to bed," Devon said, pressing a final warm kiss to her lips, as he moved past her to the door. "But first, come lock this behind me."

She did as he asked, but the metallic *snick* of the deadbolt sliding home echoed in her ears like a gunshot. Hope hated that sound. Feelings stirred inside her, giddy, and needy, and now... hollow.

"What is wrong with me?" she all but breathed into the stillness of her empty living room.

For one thing, her feet hurt.

DEVON

He hadn't said a word since he sat down, hadn't bothered looking up, but a tumbler slid in front of Devon like magic. A fair hand with short, dark nails lingered on the rim, before moving out of his immediate field of vision; the familiar sounds of the bar crashing into the void. He picked up the glass and took a long pull, followed by a deep breath. Whiskey, neat. So, it was written on his face then.

Not Cleary's had been one of his few goals for the evening. Yet, here he sat on the opposite side of the bar he had been standing behind twenty-four hours prior.

1. *Not Cleary's*

2. *Normal-ish*

3. *No dominant bullshit*—which was an extension of *normal-ish* if he was being honest, but whatever.

He was batting...nothing, or however that saying went. Devon wasn't great at sports metaphors either. He glanced at his phone, making sure Hope hadn't texted, then resumed staring at the wood in front of him.

"That bad, huh?" Nix said, lifting a bottle of Bushmills to refill his glass.

Devon chuckled weakly. "What tipped you off?"

"Probably the fact that I'm serving you whiskey while you're supposed to be on a date."

"Yeah, well. Date's over."

"Are we going to have a Pub Night?" Nix crossed her arms, creating a shelf for all the cleavage spilling out of her top. Devon answered by raising his glass. "If you end up on top of this bar, Devon Cleary," she hissed, "I'll have the boys drag you down. It's not yours tonight."

"It's always mine," he reminded her. "This," he jabbed a finger into the wood, "this is always mine." Nix glared at him. "Despite all else," he relented, "my Irish is firmly in check. Besides, you're the one pouring."

"Am I going to have to drive you home?"

"Probably." He turned up glass number two, then reconsidered. Remembering the mess he'd made at Hope's, he only drank half. "No, thanks," he said, blocking her next attempt to top him off with a hand.

Nix sat the bottle back on the counter behind her in easy reach. "Seriously, why are you here?"

Devon shook his head. Nix was one of the few people he could discuss this with, but it didn't make it easy.

"Did she puke in your car?"

Devon scowled at her and checked his phone.

"Won't see you again, unless you go to Sunday school with her in the morning?" Nix scrunched her nose, as he pinned her with a hard stare. "You know that shit doesn't work on me, Devon," she went on. "Put your dick away and tell me what happened. You're sucking down Irish whiskey like it's water, so someone pissed on your belated birthday party."

He ignored the birthday reference. Mentioning that he'd made another trip around the sun to Hope was as close as he got to celebrating the thing. "Again, you're the one pouring, and I told you no last time," he said pointedly, wondering idly about Hope's birthday. See... he should've paid attention to that, back when she was new enough to Cleary's to card. Maybe he should start a birthday rewards club or...

"Spill it," Nix pushed, interrupting his bizarre train of thought.

"I kissed her goodnight, and she ended up in subspace." Okay, so it wasn't as hard to say as he'd imagined. Devon shrugged and took a measured sip of his remaining whiskey. "Give me Coke after this. No matter what I say later, give me Coke. Or coffee," he said.

"Subspace," Nix repeated.

Devon shrugged again.

"Gotta say, I don't get the upset. I mean, doesn't that mean you did your job well? Head pats for the dominant Dom..." Nix chuckled.

"She's not a submissive."

"Then how did she end up in subspace?" Nix used the same tone you'd use to ask a kid about the chocolate on their shirt. And fingers. And mouth.

Devon scrubbed his hands over his face, then waved them around aimlessly. "That's a chemical brain thing. Science. Anyone could end up there with the right mix of endorphins and stimuli."

Nix pressed her lips tight, but the laugh burst out anyway. She cackled until tears gathered in her eyes.

"What?" he demanded.

"Anyone could end up there..." she said in a comical imitation of his voice. Devon did not find it funny. "Oh, I'm imagining Dev the Demon going all subby." She laughed again, as she carefully slid her fingers under her lower lashes, wiping away the tears before they could ruin her makeup. Devon always found it weird when people did that. He enjoyed seeing eyeliner-stained tears streaming down faces.

"Sorry to inconvenience you with my crisis," he said.

"Stop, stop!" Nix put out both hands and sucked in a breath between renewed barks of laughter.

"Maybe it wasn't even—"

"Devon," she said incredulously, barely managing to reign in her amusement. "You, of all people, know what freaking subspace looks like, and people don't just trip and land in that gooey goodness. I can't believe you spent almost a year *not* asking her out, and it turns out she's a freaking submissive. Only you could pull off something like that."

Devon shook his head, glancing at his phone. "I already told you she's not in the scene. We would know."

"Not every person who dabbles in BDSM does it through the channels we use. Most people are more private; we're kind of the minority."

"Yeah, but you didn't see her. I don't think she saw it coming or knew how she got there."

"How *did* she get there? Your lips didn't do it unless you were spouting off a bunch of growly dominant nonsense."

"I don't growl," he growled.

Nix cocked a brow and grinned. Devon sighed.

"Point taken," he conceded. "Mild restraint, and maybe a little..." He gestured vaguely. "Well, it wasn't growly. Not really. I don't think."

"The purring thing, then?" Nix gave a mischievous smile, the silver glint of her tongue ring visible in one corner of her mouth.

"Excuse me?"

She slid the barbell across her lower teeth before parking it in the other corner. "You know what I'm talking about. That thing you do when you already know you're going to get what you want."

"I wanted to kiss her goodnight," he snapped.

"Devon, I've seen you do your thing too many times to—"

"I tried to be normal."

It came out louder than he intended. Devon glanced to Lucas. The not-so-new bartender continued filling orders swiftly. He was up to his ears in customers and pretending to have no idea that his bosses were discussing something personal. He and Nix could be invisible for all the attention Lucas was throwing their way. The guy was solid; Devon had to give him that.

"I screwed it up," he said, lowering his voice. He looked down at his hands on the bar, wishing for a towel.

Nix disappeared the tongue ring and got serious. "You didn't screw her, right?"

Devon's brows ratcheted down tight. "I'm not going to fuck a tipsy woman who has no idea how she ended up in subspace. Do you think I drug drinks too?" He glanced at his phone screen. "You should help Lucas. He's drowning."

Nix rolled her eyes, then slumped her shoulders.

"Give me a minute." She walked toward Lucas and jumped into the fray. After about half-a-dozen orders and a few closed out tabs, she returned with a virginal Coke. Devon had his phone in his hand again.

"What's up with the phone? You've barely looked away from that screen, since you got here."

"I told her to text or call if she needed me," he said, taking a sip. "Thanks for the caffeine."

"No problem." She waved it away. "She was good when you headed out, right?"

"I think. I don't know," he admitted with a cringe. "When I realized what was happening, I kind of...left."

A flicker of concern went over Nix's face. "Uh...Devon?"

"Yeah..." he said, distractedly tapping the screen to see if any new notifications had popped up in the last 0.2 seconds. He didn't expect Hope to text. It was nearly midnight, so for all he knew, she'd gone to bed. But Devon couldn't stop checking for some reason, and every minute that passed fueled the compulsion. "She was doing that thing they do," he went on, "with the apologies and the clinging. I mean, they don't do that with *me* so much, but I see it all the time at Edge. She said she didn't know what was wrong with her. You know..."

"Dev," Nix repeated, more insistent.

Devon sat his phone face up on the bar and looked at his friend—who seized his shift of focus and snatched it. The phone chose that moment to buzz in her hand, illuminating with the promise of new information. Naturally. Nix glanced at the screen, then gave Devon a hard stare.

"Give it back," he said. Nix retreated a step and recrossed her arms, disappearing his phone. "I said, give it back," he said again, leaning forward on his barstool, as if he meant to come get it.

"You're going to want to settle down now. I'll give it back when I'm finished." The look on her face left zero room for discussion.

Devon let out a slow breath and splayed his hands on the bar. "Does she seem...okay?" he asked, opting to pose his most pressing question regardless. His mom hated texting, R&R was closed, and he was sitting at Cleary's. There weren't a lot of remaining possibilities other than Hope.

Nix cocked a brow.

"Fine." Recognizing the fastest route to what he wanted, Devon conceded. "But hurry up."

"Don't rush me," Nix bit out. He always found it incredible, how intimidating she could be for a curvy, under 5-foot, gothic cupcake. When she decided she had something to say, you listened.

"She's fine, Devon. Obviously," she said, taking mercy on him. "I would tell you if *your submissive* managed to break her leg while sitting in her bedroom."

"She's not—"

Nix plowed over him. "Now focus, while I lay out all the problems with this situation and the solution. The solution is simple, but you're a man, and I forgive you for making it unnecessarily difficult."

"Nix—" Devon could do without the condescension.

"Stop interrupting," she snapped. "You found a sub in the wild. Good for you. This isn't the problem." She put up a hand when he opened his mouth to argue. "This is different for you because you like her. A lot. And not because she's willing to play bottom to your top for an hour or two. She's also green, unless she's good at acting innocent. Also, not a problem. You haven't been green for over a decade, and you are more than capable of safely bringing someone into the life. If it turns out that she's less innocent than she seems..." Nix smirked wickedly, hitched up a shoulder. "Even better. The ones who play innocent are the most fun. You know I'm right. Don't argue."

Devon ran his hands through his hair. He had already ruined it at Hope's, so there was no point in resisting the urge now. He'd made it all the way through dinner, though. That was something. He tensed as he saw the protruding corner of his phone screen. "Can I check—"

Nix slapped his phone down in frustration. "Might as well. You're too distracted to hear a word I'm saying."

Devon snatched the phone off the bar and read Hope's text, a generic *Thanks again for dinner.* He sent back an equally generic *Thanks for the company* and looked to Nix.

"Better?" she asked. His phone vibrated again. "What now?" she demanded, as he frowned down at the screen.

"She, uh, says she can't wait to do it again." He texted back a quick agreement, and then looked up to Nix. "Sorry. It's just—"

"You got a green sub all hot and bothered then left her alone, and now she's texting you anything she can think of to get you to respond because she probably thinks you hate her and never want to see her again." Nix stared at him. "Now if you'll shut up and stop checking your phone for five seconds, we can finish this conversation so you can go deal with that."

Devon's eyes went wide, and he stopped breathing. "I...I left because—"

"Doesn't change anything for her tonight. You're a dominant, Devon," Nix said, some of her hard edges softening. "Not the fake kind that loses control and breaks people." He dropped his gaze to the bar and blinked back a million memories that he hated. "But not the Saturday night kind that plays around for fun, either. You're never going to be either of those things. Not the one that scares you. Not the one that can turn it off...even when you wish you could."

"I like her," he said, glancing across the bar into Nix's dark eyes. The softness of her answering smile would have seemed out of character to anyone who didn't know her as well as Devon.

"Then you can't pretend to be something you aren't. You need to trust her enough to show her both sides. That's part of it."

"Both sides?" he asked.

"Most people only get half of you, Dev. Not even that really… You have all these," she gestured around, "different pieces. The person you are here, at R&R, with your mom… The version of you that sucks down whiskey and won't get off the bar." She patted a hand on the glossy wood. "Demon," she added quietly.

Demon, he thought. The side he could only control through indulgence. That one didn't need explanation, but Nix kept talking anyway.

"Every regular at Edge knows that name. Whether they're terrified of you, want to be you, or be under you, they *know* Demon."

Devon cringed. "I can't tell her that."

Nix smiled. "You can. I've watched you negotiate scenes and boundaries more times than I've negotiated them myself, and we're rarely playing in the same place at the same time. You've got that part down to a science."

Devon shook his head and sipped his Coke. "It's not the same."

"How's it different?"

He took a slow breath. "Things get complicated when you start…you know, feeling stuff. Like with my father—"

"You've told me all about your old man. I pour, remember?" She nodded toward his soda. "But you aren't him. You need to talk to her, Dev. Sort it out, before either of you get any deeper. You can't cut that part out completely, and she deserves to know that upfront."

"I know," he said, absently running a finger around the rim of his glass. "I asked if I could see her Monday." He took another drink. "She said yes, but I don't think she was in a state to make plans."

Thus, the reason he fucking left. Hope was tipsy and subby, and Devon was way too turned on by the latter to trust himself with the former. She tasted like red wine and slid into subspace with the kind of full-body sigh that was the very definition of surrender. Devon had barely touched her. Well, not *barely*, but it hadn't taken much. The way she'd looked up at him, glassy blue-green eyes, lips parted in anticipation. All he'd needed to do was—

Leave.

"Oh, I'd put money on it that she'll still want to go. Take her to your place. Sit out on the back patio and ask if you can tie her up and play with her a while. You deserve it." Nix grinned mischievously, but Devon wasn't ready for the levity.

"I'm not saying that. Plus, it's cold outside." He glanced at his phone. Nothing new since his last text to Hope. Maybe she'd settled down.

Nix shrugged. "Well, figure it out. Right now, you're a true dominant who's been pretending he doesn't need to top for months, for some unknown reason. I don't get the denial, man." Devon opened his mouth again. Nix continued, full steam ahead. "And she's apparently an inexperienced sub who's ripe for the picking. Get it straight, before it goes sideways. You like her enough to take it slow, and you're experienced enough to keep it safe. She could do a lot worse than you."

Something ugly and possessive twisted in his gut, and Devon tamped it down fast. He told himself that he could stomach Hope ending up happy with someone else. A nice normal son of a bitch who watched football for fun and fucked in one of three positions—no gear necessary. But the idea of some misogynistic asshole or fake dom taking advantage of her nature was different. That made his blood boil and the admittedly somewhat growly thing under his skin gnash its teeth.

But like he was any better? He could behave like a gentleman dominant for the length of a scene—if he *had to*. And honestly, that shit was painful. Devon much preferred the darker scenes, the ones that left marks on his partners weeks later. Maybe he was an aggressive, abusive, possessive bastard, who'd never had a person to hurt with those tendencies. Apples and trees. Chips and blocks... It wasn't like the theory had been tested in any way that mattered, and Hope wasn't a goddamn guinea pig.

But he wanted her. God, did he want her. And not for a quick fuck or even an intense scene. Devon wanted her over, and over, and over again, in a million different ways. He wanted her to be *his*. The unfamiliar desire caused a sinful stirring of his cock in his slacks. Flashbacks of her apartment had him caught somewhere between going back and finding the nearest icy shower.

Can I take you—

Yes, please...

He'd intended to ask her out for another date, but lost sight of that the moment she cut him off. Her breathy, seductive, eager-to-please response got his dominant clawing its way to the surface. *Please* fell off her tongue like a siren song. For a Dom who had remarkably little use for begging, Devon would give her anything she asked for to watch her mutter pleases from her knees. And was that even topping? Probably not, but he didn't care.

"See there," Nix said. "You've got that look again. You can't help it. Go do what you do, Dev. And for fuck's sake, put her to bed."

"She stopped texting back. She's probably asleep," he muttered.

Nix looked at him like he was a fool. "You sure about that? You know how they are. If you don't want to go back tonight, handle it from home. Twenty says there's a vibrator in her nightstand." She jutted her chin, a movement intended to send him hoofing it out the door.

Devon tried to school his face into some semblance of civility, as he discreetly rearranged himself under the bar. "If I didn't know better, I'd think you were trying to top me," he said wearily.

"Oh honey..." Nix popped a kiss in his direction. "I'm the only one who can. Get out of here, so I can do my job. We're torturing Lucas."

DEVON

Thoughts churning, Devon stared down at the four identical pairs of black cargo pants meticulously aligned in the top drawer of his dresser. A fifth sat abandoned in his locker at the local dungeon. And for sentimental reasons, a retired pair, which saw his induction into BDSM, hung in the back of his closet.

He'd run through quite a few through the years, replacing them when their midnight black color faded to grey, or when his boyish figure developed into a man's—or when the stitching gave out. It happened occasionally when a sub got feisty, or Devon got *aggressive*. He could probably squeeze into the originals if he tried, but that first time, his straining erection was the only thing that kept them off the ground, after his belt came off.

People say that losing your virginity is an earth-shattering milestone, but Devon had virtually no memory of it. He was pretty sure she was blond, but only because nearly all the girls lightened their hair back in high school. Jessica maybe? Ashley? That experience had blurred at the edges until it was all but imagined.

But nearly sixteen years later, Devon could remember every detail of his first scene.

He could feel the cinch at his waist as he went for his belt, the rhythmic sensation of the tip slipping through each loop as he pulled it free; stiff leather in his hand, buckle biting into his skin. Devon had doubled it over and smacked it hard against his own palm. Bright pain blossomed in a hot stripe at the contact, and any question that he could do what he was about to do fell away when he uttered three words in a voice that he'd suppressed until that moment.

"Remember your safewords."

Each vicious lash tore a piercing cry from the stranger on the bench. Nothing in Devon's life had ever sounded so beautiful. Those wails flipped a switch in his brain. Turned it from a cesspool of anger, grief, and powerlessness into something...*better*. Something focused. Clear. A controlled calm. It was the polar opposite of everything he had ever known, and it tasted like salvation.

He cleaned himself up in the dungeon bathroom afterward, while someone reached their own climax in the stall beside his; he'd spend the next morning wondering if it meant he was gay; that his first sub was a guy, because that's who volunteered—that Devon had never come so hard. But in the bathroom that night, mopping spunk off his lower belly, out of pants he'd never so much as unzipped during the scene—with repetitive pleas of *Fuck me harder, Daddy*, and a whole lot of banging happening on the other side of the flimsy divider—all Devon knew was that he didn't give a shit if it was normal, as long as he got to do it again.

Wrenching his mind out of the past, Devon looked at his phone. She had to be asleep, right? It was nearly one in the morning—almost an hour since he had responded to her last text, and over two since he'd left her trying to navigate subspace. Perfect end to a first date, he thought, scrubbing a hand over his face. Just abandon her there saying she didn't know what was wrong with her. Freaking great.

But she would be asleep by now, and by morning, she'd be fine. Nix didn't know what she was talking about with all that *put her to bed* and *you know how they are* nonsense. Hope was fine. Chances were good that this entire thing was all Devon, anyway—punchy from months without a scene and projecting what he wanted to see onto the person he wanted it with. Which was all kinds of screwed up, especially as he stood staring at a drawer full of black cargo pants. He grabbed a pair and slipped them on, anyway.

Devon strode out of his room and down the hall. Reaching his destination, he brushed his fingers across the top of the doorframe for the key, then opened a room he'd hardly entered since spring. Not bothering with the lights, he settled against the headboard of the bed. Illumination from the hallway skimmed the dips and folds of the black comforter beneath his legs, its organic flow sitting in sharp contrast to the utilitarian lines of his cargo pants.

Maybe if he kept it contained—only in this room, only in *uniform*—he could keep a handle on it, he thought. How much damage could he do when she wasn't even here? She probably wouldn't respond if he sent her another text because she wouldn't see it until she got up in the morning. So, Devon could reach out a little, enough to make sure she wasn't still up, and his job would be done.

Sub settled; Dominant released from duty. Put the pants away and lock the playroom door.

Playroom...

The light coming in from the hallway caught the edges of furniture, tools, and gear. The looming bars and draped rigging of the canopy above him. And Devon called it a *playroom...* He shook his head, catching sight of the flogger hanging with everything else on the wall to his left. He stiffened.

Maybe this wasn't a harmless idea. Maybe this whole thing was a terrible idea.

He hadn't dealt well after that guy bothered Hope at the bar. The flogger on the wall served as a reminder of how bad it had gotten. She stopped coming around, and Devon got stuck in a loop of thinking about her barefoot in that short skirt and silver top, with glass number five sitting unattended in front of him—Demon screaming in his head that if he had stepped in when he wanted, the way he wanted, Frat Boy never would have happened.

He turned that situation over and over, looking for the key that would have prevented it from happening in the first place, but no matter how he played through it, Devon couldn't find the missing piece. It happened. A guy walked onto his dancefloor and put his hands on her body, and there was nothing Devon could do about it—nothing he could have done short of violating the fuck out of her boundaries. That knowledge should have made it better, but Devon's brain didn't work that way. Recourse, after the fact, felt hollow. A goddamn joke. Better to handle shit upfront because nothing ever buffed quite as shiny after life went and screwed it up.

Like the car his old man wrapped around a tree... Devon had the pinstriping redone *twice* before he gave up. Never quite right, even if he was the only person who noticed the imperfections. The *scars*.

About a week after the Hope incident, Devon ended up on the bar. As in *on the bar*. Too Irish that night, and it wasn't because of one of his predictable triggers—those spawned from times in his life where he'd failed to control the outcome. They were always there on that mental shelf in his head, but when triggered, Devon compulsively took them down one by one. He felt the ache of each again, as the familiar itch to take the control he'd lacked grew within him.

That guy grabbing Hope on his dancefloor? Huge fucking trigger. Huge. Honestly, Devon was surprised it only resulted in a Pub Night and not a string of scenes at Edge. The only thing that kept him out of the dungeon was the fear that it wouldn't work...again. What were you supposed to do when the thing that used to reset your brain stopped working, even though you still wanted it...needed it, and you were suddenly having a whole new set of dominant traits surfacing out of nowhere?

The unscheduled Pub Night did get him to pull the trigger on hiring another bartender, though. Like it or not, Devon behaved best for Nix when he was at his worst, and without a third bartender on staff, one of them had to stay until closing. That night he was wild before eleven. Nix got him down. Mark and Alex got him home, but that left Nix alone with a rowdy crowd for nearly an hour. That couldn't happen again.

Lucas Dalton, the guy he hired after the hangover wore off, was working out fine though. Nice kid. Trustworthy. Probably more than capable of closing alone if Devon could let go of the reins.

But back to that flogger on the wall... The day after his last Pub Night, Devon special ordered it. It was everything he'd fantasized about while staring at Hope on the dancefloor. Something he could swing *hard* but keep the scene alive long enough to take the edge off. The craftsperson was a leatherworker out of Oregon, and he'd waited nearly a month for the thing.

By the time the flogger arrived, Devon had calmed down enough to open it without downing a bottle of Redbreast or tracking down a handsy punk. He held it in his hands, noted the weight of the handle, felt the liquid pull of the falls toward the floor. And then, he hung it on the wall and walked away. Walked away from Hope, he realized because his sanity depended on it.

And then, she walked back into Cleary's and sat down in front of him...on his fucking birthday. He'd barely breathed, as he slid a glass of red wine in front of her. The pleasure and relief of looking into her blue-green eyes after months of her absence... Another unfamiliar sensation.

Nix was right. Something was shifting, and Devon needed to adapt. He couldn't turn it off. Not completely. Not without an outlet. Six months without a scene had him daydreaming of rigging Hope up, and that was going on long before he took her out to dinner. If he were being honest with himself, the daydreams were part of the reason for his six-month abstinence. Devon didn't need to top as badly as he needed to top *her*. Not to mention, Hope had gone a little subby on their date, and suddenly, he was sitting in the playroom in cargos... So yeah, he couldn't turn it off, but that didn't mean he could set Demon loose and let the pieces fall where they may.

If he wanted a chance at... *something*... Devon needed to bridge the pieces of his life; put them all together until there was something similar to *whole*, and then get on his knees and beg her to accept it. But with the next breath, he wanted to tell her to crawl. No... make her ask permission to crawl... The thought sizzled through his blood.

Devon never slept in this room; that wasn't this room's purpose. He didn't date the women he brought here; that wasn't Devon's purpose. He'd meant to go to his grave a bachelor with a room full of freaky shit. Let the neighbors whisper about what they find, after. His mother wouldn't get grandkids, but she could fill that void working at the daycare. Devon wouldn't hurt anyone or lose anyone. A solid plan—until he met Hope. Not that he would end up with her. She just...decimated his immunity to the desire for more than a physical or carnal release.

Pressing a thumb and forefinger into his gritty eyes, Devon remembered the look on her face when he'd left.

"She's asleep," he mumbled, as he picked up his phone. "She won't even see this until morning, you fuckwad." He started typing.

I doubt you keep bartender's hours, so you won't see this until morning. Are you still interested in doing something Monday evening?

The moment he hit *send,* a row of tiny dots hinted at an immanent response. Devon knew as surely as he knew his own name—both of his names—that she'd been holding her phone when he sent that text, and that meant she wasn't sound asleep.

"Christ," he whispered on a sigh.

I would love that, she sent back. The *When and where?* came six seconds later.

Devon considered. The necessary conversations required privacy. Nix's idea worked if you ignored the part about tying Hope up and playing with her. He glanced at the row of bundled rope on the wall and blinked away the image that popped into his head. Devon wasn't much of a rigger, but given the opportunity, he'd make do.

Dinner at my place? Pick you up at 6 or is that too early? he sent.

No, that's perfect. Thank you.

Devon relaxed a little, then frowned as another row of dots came on screen.

Can I bring anything?

Just you, he typed back.

Okay. Sounds great.

Devon waited... waited... tentatively believed that the goal had been achieved. The sub was feeling warm and fuzzy enough to settle down and call it a night, and he hadn't even suggested the use of a sex toy.

With near comical timing, his phone buzzed again.

Are you sure?

Devon sat up straighter, staring at the screen. Were they going to do this shallow back and forth all night? She had to be exhausted.

Just you, he repeated. *Now gorgeous girl, why are you still up?*

More tiny dots and then, *Sorry I got weird tonight. I think it was the wine or something.*

Not as settled as he'd hoped then. He could fix that though. Sure, he always topped in person, but he could handle this. Once he made up his mind, Devon typed the text and hit *send* without a moment's hesitation.

No more apologies, darling. I said you did nothing wrong tonight, and I meant it. Time for bed.

He watched the icon appear, disappear, then reappear as she undoubtedly typed and deleted another apology. "That's my girl," he said into the darkness, his voice taking on the edge of a dominant purring approval.

I'm having a hard time getting to sleep.

Noisy minds do that, he replied, speaking to the thing any sub would tell you if you asked them why they needed what they did.

The most seductive thing Devon offered a submissive, any submissive, was his gift for knowing which buttons to push to make their heads go quiet. In return, they gave him the thing he craved. *Control.* The chance to wield it, exercise it, let it pull against its leash until he yanked it back.

I wish I could turn it off, she responded, pulling his attention to his phone.

Let me help.

Devon watched her start to respond. Reconsider.

Okay, she sent after a twelve second eternity. The lack of exuberance in her response didn't make him feel particularly great about this plan, but he pressed on.

Are you in bed?

Yep.

Devon stared at the second single word reply in a row and felt...dirty? And not in a good way. He could get her to do it, and he knew she'd get into it. She'd sleep like a stone afterward. But it felt *wrong*, and wrong was a hard limit for Devon.

"Fuck this."

He shoved off the bed and strode out of the room, stumbling over the silvery-grey mass of Apollo, his massive pit rescue, who had abandoned his bed for the comfort of the playroom doorway. Devon pulled the door shut as he regained his balance.

"Sorry bud, but you're kind of a speedbump there. Place," he ordered.

Picking up his battered teddy bear, Devon's fur-clad roommate followed him into his bedroom. The dog walked straight to the pet bed in the corner, circled twice, and flopped down. Devon slipped out of the cargo pants and into bed.

"I'm going to try a thing here, buddy," he told Apollo. "But I have no fucking clue what I'm doing. If it bombs, let's never mention it again, okay?" The dog huffed an agreement.

He called her number and killed the lights when her voice came over the line.

"Me too," Devon said, swallowing nerves as he transitioned from their text conversation. This was going to be so much more complicated than telling her to dig the vibrator out of her nightstand.

HOPE

Everything touching her was Goldie-Locks-Zone perfect. So deliciously soft. Not too hot, not too cold. Just right. Hope rolled over, stretched, and grinned like someone who hadn't had this kind of relaxed Sunday morning in a while. And then, her entire body jerked with the ferocity of a limp corpse hit with a livewire.

Devon.

By the time she'd texted him the night before, Hope had convinced herself that he wouldn't respond. Like *ever.* And who could blame him? *Weird* didn't begin to cover the way she acted right before he rushed out. He did text her back, though, and then he called, and they ended up talking on the phone. The real deal. His voice in her ear until her eyes refused to stay open, and he hung up with a promise to text her in the morning.

Hope covered her face with a pillow and groaned, before chucking it. The pillow landed half off the bed down by her feet, denying her the satisfaction of sailing into a wall or the floor. This wouldn't be complicated if he'd been all *What are you wearing?* Or even, *Hey, can I come back?* But he didn't say anything of the sort.

Hope fidgeted in her sheets, her Baby-Bear-bed situation going hot and itchy like one of those sweaters that seemed like a good idea until fall turns to late summer at around 3 p.m. She eyed the phone on her nightstand and realized that she *wanted* him to remember to text. So, rationally speaking, maybe it would be better if he were busy at the bar and didn't think of it until evening.

As she glared at her nightstand, weighing the likelihood that a few extra hours would grant her a clearer head when it came to her dizzying attraction to her bartender, her phone buzzed. Any semblance of rationality flew out the window, as Hope launched into an army crawl over her remaining pillows, snagging her cell on the second buzz.

Her heart sank when she saw JJ's name on the screen, but she loved her brother; so, she disregarded the letdown. Strange for JJ to call though. He usually texted her unless... Her brain set off the possible-family-emergency alarm, and she answered fast.

"Hey," she said, her voice thick with sleep, despite the surge of adrenaline.

"Hey!" JJ said brightly. He sounded far away, and Hope could hear the kind of background noise you get when talking on speaker to someone in a moving vehicle. His chipper tone quieted her alarms. Emergencies rarely made people chipper. "Why did you hang up on your mom?" her brother asked.

Hope pushed herself up to sitting. "What?"

"Why did—"

"I didn't really hang up on her. I just got off the phone before I told her to go fuck herself," Hope said, pulling rogue pins out of her hair and tossing them on the nightstand. "So, she called dad, huh?" These days, her mother and father only interacted when her mom wanted to discuss Hope's shortcomings.

"Oh yeah..." JJ laughed. "And he bitched to mom, who bitched to me."

"She asked Aaron to walk me in Ashley's wedding," Hope said over a cacophony of noise and a slamming car door on JJ's end of the line.

"Aaron is a tool," he said, sounding much closer.

"Tell me about it." Hope stood and pulled on a pair of pajama pants. "I don't get her problem. It's like Christmas, but worse. It's been a year, for crying out loud. So, what are you up to this morning?"

She heard a knock, at the same time he answered. "Taking my big sis to brunch—or lunch, I guess. It's already eleven, and you can't buy a Mimosa until noon in this religiously-oppressed region."

"Dude..." She sighed. "Hold on. I need to pee."

As she ended the call and lurched toward the bathroom, Hope saw the text from two hours earlier—the one she'd slept right through—and she smiled.

Thinking about you this morning. Hope you slept well.

Not wanting to text Devon while hanging out with JJ, Hope formulated a response while standing in her bathroom. Uninvited visitors could wait. She eventually decided on, *I haven't slept that well in a long time. Thanks again.*

The moment she hit send, she heard her apartment door open.

"Don't be naked," Chloe shouted. "Your brother's here!"

Hope started down her short hallway. "So now you let other people into my—"

She came up short at the edge of the living room, where Chloe stood with one of Hope's *fuck me* heels in each hand, a satisfied smirk on her pretty face. JJ held her wrinkled dress from the night before, pinching the fabric between two fingers, like he was afraid to touch it.

"It's cool if you want to give me details after he leaves," Chloe said, snatching the dress from JJ and pushing past Hope. "But you will give them, eventually." She carried the pile of misunderstandings toward Hope's room.

"I...I just got undressed in here," Hope said to no one in particular.

"Weird place to get undressed," JJ mumbled, side-eyeing her couch. He stayed standing.

Okay. So, he was right, but to be fair, Hope *was* being weird the night before. After Devon left, she'd realized that her feet hurt. While shucking shoes, she'd ditched the dress. Then, she had a shower. Tried to watch TV... She hadn't expected company first thing in the morning.

"Not weird, if you're hooking up with a date," Chloe said, breezing back in with empty hands.

Hope choked on her own spit like the totally not guilty person that she was.

"That didn't happen," she managed.

Chloe raised a brow.

"It didn't," Hope insisted. Not that she hadn't been open to the idea.

"Whatever you say. Look, I was heading to the grocery store anyway. I wanted to see how last night went, but you aren't going to spill with him here." Chloe gestured to JJ. "I'll pop by later. Need anything?"

"Uh, no," Hope said, looking from her brother to her neighbor.

"Kay, well, text me if you think of something." And with that, Chloe was waving to JJ and out the door.

Hope's brother scanned the room. "Wait, you went on a date?"

***

Might as well keep the weird going, Hope thought as JJ pulled open Cleary's heavy wood and glass door. Sunlight glinted on gold lettering, reminding her of the way light reflected in Devon's eyes the night before. She blinked that thought away, as they walked inside.

Devon stood, diligently wiping down the bar as usual. He lifted his head the moment she crossed the threshold, mouth twisting into a wicked grin that made her feel some kind of way she shouldn't feel while out with her brother. Hope's body started toward him on autopilot. Tapping into that same energy, Devon dropped the towel, coming around the bar to meet her, tracking every move she made in the process.

Everything in Hope went warm and tingly, as he stepped in close, tucked a loose lock of hair behind her ear, and skimmed his mouth up her neck. He inhaled against her skin, like he was hungry, and she was something decadent.

"Did you miss me as much as I missed you, darling?" he said softly. Hope quivered in response. "Oh…looks like you did." He brushed a thumb over her lower lip, and brought his mouth to hers, his fingers warm and firm on the back of her neck, as his kiss made the room go quiet. Hope melted.

"Nah, it's cool. Don't worry about me. I'll wait," JJ said loudly, from his seat at the bar.

Oh right…her brother. Hope snapped back to reality, with all the finesse of a rubber band stretched too far. Devon took a step back, glaring at JJ. She could see the anger before he opened his mouth.

"I don't think you understand—"

"Uh, Devon…" Hope cut in, before anyone got forcefully ejected from the building. The hard set of his face didn't look like a thing you wanted to screw around with, and her brother was a pro at annoying the ever-loving shit out of people—especially when those people looked like they wanted to throttle him. "This is JJ," Hope said uncomfortably.

Devon squeezed his eyes tight and pressed his mouth into a firm line. "The brother?" he said, without peeking.

"Yeah…" Hope cringed.

He took a bracing breath, gave a swift nod, and opened his eyes. "Right. Great." Devon marched back behind the bar and extended a hand to JJ as Hope climbed onto her own stool. "Devon Cleary," he said as if he hadn't been moments away from hauling JJ into the street.

Her brother took what Devon offered. "Jameson James. JJ if you like."

"Jameson," Devon repeated, setting two heavy tumblers between them. "Like—" He reached behind himself and palmed a green bottle, giving it a little twist from side to side. "Jameson?"

JJ shrugged and smiled. "My parents were young. They named me after what led to my conception."

As the two of them sized each other up, Hope considered what each saw. Despite his rock star or porn star name, JJ looked like a blond-headed, blue-eyed, clean-cut college kid. He wasn't. He'd bolted from home the day he turned eighteen and bounced around Asheville ever since. He worked through a string of dead-end jobs and various roommates, while perfecting his craft, and ended up covered in ink along the way. You couldn't tell now because of his long-sleeved shirt and jeans, but no matter how far Devon's artwork went, JJ's probably rivaled it for acreage.

Meanwhile, Devon looked exactly how he'd looked every single time she'd ever seen him, save the night before. He already had his shirtsleeves rolled, that intricate tattooed knotwork making its way up his arms and disappearing under the fabric bunched below his elbows. Dark stubble shadowed his jaw, and his hair looked like he had scrubbed a towel over it, ran some styling gunk through it, and called it a day. A little rough. A little dangerous. More than a little capable of mopping the floor with a troublemaker. He tugged at his collar, then poured two fingers in each tumbler, and turned to Hope.

"Tea or wine? I'm assuming you don't want to drink to this introduction with your brother's namesake."

"How's the house red?" she asked playfully.

"Awful. But *your* house red is exactly how you like it," Devon promised, in a tone that took her back to kissing him. He slid a glass in front of her and grabbed a new bottle from the shelf. Popping the cork, he doled out a heavy pour without looking away from her.

JJ cleared his throat. "Still here," he reminded them.

"Right," Devon said, breaking away from Hope and lifting his glass. "To finding out you're the brother and not a random customer with a death wish."

JJ followed suit. "To the reason there's a wadded-up dress and heels in the floor of my sister's living room."

Thank God she hadn't sipped yet, or he'd need to wipe down the bar again. But Devon? He didn't even blink.

"Slàinte," he said evenly. "But I only had the pleasure of seeing her with them on. Sadly, I had nothing to do with taking them off."

Her brother raised his brows and nodded, as he went to take a sip.

"I didn't go yet," Hope cut in. Both men turned and waited for her to add to the toast. "To the look on Devon's face when you opened your mouth," she said to JJ.

"Dude," he chuckled, clinking glasses. "You were going to kick my ass."

Devon shrugged. "You interrupted."

"Hey, that's nice ink, man." JJ swigged half of his whiskey and put the glass back on the bar. "Really good work."

"He would know," Hope added. "He owns a shop over on Fifth."

Devon's face lit up like someone had flipped a switch. "Inky Things?" he said, tossing back his own whiskey on a oner and turning to put away the glass.

"That's us." JJ pulled out a business card and passed it over.

"I've seen your work," Devon said. "I haven't added anything new in a couple of years—my guy moved, and you know how it is—but I've scrolled your site a dozen times. My friend Nix has a couple of pieces by you."

"Nix? Hell yeah," JJ said before his brow furrowed. "Wait..." he said suspiciously, "How do you know Nix?"

"Ah..." Devon glanced between JJ and Hope. "She's one of my managers."

"Oh, right." JJ nodded. "I remember her saying she worked in a bar."

Suspicion deactivated. Hope grinned. This was going better than she could've imagined.

"Your shop is top of the list when I get the itch again," Devon said.

JJ put a hand over his heart, dropping it a beat later. "If you fuck over my sister," he said, with a placid smile, "you won't want me drawing on you."

Hope sighed.

HOPE

Sassafras, the resident queen and partial namesake of Silver Sassafras Stones and Curiosities, meowed in agitation.

"In a minute," Hope muttered.

Margo, the shop owner, left on an errand an hour ago, and even if Francis were pulled away from his sudden need to haphazardly refold every tapestry in the store, he couldn't run the register. Therefore, the woman who burst in a few moments prior took priority over Queen Sassy Pants.

Hope fiddled with the ends of her hair, unused to wearing it down at work, as the customer flitted around the store. Ninety seconds in, the woman approached Francis, Hope's less-than-helpful coworker, with three white candles and a lodestone in her hands. Hope braced herself.

"Can you point me toward your dried herbs?" the customer asked.

"Our what? We don't sell that," Francis replied gruffly, shaking out another tapestry in the woman's face. The customer took a step back, avoiding the billowing fabric, as Hope lamented the fact that she'd need to refold the lot of them tomorrow.

"Herbs are in that corner," Hope said, pointing.

Thankfully, Francis only worked two three-hour shifts a week. Regretfully, those shifts nearly always overlapped Hope's.

The woman voiced her appreciation, with a side-eye at Francis. Less than a minute later, she had added a sachet of herbs to her spoils and beelined it to the register. Sassafras yowled louder.

"Not now," Hope grumbled. "Find everything you need?" she added for the customer, who nodded the affirmative, confidently holding out her card before Hope finished ringing up the merchandise.

This woman had her shit together, Hope thought. She knew exactly what she wanted and where to find it. She probably knew what she was going to do with it all, too. Actively petitioning the universe. Manifesting her best life. You had to appreciate that kind of clarity.

Meanwhile, Hope stood there with her hair styled and makeup done, a fresh outfit waiting on her bed at home, so she could change before Devon picked her up—and a whole pile of *unresolved* hovering in the shadows in an ex-boyfriend-shaped cloud.

From Aaron's perspective, Hope screwed things up for them, and he had gallantly spent the last year taking all the necessary steps to right her wrong. They lived in the same city again, with nothing between them but walls that Hope erected, numbers she had blocked, and doors she refused to open. Aaron kept trying.

Sure, he acknowledged that he had been angry that last night, but with the passionate kind of anger. Spiraling out of love and only unforgivable because Hope insisted on being a bitch. Their regrettable one-time hookup two months later cemented his view, as did Hope's mother's attempts to get them back together. Aaron firmly believed that he was owed another chance and would either implode or explode when faced with evidence that she had moved on. That's what happened when Aaron didn't get his way.

Based on Devon's reaction the night that guy grabbed her at Cleary's, Hope didn't imagine him sitting idly by while her ex threw a temper tantrum. Guys didn't become more involved and less protective simultaneously. A couple of testosterone-fueled powder kegs in a volcano, that's what she had. One a *been there, done that* catastrophe, the other a *definitely maybe* catastrophe in-waiting.

Sassafras bellowed again, laying back her ears and narrowing her golden eyes. Her brother, Silver, appeared, purring loudly. As if apologizing for his sister's poor behavior, he wound his sleek grey body between Hope's ankles as she headed for the backroom.

"Okay, okay... It's not like it's empty," Hope said to Sass. Why did cats never eat anything touching the side of the bowl? Mysterious mysteries... "You know the hissing black cat thing is a stereotype, right?" She poured in a scoop of dry food and hurried up front at the sound of the door chime. Margo would use the back entrance when she returned; door chimes meant customer, and Francis couldn't be trusted with those for more than a moment.

"Good aft..." Hope trailed off as she walked into a whole bunch of uniform.

Aaron stared straight at her, smiling faintly at her obvious discomfort. A second cop, a woman that Hope didn't recognize, poked around the store.

"Hey, what's this thing?" the female cop said, holding up a bronze bowl.

"It's a… it's…" Hope's tongue stuck to the roof of her mouth, making it difficult to speak. She couldn't look away from Aaron to properly answer the woman.

"That's a singing bowl," Margo said, appearing from the backroom in her usual loose fitting, farmer's market-friendly outfit. She looked like everyone's heathen grandmother. "You need that to play it…" She gestured. "Yes, that… No! Don't hit it," she wailed, as the cop picked up the wooden mallet and reared back.

Margo swished past Aaron, with barely a glance, and snatched the bowl. "Like this, see?" She circled the mallet along its rim, calling forth an indulgent hum. Any other time, Margo's playing would have immediately lowered Hope's blood pressure. Actually, the whole of Silver Sassafras had that pleasant effect on her. The place was basically ambient Xanax. This time, however, the sound did little more than distract her enough to stop staring at her ex like an idiot.

"You try," Margo said, "Officer?"

"Neely, ma'am," the woman supplied, taking the items back.

Officer Neely bent her head over the bowl, a cascade of tiny black braids falling forward to frame her face. She tried to mimic Margo's movements. It wasn't the glorious auditory honey that Margo summoned, but she did make…something. "Hey! I did it."

Margo beamed at her. "You're a natural. You'll be a pro before you know it."

"This place is so cool, Marden. I'm buying this thing." She put the bowl on the counter with a smile, nodded at Hope, and resumed looking around. Margo strolled along with her, soaking up that *first-timer* energy.

With everyone else moving away, Aaron puffed up, smiled wider. "I didn't realize that you were still working here. I thought you'd have gotten this out of your system by now, or at least had to find something that pays better."

Hope smiled back, stiffly. She was tired of people telling her that she should have gotten her whole life out of her system by now. And if Aaron didn't know she still worked at Silver Sassafras, he never would have darkened the door.

"Yeah, well, I'm happy, so—"

"Speaking of paying better, I'm up for detective. I worried that switching departments would set me back, but they recognize a good cop when they see one. They'll make it official in January."

"Congratulations," Hope said.

"I like your hair like that." He grinned like he'd scored a point, while Hope wished he'd stop looking at her altogether.

"Thanks," she said, eyes following Margo's grey head above a shelf.

"You know, I was out in your part of town Saturday night," Aaron went on.

He rested one hand easily on the butt of his gun, and the other on the leather pocket that housed handcuffs—his typical, comfortable stance. The air in the room thinned. Hope crossed her arms, pinching the fabric of her sleeves and rolling it between her fingers where he couldn't see.

"I'm over that way a lot," he said. "Considered stopping in to see if you wanted to grab dinner, celebrate my impending promotion."

Hope's heart kicked hard in her ribs, and her face flushed. She pinched the fabric harder, keeping her breathing deep and even. She said nothing.

"I saw your car, so I knew you were home, but the lights were off. Didn't want to wake you up..." His blue eyes flashed with irritation, but he kept the smile in place. "You only crash by nine when you're sick or plastered."

A lie bubbled up in Hope on instinct—an explanation that she'd been hanging out with a girlfriend who lives in her building.

"I really prefer to not have unexpected visitors," she said instead.

"If you'd take my calls, it wouldn't *be* unexpected," Aaron snarled quietly. "We could set a time. I could pick you up. That's how dates work."

"I don't want to go out with you. We did that," she reminded him. "It didn't work."

"It worked great, for a year and a half. I think you *do* want to go out. I think you went out Saturday night," he said, with an accusation that he had no right to twisting his words.

Hope rolled the fabric so hard her fingers hurt. "I said I don't want to go out with *you*, Aaron. Are you shopping or...?"

"Nah. Just curious." She knew his expression too well. Aaron wasn't happy, but they were in front of people. "Neely seems to be loading up, though. If you get commissions, maybe you'll make rent," he said.

The insult landed like a stone in the pit of her stomach, as Neely put a bunch of incense and a hunk of rose quartz beside her singing bowl. With a *Seriously, this place is awesome,* she walked off again. This time, Margo stayed by Hope.

"Officer Neely says you two don't come around this way often," said Margo.

"We don't get a lot of calls over here. Got lucky today. I was telling Neely about this place. Figured we could stop in for a minute before heading our separate ways."

"She's such a nice woman. Lovely aura, really," the older woman said, shifting her feet wider as Silver emerged from the back to weave between her legs. "What was your name again?"

Hope looked down as Silver made his way to her. "This is Aaron," she said, out of habit.

"Officer Marden, ma'am," he corrected.

Silver ducked his head and bolted. Margo crossed her arms and adopted a slight scowl, as she glanced at the doorway that the cat had disappeared through.

"*Huh.*"

You couldn't miss the sudden chill in Margo's previously warm disposition. She looked like she could chew glass and spit it at you when her glare landed on Aaron and stayed. He smiled harder.

"Has Hope said something or...?"

"She's never mentioned you, *Officer Aaron Marden*. Hope, go feed the cats."

***

"So, is there something you want to talk about?" Margo asked when she called Hope back up front five minutes later.

"Not really," Hope hedged.

Margo sighed. "I saw you'd fed them when I came in," she said.

"Thanks for the out."

Today, Hope appreciated her boss's ability to read a room, even if the reading material embarrassed the crap out of her. Aaron kept his voice deliberately low through that exchange, ensuring that Francis and the other two women in the store wouldn't hear their conversation. He was good at that sort of thing. Making you feel small and alone, even when other people were around. Making you fold in on yourself and hide.

And Hope let him. She let him be quiet and sneaky, while he said things meant to upset her. It was as much a habit as her introducing him. If Margo hadn't picked up on the problem, Hope might still be talking to him—trying to act like it was normal.

"How did you... you know... *know*?" Hope asked, glancing sideways at the older woman.

"His aura is dark," Margo said mysteriously, staring across the store toward Francis, who remained quite distracted by yards and yards of fabric, his thick glasses sitting precariously at the tip of his nose.

Hope rolled her eyes.

"Stop that," Margo chided. "It's true, and your energy wasn't good around him."

"Margo..." Hope said incredulously.

"Silver left the room."

Hope nearly chuckled at Margo's admission. "That cat loves everyone," she said.

Margo nodded. "Which is why I pay attention when he doesn't."

"You know what, Hope?" Francis interrupted them in the near shout of someone who can't hear particularly well and is therefore susceptible to volume control issues. "You need a man like that po-lice." He broke the word into two hard syllables. "Clean-cut. Good job. Respectable. You aren't a bad looking woman. Especially when you clean up a little like you did today."

"Why do we keep Francis around again?" Hope asked under her breath.

Margo shook her head. "He's the only person Sass likes."

"Ahh... Right."

DEVON

I f Devon had known the day would include waterworks and demolition, he'd have brought along a change of clothes. He looked down at his black long-sleeved tee and jeans, hoping that Hope was into the do-it-yourselfer set. Bits of insulation and streaks of drywall dust morphed his date-casual look into something more like *Authorities believe the source of the explosion...* He'd told her he would pick her up at six, and without time for a change and shower at home, a brisk brush off, followed by an attempt to wash his face and up to his elbows was the best Devon could do.

At least, both bathrooms of R&R were operational again. Sure, his actual plans for the day were being pushed back, but...priorities. They couldn't discuss rearranging the various rooms of the nonprofit while a wading pool formed in the lavatory.

They would run the dehumidifier in here for a week or so to keep mildew at bay, and there would still be the matter of patching the giant hole he put in the wall to access the plumbing. Finishing work after that... But if nothing started spraying water again, they were on the road to recovery. Which was the whole point of the place, wasn't it?

"The goal was to fix the bathroom, Devon. It looks like a bomb went off in here," Monique Franklin, one of Redact and Recover's two resident counselors, said over the obtrusive hum of the dehumidifier. Devon winced. Her declaration added weight to his suspicion that he looked like he had been near an explosion.

While the outfit changed daily, Monique always looked like herself. Today, that meant a coppery headband held her halo of curly black hair away from her face, her blouse a rich purple that caught the light with a sapphire sheen. Bright red lipstick contrasted vibrantly against her deep brown skin and perfectly matched her nails.

"Unfortunately, this is one of those *make a mess to clean it up* situations," Devon said regretfully. "But the leak is fixed, and the toilet works. Once we get this place dried out, the dehumidifier will go back into storage, and I can patch the wall."

"You can't leave it like this." She cringed.

"I'm sorry," Devon said, walking out with Monique on his heels. "I'll fix it next week."

"Next week! What if a horde of spiders crawls out of the wall while you use the facilities?" she demanded.

Sydney Malone, their resident attorney joined the exchange in R&R's small lobby.

"What's going on?"

In some ways, Sydney reminded Devon of Nix, though the two looked nothing alike. Whereas Nix had a gothic creampuff vibe, with a jet-black pixy cut and a mean right cross, Sydney Malone was all long and lean, with pale blond hair that, even in a high ponytail, fell well past her shoulders. Always immaculate, with a tailored suit and perfect manicure, he doubted her right cross would hold a candle to Nix's. But Sydney's strengths lay elsewhere... Specifically, in the way she made grown men sob in courtrooms. Both women were deceptively capable of putting people in their place— or performing castrations. Whatever the situation called for.

R&R never could have afforded Sydney's services if she charged her regular rates, but she had a soft spot for the cause. In her case, a sister who was, thankfully, alive and healing. Devon had watched Sydney hold hands with teenage girls while calling the police, and he'd watched her walk adult women through their worst nightmares. When a mother lacked the strength to do what needed to be done, Sydney, despite having no children of her own, picked up the mantel until they could lift it again. And in court, she was a pit bull. Viciously protective. Unflinchingly loyal.

Devon had a thing for pits.

He turned to answer her, still backing toward the door. "I fixed the leak. I don't like mold, so the hole stays until we get it dry in there. But it's functional, and I'll patch up the cosmetic stuff next week. Also, apparently Monique thinks spiders travel in hordes."

Monique scowled at him. Sydney's eyes narrowed.

"Why are you in a hurry?" she asked shrewdly. Sydney would make an excellent dominant, Devon thought. The woman dripped authority and never missed a thing.

"Because I have a date, who I'm supposed to pick up in about fifteen minutes," he said.

"You're covered in filth," she observed.

"I noticed."

"Name?"

Devon rolled his eyes. "Are you planning to run a background check on her?"

"Would that cause a problem?" One blond brow jacked up into an angle as sharp as her wit.

Devon snorted. "I suspect hers would look better than mine. Her name is Hope. Hope Lawson."

Sydney stared at him for a moment. "You should bring her by, sometime."

"Maybe I will."

Devon realized, quite unexpectedly, that he meant it. Perhaps he could do this whole *bridge the different Devons* thing. But that was dependent on a host of stuff going how he wanted, and he couldn't get his hopes up yet. R&R was private like his BDSM life, but in many ways more intimate. The more Devon thought about it, the more he was forced to admit that the way he'd always handled playdates wasn't intimate at all. It could have been. He knew people who had insanely intimate dynamics. And they unnerved the crap out of him.

Devon didn't like digging into the specifics of what R&R was, how it came to be, or the role they served because it reminded him of things that hurt. He could work here for hours, but that didn't mean he wanted to talk about it. The bi-weekly group meetings he attended were laced with things they all needed to get out and never wanted to acknowledge. The dichotomy of that often felt like a vicious ripping inside his psyche.

Well... that sounded dramatic. True, though.

It got messy in his head sometimes. Was it harder for the group members supporting shattered loved ones, or those like him? Death made Kelly untouchable. She was far away from the hurt that destroyed her, but Devon would never see her heal. His mom would never see it either. Her tragedy was both over and perpetual. *Schrödinger's Trauma.* Trying to pick apart the *hows* and *whys* inevitably set off a Pub Night, and Devon wasn't looking forward to the possible repercussions of having those conversations with Hope, even if she responded well.

He also hated scuffing his bar.

"Would that be alright?" he asked, pulling himself back to present. "We could have her sign an NDA if necessary. She's a teacher...or was..."

"Bring her!" Monique beamed. "It's about time you found somebody."

"What kind of teacher?" Sydney asked.

"I'm not sure..." Devon said, realizing that whatever subject Hope taught hadn't come up. "She moved here for a job at a school... Costings Academy? But she ended up not taking it."

Sydney pressed her pink lips together for a moment, a world of clever calculation hidden behind her eyes. "That's excellent. Her experience will be especially useful."

"I wouldn't be bringing her to volunteer, just to show her the place. You know, the kind of work we do..."

Devon didn't know why he was discussing all this with them when so many other things remained unknown, and he had no idea how to sort any of them. Hell, he was picking her up in fifteen minutes, and he hadn't even figured out how to cross the first bridge toward a relationship with her without freaking her out. With the physical chemistry between them and the fact that *physical* was the single word descriptor of every interaction—they didn't count as relationships— he had before her, it should be easier to talk to her about this one thing. Devon glanced down at his streaked and sweaty shirt. He wasn't even wearing clean clothes.

"It's early though. I'm not sure how it'll go," he added awkwardly.

Now Monique studied him. "Well, I'll be. You see that Syd?"

"Oh, I see it alright," the blond agreed.

"What?" Devon held out his hands, looked them over too.

"Nothing, honey." Monique smiled. "You go on your date. Everything's going to be fine."

HOPE

"**T**his is Apollo," Devon said, patting the massive chest of a dog that was trying to get close enough to stand *inside* him.

Apollo turned his attention to Hope, giant body coiling.

"Heel," Devon snapped. The dog, excitement barely contained, managed to stay beside him, butt hovering an inch off the floor. "Remember the rules, buddy," Devon said, affectionately. "Don't smush her. You are big." The dog cocked his boxy head from side to side, staring up at his master with intelligent eyes.

"Sorry," Devon said, bringing his focus back to Hope. "I don't think I mentioned him."

Hope smiled down at Apollo. "I surprised you with my brother yesterday. This is way more forgivable."

Devon smiled a little. "Seemed like a good guy."

"He liked you too," she said.

Devon scrubbed his palms over his thighs. "Well, that's a relief. If you don't mind, I'm going to—" He gestured toward the hallway that led away from the living room.

"Yeah." Hope waved him off. "Go ahead. Apollo and I will get to know each other."

"You need anything before I go?"

"I'm fine," Hope said, putting her hand on Apollo's head. His fur was softer than expected. The dog wagged his tail so hard that his entire body wagged with it, a slobbery, happy grin on his face.

"The kitchen is right in there," Devon pointed, "if you want a drink or something. This," he added, thumb over his shoulder toward the closed door situated between the hallway and kitchen, "gets you a dangerous set of stairs and the washer and dryer, so if you need to do laundry for some reason while I'm gone, watch your step." Hope giggled. "Guest bathroom is down the hall. First door on the right," Devon said, with a grin. "I'll be quick."

"Thanks," she said, settling on the couch with Apollo, who promptly lay his five-hundred-pound head in her lap.

She watched Devon slip down the hallway and disappear into what she assumed was his bedroom at the far end. A moment later, she heard a second door close from behind the first and the distant sound of a shower. Hope stroked Apollo's soft fur and looked around.

The house was...unfussy. Tidy. Not utilitarian but lacking frivolous decoration. A weight bench sat in one corner, a dog bed in another, and a leash hung on a hook by the door. The charcoal grey couch only showed stray Apollo hairs when the light hit at the right angle. TV, speakers, the occasional wooden end table, or chair for company. It was a place to live, but nothing one would consider unique. Unless you considered a bachelor keeping a clean house unique. Sort of how, at Cleary's, the warm, glossy wood of the bar, sparkling bottles and glasses, and sturdy furniture doubled as decoration—aside from an occasional salvaged liquor sign on the wall, or that one sign that hung above the bar. Its charm, its beauty lay in the simplicity.

Devon said he'd been working at the nonprofit most of the day...*R&R*. He apologized when he picked her up, worrying she wouldn't be into the idea of him popping off for a shower and change when they got to his place. He'd smelled of cologne, sweat, and dust. Hope wanted to crawl into his seat and straddle him while burying her face in his neck.

She did not, of course.

"I really like him," she whispered to Apollo. He looked up at her, and for the first time she noticed the uneven edges of his ears, the puckered scar that disturbed his fur in a long line from the corner of one brown eye, down the length of his jaw. "What's this?" she asked, gently sliding her fingers over the place.

Similar scars marred his massive chest, especially visible where his solitary white patch met the more-abundant grey. Searching turned up others on his haunches, his sides. "You're covered," she said to the pup, who seemed unconcerned, so long as she kept petting him. "What happened to you?"

"He had a rough start," Devon said, startling her.

Hope looked up to find him barefoot, in jeans and a white t-shirt, rubbing a towel in his still-damp hair. The ink that wound its way up his forearms continued at least as far as the edges of his sleeves, distracting her with the mystery of where it ended.

The scent of *clean male* washed over her, and Hope found herself looking to the pale wood floors. Focused on Apollo, she hadn't heard Devon return. But to be fair, he had taken a very quick shower.

"He's never been aggressive," Devon said quickly. "Someone probably planned to use him for fighting, but he was still small when they..." She watched his chest heave with a breath. "Well, anyway..." He trailed off, gaze landing on Apollo, face grim.

"He's precious," Hope said, wrapping her arms around the teddy bear of a dog.

"Most people are afraid of him. He's a good boy, though. I don't think he'd hurt a fly. Might squish it to death trying to snuggle, but that's all. There aren't many homes for dogs like him," he explained. "I live alone, and I'm more than big enough to fend for myself," he added with a grin that faded into tension. "He's a good boy," Devon repeated, determined to sell her on this dog. Apollo licked her face, more than capable of selling himself.

"Hey now, not Apollo's," Devon scolded. "Place."

Crestfallen, Apollo lumbered off the couch and plopped onto the cushion in the corner.

"He's so well behaved," Hope said.

"We've worked hard on that. If you intimidate people, it's safest all around if you know how to act. You want wine, cider, beer? I also have water and probably soda," he added as an afterthought.

Hope put a hand to her chest in mock shock. "Did you forget what I drink?"

Devon smiled and shrugged, but it lacked the ease she had come to expect from him. Was he nervous? "You might like to try something new," he ventured, his inflection lost somewhere between a suggestion and a question.

Hope thought of her unsettling interaction at work, and how nice something new could be sometimes. She knew exactly what she wanted to try.

"The cider, then."

Devon chucked the towel he'd used to dry his hair down the stairs, on the way to the kitchen. He returned with beer in one hand and hard cider in the other.

"Hopefully, my company will be an acceptable replacement for Apollo's. He's a charming oaf." He handed her the bottle.

"He put his head in my lap," Hope said. "We're besties now."

Devon raised his brows and looked to Apollo. "Traitor."

Hope laughed, then took a sip. Sweet, tart bubbles danced over her tongue and down to her belly in an icy slide. "This is really good," she said.

He gave a nod. "You can't trust him, just so you know. He's an attention whore. It's the reason he's still alive." Devon raised the beer in his hand toward the dog. "The people at the shelter couldn't stand putting him down while he was loving on them. Stitched him up instead. You should have seen him. Gangly. Shaved. Black and blue stitches everywhere because they ran out of one color halfway through."

"Thank goodness he was lovable," Hope said, bringing her bottle up again.

"If you need me to put my head in your lap to prove my affection, I can," Devon said, "but my hair's wet, and if I lay down, I might not get up to cook dinner. It's been a long day."

Hope nearly spit out her second swig of cider. "I can help with dinner," she managed between coughs.

Devon pulled on a thick sweater to go put steaks on the grill in the backyard. They wouldn't be eating out there. The end of November was reminding them that *almost winter* was a thing, especially this year. The thermometer sat much colder than it had all weekend, and temps weren't supposed to make it out of the forties again until Friday.

They worked around each other in the kitchen, putting together the salad, Devon cursing under his breath when he realized that he forgot to start the potatoes earlier, and Hope laughing and asking why he was so distracted. Apollo huffed from time to time, offended by the lack of food being thrown his direction. French bread went in the oven, Devon retrieved the steaks, and in under half an hour, they were sitting across from each other at a small kitchen table with a meal between them.

"So, how was work?" he asked, putting a napkin across his lap. "Weave any magical spells? Break the record for the most incense sales in a day?"

Hope laughed. "It was okay. I sold a witch the ingredients to summon a spirit...or a lover. My ancient coworker poorly refolded the tapestries, so I'll have something to do tomorrow. And he suggested that I might be able to get a man if I wore my hair down more often." She skipped the part about Aaron because... well, she didn't really know why. Maybe because she didn't want to think about him or didn't want Devon to. There were much more pleasant things going on than Aaron's intrusions.

Devon smirked. "If my opinion has any value, you do look beautiful today. But I've never seen you not look beautiful. If you want me to help you shave it off to spite him, I have clippers in the bathroom." Hope grinned. "Short hair has its perks," he said, scrubbing a hand through his own.

"Noted, but I think I'll pass for now, thanks. So, what's with the construction debris?"

Devon shook his head. "Busted pipe at R&R. Cheaper for me to fix it than hire someone."

"A man of many talents." She skewered a bite of her steak.

His eyes flicked up to hers, dark and seductive. "I'm good with my hands," he said, without a hint of shame. Hope swallowed hard, then watched his bravado falter. "Minor carpentry, automotive," he explained, looking down to his plate. "It's the only thing I had a knack for when I was a kid. I didn't play catch with my old man. He owned a construction company. More of the *I said a five-eighths...* with a sharp smack upside your head type," Devon said, pushing salad around his plate with a fork.

"I'm working on this place." He gestured around to the house. "But it's slow. That's why the kitchen looks like it was puked out of the seventies. The guest bath isn't any better. Did the floors myself, before I moved in though." Pride flashed on his face at that. "The entire house was carpeted in green and gold shag. Even the bathrooms." Devon shuddered. Hope didn't blame him.

"They're really beautiful," she said earnestly, looking down at the blond wood.

"You're beautiful." He tucked into a piece of bread.

HOPE

The meal was as delicious as the way it had gotten on the table. Simple, comfortable. Even with the missing potatoes. Hope sipped her cider, letting it go warm, waiting for a moment when she might find a reason to not fall for him. It all fit too well, like a glimpse of something lasting. Hope refused to think about the last time she considered that possibility; she wouldn't let it ruin this evening with him.

When they finished, they stacked the dishes in the sink and retired to the couch. Having long since ditched her boots, Hope gave Devon the corner and scooted in beside, her knees tucked up beneath her. He wrapped an arm around her and pulled up music with his phone. Something instrumental thrummed through the speakers in the house.

"Can I tell you another secret?" he said abruptly. She felt his body tense beside her and wondered what had him so edgy.

"Is it the deep, dark sort?" Hope asked in a conspiratorial tone. The tension in him didn't relax. If anything, it coiled tighter. "Devon?" His name came off her lips, tinged with worry.

"This is the best evening I've ever had in this house," he eventually said.

"Me too," Hope countered. Warm relief flooded her, as he chuckled and kissed the top of her head.

"Thanks," he said softly.

"For what?"

"For letting me see you tonight."

Hope turned her face toward his and looked into his eyes. She didn't know what she wanted to say, or the best way to say it, so she opted to act on her impulse from the car when he'd first picked her up. Pressing her mouth to his, she swung one leg over his lap, straddling him. Devon made a muffled sound of surprise, his hands settling too carefully on her hips.

The heat of his palms seeped through Hope's thin sweater, as she slid her hands into his hair, tilting her head to kiss him deeper. Opening more for him, reveling in the sensations of his tongue against hers. Her fingers felt the new sheen of sweat over the nape of his neck. The growing evidence of his desire was an iron rod against her core, and she could feel the enormity of his need the moment his hips reflexively ground against her, raising, and lowering her in a smooth, powerful undulation as she sat atop him.

The seams of his jeans chafed the inside of her legs during that deliciously slow rollercoaster ride, reminding her of how little lay between them. And the oddest thought went through her head. Devon was in control, even as he came undone.

His kiss grew more insistent, more demanding, drowning her in the intensity. No longer was Hope goading him on with her body. Now, she was breathless, soaking wet with desire, and trying to keep up. Suddenly, it was her hips rocking, but Hope lacked his delicate control. Her body sought friction...release. A needy, hungry, search for him.

Touch me. Please, touch me. She wanted to beg.

Devon made a sound of amusement, entertained by the way the tables had turned. His hands slipped under the edge of her sweater, the thin fabric of her leggings, and a lacy thong offering no protection. He found that place on her hips where his hands fit perfectly again and dug his fingertips into her flesh.

Hope came up for air on a gasp of pleasure and pain, one hair's breadth from climaxing in her leggings. Her eyes fixed on his, shocked at how close she'd come. She recognized the expression looking back at her as the same cocky, seductive gleam from Saturday night. The one that made something inside her unfurl into a sopping wet mess of *Please...*

"Sorry," he blurted, giving his head a forceful shake, and pulling his hands out from under her sweater. "Sorry..."

"I kissed you," Hope said, an insincere laugh bubbling out of her.

While she'd instigated their brief make out session, by the end, there was no doubt who was driving whom. Hope was on top, but Devon had the upper hand. Devon stopped them.

"Devon?" She tilted her head and bowed her body forcing him to look at her, because he still hadn't responded. "What's wrong?"

He scrubbed his hands over his face. "Nothing. Nothing's wrong."

"Then, why do you keep doing that?" she asked.

"I just... I need to talk to you about some stuff."

"Okay... I'm listening."

When he shook his head again, she started to worry. Hope tried to think through everything he could possibly want to say that they hadn't already covered. Something he would want to address before they got more involved physically... And then it hit her. There was still that one conversation that they hadn't had, and no one wanted to have it when they were already ripping off clothing.

"I...I haven't been with anyone in nearly a year... I mean, other than kissing Chloe sometimes," Hope said. "I had them run all the majors six months ago." Devon looked up at her and chewed his lip to tame a smile. "And...that wasn't what you needed to talk about," she said, with a dull horror.

"No, but it's another conversation that needed to happen. I got the all-clear two months ago. I haven't had sex in... God, it's been more than six months. Seven, at least, but I don't think eight. I'm also careful, for what it's worth."

"I thought... Right." Obviously, he wasn't a virgin. Obviously. "Just no relationships..." She chuckled at his wicked, wicked grin, grateful that he was relaxing enough to flash it. "So, say the thing," Hope urged. "Whatever it is, say it."

He scooped her up and put her beside him, with less effort than she expected. "It might be easier without you straddling me." He took a contemplative pull from the bottle of beer on the side table. "Nope," he said. "Doesn't help at all, actually."

Hope dug through her bag of mental tricks to make uncomfortable topics easier. Maybe a game or...

"Have you ever played *Never Have I Ever?*" she asked. Hope never would have gotten a therapy client tipsy to get them to open up; but Devon wasn't a client, and this wasn't therapy.

Devon eyed her warily. "I don't—"

"It'll be fun," she said, hopping off the couch and gesturing to his drink. "Are you almost out?"

"No, I'm fine—"

Hope grabbed his bottle, noted the tepid liquid in the bottom two inches. "This won't work," she said, shoving it back into his hand. "You polish off this, and I'll grab us both another."

"I have to drive you home," he reminded her.

"Not yet," she replied. "Take small sips. You only need enough for the game. Where's your bottle opener?"

Devon shook his head. "Side of the fridge."

Hope returned with a fresh bottle for each of them. "We take turns," she said. "One of us says *Never have I ever*...and then finishes the sentence. If you've done it, you drink, and if you haven't, you don't."

"Hope, I know how to play. I just—"

"Great, then it'll be easy. I'll go first. Never have I ever kissed a girl." Hope grinned and took a sip. Devon reluctantly followed suit. "Now you."

"Never have I ever..." he began, "played a team sport."

This time neither took a sip.

"Really? No baseball? Kid's soccer?" Hope asked. "They shove that stuff on little boys." He shook his head in response. Her dad was going to hate him, assuming they ever met. "Okay, then," she continued. "Never have I ever had sex in a car." Hope did not sip.

Devon's eyebrows went up. "Really?" Hope shook her head. Devon swigged his beer. "You should know that I have a pretty high alcohol tolerance."

"I'm after information. How much you drink is up to you."

"There seems to be a pattern to your statements," Devon said, picking at the label on his beer.

"Really?" Hope said. "I've only gone twice. That doesn't seem like much of a pattern." She watched him smirk. "Take your turn," she said, giggling.

"Never have I ever—" He stopped and stared at her. "Never have I ever wanted..." She watched him wet his lips, swallow hard, then lose his nerve as plainly as if it had fallen onto the floor in front of her. "Never have I ever had a date over for dinner." Hope sipped, but Devon didn't move. Still as a statue, he stared at her.

"Until tonight." Hope said. Devon blinked and brought the bottle to his mouth.

"Until tonight," he agreed.

This wasn't working. Whatever he was afraid to say had him clamming up every time he tiptoed near it and stopping short every time things heated up. It seemed out of character. In the near-year she'd known him, he'd never had a hard time saying what he meant, and his hands were too skilled in what little they'd done together to believe that he was a shy lover. Not to mention the various pulse-spiking things he'd growled or purred against her ear on Saturday.

Impatient little thing...

Hope's heart tripped over its own feet, and every muscle in her pelvis clenched at the memory.

"I'm sorry," he said from beside her, yanking her attention back to present. "I know what you're doing, and I'm not making it easy. I don't know how to start."

"It's okay," she said, getting to her feet. "I get it. There are things I have a hard time talking about too. There's always next time." He genuinely grinned at that. "I'm going to go check out your seventies bathroom," she said. Hopefully, it would distract her from...him.

"Ugh." Devon groaned. "You might ask me to take you straight home."

"I hope there's a green toilet," she said, giggling.

He shook his head. "You're going to be pleased, I think. I'll run Apollo out back, while you're checking out the antiques. He won't go when it's cold, unless you make him." Devon headed for the sliding glass door by the kitchen, Apollo on his heels.

Hope heard the door open and close, followed by Devon's muffled voice drifting in from the backyard. She walked into the hallway, squinting into the low light. What did he say earlier? First door on the...? Whatever, she'd find it.

Coming to the first door on the left, Hope pushed inside a room dark as pitch. Something rolled in her gut, an unexpected hit of *You-are-in-the-wrong-place* intuition flooding through her.

Hope was trying to be more mindful of her intuition these days; although she had a terrible habit of being all, *Oh hello. You have concerns? Noted.* And then, to her detriment, plowing onward.

This instance was no exception. She chalked it up to being out of sorts from her earlier interaction with Aaron. The unsettling shiver that creeped through her as she slid her hand along the wall in search of the light switch didn't stop her either. After several swipes of her hand, she bumped up against the slick plastic plate and flipped the switch, flooding the room in harsh light.

This was not a bathroom.

DEVON

Devon stood in the fenced lot behind his house, waiting for Apollo to choose a place to piss. Apollo circled aimlessly, exhaling billowing puffs of white, as if no mere patch of earth would ever be worthy of his urine. He seemed utterly oblivious to Devon's desire to get back inside.

"Come on, man. Help me out," Devon grumbled, the air around him so frigid that it felt like sucking shards of ice down his nose and throat, rather than breathing.

At least, there were benefits to freezing his balls off, he thought as his head cleared and his cock eased its escape efforts. Then, he flashed to Hope grinding against him and swore under his breath, when the thing once again tried to mind-over-matter his fly. *Cold, cold, cold*...Devon focused on the one thing that might help him resolve the issue...again.

"Pick a fucking spot, dude," he snapped.

Freezing and frustration did nothing for his patience. Did the dog roll his eyes? Probably. He needed to stop worrying so much about Apollo and come up with a plan. How in the world could he, Devon Cleary... The Demon of Edge... Dominant right down to something in his DNA... not be able to articulate to a woman what he was into? Hope had his head in knots, and not the intricate, symmetrical Shibari sort.

He sighed.

Maybe he didn't need to *say* anything. He could get the conversation started by showing her the playroom. *Hey, look in here...* No... That would send her running. *So, I like kink...* No. Not that either. He paced a few feet and back again. *How do you feel about kink?* But while they were sitting somewhere innocuous like the couch or the kitchen table. Yeah, open invitation. That might work. If he got lucky, she'd be all *I thought you'd never ask!*

Devon shook his head in the darkness, icy air crawling down his collar with the movement. She wasn't going to say that. If he hit the lottery, he might get an *I don't know. What did you have in mind? Yeah, fuzzy pink handcuffs sound exciting...* Shit. He didn't own fuzzy anything. He did have metal cuffs, leather restraints, zip ties, miles of rope, various harnesses, bars, and positioning aids. The leather would be comfortable if the aesthetic didn't make her nervous, but they looked like the real deal—because they were. Inferior gear was a waste of money, and while the occasional snapped restraint was erotic as hell, Devon needed to know that it took a ton of effort to get there. Otherwise, it was just cheap gear fucking up his scenes, and that was a huge turnoff. And dangerous, on the rare occasion that he did any kind of suspension.

Devon had spent over a decade and a half layering his preferences and building—quite literally in many cases—his collection of deviant playthings. It would be a lot for anyone to take in all at once, and she seemed so... soft.

Maybe he could dial it back, focus on the part he couldn't turn off. He didn't need the gear, but he was never going to pull off a scene—*an intimate encounter*, he corrected himself—without some level of dynamic. That wasn't realistic. An underlying thread of power exchange wove through their conversations and kisses already.

If I fuck you, you're going to end up with your arms pinned over your head or behind your back at some point. Devon cringed and tried to ignore the visual image of when he'd done exactly that on Saturday. He'd only meant to kiss her, really.

"Apollo, man... seriously. I don't care if it's on the side of the patio furniture, just go already." He ran his hands through his hair, took a breath, and searched desperately for his center.

I need to ask how you feel about consensual kink. I tend to be a little dominant during play...during... during— Fuck.

Big deep breath.

I need to ask how you feel about consensual kink. I tend to be a little dominant in the bedroom, and it's important to me that I know your boundaries before we go any farther. I don't want to do anything that you aren't comfortable with.

Okay, that wasn't half-bad, even for a newbie. Ignoring the fact that there was nothing *little* about his inner dominant, it was also honest. Devon repeated it in his head again, and again. When Apollo finished up, he would march back inside and rip off the bandage. Yep. He repeated the words one more time, lips moving mutely. Mmm hmm. He could do this. Then, who knew? Maybe pull her back astride his hips and... Not helping.

"Finally," Devon breathed, as the pup graced a tree in the corner of the lot with a golden shower.

HOPE

A dungeon.

Hope didn't know another word for it. Ropes and pulleys hung from the ceiling. Panels with steel rings adorned the walls. The bed... Holy shit. *The bed*. A canopy-framed monstrosity with some sort of rigging suspended from the top and thin, metal bars around the bottom like a cage. Beneath the bed was a *cage*. Light glinted off more shiny metal rings, as her eyes skimmed over various pieces of... furniture? For tying off, she realized, a dull buzzing growing louder in her ears.

Most of the furniture, and harnesses, and *things* had discernible uses, even if Hope had never been in the same room with their like. One only need know the shape of your average human to understand that this one exposed the back, butt, and thighs, folding the body onto all fours. That one got you spread-eagle—Hope recognized it from spicier porn. Others were harder to figure out, though. The thing that looked like a short, wide ladder? Its purpose eluded her.

Do you want me to let go, darling, or do you like the sensation of not being able to get away?

Heat flushed through her.

One wall displayed lines of carefully arranged items. Wide leather cuffs with heavy hardware. Belts, crops, canes, and...other things that she could only guess the names of but were clearly intended to inflict pain. Rope...so many neatly tied bundles of black rope, ordered by size. Actual handcuffs... Not toys, but the real deal. No pink fuzzies or dainty little chains in sight. These had thick hinges connecting the parts that clasped around your wrists, so you couldn't twist your arms. The kind Hope recognized. She shuddered and imagined Devon differently than ever before.

She could see him there, feet bare, hair damp from the shower, the fabric of his shirt pulling taught across his back as he reached for one of those bundles of rope—the visual enhanced by the multitude of times Hope had watched him reach for bottles of liquor at Cleary's. She knew what he would look like. He would turn to her with his signature wicked grin, and—

Shiny, biting, metal cuffs.

Hope looked away, only to catch her reflection in a large, framed mirror leaning against the wall. Nothing about her looked like it belonged in this room. She wasn't supposed to be here. She didn't have permission. People got pissed off when you trespassed through their private spaces, and rightly so. And pissed off people did all sorts of out of character things.

Snick, snick, snick, snick, snick...

Stop it. Quit...struggling. You don't get to say that shit, then walk out on me.

Hope shook her head at the memory—at the cold, unforgiving steel against her skin and the weight of a body crushing the air from her lungs. Everything in front of her pitched like a snow globe before righting itself. She took one step backward, and then another. The third had her out in the dim hallway and bolting for any door on the opposite side. Bathroom...she had to find the bathroom and hide until her head stopped screaming *RUN*.

Hope found it on the right side of the hall, a few feet past the room she had entered. The door was open and inviting, and if she'd noticed it earlier, she would have walked the extra four feet to check there first. She wouldn't even know there was a dungeon.

There would still be a dungeon across the hall, and she would have no clue.

Who has a dungeon in their house? she thought, as she flipped the inadequate lock. Someone Hope would end up falling for, seemed the most obvious answer. And wasn't that a kick in the ass? She couldn't hide forever, but how was she supposed to go back out there and face him? She needed a plan.

No... wait. She already had one, because she'd walked on eggshells before. Devon was out back anyway. He had no idea that she'd seen that room. She could pretend everything was normal. Keep calm; keep him calm. He never had to know. Hope would walk back out to the living room and ask him about Apollo or the nonprofit. He'd take her home later, and then she'd figure out where to go from there. But she did need to move. The longer she hid, the weirder it would be when she came out.

Hope did her business, in a toilet that numbly registered as mustard yellow. She scrubbed her hands a bit too long in a sink that matched, garish green and gold wallpaper framing her image in the mirror, as she did. The color combination did nothing for her fair complexion. Neither did her nervous stomach.

This was fine, she told herself. He had no idea. This was *fine*. Straightening her spine, and plastering on a mildly pleasant expression, Hope left her hidey-hole.

Act normal. Just like old times. I got this.

It took a few seconds to register all the light in the hall. Hope stopped cold the moment it sank in. She told herself to smile, told her feet to keep moving, one in front of the other. But something around the base of her skull interrupted the signal, her body refusing to comply with her commands.

With thinly veiled terror, she looked to Devon, who leaned against the jamb of the first door she had entered with his arms crossed over his chest. The dungeon door. The fucking dungeon. Hope's eyes went from Devon to the now darkened doorway beside him and back again, in what felt like an impossibly sluggish shift of focus. She swallowed hard, finding her smile far too late to be convincing. Despite the casual arrangement of his limbs, tension rolled off him.

He knew.

"Trouble finding the bathroom?" he queried.

Hope couldn't read his tone, and she knew exactly why that unnerved her. The memory of Aaron cut in again as unwelcome as it was unbidden, as she mentally scrambled for a way out.

"I found it fine," she lied, her voice a solid octave too high.

"Really?" His brows rose. "You left the playroom door open. You left the light on."

Playroom?

His body shifted. Hope took a stumbling step back, jerking her hands up reflexively, as her smile faltered. He'd only gestured to the room. He wasn't stepping toward her; he was just... just gesturing. What flashed on his face told her that he didn't miss her slip.

"I... I'm sorry," Hope blurted, deliberately lowering her hands back to her sides. There was no salvaging this. The train in this wreck was hauling explosives when it went off the rails and plowed through a forge.

Devon studied her for a moment, a muscle twitching in his jaw. "No apologies, darling," he said, his voice deceptively soft. He put his hands up where she could see them, dropped his gaze to the floor, and slowly turned to walk toward the living room. Hope could barely breathe.

When she got up the nerve to follow him out of the hallway, she found Devon carrying their unfinished drinks toward the kitchen. Apollo sat quietly on his cushion, a tattered, one-eared teddy bear between his front paws. His eyes tracked Devon as he moved, like the dog could read the tension in the man.

"Are you ready to go?" Devon asked, as he returned.

"Uh..." Hope glanced around uneasily. As if that were answer enough, Devon nodded.

"Do you want me to get you a ride, or do you feel comfortable with me taking you?" he asked in that unreadable tone. No more dramatic than *Do you want fries or onion rings?*

"I'll go with you if that's okay," she said, hesitantly. He gave another curt nod and sat down to pull on his boots. "Devon," Hope said, noting the stiffness of his shoulders, the way he struggled with the laces. She should leave this alone. He wasn't raging, even if he was upset. She really shouldn't poke at this— "Are you alright?"

Hazel eyes shot up to meet hers. "Are you?"

"I, um... I didn't mean to..."

"It's fine. I'll take you home." He fumbled the laces on his second boot, cursing under his breath as he tried again.

He didn't say a word in the car until he asked if she'd like him to walk her up. And when Hope said he could drop her off at the curb, he didn't say a word then, either. It felt like there was a chasm between them, when less than an hour earlier, she'd been straddling him. Why did she have to go left? And why in the hell was it Aaron's voice that echoed in her head in that room? Aaron was the one who couldn't move on, not her.

But Hope knew why, didn't she?

"Thanks again," Devon said as they pulled to a stop in front of her building. "I'm sorry about... everything." His tone had gone from unreadable, to defeated.

"It's fine."

She cringed at her too high voice. He was leaving again, and Hope wanted... She wanted to be back on his couch. Rewind all the way back to the moment he dug his fingertips into her hips, but instead of coming up on a gasp, she wanted to push so close that he swallowed it. Willfully reckless at best.

Devon pressed an awkward kiss to her cheek before she got out. Hope climbed the stairs to her apartment alone. Letting herself inside, she locked the door, put her shoes and coat in the closet, and stood in the stillness wondering how the hell she had gotten there.

HOPE

Fifteen minutes later, Hope still paced the no man's land between her living room, kitchen, hallway, and dining area—her mind restlessly circling everything that had happened since she got up that morning.

He called it *the playroom*. There was a cage under the bed. There were so many ways to tie a person up or strap them down. And Hope knew, marrow-deep she knew, that Devon wasn't on the receiving end of any of it. She'd seen it that night at Cleary's when a stranger grabbed her, though she hadn't known what it was. She'd felt it at the restaurant on their first date, and later when he had pinned her arms behind her. His voice echoing in her ears, mouth and hands ravishing her body until something snapped in her brain. Everything went all warm and fuzzy that night, turning her into a needy, desperate... Hope swallowed hard.

Devon liked control. Commanded it. Even without walking into that room, this was no surprise. Maybe she should have given more thought to why she was so attracted to *him*, specifically. Stupid, stupid girl.

Her phone buzzed, so Hope reluctantly pulled it out. An unwelcome text notification from her mother appeared asking when the wedding escort situation would be sorted and offering to reach out to Aaron again if it would settle things more quickly. Hope considered throwing the phone at the wall, but unlike Aaron, she had a modicum of self-control. Her shrinking bank account helped fortify her resolve. Her mother would have to wait. Hope had bigger things on her plate, tonight.

She had already moved to escape someone addicted to control. *Escape?* Was she using that word now? Even if it did constitute an escape, she had failed horribly. She fucked Aaron on her couch two months later, and now he worked in Asheville, lived a few miles down the road, and made no secret of wanting her back. He showed up at her job today, for crying out loud. Hope didn't know how to fix that mess. She was tired of trying.

She didn't know how to fix what happened with Devon either. Now that she was back in the security of her own space, she wished he hadn't left. Maybe... It was confusing. Aaron liked to...control things when they were together. It had been fun at first—the kind of fun that made her burn with shame when she thought of how it ultimately played out.

He didn't have a dungeon in his house, though. Devon had a dungeon—in his house. Wasn't a literal dungeon like a giant *Don't Go There* sign, especially after what she went through with Aaron?

A knock at the door had her jumping out of her skin. Her bestie from across the hall was one of the nosiest people she had ever met, and Hope had zero desire to talk, tonight. How could she explain what sparked the abrupt end of the date without violating Devon's privacy on a level that he didn't deserve? He hadn't done anything inappropriate. Hell, he took her straight home. But everything in that room— She shouldn't have been in there, anyway.

The knock came again, a bit louder. If she waited long enough, Chloe would go away. Or more likely, she had already spotted Hope coming in alone, and would therefore knock louder, and louder, and louder, then leave and come back with her key. After weighing her options for longer than necessary, Hope walked over and pulled open the door.

It was Devon who turned toward her, one foot already on the stairs to go.

"I—" He shut his mouth and stared at her.

"I thought you were Chloe," Hope said, silently cursing herself for the lame announcement.

"I should've gone." But he didn't move. He stood there frozen, waiting.

Anxiety coursed through Hope, making her hands tremble. What's it called when you see the bad choice, and you choose it anyway? Not brilliant, that was certain. She clenched one hand on the edge of the door and the other at her side. Devon would go if she told him to—because he wasn't Aaron, he'd go.

"Can we talk?" she said.

Devon's brows pulled down over his eyes before astonishment sparked. "Really?"

Hope nodded and pushed the door wide. She needed to figure out how she felt, and Devon was a complicating factor more easily—and probably dangerously—studied in person.

He left as much space as he could between them as he passed, eventually stopping deep in her small living room. He wasn't close to her; he wasn't blocking the door or getting near the hall to her bedroom. The familiarity of her environment and roughly six feet of empty air stood between them. Every movement he made was a deliberate statement. *Nonthreatening. Safe.* It made that weird tingle at the base of her skull stir to life again, but Hope ignored it. She dug her sock-clad toes into the carpet and took a breath.

"Is there a place you'd like to start?" Devon asked, head slightly bowed, eyes trained on her. God, did he have to look at her like that?

Hope wet her lips and went for it. "There's a dungeon in your house." She watched him give a resigned nod.

"I call it the playroom, but yeah… I never meant for you to walk in there before I got a chance to talk to you. I *was* going to talk to you," he said. "I just…didn't know how. The light caught my attention. I should've stayed in the living room. I'm sorry—"

Hope's apology poured out reflexively. "No, I'm sorry. I wasn't trying to snoop, really…" She trailed off as his brow furrowed.

"I'm sorry I scared you," he breathed. "Christ, Hope. You have nothing to apologize for. First time in my house. You opened the wrong door because I forgot to lock it." He shook his head. "But the way you backed away from me— Did you think—" Devon stopped talking, scrubbed his hands over his face. "Sorry."

Tears pricked her eyes—something that felt silly and irrational. In her day of unexpected surprises, Apollo ended up being the only good one. Hope was *tired*.

"I guess I thought..." She twisted the hem of one sleeve between her fingers. "You told me where the bathroom was, but I forgot. I know that room was...private."

"You thought I was mad." His deceptively calm voice might have convinced her if she couldn't see his eyes. Hope nodded minutely. A muscle in his jaw twitched. "Where did you learn to cower when you think a man is angry, darling?"

Answering that question honestly felt like an admission of her own mistakes, so she said something horrible instead.

"Well, I've seen you mad."

The moment it was past her lips, Hope wanted to snatch it back.

"Then, I'm sorry for that too," he said softly. "I never— I wouldn't—"

She couldn't stand this. Devon was the first guy in over a year who made her feel safe. He was steady as a stone and willing to physically remove anyone who compromised her if needed. He had throttled their physical relationship because he wanted her to have all the information, while also agonizing over how to deliver that information. So much so that she beat him to the punch and set off this mess because of some residual handcuff-triggered hang-ups. And now, she had turned his concern into a weapon to avoid talking about her baggage.

"It wasn't you," she uttered. "I'm sorry. I'm so sorry. You've never given me a reason to fear you. It was me. Stuff I need to figure out in my head..." She brought her hands to her temples, as she barreled on.

"Stop," Devon said, his steady voice cutting clear through to her center.

Hope tried to swallow, but her mouth had gone dry. "I'm—"

"Darling, stop." So calm. "Stop apologizing. If you want to talk about," he gestured broadly, "whatever...*whoever* caused that kind of conditioned response in you—and trust me, I know a conditioned response, when I see one— I'll listen all fucking night. And possibly track them down, after," he added as an afterthought. "Don't apologize to me again. I can handle anything you throw at me. Anything. And if I can't, I'll figure it out."

"Okay," she squeaked.

"I like you, Hope. I really like you, in a way that..." She watched him search for words. "I don't want to stay where I am. I want to move forward when I'm near you."

Hope's brow knit tight. Devon huffed in frustration.

"This isn't coming out right," he said.

"It's okay," she said, reassuringly. "I'm listening."

Devon nodded and started again. "My life is divided in segments," he began. "The bar. R&R. The stuff I do privately." Hope could figure out what he meant by *privately*, after seeing his playroom. "You're the first person that I wanted to share all of that with. Like...one me." He put a hand over his heart, dropped it again. "It's different, scary, and honestly, I didn't have the best role models when it comes to healthy relationships. But when I'm near you, I want to get it right. Or at least, have a chance at that."

The more he spoke, the more insistent that tingle at the base of her skull grew. His deep, soothing voice beckoned her to curl into him, to deal with the consequences when they came.

"Bringing those parts together is challenging though."

"How so?" she heard herself ask.

"I told you I've never dated someone, right? I mean, yeah, back when I was sixteen, seventeen... But the rest has been a steady stream of mostly one-off play partners. I can't even tell you how many. I knew what I was from a young age, and I went with it."

"And that is...?"

Devon straightened his back, widened his stance. While Hope tracked every infinitesimal change in his posture with intense awareness, he seemed unaware that he had moved. It was like watching something beneath his skin stretch its muscles, as it waited to hear its name. Anticipation rolled in her stomach.

"Dominant," he said. "Very, very dominant."

That probably should have had a different effect on her, Hope thought, as a distracting heat kindled between her thighs.

"And the thing is..." Everything in her body tightened as he went on. "Keeping that part of myself on a leash used to be easy. I let it out in the playroom or similar places, and in other ways—when I needed to get something accomplished at the bar or the nonprofit. But now, it feels like this thing in my brain is constantly looking for you." Some dam broke in him, *feeling* pouring out along with his words. "Like I need to *do* something. Not just this week, but for months now. That night at Cleary's, I was barely holding it together. You kept leaving your drink unattended. I wanted to scoop you up and... I don't know."

He did know, she thought, as he ran his hands through his dark hair. He didn't want to say, but he knew.

"It wasn't safe," he said, his eyes pleading for understanding. "I needed you safe. Then that guy pulled his stunt, and I wanted to pull him apart." The raw gravel in his voice didn't sound hyperbolic, as Devon's hands clenched and released at his sides. "It's driving me crazy. It makes me want...things."

Hope watched him wet his lips, as his stare bored into her. She could barely breathe, with him analyzing every detail of her, every expression, every gesture. She felt a crushing vulnerability under his gaze but bet it had nothing on how vulnerable he felt right now.

"What kind of things?" she asked. Part of her wanted him to say something terrible, something that made it easy to ask him to leave. Another part dropped to its knees and prayed for him to get it right.

"To tell you about my day," he said hesitantly, "and ask about yours." He shrugged, but the motion seemed forced. "I want to tell you about R&R, or Cleary's, and you can tell me about the guy who screws up the tapestries. I could introduce you to my mom maybe?" His cheeks pinked. "Everyone loves her. And I want to feed you. Pull one of my sweaters over your head when you're cold. I want to skim my hands under my own t-shirt to get to your bare skin, and kiss you in the morning, and pummel anyone who hurts you... Okay, that last part might be a Dom thing, but what I need you to hear is that, with you, I want more than what I get in that room."

"You want to date me," she said.

He nodded. "And..." he added darkly, canting his head. Hope stood silently, expectantly, breath coming faster with each rise and fall of her chest, as she watched it shift in him again—the thing always waiting to come out and play. "I want to bind you so tightly that the rope leaves patterns on your skin."

Hope trembled.

"Run my fingertips over the impressions after, trace them with my tongue until you pant my name. I've heard you pant my name," he said. "I like it."

Her cheeks burned.

"I want to strap you to a St. Andrews," Devon went on, "and hold a vibrator between your thighs until you're slick with all you've given me." His gaze darkened. "I want to leave marks that you'll see for days, so every time you undress, you shudder with the memory of the pleasure I wrung from you." His hazel eyes found hers, flashing with heady lust. "I want everything, you see. And I've never wanted everything before."

Hope noted the rising desire in him—the tension in his body, the increased rate of his breathing.

"That room," she said, unable to hold it in any longer, as he stared down at her. "It makes me think of things I want to forget."

His jaw tightened until a muscle twitched. "You never have to go in there again. Not unless you want to."

"But all that stuff... You want to..." Hope looked down at her fingers, twisting in the teal fabric of her sweater.

"It doesn't matter," Devon said. "I don't need anything in that room to be with you. Those things are fun, but they're just things, and if it's not your thing, that's okay."

"Do you like to hurt people? Is that *your* thing?" Hope asked in a rush. A complicated twist of fear and desire sizzled in her chest as she awaited his response, something Hope didn't understand at all.

"Do you want the quick and dirty answer or the other one?" he asked, hands hidden behind his back, as if reminding them both that he was choosing not to touch her.

"The fast one," she decided. Devon winced, and Hope's heart sank.

"Then yes, I do," he said.

"Maybe... Maybe a slightly longer version," Hope said softly. Devon's lips quirked up in amusement, as he let out a relieved breath.

"Thank you," he said, then steeled himself. "Yes, I hurt people," he explained. "That's one of my things. However, pain and pleasure can go hand in hand—when done well." His eyes went half-lidded. "I can take you to the peak, play with you until I decide to tip you over the edge, and catch you when you drop. Not a brag but a promise. I'm good at it. I can do it until you lack the strength to stand. But I don't need to hurt you to accomplish that, any more than I need to tie you up. I'm dominant to my core, but pain and bondage are only acceptable when everyone's on board.

It's the control I crave most, darling, and I'll manage that, within your boundaries if you're willing."

Okay, that sounded less scary, but still complicated. "How?" Hope asked. "Like, what would you want to *do*?"

"There are other ways to..." Devon began, then wet his lips, hesitating long enough that she thought he might shutdown. "How much do you know about BDSM, power exchanges, that sort of thing?"

"Mostly what you see in porn," Hope admitted, with a hard blush.

Devon nodded. "Unfortunately, BDSM porn is about as realistic as pizza guy and yoga instructor porn. Do you know what subspace is?" Hope shook her head and watched him falter. "Would it be okay...?"

"Please." She gestured for him to go on.

"Okay. So, subspace is something that happens when an s-type— a submissive— I mean, I'm not trying to imply— It's mainly a chemical thing—Christ, this shouldn't be so hard for me." He took a breath and began again. "Subspace is an altered mental state that many subs fall into during BDSM play."

She nodded, ignoring her scorching ears.

"It's all about endorphins, and opioid receptors, and...magic." Devon gestured vaguely, before shoving his hands behind his back again. "I don't think anyone understands it fully, but most subs enjoy it. Like a high, almost. And for a Dom? Let's just say that it's satisfying to put someone there, to have that level of control over them."

"And you want to see me in *subspace*?" Hope said. Sex on a natural high seemed like a decent sales pitch, assuming she could get it without handcuffs.

Devon rolled his lower lip between his teeth and took a measured breath. "I think I already have," he said.

Hope blinked at his anxious, searching expression.

"You probably felt fuzzy, disconnected, but maybe really connected to... well, to me?" he said, his voice lilting up with the question.

Saturday. He was talking about Saturday night—about the reason she'd felt so out of sorts.

"You left," Hope said as the realization struck home.

Devon's mouth quirked into a sympathetic smile. "I had no right to stay."

"I *wanted* you to stay."

Devon shook his head. "I'm sorry for the way I left, but not for leaving. I literally defined subspace for you thirty seconds ago. You'd had three glasses of wine, and we've never had sex. We've never talked about what you feel comfortable with. That isn't an acceptable level of consent for me."

"Are you capable of having sex without a bunch of dominant BDSM stuff? Because I was more than willing to sign up for that," Hope snapped. Devon flashed a wicked grin at her intensity.

"I can cut everything but the dominance. That's in my nature, and it's the thing about me you respond to most. You'd miss it."

"I don't think that's true." Or she didn't want to admit it to him right after he said he had intentionally left her high and dry... or wet? *Oh God.*

"Moth to a flame," he said.

"That's ridiculous," Hope countered.

Devon raised a brow. "Says the woman standing less than a foot from me."

Hope looked down at her sock-feet, the tips of his boots roughly five inches from her toes. If she had to guess when she'd started unconsciously moving toward him, it was likely somewhere around *Dominant. Very, very dominant.* Honestly, it might have started with the shift in his stance.

"Are you going to leave if that subspace thing happens again?" she asked.

His forehead creased. "Tonight?" he asked. She couldn't stand the weight of his gaze, so she nodded at the floor. "Don't worry about that. I won't touch you. Responsive as you are, it still takes some effort."

Hope swallowed hard. "You could, you know..." She glanced up. "Touch me."

Devon's hands dropped from behind his back to his sides, but he didn't reach for her. "Hope..." His voice dripped a warning, one Hope ignored.

"You've told me the deep, dark secret. I've seen your dungeon... er... playroom. I don't know if I want to go in there again, but I know any hangups I have aren't because of anything you did." She looked up into his eyes, watched the light glimmer over the flecks of gold as if fire animated them.

"It's been a long day," he said, without an ounce of conviction.

"I know." She went on. "I've had one and a half hard ciders over the last three hours, and if I land in subspace, I'm saying right now that I'd prefer to be in it with you because being in it without you was…"

"Disorienting," he breathed when she let the sentence drift. "Because you didn't know."

Hope nodded. She'd felt hollow after he left on Saturday, and the endless, empty ache nearly burned her alive until his voice came over the phone. But talking to him had been a bandage, not a cure.

"Don't go," she said, her voice tinged with a desire whose flames licked through her. "Tell me I pass your rigorous standards for consent, because I want you to stay."

Needed him to stay. Devon fisted his hands at his sides, an outside representation of his inner restraint.

"We don't have to—"

"I want to."

She watched the slow, steady inhale. His broad chest rising and falling close to her own. His voice slipped further into that timbre that caused her body to quake with anticipation. "What is it you want, darling girl?"

Hope looked up at him through her lashes, utterly certain and unafraid. "Kiss me in the morning," she said. "Please."

HOPE

Devon's gaze settled on her mouth. "There you go again," he said. A delicious shiver crawled down her spine, and a thrum of energy pulsed up through her core at the sound of his husky voice. "Having no idea what you do to me..." He slid a finger gently down her cheek and under her chin, tilting up her face. Hope's breath came quick.

"Mmm... You've gone quiet," he said, his lips inches from hers. "I bet I can make you make all sorts of sounds." The air rushed out of her lungs. Devon's lips twitched in amusement. "But I'm going to need a promise from you first."

"Yes."

Why on earth did she say it like that? Like *Yes, I promise. Whatever it is, I promise...*

Devon chuckled darkly, fingertip trembling under her chin. "So willing..." he said. "Promise me, darling. Promise me that you'll tell me if something feels wrong."

"Devon..." her voice came out needy and strained, laced with every bit of anxiety that she'd fought through the evening, through the day... She wanted him against her. His mouth on her, his hands...

Devon clicked his tongue. "You want me to touch you. You want it *so badly*. I worry you'd agree to anything to make that happen, and I can't have that," he said gallantly. "So, I'm going to take advantage of that desire. You will promise to tell me if you want me to stop, want me to behave differently, or are uncomfortable for any reason, and I'll make sure you blush at work tomorrow when you think of me. Deal?"

"Yes," she said breathlessly, though he was right. She would agree to almost anything to close the inches between them. "I promise I'll tell you, but please—"

He cut her off with a kiss. His tongue sliding into her mouth, as the hand that had been under her chin slid to the back of her head. Hope grabbed for him too, fisting her hands in the fabric of his sweater to pull him closer. With a disorienting pivot, he shifted them around. Then sitting back on her sofa, he pulled her down to straddle him.

"I've wanted back between your legs since you got off," he growled.

She thought about how he'd changed their trajectory earlier in the evening. But all that came out of her mouth was something that sounded like a whine, as her hips involuntarily moved against him.

"Mmm..." he said, the sound reverberating from somewhere deep in his chest and stilling her. "Do that again." As Hope's cheeks flushed with embarrassment, Devon cocked his head. With the hint of a smile playing at the edge of his mouth, he gripped her hips. "This," he said, rolling her pelvis, watching pleasure flood her face. "Do *this* again."

Hope's mouth fell open. She didn't know how much more she could stand before she came apart— while he watched her. After one painfully slow forward and back, Devon released her, resting his hands on her thighs, thumbs dipping toward center. He stared at her expectantly.

"Again," he said. No request in it.

Hope chewed her lip, and tentatively rocked herself against him. The shot of pleasure through her core paled in comparison to the one triggered by his wicked grin.

"Do it again," he ordered.

Breath coming harder, she rolled her hips outright—her sex slick and hot as she followed the hard length of him beneath his jeans. Though it occurred to her in a rather dazed way, that it would be embarrassing to soak through both of their clothes, the potency of what he called out of her had her arching her back and bracing a hand on his chest to steady herself. Without taking his eyes off her face, Devon gently took her bracing hand, lacing their fingers together.

"Again," he said, pressing a kiss to her knuckles. "For me."

Hope's body began moving before he fell silent. She gripped his hand tightly, using it for support. She could hear her own panting breaths, the rustle of fabric between them. Too much fabric, too much... The incessant thudding of her racing heart... She needed this. Needed him. Like breathing.

That far away feeling flitted at the edges of her awareness, but something in the back of her brain pushed back, unwilling to fully let go. The spacy, floaty sensation persisted, threatening to pull her under.

"Ahh... that's my good girl," Devon said, voice dripping a flavor of seduction that Hope craved, even if she didn't understand why.

With a tug of fabric over her head, her sweater was gone. Hope looked down at her lacy black bra and leggings—the latter plastered to her from all the mindless grinding. Devon skimmed his gaze over her, licking his lips.

"Oh, gorgeous girl..." he said, huskily. With a swift move, he hooked an arm around her waist and brought his mouth to hers again, kissing her like he owned her.

"I need to get inside you," he growled, rolling her off him, and crawling up between her thighs as she landed on her back on the couch.

And that's when reality had the audacity to smack her in the face.

The couch. No, no, no, no, no... The thought reverberated through her mind, through the delicious sensations and the insatiable need, like nails on a chalkboard. As Devon reached for the waistband of her leggings, Hope's body shot backward, scurrying away from him before she knew what was happening. Devon yanked away his hands, scrambling back to his haunches.

"Are you okay?" he said, honest concern drowning out any unsatisfied desire. She could have loved him for that—for looking worried, instead of disappointed in that moment.

"Not here..." Hope stammered. "I just... Not here, please."

Devon stared at her, weighing her state and his options. Then, he stood and extended a hand. When Hope clasped it, he pulled her up against him. Her legs wrapped around his waist, as he scooped one hand under her ass, and slipped the other arm behind her back. He kissed her again, a deep, lazy thing that made her thighs tighten and her core open. Languorous. Thorough. It washed away the intrusion in her mind leaving only him. Only Devon.

"Better?" he asked, coming up for air.

"So much better," she breathed. "Thank you."

Devon nodded and raised a brow. "Bedroom?"

"Yeah."

He kissed her as he carried her, only stopping to curse under his breath as he pushed them through the bathroom door. In Hope's apartment, the first door on the left actually *was* a bathroom. She laughed, as she pressed a row of kisses down his neck.

"You think it's funny until I take you on the counter," he said, stumbling back out into the hall.

"Last door—" she got out before his tongue reclaimed her mouth.

Devon groaned with relief, as he lowered her to the bed.

"Do not move," he said, pushing himself to sit on the edge and slipping off his shoes. "Sorry, I tromped through your bedroom in boots."

"I'll forgive you if you get back over here," Hope said, smiling up at him in the low light from the hallway.

Scooting closer, Devon splayed a warm hand across her stomach. Eyes on Hope's, he slid that hand to her hip, then caressed a fingertip down her other side, hooking the waistband of her leggings. His hands warmed a trail down her thighs, her calves, as he slowly peeled off everything but her thong in one steady motion. The whole mess sailed over his shoulder to the floor. Gooseflesh erupted across Hope's skin, her nipples tightening in her bra even as her sex remained a pool of molten need. She waited; watched him watching her.

He touched her tenderly. As if he'd leashed—at least temporarily—that part of himself that needed to dominate. With a shaking hand, he tucked a rogue lock of hair behind her ear. "I will remember you like this for the rest of my life," he said, pressing a reverent kiss to her forehead, her lips.

Hope kissed him back, pushing herself up to sitting as she did. When she reached for the hem of his sweater, Devon obliged by raising his arms, then removing the white undershirt that she had left behind. Her hands slid through the light smattering of hair on his chest, over his stomach, down, down until she caught the front of his jeans. Devon pulled in a sharp breath.

A moment later he was out of his pants, his erection springing free. Hope's legs parted at the sight of his naked body; she couldn't help it. Devon didn't miss the reaction, and his wicked grin returned. As he wedged his knees under the bend of her legs, on either side of her ass, and caressed fingertips up her inner thighs, his hands no longer shook—but Hope's entire body trembled.

"Kiss you in the morning, you say?" he asked, playfully.

"Please, Devon…" she whimpered, anticipation suffocatingly thick.

"I'm going to kiss you now." He slid a hand behind her back, and the tension of her bra released. Tossing it to the floor, he left her exposed in the dim light. "Maybe here?" He cupped a hand beneath one breast. Her back arched as he circled a thumb around the tight nipple. "Or here?" he said, dropping his head.

His deliciously hot mouth suckled at her— nipping… licking… suckling again…

"Please…"

Hope gasped, her thighs alternately pressing against his flanks, then spreading wide, her body threatening to implode. In desperation, she wrapped her legs around his waist and pulled. She met an immovable wall. Devon chuckled. Putting a hand on her chest, he sent her flopping back into the pillows, before scooting his lower half back. Hope stared down her stomach; one of his arms running up the middle of her torso, and the other crossing her pelvis. The bulk of his upper body pinned her legs open. Devon's eyes, black in the dimness, held an expression that told her he had her exactly where he wanted her.

"I'm going to kiss you here now," he said, tracing a finger down the center of her black lace thong. Hope's body bucked; Devon's grin spread. "Would you like that, darling? If I can't wait until morning, would you like me to kiss you here now?"

Her legs jerked. "Devon, please…"

For all her pleasure, the burn bordered on excruciating. Hope wasn't sure coherent words were coming out of her mouth, at this point. She'd never had a guy drag out foreplay until she begged. Usually, they were more than happy to get their dick wet at the first available opportunity.

"God, you're so wet," he drawled, as she panted. He traced and retraced that line with his fingertip. Hope writhed. "How did you get this wet? You must be *aching*, you beautiful, greedy, impatient little thing…"

She mewled, pitifully. Then on a downstroke, Devon hooked a thumb under her panties, pulled them to the side, and latched on, his tongue lapping over her, laser focused on that most sensitive spot. Hope's hands shot into his hair, as she helplessly opened for him.

"Devon… God… Devon…"

"Say it again," he said against her sex, before diving back in. Licking, sucking… feasting on her as if she were the only thing on earth that could satisfy him. A guttural noise of indulgence vibrated in his throat, piercing straight through the core of her, and without warning, Hope tipped off a cliff. With her thighs clenched around his head, and her hands in his hair, she came shouting his name. She stayed there, desperately clamped onto him, utterly unable to let go until he pulled her thighs away from his ears to take a breath.

"Sorry… I… Sorry…" Hope murmured anxiously.

"Don't you dare," Devon growled, prowling up her body, before freezing. "Shit…" He whipped his head around. "Where did we throw my jeans?"

"Your *jeans*?" Hope repeated in stunned panic.

He looked back to her, smiled mischievously. "I need a condom, darling." It took her a few seconds to process, but the issue eventually sank in.

"Nightstand. Top drawer... Wait, check the date." God knew she hadn't looked at that box, since she moved in.

Devon pressed a quick kiss to her mouth, leaving the taste of her own sex on her tongue. The hallway light washed over him as he turned for the nightstand, illuminating where all the ink ended. The intricate designs that first caught Hope's attention when he rolled up his sleeves at Cleary's continued up his arms, over his shoulders, and converged into the head of a wolf that covered most of his mid and upper back.

It stared back at her, as realistic as a black and white photo, but with the same black and grey lines from Devon's arms cutting through its detailed fur. They highlighted the ears, framed unreadable eyes. There were no cartoonish fangs or curling lips. No foaming at the mouth. The wolf didn't need to snarl to prove he was dangerous. And the only thing holding him back? All those pretty lines that Devon had commissioned to restrain him.

"Your tattoo..." she said, reaching over to trail a hand down his back.

Devon stiffened. He angled the box of responsible choices toward the light from the door and squinted. "You're good until July," he said.

He was back over her a split second later, staring down at her as he stroked a hand up and down his thick shaft and deftly rolled on a condom. Hope squirmed against the sheets, promptly shelving the sight of his tattoos in favor of the sight before her. God, he was glorious in the low light. Dark hair tousled and wolfish eyes gleaming.

"Do you want to come again, darling?"

"Please…"

Devon closed his eyes. "I'm addicted to the way you say that word," he said before his tone turned darker. "Someday, I will torment you for hours while you repeat it, but tonight…" He sucked in a breath. "Tonight, I can't wait another minute to bury myself in you."

With that, he braced one hand by her head, the head of his cock pressing insistently against her still pulsing sex. Devon watched the expression on her face shift with each inch he slid inside her, stretching her, filling her, erasing every sense she had beyond the way his body felt in hers. Hope couldn't have hidden from him if she'd tried.

With the aftershocks of her first orgasm still tightening against him, Devon began to move. Slowly at first, exquisitely slow, but with ever-growing need. His kiss shifted intensity along with his thrusts, building from gentle to possessive. Unable to speak with her mouth full of his tongue, Hope wrapped her legs around his waist and threw herself into matching his rhythm. It was every-thing. He drove her to the edge again, and she slipped over in the way water tumbles over a fall— without a moment's hesitation to wonder if there are rocks below.

Then his mouth left hers. Devon rocked back onto his knees, dug his fingers into her hips for leverage, and pounded harder.

Hope cried out, as orgasm after orgasm quaked through her body. She could hardly get a breath between each cresting wave of pleasure. Each desperate, inarticulate exclamation, he called out of her.

Devon's fingers bit deeper into her sweat-slicked skin, pulling her into him with every powerful thrust. Everything between them was a hot slide of flesh in flesh, as he looked down on her with the eyes of a predator sighting prey. He could eat her alive, she thought, as another climax ripped through her. He could have every bit of her.

Devon's rhythm shifted again, slowing in favor of greater impact each time he bottomed out in her pussy. Then it happened. He stretched out over her, catching her wrists with one hand and shoving them into the pillows above her head. His other hand clasped her throat. The move startled her but didn't scare her, and Hope didn't know why. With his face inches above hers, he need only squeeze and not let go. She would have no way of stopping him. That should terrify her, she thought as her body arched into every point of contact between them. Closer, closer still...

"Please..." she whimpered, searching for an unknown horizon. The hand at her throat tightened slightly, and Hope's eyes rolled back in pleasure. Her entire body tingled with another building release.

"Ah, there you go," Devon gritted out. "That's my good girl. I'm going to come in you now, darling. And you're coming with me."

A cascade of sensation flooded Hope's body as Devon relaxed the hand at her throat and his mouth claimed hers. He plowed into her, yanking her close as he buried himself to ride out his orgasm.

Hope groaned a final release with starbursts dancing behind her eyelids.

DEVON

Devon awoke with a throbbing cock sandwiched between his stomach and Hope's thigh. He chose to ignore that fact. There were things he needed more than sex, at the moment—things he had never experienced.

The morning light filtered through not-quite-pink curtains, making the room feel...well... *rosy*. They lay in a nest of once crisp white sheets patterned with beige and grey moons and stars, and a plush comforter that matched the drapes. Dusty rose? Ballet pink? Freaking mauve? There was probably a name for that color, but there were no words for the way it brought out the dewy flush on her cheeks as her head lolled on his shoulder. Her hair twisted over the pillow in a dark tangle, a perfect complement to her smudged mascara.

Glorious ruination... The room, Hope, and Devon on levels he never knew existed.

Her breasts shifted against him with each smooth rise and fall of her chest. His heart thumped under her palm. Devon wished he could step out of his body and stand over them. Wished he could see the entirety of this beautiful mess they'd created. He'd never helped make anything like this. Ever.

She had slept tucked against him since they'd crashed together the night before—with the exception of a half-hour window around 2 a.m., when her insistent grinding against his hip had Devon reaching for the box of condoms in her nightstand and sliding back inside her. Discarded clothes littered the floor, and the air smelled of sex layered with *his* and *hers* bodywash. He had never woken up beside someone before—never wanted to—but Devon could get used to this. He didn't want this to end.

Unfortunately, life didn't come with a pause button. Hope shifted against him, heaved a deep, lazy sigh, and lifted her head. When she looked at him with bleary eyes, Devon felt the strangest pang in his chest.

"You're watching me." She grinned, drowsily, as he smiled down at her.

"My favorite view," he said.

"Mmm..." Hope purred, pushed up to straddle him, and stretched like a cat. If it weren't for round two, Devon might have ejaculated up his stomach like a virgin, what with his cock nestled under her silky wet sex as she arched. "Still a good view?" she asked.

It wasn't yet seven, and they'd burned a few million calories throughout the night. But on went the necessities, and then, she laced her fingers in his and bounced until he came inside her, her core gripping him as he did. Holy fuck, she was gorgeous— her head thrown back in absolute abandon. For him, he realized. He got to see her like this. *Feel* her like this. Something no one could ever deserve, least of all him. *Grateful* didn't touch it.

Hope collapsed on top of him, his cock still twitching inside her, as Devon pressed lazy kisses to every part within reach.

"I don't want to get out of this bed," he groaned, trailing a hand up and down her back.

"I could be sick," Hope offered.

His excitement surged at the prospect of staying exactly where he was until reality set in. Aside from their responsibilities, you probably weren't supposed to spend every waking and sleeping moment with someone you had technically been on one and a half dates with. Devon sighed.

"Apollo will need out, and if you skip work, you won't get the opportunity to blush in front of people every time you think of me inside you." He rocked his hips for emphasis, smiling and kissing her temple when her pussy clenched his cock.

"Fine," she pouted, rolling off him.

Locating everything but his t-shirt, Devon headed to the bathroom. Hope scooted around him, as he fastened his jeans. Pulling yesterday's sweater over his head, he realized that she had sat down to pee. Devon studiously looked at anything but her. His face heated.

"What?" she asked, flushing the toilet.

He didn't understand his embarrassment over something so innocuous. Maybe it was because the last time a woman peed in front of him, it was under threat of denial. Waterworks wasn't really

Devon's thing, but watching a sub dig for that level of submission when it wasn't their thing either could be delightful.

"You found my t-shirt," he said, pulling his attention from the thoughts swimming in his brain and focusing on what she was wearing. *All she was wearing...* he noted, as she hopped up on the counter beside him, deliberately spreading her legs as she leaned for the faucet.

"Christ," he breathed.

Hope ran her hands down her breasts and stomach by way of drying them, and again his fly was pulling double duty as a retaining wall.

"What did you call me last night?" she said, hooking his waistband with one hand, and snagging the wallet from his back pocket with the other. Hope riffled through the contents as he watched her, holding up the shiny gold square when she found it. "Greedy? Impatient?"

Devon raised his brows. "Did I make it to *bratty*, darling?"

"Hmmm... I don't remember." She lifted her eyes to his. "But you definitely mentioned this counter."

Devon leaned into her. "Did I now?"

***

The two things Devon learned before leaving Hope's still preoccupied his mind as he walked into Cleary's.

Firstly, her bathroom counter sat at the perfect height for him to bury himself to the hilt—even if his knees did bang the ever-loving fuck out of the cabinet beneath. Additionally, he hadn't hit his orgasm limit for the day. Then again, neither had Hope. So, maybe he'd learned three things.

"You're early," Nix said, as he cut through the main room. "I thought you had stuff to do at R&R."

"I'm going over there before Mom's tomorrow. I already texted Dre," Devon called over his shoulder as he headed for the safety of the office. Nix would assume he needed to stow his stuff, do some bookkeeping, whatever... while he got his head on straight again.

He'd already texted Hope too. Asked about her schedule and arranged to pick her up at one tomorrow—because apparently Devon couldn't make it more than a few hours without lining up his next hit. The next twenty-six hours might as well be decades, every time he thought of her straddling him in the pale light of dawn, though. And that's why he picked Cleary's over R&R.

Normally, Devon found satisfaction in his handyman, cleanup guy, *what-can-I-do-for-ya?* role at the nonprofit, but his next big project required facetime with Dre, R&R's second counselor; which was fine, great even. Devon loved planning with him, putting their heads together to make R&R work.

Just not today.

Devon felt raw, and not because of round after round of fun with Hope. Their amorous evening, morning, middle of the night...bathroom freaking counter adventures left his body loose and relaxed. But his head couldn't put away the image of her flinching back from him outside the playroom, or the way she bolted out of his reach on her couch. Then, there was the feel of her warm and wet and open for him. The desperate, needy sounds she made when she was utterly undone.

The fucking flinching…

Was emotional whiplash a thing? Devon felt like it was a thing.

He squeezed his eyes tight and scrubbed his hands over his face. *Way* too many feelings to spend the day talking shop with a therapist. So, he'd picked Cleary's, instead. If Nix pushed too hard, he could fire her. He didn't have that level of control at R&R.

Making his way to the bar, Devon dug out a clean cloth and got started.

"You know we've only been open fifteen minutes, right?" Nix said, pointing toward the bottles on the shelves one by one with the pen in her hand, listing what needed to be pulled from the back on the notepad they shared.

Devon turned to face her. "Is there a problem with me wiping down a bar *that I own*?" Okay, that came out harsher than he'd intended.

Nix arched a brow. "Nope. You putting margaritas on Happy Hour tonight?"

Devon forced his brain to focus on liquor, instead of flinching. He shook his head. "Do something with rum," he said. "We're drowning in it." They'd been tripping over cases for six months because Hope wore a tank top one Saturday in May, and Devon managed to order cases instead of bottles. He wouldn't live it down until he got rid of the evidence, but the stuff just would not move.

"Okay, but it's Tuesday," Nix said, making a note.

"And that matters because…?"

"You know, Tuesdays… Tacos… People expect tequila," she said.

"What people? We're dead, on Tuesdays," he groused. Nix waited, saying nothing. "Fine." Devon relented. "Do margaritas tonight, but something with rum the rest of the week. Why does no one in this town drink rum anymore?" This much frustration couldn't be normal, for a guy who'd gotten laid more in the last twelve hours than the last seven months.

"So, I'm going to assume you didn't tie her up and play with her," Nix said.

Devon huffed out a laugh, turned back to the bar and started wiping again. "It was fine," he said. "More than fine."

"Says the guy chewing my head off. Don't know what we'd have done if you'd showed up in a *bad* mood."

Devon sighed and kept working on his pointless task. The wipe down thing soothed him. It was also the least extreme outlet in his arsenal. "I'm sorry. I'm being an asshole."

Nix laughed. "Oh honey, you aren't going to hurt my feelings, today. I don't get it, though. You say things went well, but you're in this sour-ass mood."

Devon shrugged. "So, I'm moody."

"You're also avoiding Dre," she said. "Something happened."

"Shit," Devon mumbled. He pressed his mouth into a tight line. "Hope walked into the playroom," he said, "while I had Apollo out back—before I talked to her."

Nix came into his periphery and leaned against the bar. "How did that go?"

Side-to-side with that clean, white towel…

"It scared her," he said. "Not just the room, but...*me.* Like I would flip out about her accidentally walking in there, and I might—"

Circles. He switched his technique to circles as the muscles in his jaw and shoulders tightened. Even if they got faster or harder, circles were still soft. Not the harsh, slicing movements his side-to-side efforts were devolving into.

"Did she say that?"

Devon laughed harshly.

"The way she stumbled back and put her hands up when I moved made it pretty fucking clear." He squeezed the towel for a beat, then revisited his circles technique. "I took her home, but then we talked, and one thing led to another."

"One thing led to another, like...?"

"Pretty sure Apollo slept on my bed. He knows he's not allowed up there, but I guess I can't blame him when I abandoned him. At least, he didn't pee anywhere, or if he did, I haven't found it." He glanced up to find Nix biting back a smile.

"Then why are you so... you know... like this?" she asked.

He shrugged again. "She's—" Devon searched for a word, and when nothing useful presented itself, he made one up. "*Flinchy.* In my hallway, on her couch after we smoothed things out. I can't focus on everything else we did, with my head tripping over that." He blinked, realizing that he hadn't intended to have this conversation. "It's stupid." Devon clammed up and redoubled his efforts on the already clean bar.

"That's not stupid, man," Nix said. "That's Relationship:101. Concern for the other person is part of it."

"I care about other people, Nix. Contrary to popular belief, I have human emotions pretty frequently," he said, not bothering to hide the insult.

"Yes, you do. You have the biggest heart, and a dominant streak a mile wide that gets shit done. You'll go over and above for me, the staff," she gestured to Cleary's seating area, "R&R. You'd do anything for your mom... And you'll do the same for a sub—for as long as it takes to run a scene and get them straight after. But you don't come in here worrying over a girl from last night. It's not what you do."

Devon considered. "Devil's advocate—"

"Do not," Nix warned, launching a paint-stripping glare at him.

"I mean," Devon said, retreating from that landmine, "from a dominant's perspective, knowing a partner's triggers matters, and I'm nothing if not a dominant."

"You Devil's-Advocated without saying it." She glared again.

"Hello. *Demon*," he said, gesturing to himself. "You know it's true, though."

"So, you're doing the dynamic thing with her, then?" she asked.

"No," he said. "Not exactly."

Nix's brows pulled together. "What does that mean?" she said.

"What the fuck do you think it means? As you were so kind to point out Saturday night, I can't turn it off." He took a breath and spoke more calmly. "We talked. I told her I would always have those *tendencies*, but that I could work within her boundaries—and I will. I still want to know why she thought I was going to grab her when I barely moved, though."

"Okay, but can you keep it on her level?"

Agitation fanned through him. "Are you serious?"

"There is a certain... Let's call it a quota," Nix hedged.

"Let's not," he shot back. Nix plowed onward.

"One she's not going to be able to—"

"There is no goddamn quota." Devon resisted the urge to drum a fist on the bar.

So, now he was an emotionless robot with a BDSM *quota*, who was incapable of dating someone if he couldn't cane the ever-loving fuck out of them from time to time? *Right...* This whole conversation could go rot in a trash heap.

"Okay," Nix said, with none of the inflection of someone who intended to stop talking. "An *intensity,* then. You can't cold-turkey the thing you've used to keep your head straight since you were wet behind the ears while fixating on why she's flinching. You need the outlet."

"It's not like I stopped going to Edge because of her," Devon lied. "I haven't run a scene with anyone, in over six months. And we both know what a conditioned response looks like...I can't watch her all but run from me in fear, *repeatedly*, and ignore it."

Devon didn't understand how a dominant, how *anyone*, could do that. The time on her couch, it wasn't even because she thought he was angry, which he found equally disturbing. Devon wanted his girlfriend going all Pavlov's Puppy in a manner that left her sitting in a puddle of her own fluids, not backing away from him like—

Devon froze, threw his train of thought into reverse. Did he... Did he really just...

"I know." Nix pinned him with a stare, but Devon had lost the thread of their conversation.

"I'm, uh, going to pull stock," he said, heading for anywhere without an audience. She let him make it three solid strides.

"You'll need the list," Nix said, tearing her slip of paper loose and holding it out for him.

HOPE

Nope, Hope thought as Cleary's heavy wood and glass door closed behind her.

Devon stood behind the bar, working his way through an assortment of bottles for a couple of customers, with all the showmanship of someone who knew where the tips came from. Given that she would see him the next afternoon anyway for what Devon deemed *a boring surprise, so don't get your hopes up* and the fact that he'd been screwing her on her bathroom counter 14 hours earlier, interrupting him at work suddenly struck Hope as embarrassingly desperate.

She hedged back toward the door, but another entering patron blocked her progress. Hope shifted her weight from foot to foot, awaiting her chance to cut past them, as Devon handed over the drinks he'd constructed. Except then, like he had some sort of *Hope Radar,* he looked directly at her and... Well, he didn't grin exactly, but he certainly looked pleased. Reaching beneath the bar, he pulled out a bright white cloth and gestured to the stool directly in front of himself. He didn't take his eyes off her, as he made slow passes over the bar.

Busted, Hope thought. She wet her lips, then walked toward him, shrugging out of her coat. She slung it over the back of the barstool, on her way past.

"Hey, uh... sorry for—" she stopped short when Devon set the cloth aside and patted the bar expectantly.

"Come here," he said in firm, but gentle command.

Some invisible tether had her standing on the lower rung of her barstool and leaning forward before she considered the logistics of reaching him across the high bar. Devon met her in the middle, framed her face in his hands, and put his tongue in her mouth, not giving a damn about onlookers. He smelled like he had that morning when her entire body was pressed against him.

"Are your feet still on the barstool?" he asked, backing away.

"Umm... No." Hope blushed, lower half dangling from the edge of the bar.

"Don't fall," he said, pressing another kiss to her forehead.

"Right. Thanks." She dropped about eight inches, before climbing back onto her seat. Devon produced a wine glass and reached for a bottle. "Actually, can I get ice water? Or tea if you have it," Hope said.

Devon inclined his head and slid a glass of iced tea in front of her. "You came to a bar for tea?" He raised a brow, mischievously.

I came for you, she wanted to say. "I went for a walk. Thought I'd stop in and say hi." She reached for the glass.

"Where's Chloe?" Devon asked, scanning the room.

"Work." Hope shrugged and took a sip. It was cold and sweet but didn't extinguish the fire from that kiss.

Devon pulled out his phone, frowned at the screen, and put it away again.

"Something wrong?" she asked.

"Ah... It's nothing," he said. "Hungry?"

"I ate at home." She'd barely sat down, and he was already checking the time. Time she'd been eating up every day since Saturday, or Friday...technically. "Hey, you know what? You're busy. I'll be out of here, as soon as I finish this. Can you ring me up?"

Devon smirked. "First of all, I'm walking you when you go, and secondly, the drink is on the house."

"No, I don't want to... I didn't mean..."

Great. Interrupting his entire evening, freeloading, and pulling him away from his job... More desperate by the moment. She twisted the hem of her shirt and bounced a foot on the rung of her chair. Devon pressed his mouth into a firm line. Hope stopped fidgeting.

"Sorry," she said.

Leaning across the bar, Devon spoke low. Hope's pulse spiked again at the scent of him, the proximity. "You believe that we have a problem here, darling." He canted his head. "And we do. But it isn't what you think it is."

Hope's brow knit. "Okay..."

A guy in khakis and a light blue button-down walked up to the bar a few feet over from where she sat. He waited patiently. Devon sighed.

"I'll be right back. Do not leave that stool." His last sentence landed with all the weight of a gavel. Deliciously final and non-negotiable.

"Yes, sir." Hope giggled. Something flashed in his eyes.

"Stay," he said.

Devon approached his customer, glancing over periodically as if Hope couldn't be trusted remain where he'd left her. She stuck her tongue out at him and sipped her tea. As Devon strode back from the other end of the bar, Nix sauntered up beside him.

"God, it's slow tonight," she said. "Four of the big tables are empty, and two are about to tab out. I'm sending Brandy home."

"Typical Tuesday." Devon shrugged, crossing his arms over his chest, and pinning Hope with a hard stare. "Don't cut her loose yet. I need to handle something."

Nix cocked her head. "What kind of thing?"

Devon heaved an exaggerated sigh. "Hope walked over here all on her own for a surprise visit. Didn't even text that she was on her way. I looked up, and there she was. *All alone.*"

"Oh." Nix grimaced. "Right... Where's Chloe?"

Hope opened her mouth, but Devon beat her to the answer. "Hope says she's working." He smiled, tightly.

Nix adopted a wicked grin. Her stance widened a fraction, and she crossed her arms, morphing into a miniature, busty version of the guy beside her.

"Did anyone ever tell you two that you stand the same?" Hope said, with a chuckle. Actually... She looked from *tall, dark, and dominant* to *short, dark and...* Her chuckle thinned to silence as Nix and Devon side-eyed each other.

"Perceptive little thing, isn't she?" Devon said.

"Not all that perceptive, if she doesn't see what I'm seeing," Nix replied with a snort.

Unease washed over Hope. "I didn't mean that as an insult. I just thought—"

"Again, darling, the problem isn't what you think it is." His eyes glittered.

"Demon goes to work..." Nix said, shaking her head. "I can stay late, but I'm not closing for you." She clicked her tongue but didn't say another word, as Devon stepped out from behind the bar, caught Hope by a wrist, and tugged her toward the back.

"My coat..." she said.

Plowing forward, Devon didn't spare her a glance.

"Nix will watch it," he promised, as Hope stumbled along after him.

"Where are we—"

Without preamble, Devon pulled her into a tiny office housing a mammoth metal desk painted army green, a filing cabinet, and a single office chair that had seen better days. The beige walls could do with a fresh coat of paint. He closed the door and locked it.

"I'm sorry, are you..." Hope trailed off as Devon began stacking the various paperwork and junk from the desktop, shoving it into drawers. "What are you doing?" she asked.

Only the muffled drone of music, voices, and kitchen sounds forcing their way into the room answered her. Devon closed a laptop, put it atop the filing cabinet, and then swiped his hand over the desk.

"Do you have any aversion to office furniture that I should know about?" he asked.

"Um... No?"

Sinking into the chair, he patted the newly empty surface in front of himself.

"Then sit," he ordered.

Hope reluctantly circled the green monstrosity and hopped up in front of him, staring down into his upturned face.

"I don't like the idea of you walking around town alone at night. Especially if no one knows to check on you if you don't show up," he said without preamble.

"Okay..." Hope trailed off as Devon unfastened the snap on her jeans.

"And that makes me want to convince you to never do that again."

He tugged down her zipper, rested his hands on her knees. Hope thought of the way he and Nix had spoken at the bar, of all the crops and canes in that room of his. She chilled.

"But because consent is everything," he went on, "and we've never talked about how utterly terrified I am at the thought of something happening to you, I think the best way for us to approach this situation is through positive reinforcement."

"I'm sorry, what?" Hope said.

Her core pulsed and tingled as he deliberately licked, then bit his lower lip, staring up at her through dark lashes.

"Seeing you unexpectedly brings me intense pleasure." He pulled off her tennis shoes one by one. "And I never want you to feel punished for the things you want or need, especially when you want me. Or did you come because you needed me?" Devon flashed her a devastating smile. "So, *very* positive reinforcement. That's where we are, I think." His tone turned contemplative. "But with a side of delayed gratification. I need you to learn this lesson, darling, to think about what you've done."

Hope's breath caught and everything between her thighs heated.

"Take them off," he said. "Now. Please."

Hope was numbly aware of the absurdity of leaving her jeans, socks, and panties in a pile between his feet, so she could put her bare ass on a frigid metal desk—all while a bar full of patrons and staff continued existing on the other side of the door. She sat in front of him, nervously, knees pressed together.

"There we go," he said, sliding warm hands up and down her thighs.

Devon locked eyes with her, as he spread her legs. Standing, he leaned into her, rough denim brushing her most sensitive skin, as he lowered her back on the desk. He looked down at her for a moment, before reclaiming his seat, leaving her open and vulnerable as she stared into a drop ceiling.

"Devon, this is—"

"Beautiful," he breathed against her sex. Hope's brain went fuzzy. Her body spasmed. "You smell like me, like us," he said.

She blanched. "I was running late for work, so I didn't—"

"Hush. I love that you smell like I fucked you." As if to prove his point, Devon leaned closer, letting his breath tickle her with every exhale. "Let's talk about why you're leaking on my desk." Horrified, Hope started to push upright. "Did I say sit up?" he demanded. She settled back again, eying him warily. Devon inclined his head.

"You *yes, sir'ed* me," he said, his tone accusatory as he trailed a maddeningly light finger down her center. "I thought I could ignore you skipping through the dark without letting anyone know your plans—casually mention it later and ask you to do things differently next time. It's probably what another man would do. But then..." He sighed heavily. "You *yes, sir'ed* me."

"Wh...what?" Hope stammered. Was this about walking here alone? Or how she responded when he told her to stay put while he helped that customer? Or was it strictly because Devon was, by his own admission, *very, very dominant*, and every time he started growling orders in her ear, her knickers dampened?

Devon lapped his tongue over her once, as if she were an ice cream cone threatening to drip. One powerful, flat sweep, and then the heat of his mouth gave way to the chill of empty air. Hope whimpered softly, legs trying to close. Devon gently pushed them wider.

"You said it as a joke," he said. Hope felt that other delicious tingle, the one at the back of her skull that she was starting to associate with— "The next time you *yes, sir* me, it won't be a joke," Devon promised.

As he flicked the tip of his tongue against her clit, Hope reached to bury her hands in his hair. Devon caught her wrists, and pinned them on the inside of her thighs, using his hands and hers to part her. He clicked his tongue.

"Impatient..." He sighed. Hope twisted against him, needy and breathless. "The only thing you control here is whether we stop, understood?"

"Yes..."

"Yes, what, darling?" he drawled wickedly, eyes glittering up from between her legs as she lifted her head to look at him.

"Do you really expect..." Hope trailed off as he licked her again. Painfully slow. "*Fuck...*" she whispered on an exhale.

Devon's upper body vibrated against her with a laugh. "It's a slow night. I can do this for hours," he said. "So, I say again, the only thing you control here is whether we stop, yes?"

"Yes... Yes, Sir." Hope panted, cheeks flushing at her own desperate voice. He was right. There was no mistaking it for a joke this time.

He licked again—the sound of wet lapping nearly as seductive as the heat of his tongue. "God, the taste of you..." Another lick left her moaning and shuddering. "Whoa. That was fast. Okay, we'll back off that for a minute," Devon said.

Hope whimpered and squirmed.

"Darling girl, do you want me to stop?"

"No, Devon—"

"No, what?"

"Sir! No, Sir." She writhed on the desk; the once icy metal warm beneath her.

Devon started licking again, a faster pace which he alternated with gentle sucking. The muscles in her core tightened and coiled, ready to shatter. Then he stopped, leaving her lingering on the edge.

"Oops. Almost got carried away there, didn't I?" he said, from between her thighs.

Hope's head thumped back onto the desk. "I don't understand what you want," she whined.

"Oh, darling. It's what I *don't* want that has me licking your pussy right now. You walked here alone, at night, without telling anyone. Don't do that again." Devon released one of her hands and skimmed a finger over her clit as he spoke, the muscles of her sex contracting lightly each time he did. "Aw, cute," he said, stroking again. "What an eager little hole." Hope instinctively reached down, but Devon snatched her hand again, putting it back on her inner thigh. "No touching," he admonished. "You'll ruin it."

Hope's laugh caught in her throat. Her threatening orgasm loomed out of reach. The perpetual buildup grew more intense, with every touch, and his pauses pushed the finish line back farther. Keeping her free hand off her clit was an exercise in self-control, the likes of which she had never experienced. Why in the world wouldn't he...?

"Wait... Are you *punishing* me?" she asked suddenly. "You said you didn't want me to *feel* punished, but—"

Devon laughed; a vibrant, luscious thing.

"Such a soft little kitten, aren't you?" He leisurely slid one finger inside her and pulled it out again. Hope squirmed pitifully. "I never realized how fun it could be to play with soft things," he said thoughtfully, as he put his now slippery finger against her clit and rubbed a few solid circles. Hope arched and panted; Devon stopped again. "This isn't a punishment, darling. This is a lesson. I'll let you finish..." He pressed a kiss to the top of her sex; her head bounced on the desk in response. Devon laughed again. "Eventually."

"Fine, you've made your point." Which was something about walking alone and calling him *sir*, she thought. Maybe...

"How about I let you know when I'm finished making it?" he said, amused.

He put his mouth on her again, Hope's eyes rolling as she urged her body to get with the program before he stopped. The second her legs went rigid, Devon pulled away. Hope grasped at the edges of relief, nearly sobbing as it slipped through her fingers.

"Please." Her pride leached out like the wetness between her thighs and the puddle of clothes between his feet. "Sir, please..." she begged. Devon ignored it.

"Now that I have your full attention," he said, "let's lay down some ground rules. Next time you want to see me while I'm closing, and no one is available to walk with you, you will text or call first. Just to be safe, yes?" Hope nodded, frantically. "What was that?"

"Yes, Sir," she managed, as her legs clamped harder against their joined hands on one side, and his elbow on the other. "I'll text or... something, Sir."

"There's my good girl," he purred.

Good girl. Good girl. Good girl...

Hope's excitement climbed with the tension in her body, as Devon dropped his head and made lazy, slow strokes over her clit, like he had all the time in the world. Then, when she was dizzy and panting from pleasure, he pulled one of her hands to the top of her cleft and pressed her own fingers into her flesh.

"You rub here," he ordered. "But don't you dare come." Hope's body bucked, and Devon chuckled, turning his head to lap across her fingers as she circled them.

"I don't think—"

"Do not stop and do not come."

"But I need—"

"You will not stop, and you will not come without permission," he said, voice stern. "Don't make me say it again."

Something in his tone got her fingers moving and made her start singing the *ABCs* in her head. *A, B, C, D...Don't stop and don't come. E, F, G... Don't stop and don't come.* Hope broke out in a cold sweat. She shook her head, fighting the inevitable.

"Oh, fuck," she whispered.

And then her hips were rolling; she couldn't help it. He had her laid out on a desk, naked from the waist down, and bathed in fluorescent light, lapping at her as he watched her touch herself. She should be horrified, but she couldn't stop. Only a door separated them from the staff, the customers, and she could not stop. Maybe she was greedy, impatient...

Hope clamped a hand over her mouth, as a whimpering moan came out of her. Devon caught it and pulled it back between her legs.

Raising his head, he said, "I want to hear how hard this is for you."

A host of thoughts flashed through her brain in quick succession, ranging from where they were, to what they were doing, to all the random people who might hear. But then, everything went kind of floaty. "Yes, Sir," she said, opening wider for him and throwing her head back with a string of rhythmic, needy sounds—struggling to keep the ever-building orgasm from flooding through her body as she rubbed a disjointed rhythm for him.

Don't stop and don't come. Don't stop and don't come. Don't stop and don't come.

"Mmm... So close, aren't you? Don't come," Devon warned. He repositioned, using one hand to part her sex, while sliding the fingers of the other inside her. Hope shuddered, heat searing through her. "Look how hard you're trying. You're shaking like a leaf." His voice nearly undid her. She scrunched her eyes tight, panted hard, and started singing in her head again. Devon laughed. "Okay, okay... You can stop," he said, pulling her hands away and sitting her upright on the edge of the desk. Hope swayed, dizzy and disoriented.

"Sorry, Sir. I was..."

"Practicing your ABCs?" He grinned at her. "You were trying so, so hard to follow commands, and you were about to fail beautifully." Hope shifted uncomfortably, her sex sliding against the now gooey surface of his desk. "I think we've succeeded at the delayed gratification portion of this lesson. Now we're going to get you dressed, get you home, and get to the positive reinforcement part."

"You're taking me home?" she whimpered.

Devon smiled. "The walk will give you time to think about how you are never going to risk bodily harm by walking alone at night without letting anyone know, right?"

"Yes, Sir." She studied her fidgeting hands. "But... are you going to..." Hope trailed off, unable to spit out the question.

"No more edging tonight. Promise," Devon said, with an expression that assumed she'd be happy to hear it.

Hope's brow furrowed. "Edging?"

"You don't..." Devon frowned, scrubbed his hands over his face, then shook his head. "I mean that I won't stop you again. I'll let you come until you can't, but only after we get you home. But remember—"

"I won't do it again, Sir," Hope mumbled, the words tumbling over each other. "Sorry, Sir. Thank you, Sir."

Devon cocked his head. "How are you so good at that?"

HOPE

"No, Sir. I won't do it again," Hope mumbled, rocking her butt side to side, before jolting awake.

The noise that woke her sounded nothing like a hand on a backside. It did, however, sound like a disappointing interruption to a rather interesting dream—one that was currently slipping away faster than she could commit it to memory.

Disoriented by the sensation that she might have been asleep for seconds or days, Hope fumbled for her phone. Less than fifteen minutes had passed since she'd pointed Devon toward the extra set of keys on the purple stretchy thingy in the kitchen drawer so that he could lock up as he left. Hope desperately wanted to sink deeper into the covers he'd tucked around her, but the person in the hall might as well pound directly on her brain.

Pushing herself upright, she stood on shaky legs. After being held at the edge of her orgasm for an eternity, then coming hard and fast too many times to keep count, she needed more than a ten-minute power nap.

Unfortunately, the noise-maker down the hall didn't seem to care.

Hope pulled on pajama bottoms and a t-shirt, the pounding increasing in volume with every echoing *thud,* as she dressed. Closer than down the hall... Was it someone at Chloe's? That would explain the volume, but Chloe was working seven to seven. She wouldn't be home until morning.

Hope got moving. Halfway through her apartment, it became fully evident that her own door was the victim. The pounding so violent that if she didn't hurry, the hinges might give up. Who in the world would bang on her door like that? Especially after ten.

"I'm coming," she yelled, *twice,* because the first time did nothing to stop her visitor.

Considering the situation, Hope backtracked for her cellphone. If she found an axe murderer out there, she might need to call someone—even if she didn't want to deal with them. Inching toward the door, she looked through the peephole, and got a fish eyed closeup of Aaron—full-uniform and fuming mad.

"*Fuck,*" Hope whispered to herself, before calling out to him. "What do you want?"

"To make sure you're alright," he bit out.

The radio clipped to his chest chirped and a grainy voice broadcast something about a 10-16, and a request for units to respond. Chloe wasn't kidding about their paper-thin walls. Hope could make out nearly every word. A voice Hope thought might be Officer Neely came back immediately, rattling off a unit number and acknowledging that they were en route. Aaron ignored the entire thing.

"Open the door, Hope."

"No."

She gripped the phone in her hand, watching him through the peephole. Aaron paced two steps down the corridor, two steps back. He turned to face her door again, hands on his hips. Hope watched his chest rise and fall with a deep breath, but the expression on his face betrayed the futility of his attempt at calming himself.

The dispatcher spoke again. *9982, please respond...*

"Open the fucking door," Aaron snapped, slamming a fist into the wood. Hope jumped back.

"NO." She sent up a silent thanks to the universe that her denial came out with so much force, even as her heart raced, and her hands shook. "I'm fine, or I was until you showed up. Go away, before I call the police." She watched him wet his lips, shake his head.

"I *am* the police," he said, closer to the door again, calmer. He scooted in until she could no longer see him. She heard a soft *thump* against the door, as he rested a hand...his forehead...? "Let a guy check on you, Hope."

"Well, you've checked. I'm fine. I'm not opening this door, Aaron."

She staggered back, as his fist made another jarring impact. Hope's heart jackhammered in her chest. If he kept doing that, he'd break the door down. It wasn't a question of *if* but *when*. There'd be nothing between them. Chloe wasn't home, and Devon had left, and—

"I swear to God, Hope," Aaron snarled, "if you don't open this goddamn door—"

Panic ricocheted through her, as she fumbled with her phone. This was his beat, so who knew how long it would take a different officer to arrive.

9982, what's your location? Aaron's radio chirped again, and he went silent. Hope eased to the peephole, ready to retreat if he tried to force his way through. She watched him eyeball her door like he was weighing the pros and cons of kicking it down, but some of his rage was dissipating.

With a heaving breath, Aaron grabbed the radio and turned for the stairs. "9982 en route."

With every step Aaron's legs carried him away, Hope's own grew weaker. Her hands trembled; her stomach churned. All the well-fucked, snug, and sleepy goodness that Devon left her with transformed into edgy energy crawling under her skin. She looked back to her phone, exiting out of the emergency call she hadn't sent. With Aaron gone, what was the point? Maybe it was an overreaction anyway.

But why tonight? The pieces started coming together, heightening her angst. Was Devon the reason Aaron showed up at her door? Had he followed them? Watched Devon leave?

She glanced at her screen again, then quickly pulled up her text thread with Devon.

Got up to brush my teeth. Thanks for walking me home. Hope the rest of your shift goes well.

Guilt and worry warred within her, but she needed a response, without panicking Devon. She stared at her phone for a grueling five minutes, before it vibrated. They'd had a bit of a run on the bar, he said eventually, but all was well, and he couldn't wait to see her tomorrow. Funny way to say *Your ex hasn't yet identified, followed, harassed, arrested, and/or shot me,* but Hope would take it. She did end up brushing her teeth, and grabbing a shower, but sleep eluded her for hours.

***

Half a pot of coffee the next morning made up for Hope's late night. As promised, she arrived at Silver Sassafras an hour before opening. With Margo gearing up for the holiday surge, new treasures needed shelving. Hope loved the morning quiet of the shop; the scent of herbs and incense in the air; the soft swish of the broom across the tile. She petted a purring Silver, waited on an indignant Queen Sassafras, and pretended the night before consisted of only good things—endorphins and orgasms, not exes and anxiety.

Devon also survived until daybreak. He'd texted her a good morning reminder that he'd pick her up at one for their *boring surprise.* Hope felt more guilty over not telling him about Aaron's visit than giving away half of her shift, but that made sense. Her bank account was screwed regardless, so why dwell on a few lost hours?

Naomi, the Art History major who worked weekends and school breaks at the shop, would relieve her at noon. She might regret snatching up Hope's hours, though. Extra pocket money or no, Francis worked noon to three today, and his company could be downright torturous.

Hope looked up as a young guy with spiky, pink hair walked in. Only her third customer of the day—and the other two came in together, so maybe they should count as one. He wore all black, his coal-lined eyes nervous but kind.

"Good morning. Can I help you find anything?"

"Obsidian?" He smiled shyly. "Doesn't have to be very big. Rough is fine, or tumbled—but small," he tacked on quickly.

Familiar with the code for *Cheap, please*, Hope ushered him to the *by-weight-bargain-bin* and ensured that he could identify the stone he needed, before leaving him to treasure hunt in peace.

She went back to tidying, idly wondering his age. Out of school unless he was skipping or between college classes. He couldn't be more than twenty. A row of thick hoops ran up one ear, but he had no visible ink. He looked like the sort who would have visible ink the moment he had the cash to cover it, though. The kind of kid she'd thought she might be able to help not long ago. Thus, her foray into sociology, education, and eventually counseling.

Things were clearer now, though. Hope couldn't be trusted to give herself solid advice, much less someone else.

The kid made it to the register, handing over his stash and a debit card. Hope returned the goods—a single white candle, and a tiny chip of obsidian—in a paper bag. She didn't bother weighing the stone. Instead, she threw it in for free with all the honest to goodness hope that he won whatever battle he intended to wage with such meager weapons. Faith came in all flavors, but from where Hope sat, it was still mostly luck of the draw. The culmination of choices and experiences. Comfort was sweet, though, and she hoped her young customer found some of that.

He thanked her and turned to go, stopping short a few feet past the glass store front, ducking his head, and hurrying off in an arc. The copious amount of merchandise on display blocked much of her view, but Hope recognized *spooked* when she saw it. She dropped her brows, and worried over his obvious discomfort. *Broom closets* were real, especially in the south. Hopefully, he hadn't spotted someone he'd rather not run into while exiting a metaphysical store.

Silver wove through her legs, distracting her from her pink-haired patron. As Hope leaned down and stroked a hand over the cat's back, the bells on the door chimed again.

"You get the strangest types in here, huh?" came a voice she knew intimately.

Hope surged to her feet, eyes skimming over him, analyzing the threat. Aaron stood alone, dressed in jeans, with an unzipped leather jacket— not on duty. She had no doubt he was armed, though. He left that jacket unzipped for access more than anything.

He smiled. "Easy, babe. I came to apologize."

"Okay," she said carefully. Hope hated it when he called her that, but not enough to start a fight over it.

"I understand that it was probably scary when I showed up last night," he said like someone repeating something they heard a therapist say once.

Hope crossed her arms. "Yeah, it was," she agreed.

He smiled again, pleased with himself. "That wasn't my goal. Look, I saw some guy pulling you down the sidewalk and—"

"Aaron..." If he'd meant that as a reassurance, he'd missed the mark by a few million miles.

"I know how that sounds, but I saw you when I rolled through on patrol," he said quickly. "It was a coincidence. I tried to let it go, but I couldn't stop worrying about you. So, I circled back to check-in."

It sounded rational when he said it like that. He looked at her, big blue eyes pleading for her to see his sincerity. It filed the edges off her anger, even though Hope knew how easily Aaron said the right things after he'd crossed a line.

"It's not your job to check on me," she said, more exasperated than angry.

Aaron smiled wider. "Actually, it is. Cop, remember?" He tapped a hand on his chest. "I get paid to check on things that look shady. I saw a guy dragging a woman from a bar, and I checked on the possible victim."

Some guy dragging a woman out of a bar... Hope wondered if that was what the outside world saw when they passed Devon escorting her home for a string of mind-blowing orgasms. She'd felt nothing but impatience and lust, as they'd made their way from Cleary's to her place. Well, that and the seam of her jeans, since he'd pocketed her panties in the office. *It will help you remember*, Devon had promised. And here she was thinking about it again, so maybe he'd been right. She shelved the thought for later.

"And the fact that it was *me* didn't come into play at all?" she asked, arching a brow at her ex.

"Of course, it did," Aaron retorted. "Because it's you, I didn't just *wonder* if that was unusual; I *knew* it. But that's not why I'm here anyway. I won't apologize for checking on you, even if it pisses you off." He stared at her intensely. "I will apologize for the other part though. I was pissed when you wouldn't open the door. I panicked a little. Dispatch kept calling, and I didn't have long unless I told them what was going on. Figured you didn't want a record of the police coming to your apartment for a wellness check." He wet his lips. "I raised my voice," he said, with a shrug.

Hope's eyes went wide with disbelief. "You *punched my door*."

"I knocked. *Hard*. You wouldn't let me in." His last sentence was an accusation if she'd ever heard one.

"I told you I was fine," Hope said, her voice rising with her frustration.

"And if some asshole is in there with a gun to your head telling you to say that?" He arched a blond brow. "I was pissed...so fucking pissed off at you because you don't *think*, Hope." He closed his eyes for a beat, tamping down his agitation. Hope searched for a way to hold her line, without causing him to explode.

"Not that it's any of your business," she said carefully, "but I'm not bringing a stranger to my apartment, and he certainly wasn't forcing me there. You have to let this go, Aaron. You saw what you wanted to see because you didn't like the alternative."

"Which was what, exactly?" he snapped.

"I just told you." Hope shook her head.

Aaron shoved his hands into his jacket pockets, yanked them out again. "You're seeing him. Like actually *seeing* him."

"I'm allowed to do that," she said, as calmly as she could.

"I thought..." He pressed his mouth into a tight line and huffed. "I gave you time to *find yourself*, or whatever..." he said, waving his hands around, as if he were batting at a swarm of gnats. "And you—"

"We broke up a year ago." Hope cut in. "I moved away."

Aaron blinked at her. "You fucked me on your couch. *Here*. In Asheville. I moved here for *you*." He pointed to the ground beneath his feet, then at her with sharp movements.

Hope set aside the fact that she had sex with him after a ridiculous amount of wine. Wine she drank after trying, unsuccessfully, to get him to leave her doorstep when he'd showed up begging her to talk. They used coffee mugs Aaron dug from one of her moving boxes because she hadn't finished unpacking yet, and she took a morning after pill the next day because she had no idea if he had worn a condom. The whole thing was cringe-worthy, and Hope wasn't going to pick it apart because it wouldn't change a thing. Instead, she focused on what she said after.

"I told you that was a mistake," she said, looking directly at him. "I never asked you to move to Asheville. I asked you to leave me alone."

"Queen of mixed messages over here," Aaron said, through gritted teeth.

"What mixed messages?" Hope asked. "I consistently say that I'm done. You won't listen."

His cheeks reddened with his rising temper. "I never cheated on you," he snapped. "I took you out. I bought you flowers and remembered your birthday...our anniversary. I fucked up *one* time, Hope, and it wasn't even—"

"You *attacked* me," she said. "You didn't want me to leave, and you attacked me, Aaron. You still won't let me go now. I start seeing someone—someone I really like, and you're snooping around my apartment and stalking me at work." Instantly seeing her mistake, Hope slapped a hand over her mouth. Aaron's chest heaved. Rage curled his upper lip.

"You and I have very different definitions of the word *attack*," he bit out. "If you want to push me to my goddamn limit, then blame *me* for not giving up on *you*— Play victim while you go whore around with some inked-up bartender, then you're crazier than I thought."

The sound of her own pulse rushed in Hope's ears. "Why did you say that?"

Aaron sneered. "I'm a cop, Hope. Do you really think I can't figure out who you're fucking? It wasn't even hard. Just look for the thing dragging itself out of a bar three blocks down, sniffing around for a bitch in heat."

A white-hot rage coiled and gnashed its teeth in her chest. It was volcanic, and it wanted out. But rage was an unsafe emotion to indulge in while alone in the store with a very angry Aaron. "Leave me alone," she said. "Leave *him* alone. Don't bother me again."

"Or what?" Aaron countered.

Hope tilted up her chin in defiance. "I'll file for an order of protection."

Aaron flashed a saccharine smile. "And how did that go in Charlotte? Oh... right... It didn't. Because you're full of shit, and everyone knows it. No one wants to ruin a good cop's career over the lies of a vindictive cunt."

Even with the counter between them, Hope flinched back as he took a single, deliberate, quick step toward her.

"See?" Aaron said. "*That.* You play your little whiny victim card. Act like me *breathing* near you is a personal attack. I come to make sure you haven't been drugged and raped, and you somehow twist it in your head so *I'm* the bad guy. But it's your twisted head, Hope." He jabbed a finger into his own temple. "That's why no one believed your sob story last time. I feel sorry for that stupid son-of-a-bitch. He has no clue what he's gotten himself into. Maybe we'll have a drink one day and talk about how damaged you are."

"Leave me alone," she said again, voice wavering from all the fight or flight surging through her.

Aaron gave a derisive laugh. "Remember who caused this, babe."

DEVON

Devon spotted it the moment she opened her apartment door. Hope was twitchy, anxious... *Off*. He held out the spare key he'd used to lock up behind himself the night before and watched her reach for it, pull her hand back, then ultimately take it. Every movement appeared painfully considered and carefully executed.

"So are we on a schedule here or..." Hope grabbed her coat from the closet, trailing off as Devon pulled it from her hands.

"What's wrong?" he asked, dropping the coat on the arm of her couch.

During her pause, Devon created an entire imaginary storyline in which she told him that the night before was too much. The fact that she was frightened by her desire to seek him out, by the marks he left on her when his fingers dug too deep, the way his inner-dominant put her inner-submissive on its knees with only a flimsy office door separating them from the rest of the bar. By the intensity of it all. Devon crafted a nightmare in six seconds flat.

"I need to tell you something," she said, and he watched her anxiety reach fever pitch.

Without a conscious thought, Devon pulled her to his chest, tucking her head beneath his chin. "I'm listening."

"You're going to be mad."

Her body trembled against him. His heart thumped uncomfortably in answer. Devon held her tighter, as he thought of all the things that she could tell him—things that would make him mad—and resigned himself. He wouldn't yell. He wouldn't stomp, or rage, or slam doors, and there was no way in hell he was going to throw anything. Not a lamp, and not a punch. There wasn't a thing in the world that she could say that would make him give her a reason to flinch.

"Maybe," he said roughly. "But you can still tell me."

Hope spoke in a small, cautious voice, her body going very still as if she worried that any movement might trigger a catastrophe. "Aaron came here after you left last night."

Anger scorched Devon's ears and face, as his head started doing all kinds of math. "Your ex," he said. "The cop." There was a cop in Cleary's the night before, but he came in when they were already closing. He'd wanted to order, but Devon gave him a soda on the house because the kitchen was clean. If it was the same cop, that was a whole lot of time between Cleary's and her apartment three blocks away.

"I didn't let him in," she said, in a rush. "He saw me with you and said he wanted to make sure I was alright."

Devon relaxed a fraction. "I'm not saying I like it, but it's nothing to be angry over. Especially, not angry at you."

"He came by the store today, too."

And… now Devon wanted to hit something.

"He said he came to apologize, but we got into it a little."

"Okay…" Devon managed. "Do you feel like it's handled? Do you want it addressed formally? We could… I mean…" *Shit*. He thought back to that night at the bar when she'd all but begged to go home and be done with it. Devon had been convinced that if their relationship were…more like what they'd started now, that night never would have happened. So, what was his excuse today?

"I told him I was seeing someone," she said, in a tone that bordered on questioning. "I said there was no reason for him to worry, and it wasn't his business."

"Is that why you got into it? Because he doesn't approve of you seeing someone?" When she didn't immediately answer, Devon decided her silence said enough. "It sounds like you made things clear," he said. Hope stood rigid against him— holding onto way more than she was letting go. "Is there anything else you needed to tell me?" he ventured.

"No…" she hedged. "No. I'm sorry my past is causing drama."

Her arms remained tight around his waist; her head pressed firmly to his chest. And that thing in Devon bristled, because it didn't like her lie either. Hope was this weird mashup of Devon's dominant desires, his everyday life, and something else that was suffocating and didn't seem like it would fade anytime soon. When they stood there in her living room and she held onto him like she did, he could feel the shape of everything she wasn't saying, even if he had no idea what the words might sound like. It ate at him.

"Do I still get a boring surprise?" she asked, pressing closer to him.

"Two," Devon said, still running on instinct. "If you'll let me keep you for dinner, I'll give you two boring surprises." She looked up at him with tears on her face and a smile that made his breath hitch. "Come on, let's get your coat on. It's cold."

HOPE

Devon stole nervous glances in her periphery. Whatever he'd planned had him nearly as uneasy as that time he tried to tell her he liked to tie people up. Which was all very odd because, honestly, if you'd spent years casually negotiating restraining people and whacking them with stuff, wouldn't the nerves wear off at some point? Hope reached for the hand resting on her thigh and clasped it. Devon squeezed back.

"There's some stuff I need to do today, but if you get bored or want to leave, I can run you home," he said.

Hope smiled as he swung the car into a parking lot neighboring a squat, brick building. The sign above the door read *Redact and Recover*. "The nonprofit..." she said aloud, as the realization landed.

Devon looked over at her. "If it gets uncomfortable, I'll take you straight home."

"You already said that," she reminded him, grinning wider.

His cheeks flushed. "You want a safeword?"

"A what?"

"So, we haven't covered the basics yet. Got it…" Devon smiled stiffly. "You know, like a code word you say so I know you want to stop."

Hope giggled. "It'll be fine. Really. I'm excited." He put the car in park and stared at her. "Fine. I swear I will tell you if I want to leave," she said, putting one hand on her chest and raising the other all official like. "But I won't… Sir," she added with a wink, as he climbed out of the car. It earned her a sideways glance.

A six-foot-something Black man wearing a lavender shirt and grey slacks came hustling toward them as they entered the small lobby.

"Devon, my man," he exclaimed. The two clasped hands and exchanged a quick slap to the back in the way virtually every set of guy-friends on the planet said hello. "I have fifteen minutes, so introductions, then let's do it."

"Hope Lawson," Hope said, putting out her hand.

"Andre Young but call me Dre. I'm one of the counselors here," came the response, as he slid his hand into hers.

Dre sported a winning smile and the eyes of someone who—as often happened in social work—had seen too many terrible things to count but continued making a difference, one session at a time.

"Hey, is Monique around?" Devon asked.

"With a client," Dre said. "She's still pissed about that hole you left in the bathroom."

Devon cringed. "I swear I'll get to it, but we need it dry in there, first."

"I know you've got it," Dre said, with a grin. "But let's go do this before she walks up here."

Devon and Dre moved through the building, chattering about where to move what. Hope followed, listening and watching. Apparently, a shift of rooms was necessary because of the rate of growth. Too much need, too few resources— the bane of every nonprofit's existence.

Both men worried that the team giving up the larger room wouldn't appreciate the interruption, and there was some discussion about whether they could be employed to help, or if it would be better for Devon to suck it up and move it himself during off-hours. Dre rushed off to his appointment, shouting a quick *Nice to meet you* to Hope as he vanished.

When they were alone, Devon hopped up on the edge of a desk, looked out at the large room containing a smattering of computer workstations, and sighed.

"So... we need to move something?" Hope nudged.

Devon closed his eyes, running his hands through his hair. "Nah. I'm just making a plan." He continued to scan the room, glanced to the clock on the wall, the door, back to scanning.

"I could do it in a couple of hours," he said, "but they're never going to agree to it. They'll say we can't have the whole tech team down at once. They'd have to make time to run cable to the old group space." He shook his head. "No one likes running cable. The only reason they're in this room is that it was wired when we moved in." Again, with the hands. Up his face and through his hair, this time linking behind his neck for a moment. He looked tired. "It's not hard, but it's a lot for one person," he said.

"Especially one person who has another full-time job and doesn't get paid to be here," Hope said, lifting a brow. "This? This is the tech team?" She gestured around the room.

"Yeah."

"Where are they?" Hope asked.

"Probably at lunch. They make their own hours. The counselors and Sydney—she's legal—they keep to a schedule. But tech doesn't have to worry about appointments, usually. They show up when they want or when they're needed."

Hope pursed her lips and considered. "How much of this stuff do you think we could move before they got back?"

His eyes met hers, wickedly devious. "Why darling, are you suggesting that we move their equipment without asking?"

"Not at all, Sir," she said, batting her lashes coquettishly. "I'm only suggesting that we move the furniture. Totally different. They can move their equipment over whenever they're ready," she said, shoving a rolling chair toward the door.

"You are delicious," he replied.

Hope smiled down at the floor. "Which room are we moving to?"

Through sheer force of will, they were strong-arming the last desk down the hall when Luca, Syl, and Jackson, AKA: The Tech Team, returned. Hope could feel Devon's smirk as she slapped on a smile, introduced herself, and excitedly told them how they'd managed to move everything but the computers to the new space—as if it were a praise-worthy achievement and not a massive, though necessary, inconvenience. Hope restrained her giggle through their stunned blinking and strained thanks.

"We make a good team," she said breathlessly, as they brought the first load of chairs into the new and improved meeting room, stepping carefully around the computer equipment still in the floor. She suspected cabling would be run quickly, as the tech team would want their babies back on their desks ASAP.

Devon closed the door, sat down in a chair he'd carried in, and patted his knee. "I'm as impressed with your deviance as your ability to feign innocence." He chuckled as she sat on his lap. "I'll have to remember that about you," he said, hooking an arm around her waist. "Five-minute break, then we knock out the rest of it?"

Hope nodded. "All that's left are the chairs and the tables, right? It's not much."

Devon sighed. "Yeah, that's my next task. We need more seating for this room. We're overflowing in most of the groups as it is, but at least there's more space in here. Maybe one day we could have conferences, build better community safety nets, and keep people from needing these services in the first place. One step at a time."

"So, you never told me what Redact and Recover does. They have counselors. Plural? And legal, and at least three IT people..."

Devon put a hand on her knee, rubbing his thumb back and forth. "You know, it's strange. I volunteer here almost every week, and Mom and I technically got the place started. We're both on the board." He laughed. "But I'm better at moving furniture and fixing leaks than explaining it all."

Hope put an arm around his shoulders. "Does it remind you of your sister?" she asked, remembering him saying that they'd started R&R to honor her.

"Kelly," he said, voice barely audible.

"Kelly," Hope repeated with a soft smile.

"Talking about what we do here reminds me of what we didn't do for her if that makes sense..." His chest rose and fell in a deep, steady breath. "The condensed version is that she overdosed." He glanced at Hope, sidelong, before adding, *"on purpose.* She was eighteen; I was fourteen. I thought she was the coolest person alive. I know that sounds ridiculous, but it's true. We got along. My dad was..." He looked around the room, something Hope suspected helped him avoid looking at her. "Kelly and I were close. She was always in my corner, and then she was gone."

Hope passed a hand over his back in slow circles.

"So anyway. After my father died, Mom and I used some of the insurance money to start this place. Everyone on staff has experience dealing with victims of sexual assault, trafficking... Specifically, anything that involves imagery. *Redact* for getting content out of the public eye—"

"And *Recover,*" Hope said, "for healing."

Devon nodded. "Monique and Dre do the counseling and group sessions, Sydney all but gives us two days a week for the legal stuff, and Luca, Syl, and Jackson scour the web removing content and gathering evidence. They also play *Expert Witness* when necessary."

Hope added up everyone's specialties and made some assumptions about what triggered his sister's suicide. "So, Kelly..." she prompted.

"Kelly didn't get the support she needed," Devon said. He blinked fast. Hope pressed a kiss to his temple on impulse, as he began talking again. "Some shit happened. There was a video that got passed around. You don't have to physically hurt a person to destroy them," Devon said. "Although... having seen part of the video..." He went a bit green and shook his head forcefully. Hope's heart ached.

"But anyway." Devon deliberately shifted trajectory. "I like to believe that a place like this would've made a difference for her. That, if there's some sort of *existence* after death, she sees this and knows I would've helped if I'd known—if I hadn't been a kid. And that I don't blame her, like I don't blame the people who come here. I think Kelly felt like everyone thought it was her fault. That's why we didn't know about any of it until after she was gone. Maybe *she* thought it was her fault," he added, quietly, "and that kills me."

"I'm sure she knows," Hope said, continuing to stroke his back.

"Yeah, well." He passed a quick hand under his eyes and scrubbed it on the flank of his long sleeve t-shirt. Hope pretended not to notice. "It's good for Mom," he said. "She doesn't come here much, but she needs to know it's here and working."

The door to the room swung open, and a burst of color and personality blew in with a human Barbie tight on her heels. Devon took a single breath and smiled, as if he hadn't been dissecting his heart in the new group space moments prior.

"You did not tell me." The woman in front scolded.

Devon put Hope on her feet and stood beside her. "We figured if we moved the furniture fast enough—"

"Not about the move!" she said, cutting him off. "About this," she gestured to Hope and smiled, reaching for both of her hands.

"Monique, this is Hope; Hope, Monique Franklin," Devon said, executing his due diligence.

"It is so nice to meet you." Monique squeezed Hope's hands in her own, as she spoke.

"It's lovely to meet you too," Hope replied.

"And this is Sydney Malone," Devon added, gesturing to the slender blond. "She's an attorney, but we like her anyway. Wait..." he said, turning to face her. "It's Wednesday. Why are you here?"

Sydney waved that off. "Only for a minute. I needed something for a hearing tomorrow. But look at my timing," she said, holding her hands out toward Hope like a gameshow host showcasing a prize. "Devon says you teach."

"I did not," Devon corrected, quickly, before looking at Hope. "Not exactly."

"It's alright. It's true, or was, anyway. I taught English Lit in Charlotte. I moved here for a job at Costings but ended up passing on it. Now I'm figuring things out." Hope shrugged. "This set up is amazing. So, you all offer group sessions and one-on-one?" She asked, shifting to what interested her.

"Oh yeah, honey." Monique beamed as she answered. "Dre takes most of our male clients and any of the older women who aren't uncomfortable with men. He also does a lot of the office work. I see the kids and the rest of the adults. And we each host a group or two." So full of joy, for someone talking about counseling the child victims of atrocious crimes... "Busy, busy, busy..." Monique said.

"Sounds like you've built an incredible support system."

"You look familiar," Sydney interjected. "Where did you go to school?"

"USC," Hope said, wondering why Devon looked increasingly frustrated.

"I spent some time at USC." The blond smiled. "Maybe that's how I know you. Did you have Professor Anderson?"

Hope tried to remember, but the name didn't ping for her. "I don't think so. I spent most of my time in the sociology department."

"Syd—" Devon tried but failed to cut in, as the woman plowed onward with all the patient, unyielding tenacity of a moving glacier.

Hope doubted anyone ever got Sydney Malone to change course, unless she chose to. Even Devon had no effect, and she'd seen him hush an entire bar with a single command. *And*...now she had that tingle going on again.

"I thought you said you taught English?" Sydney's brows cinched together.

"Well, yeah, but my master's is in social work. I'm no longer working in a school, but I was moving out of teaching, regardless."

"Really?" Sydney lit up with curiosity. "So, what did you plan to do at Costings? Before you decided against it, I mean." She stared at Hope, expectantly.

"I was supposed to be the new counselor. The current counselor would've mentored me until I had enough hours, then she planned to drop down to part time," Hope explained.

"I'm sorry." Now it was Monique who cut in. "You have a master's in social work and a counseling license?"

Devon kept looking from Hope to Monique, with an occasional evil eye shot at Sydney. He'd stopped trying to cut in.

"I need to log my hours for full licensure, but technically," Hope said hesitantly.

"Alright, well, I'll let you all chat. I'm out of here. Nice to meet you, Hope," Sydney Malone said. And with a flip of her ponytail, she clicked away on red-bottomed heels.

HOPE

"Did you get the feeling that Sydney planned that whole thing?" Hope asked later, as they drove to whatever second *boring surprise* Devon had in mind.

Not that R&R was boring. Hope enjoyed getting back into that environment. It reminded her of her favorite internship—transitional support for victims of domestic abuse. Incredibly hard, but so rewarding.

Devon slid the hand on her thigh further between her legs. "Sydney always has a plan. She'd already looked you up and knew exactly what she wanted you to say." He shook his head. "You have a master's," he said. "And you're a counselor." The awe in his voice unsettled Hope.

"Technically," she repeated.

"Why do you keep saying that?" Devon asked. "It's not *technically*; it's *literally*. You *literally* have a master's in social work and a counseling license."

"I still need to log the hours, before I'm fully licensed."

Devon grinned. "You're amazing. I barely survived two years in community college, and those two years took me *four*. I'm surprised Monique let you escape."

"Are they really that hard up for another counselor?" Hope asked.

"It's complicated." Devon put on the turn signal and made a right. "There isn't money for another fulltime counselor, but we could more than fill the hours if we had one."

Again, she noticed him shifting between *we* and *they*. As if R&R were an integral part of him, yet something he tried to separate himself from. Hope had the feeling it wasn't the only integral part of himself that Devon silenced.

"The group sessions are bursting at the seams because they prioritize the one-on-one availability. R&R *needs* another full-time counselor or even two; they can *afford* someone two, maybe three, days a week. That's the reality. It's hard to find a good fit who's okay with the limited hours. Plus, the work is hard— I mean, they're stretched thin, it's emotionally draining, and if we did hire someone, we couldn't give them more than a few days a week and almost nothing for benefits. Not exactly a sweetheart gig."

"At least there's room for the bigger groups, now." Hope smiled stiffly.

"That there is." He grazed his thumb on the outside of her leg. "Are you ready for *Boring Surprise: Round Two*?"

"Ready as I'll ever be." She smiled outright.

"Good, because we're here."

"And here is?" Hope looked up at the apartment building beside them.

Devon swallowed hard, wet his lower lip. "Uh… My mom's?" Then, he cringed.

Hope's first thought was that the now somewhat grimy jeans and magenta pullover she had worn to R&R was the last thing she wanted to wear to meet his mother. She wasn't even wearing her lucky ankle boots. She had on trainers, for crying out loud. But Devon was dressed similarly, and he looked so sheepish that it took some of the edge off. Plus, there was that time she dumped her brother on him the day after their first date, so she totally deserved this. The Apollo surprise was nowhere near the level of a brother. She had this coming.

"Are you sure this is okay?" she said, gesturing down to herself.

"Clothes won't be the deciding factor here," Devon said.

"What will?" Hope asked hesitantly.

"Mostly whether you like Mexican food."

Her stomach responded with a growl, then they were on their way. Devon came around the car, taking her hand. Once inside, they took an elevator to the fifth floor, then followed the sound of music to a door down the hall. Hope shifted her weight from foot to foot, as Devon knocked.

"One second," came a softly accented voice. The music quieted, and a moment later, the door swung open. "I hope you're hungry. I've made too much," Devon's mother said, as a mouthwatering bouquet of spices promised that the woman made culinary art in there.

She was at least six inches shorter than her son, with the same dark hair, though longer and twisted into a braid. Matching full lips, but Devon had fairer coloring. His hazel eyes definitely didn't come from her side of the family. She stood barefoot, wearing a yellow top and black lounge pants.

"What's this?" she asked, smile faltering as she focused on Hope—who pretended that she didn't want to hide in a hole. This woman clearly had less warning about this meeting than Hope did, and they were at her home to eat her food. A small fire ignited in Hope's face.

"I'm sorry," she muttered.

"Mom," Devon cut in, "this is Hope."

"And Hope is...?" His mother arched a brow—morphing her features into the exact expression Hope had seen on her son's face a thousand times.

"Having dinner with us," Devon said nervously. His mother smiled.

"I'm kidding, hijo," she said, pulling him down and kissing his cheek. "But you should have told me. Go set a place for her."

"Come in, come in." Scooping an arm around Hope's shoulders, she guided her into her home. "My name is Maria," Devon's mom said, rolling the *R* softly as Devon abandoned them without a backward glance.

"I'm really sorry," Hope said, glancing down at herself. "Devon said dinner was a surprise." Okay...he said a *boring surprise*, but Hope wasn't about to tell Maria that her son called her boring. "We've been moving furniture at R&R all afternoon and—"

Devon returned, stopping beside his mother who had gone utterly still.

"Sorry, is something wrong?" Hope looked between the pair.

Maria recovered, smiling indulgently. "Don't worry a thing about it. I'm basically in pajamas." She laughed. "You two must be hungry, after all that work."

"It smells delicious," Hope replied, swallowing her pooling saliva before she drooled in front of Devon's mom.

Her stomach had been uneasy at both breakfast and lunch thanks to Aaron's unannounced and unwelcome visits. Then she'd moved furniture at R&R with Devon until her muscles ached. Hope could eat a shoe if that shoe smelled like whatever Maria had in the kitchen.

"Ask Devon, I always make too much." Maria grinned and herded everyone toward the table.

Devon polished off three helpings of chicken mole, and Hope and Maria each had two, but there was still food to pack away. Then it was Hope and Devon, elbow to elbow at the sink, while Maria begged them to leave it for later.

"You cooked, Mom," Devon said. "Sit down."

Whether at the bar, his house, or out and about, he was always picking up or wiping up something. Energy that needed to go somewhere. Maria had to know that too. She grumbled, but she sat at the table and asked questions to keep the conversation flowing. Mostly things like where Hope was from—*Here, originally. I went to college in Charlotte and stayed but moved back to Asheville a year ago*—and what her family was like. *Not like you*, Hope thought.

She gave a mind-numbing rundown of spouses, jobs, and stepsiblings, which gave the impression of depth.

With cleanup concluded, Maria turned the stereo back on. Music filled the empty air between their sentences, as she passed out bowls of ice cream. Hope watched Devon light up like a child—up until he caught her eye and licked his spoon in a manner that was anything but innocent. Hope blushed into her bowl.

"I would offer you two a cocktail," Maria said, either oblivious to her son's flirting, or studiously ignoring it, "but Devon needs to drive home." She narrowed her eyes, shrewdly.

"The soda is great, thanks," Hope replied, already stuffed and sleepy.

"Mom, you know a drink or two after dinner isn't going to do it, right?" Devon joked.

"Dios mío, hijo." Maria glared at him. "You're a grown man, and I don't often get a say anymore, Devon, but you will not be driving home drunk from my house."

Devon put up his palms, still holding a spoon in one hand. "I surrender," he said, with a laugh, snagging another bite of ice cream. "You probably only have vodka and cranberry juice anyway, and I'm not a Cosmo guy."

Maria huffed. "Hope," she said, adjusting her attention accordingly. "What are your thoughts on drinking and driving?"

With no other option available, Hope stepped into the odd thing passing between them. "Oh... that's a no for me. I met Devon at Cleary's, but I walk there with my friend Chloe. No driving necessary." She must have gotten it right because Maria nodded approvingly.

"See Devon," she said. "Hope doesn't joke about this sort of thing. If she plans to have a drink, she *walks.* Hope doesn't go driving around impaired in a muscle car. She's a smart girl. You could learn a thing or two from this one."

Devon slumped in his chair, poking at the ice cream in his bowl. "I know, Mom."

Great... now he looked pitiful, and Hope felt compelled to fix it.

"Um..." She regretted opening her mouth, as they both turned to her. "Devon's pretty particular about when and how much he, or anyone with him, drinks," Hope said, clumsily, ignoring that a good portion of her experiences with that revolved around his firm views on consent. His mom didn't need details about her son's sex life, even if his principles were sound. "It's something I appreciate." She caught Devon's eye, and his nearly imperceptible smile made her nape tingle. It felt like a secret—the hint of pleasure, just for her.

"Well..." Maria said. "I am glad to hear you say that...even if he makes jokes that he shouldn't. You aren't very funny, Devon," she scolded.

"I know, Mom." He took another bite of ice cream.

***

Hope felt strange as they climbed into his car. Maybe it was because her day drudged up everything she should have already sorted. The dichotomy of Aaron and Devon. The nurturing warmth of Devon's single, living parent when compared to Hope's horde of distant, superficial, place holders. Her current job, previous job, and the calling that she would never answer. The last thing someone in crisis needed was guidance from a person who couldn't manage herself.

But R&R was incredible, and Maria was a treasure. Whatever she'd uttered in Spanish as they had walked out the door turned Devon's face crimson and had him glancing at Hope. She didn't know what Maria said, but his embarrassment registered loud and clear. Then Maria wrapped her in a hug and informed her that dinner was every other Wednesday.

It had been a very long, very complicated sort of day.

"So?" Devon said, from the driver's seat.

Hope sighed. "Your mom is amazing."

"I know." He smiled. "Do you forgive me for not telling you?"

"Assuming she didn't hate me. But if she doesn't let me in for dinner next time, I'll cry. That mole was freaking incredible."

"She doesn't believe in store bought mole," he said, putting on a turn signal. "She loved you." He threw a quick glance Hope's way, and a prickle of something that she didn't want to look at too closely went through her.

"Well, she has firm views on drinking and driving." Hope chuckled, as she shifted the topic. "Which is great, but does your mom think you're a lush who drives around tipsy?"

When Devon didn't immediately answer, Hope looked out the windows at the passing streetlights, feeling lazy and content. His voice brought her head back around.

"It's how he died," he said.

"I'm sorry?" she asked, hearing the words but needing a moment to process them.

"My dad," he said. "That's how my dad died. She's right that it isn't funny when I joke about it. I don't know why I pick at her like that. It worries the shit out of her." Devon kept staring at the road like it might disappear if he looked away. "He used to get drunk, and he… he wasn't a nice drunk, you know? Anyway, five years after Kelly died, he was being his usual husband-of-the-year self. We had some words, during which I broke his nose, and he took off. Ended up wrapping this car around a tree, while he wasn't wearing a seatbelt. Fucking idiot." Devon shook his head in disgust.

"I'm…sorry." Clearly, he had some major hang-ups about his father, but what else could she say? Devon laughed harshly.

"Sorry about what? That he was a shitty father and a shittier husband? That I spent six months of my free time and more money than it was worth putting this bitch back together to spite him? He probably rolls over in his grave every time I slide behind the wheel, and I feel nothing but satisfaction that he can't do a goddamn thing about it." He grinned wickedly, then glanced over at her. "Sorry…" he muttered. "And thanks. It's just…the fact that he's gone isn't something I cry about, you know? I was nineteen, already grown, and Kelly was gone. He threw himself through a windshield and *Boom*. Nobody beats the shit out of my mom anymore. Only sad thing about it's that he took so long to do it. Christ, this is heavy... Change the subject, but don't apologize first. Please."

"Ye—" Hope bit off her *Yes, Sir.* It didn't fit their conversation, and she had no idea where it had come from. She cleared her throat. "What did your mom say when we were leaving?" she asked, thinking of the way he'd blushed. It was an adorable thing, watching Devon go red to his roots. A proper distraction from anything heavy.

"Don't speak Spanish?" he asked mischievously. Hope shook her head. "Neither do I," he said, laughing as Hope swatted his arm.

"Liar. You *blushed*."

"You'd be embarrassed too if you couldn't interpret your own mother."

"Devon..."

"I don't know what to tell you." He shrugged. "I'm not fluent. I guess we'll never know."

Hope giggled.

"Can I take you home?" he asked, exhaustion sneaking into his voice.

"Yeah. I'm beat, too. You can drop me off out front if you want."

Devon took a slow breath before he spoke. "I don't think you'll ever convince me to drop you off at a curb again. I've done that twice. I hated it the first time, and the second was worse."

DEVON

How would vanilla people handle it? Devon brought the bar down to his chest in his dark living room, considering. Surely, this happened to them too. Probably more often than in the kink community, now that he thought about it. Kinky folks live and breathe the whole *safe, sane, and consensual* thing. If someone stopped playing with you, you left them alone, or ended up banned. Posers and fakes aplenty, but the community didn't willingly tolerate abusers. Yeah... Maybe this was a vanilla problem in need of a vanilla solution.

So, a couple of them start up a relationship, realize the ex is a problem, and then... What? What did they do? Because Devon wanted to kill someone, and that couldn't possibly be normal. Or advisable.

The bastard went to her apartment, right after Devon left her a mewling pile of *Yes, Sir. Thank you, Sir. I'll never scare you like that again, Sir.* He could be stalking around her building, right now. Okay, that train of thought wasn't helpful. Devon had to focus on something, anything but that.

He pushed up with an exhale, then inhaled slow and deep as he brought the weight down again. Back up, like all the times before. Back down, just the same. Enough weight that his arms and chest burned—but nothing that required a spotter. Apollo didn't understand the concept of *Don't let this thing crush me to death*, and given the snoring coming from the corner, the mooch might not even wake up to cock his big-ass head and stare at Devon as he turned blue.

More with the inhale, exhale. Up and down.

Devon was never going to be a washboard stomach guy, but he paid attention to the areas needed to break up a bar fight or fuck properly, so his bench and squat games were decent. Especially since he'd stopped going to Edge. He needed an outlet, and this was as good as the next option.

Not good enough tonight, though.

He needed to go get her; that's what he needed to do. No...wait. Devon *wanted* to go get her. The thing he *needed* to do was keep fighting gravity on this weight bench and remember the difference between a want and a need.

Hope made things foggy like that, twisted up his head. Right now, for instance... It used to be that when Devon had this much buzzing around his brain, he itched to get to Edge and be Demon for an evening. And yeah, tonight he wanted to snatch that control and handle shit, but he didn't want to look for it at Edge.

That girl was a dog whistle for his dominant side, but when the thing showed up, it was smitten with her too. Made it damn near impossible to think, let alone *act*. Devon had tagged in Demon every time his emotions got the better of him since he was eighteen years old because Demon handled shit. Demon knew what he wanted. He was cold, calculating, and did what needed to be done. But Devon and Demon were on the same page, tonight. They both wanted to get in the goddamn car.

Racking the bar, Devon shook out his hands. "Christ," he whispered into the shadows. Apollo shifted in the corner, rustling his bed and teddy bear.

He'd planned the R&R trip, but the rest of the day went off-script in the weirdest way. It started in her apartment when Hope admitted that Aaron came by the night before, and it snowballed from there. Next thing Devon knew he'd decided to take her to his freaking mother's for dinner because he didn't want to take her back home. It didn't even occur to him to warn his mom, but it turned out that didn't matter.

Devon's Spanish was atrocious, but he could absolutely understand his mother. With first generation parents and a Spanish speaking home, Maria Cleary didn't use English when telling him to straighten up out in public as a child. And Devon had been more than one handful since his birth thirty-four years ago, so he'd had plenty of opportunity to learn her ancestral tongue. When she looked at him right in front of Hope and said *Marry the girl before someone else does*, he'd nearly swallowed his own tongue.

Not that *that* was going to happen. Ever. Hope said herself that she didn't do live-in situations, and Devon didn't even do relationships. Or maybe he did now... The point was that his mom wanted a daughter-in-law, grandbabies. The peaceful normal that his father had stolen from all of them. She would have to settle for a girlfriend, provided Devon didn't screw it up.

And his whole *Woman I've been dating less than a week, meet my mom!* routine wasn't all of it. Hell, it wasn't even the start of it. Devon could have explained R&R without talking about Kelly. Certain topics were better left deeply suppressed because no one wanted to deal with the fallout when he let them surface. But covered in sweat from shoving furniture around, seeing her care about a thing that mattered to him enough to roll up her sleeves and work for it made him want to... Devon didn't know. Tell her why it mattered? Maybe that was it.

And the pièce de resistance? All that shit about his dad. Where did that come from? Devon's thoughts about his old man were messy, aggressive, borderline violent on the best of days. Not casual date conversation. And he'd blabbed it out there like they were in a Locker Room meeting at R&R, and he was *talking* for some unknown reason. At least he hadn't been drinking. Not a pretty conversation when he was drunk.

The heat kicked on. Moving air cooled the thin layer of sweat coating his bare torso, trying to lull him into a false sense of security. He wasn't falling for it. In under five minutes, that breeze would go from refreshing to stifling.

Getting off the bench, Devon headed for the thermostat in the hall, eradicating one source of discomfort that he could still control. Pacing through the dimness, he replayed it all again. He'd opened nearly every remaining facet of his life to her in the span of a day and then dropped her off at her apartment—the apartment her ex came around the night before. The way he felt about that, the desire to go back, was alien to him on so many levels.

When Devon asked if he could take her home, he meant *here*. *His* home, *his* bed, shove himself inside her until she came calling his name, and the thing in his head calmed down a little. Less to worry about when he could reach out and touch her at 3 a.m.

Pulling out his phone, Devon stared at the screen. Best not call someone this late on a weeknight. He rolled his shoulders, shook his head. Even Nix would be asleep at this hour.

More pacing. Impulsively, Devon typed a text.

I can't stop thinking about you.

He regretted the vulnerability of that sentence the moment he hit *send*. Except then the row of dots indicated an incoming response. Devon held his breath.

Funny coincidence... she replied.

Forty minutes later, Devon lay sound asleep under a some-shade-of-pink comforter, Hope's head on his shoulder.

HOPE

Less than ten days later, on a busy Friday night, Hope sat at Cleary's bar with her best friend. Sipping her wine, she contemplated all the things that could change in the span of a few weeks. For one thing, her sex life was no longer a desolate wasteland of self-pleasure and fantasy. In fact, she was starting to think that she wasn't single at all. Go figure.

On a more mundane front, the Seldena... Saldovo...? It no longer showed up as *House Red* on the tab because it wasn't on the tab at all, and Devon no longer made excuses about mistakes in the kitchen when he slid food in front of them. He liked feeding her, simple as that. If she could get her mother to stop texting her about finding an escort for Ashley's wedding, life would be grand, but as it stood, things were looking pretty good.

"This has perks," Chloe said, snagging a tortilla chip and scooping spinach artichoke dip into her face with all the grace of someone filling a pothole.

Hope stiffened as she watched Devon reach for a high bottle. She bet he looked like that when he'd pinned her arms above her head against her living room wall two nights prior, when he'd walked through her door after a meeting at Redact and Recover, already ravenous. They hadn't made it to her bedroom. At least, not for that round.

"Hell yeah, it does," Hope said. Chloe pivoted her entire upper body and popped her brows. "Sorry..." Hope sipped her wine, savoring the familiar flavor.

The wanting him hadn't faded. If anything, it intensified. Every time he shifted his stance, or changed his timbre, something in her hit its knees. *Take me*, it said, and Devon usually obliged.

In the short time Hope had been seeing him, he'd had her on nearly every flat surface in her apartment and against a good portion of the vertical ones too. He'd made a habit of crashing in her bed for a few hours afterward, pressed to her close as her own skin, before letting himself out to go take care of Apollo. Devon gave her key back every time he saw her, and Hope took it, knowing that he would have it again in under twenty-four hours. Someday, she would get up the nerve to tell him to keep it.

Hope had been to his house once more as well, but that was all food and couch cuddles and petting the dog—after Devon's awkwardness dissipated. They hadn't had sex there. Hope had never fallen asleep there. The door to the playroom had been closed, and she suspected locked.

When she walked past it on the way to his time-capsule guest bath with the green and gold decor, Hope could feel Devon's eyes on her—his energy a charged combination of edgy and anxious. He wanted her in that room, and he was terrified of opening that door for her again. When, unsurprisingly, his dominant side raised its head that evening, Devon leashed it fast. He took her home and dropped her off with a kiss at her door like a proper gentleman.

She hated it.

"But, I mean, he's good right? I bet he's good," Chloe said surreptitiously, as they watched him stand shoulder to shoulder with the newer bartender, Lucas—a young guy with spiky blond hair and a painfully obvious crush on one of the servers. Devon mixed a drink, nodding at a customer down the way as a bill went in the tip jar.

"Like a drug," Hope said, thinking about so much more than the sex. She sighed.

"Huh?" Chloe leaned closer.

"Yeah, the sex is great." Hope knew she was only getting the tip of that iceberg, much like she'd only gotten the superficial introduction to everything else. So much depth and darkness to Devon Cleary, that even he had probably never seen the bottom.

"Hey, bitches," Nix said, sauntering up behind the bar with a tray and a couple of debit cards.

"Hey, babe." Chloe grinned. "We were discussing the finer points of your boy over there."

Nix snorted. "Only thing I care to add to that conversation is that he's not my type."

"Mmm..." Chloe purred, and Hope recognized that her friend was doing that thing she did right before they usually ended up making out. "What is your type, then?"

Nix straightened slightly, lifted her chin, and donned a small smile. For some reason, Hope's heart beat hard in her chest. Eventually, Nix cocked her head and said, "I prefer blonds."

Chloe let out a decadent laugh.

***

"Can I ask you something?" Hope said, as Devon locked her door.

He'd walked her home when he got off at eleven, but tipsy-Chloe stayed behind. Devon had been on Hope's side, oddly oppositional to that until Nix said she'd make sure Chloe got home safely. She would have Alex keep an eye on her from the door or walk with her if Chloe made it to closing. Apparently, Devon's *No woman out alone* routine didn't register Nix in the same way it registered Hope and Chloe. And that was what she wanted to talk about.

"Anything," Devon said huskily, stepping into her and pulling her body to his.

"How did you meet Nix?" Hope asked, against his lips.

He froze for a beat, then stepped back.

"Sorry. Is that..."

"No, no, it's fine." He shook his head, hazel eyes going more serious than lusty.

"I've noticed that she's a lot like you," Hope ventured. "I mean... *a lot.*"

Devon bit down on his lower lip, fighting a grin.

"And that night I came to see you at work—I forgot to bring it up because things got so weird..." Hope didn't have a better descriptor for her ex's appearances at both her apartment and her job after he'd seen her with Devon. "Nix called you..."

"Demon," he supplied. "It's a... a nickname. A *scene* name." He pulled his hands from her hips to run them through his hair. "Do you want to sit down?"

"Uh, sure." Hope moved toward her couch before rerouting to the kitchen table. "You hungry? Want a drink?" she asked. She didn't want to assume he'd eaten at work if he was secretly starving. Devon shook his head as he took Chloe's usual chair.

"I wanted to talk to you about this, anyway. That night you came into Cleary's, and I took you to the office... But like you said, things got weird, and it didn't come up." He glanced up at her. "I don't know how much I'm supposed to tell you, or how fast, but this has been bothering me. Not that it's bad," he said. "Just..."

"Devon," Hope said, smiling softly.

"Right... Right." He took a slow breath and started again. "I met Nix the year before I opened Cleary's, through the local...community."

"The local bird watching community?" Hope asked, earning a smile. The visible tension in him relaxed a fraction.

"You say she's a lot like me, and you're right. She's one of the few people who can occasionally put my top in its place when I'm...you know." He smirked. "Oddly enough, we get along. We work well together at the bar, and we know that a scene together would be a disaster. It's fun to watch her though, and we've handed off to each other from time to time." Devon met Hope's gaze for a moment before aimlessly tracing a finger over the woodgrain of her table. "Nix is a skilled dominant. Makes a lovely sub, too, when she feels like letting her partner pretend for a bit. Then she flips it, and—" He looked at her outright. "Nix isn't my type."

"She says the same about you." Hope laughed, but Devon didn't.

"She isn't the only person from work that I met through those channels, and I think you deserve to know what my past looks like when it comes to people that I still see regularly."

"Okay," Hope said hesitantly. "So, you're saying that you've never had sex with Nix, but someone else at Cleary's?"

He swallowed hard. "There have been a handful of servers over the years...not while they were employed. I don't play with anyone who works at the bar. That was a personal boundary for me, long before you came along." He pulled in a breath. "I also met Mark and Alex through the local club."

Hope nodded. "You've never had sex with Nix, but Mark? Alex?"

His brow furrowed slightly, and he tapped a finger on the table. "Would that bother you?"

"I don't think so. I mean, you aren't having sex with anyone else right now, right? And you don't *play* with anyone from work, anyway."

Devon pressed his mouth into a tight smile. "I was actually curious if you'd freak out if you thought I was..."

"Bi!" Hope finished for him in sudden epiphany. "Or pan? Sorry, I thought you were worried about the working with someone you'd slept with part. No, sexuality's not a deal breaker for me." She reached for his hand. He looked uncomfortably at their intertwined fingers.

"I've never had sex with them either, but...um..."

"But you're bi? Really, that's not a thing for me. I make out with Chloe all the time."

Devon let go of her hand and went back to drumming the table. "It's not that, exactly."

"Okay, but it's something. Just say it, Devon. I'm pretty open-minded." Or she tried to be when her own triggers didn't get in the way.

He nodded, seeming to make up his mind. "Nix says I'm *pan-dominant*." He chuckled weakly. "I'm not a hundred percent sure that's a real word." Devon glanced up at her, back down to the table. "I've topped for Mark a handful of times. Stacy gets a kick out of watching, but that was years ago. I'm really good at putting a sub in a proper headspace when I'm in the mood."

Hope sat quietly, trying to look accepting and supportive—trying to take in the tide of Devon that she could see preparing to overflow. His gaze drifted up until his eyes fixed feverishly on some middle ground between them, staring into nothingness as he saw something entirely different than her sitting at her kitchen table. His spine straightened; the drumming finger stilled.

"Give me a willing submissive, I'll hand back a mewling kitten," he promised, voice wickedly even. "And I don't give a fuck about the identity of that sub, as long as everyone is a consenting adult. I also don't need to be sexually attracted to someone to get off on—" He blinked, swallowed, refocused on Hope. Watching him lock up tight what he'd barely opened for her stung, but she let him. Some things took time to share. "The point," Devon went on, "is that I need to top sometimes, even when it doesn't involve sex. And I'm good at it."

"So, that's why you said you couldn't turn off the dominance stuff, because it isn't necessarily sexual for you. It just *is*." *Demon*, the alter ego that needed to get out sometimes. The one she'd caught glimpses of for as long as she had known him.

The one that Hope secretly found as titillating as she found Devon, even if the idea of it scared her senseless.

"Right," he said. "But I'd be lying if I said that I could separate dominance from sex. I can do dominance without sex, easy. Sex without dominance is a hell of a lot harder." She watched him wet his lips and force a smile. "And explaining this to you is hard. I can negotiate the fuck out of a scene, but... I don't want to screw this up."

"Do you think I'll be..." Hope rolled the hem of her shirt between her fingers, under the table. "Enough? Because if you need to—"

She watched the breath go out of him.

"God, yes," he said. "If you can't give me something I need, I'll stop needing it."

Hope didn't like that answer. His concern was touching, but Devon had overlooked a glaring truth. She wasn't *enough* if he had to erase a part of himself to be with her, and Hope didn't want parts of someone she cared about erased. She didn't want this part of *him* erased.

Hope stood and moved around the table. Devon shifted in his seat to face her, blinking fast as she knelt between his feet. When she put her hands on his knees and pushed them wider, the blinking stopped, and his eyes went wide too. A quiver went through him, caressing her palms. "Am I supposed to call you Demon?" she asked. His lips parted at the sound of that name.

"Devon," he eventually managed. "Call me Devon...or sir. Just... don't call me that. I don't know how I feel about it."

"Yes, Sir." Hope forced a nervous smile. "Don't assume, okay? I know you think I can't handle...whatever you want, but I might surprise you," she said softly, as a blush flushed her face.

Devon brushed a thumb across her lower lip. "You often do, darling."

***

Hope awoke in a tangle of sheets that smelled like cedar and sandalwood. Like *Devon*. She breathed it in, comforted by the familiar. He headed home at around three. Something Hope only knew because she had rolled over to check the time as he kissed her goodbye.

At 10:30 a.m., Chloe showed up for post-night-out breakfast. She picked at her toast and skipped the eggs and coffee completely, while chugging about a gallon of the electric blue Powerade she had lugged over from her place directly from the bottle. Hope quietly sipped her coffee, content in the knowledge that Devon would be finished at the bar soon. Even if Chloe remained miserable, Hope would have someone to hang out with. Endless hours alone didn't hold the thrall they had a few weeks prior.

"Ugh…" Chloe groaned. "The smell of that is making me ill."

Hope chuckled. "I don't think my coffee is the problem."

"Oh no… Hold on…" Chloe bolted for the bathroom, turning on the faucet and slamming the door. She reemerged ten minutes later, the color of pea soup. "I'm dying," she said.

"You're hungover," Hope replied dryly.

Chloe put her head in her hands. "I'm never doing this again," she groaned.

"You always say that."

"Will you be around later? I'm going back to bed. I'm still out of sorts from working thirds last week."

"Plus, you're pukey." Hope grinned, as Chloe dry heaved.

"Oh my god, why would you say that word. You're a bitch, but I love you." Chloe pushed to her feet and shuffled away, carrying her Powerade under her arm. "Aw," she said, opening Hope's apartment door so she could escape back to her bed. "He got you roses. Romantic."

"He what?" Hope stood and strode toward her friend. Sure enough, a bouquet of red roses lay on her welcome mat.

"Okay, I'm going. I don't know if I can do the whole vicarious movement thing of watching you bend over to get those." Chloe made a gagging noise, as if gravity were the only thing keeping her from vomiting again and stepped over the flowers.

"Hey..." Hope called after her. "So, these weren't here when you came over?"

"I'm hungover, not drunk. There's a difference," Chloe said, as she let herself into her own apartment. "I'm going to go die, now."

"Rest in peace," Hope called after her.

She looked down at the roses, intuition prickling. It wasn't that she didn't think Devon would buy her flowers. It was just that he should be at Cleary's, and even if he wasn't, why make the extra trip by her place to drop them off when he could have handed them to her in person later? Something felt *wrong*.

Her phone buzzed at the small of her back, so Hope pulled it from the band of her yoga pants.

Nix is running late. I'll head your way by 3. Right down the street if you need me. XX

Hope looked from Devon's text to the roses and back again, before grabbing the bouquet. She didn't like touching them. *Bad energy, dark aura*, as Margo would say. Did roses have auras? Hope wasn't even convinced people had them. She dumped them on the counter in her small kitchen. Snatching the folded cardstock from between the stems, Hope flipped it open, anxious to prove the depth of her overreaction, but it didn't play out that way.

Familiar handwriting gouged the paper in an angry scrawl. Harsh and sharp and *Aaron's*. Hope dropped the card on the counter, glancing toward her living room.

Locks.

Rushing back to the door, she looked through the peephole. Satisfied with the vacant hallway, Hope unlocked and relocked the knob and deadbolt, shivering at the metal *snick* of the mechanisms sliding into place. She twisted the knob and yanked against the unyielding barrier.

"It's locked," she whispered, hand still gripping. "I've checked it. It's locked."

Reluctantly, she headed for the kitchen and reopened the card.

What if they found out you loved it? Happy anniversary.

Her eyebrows lowered. Loved what? If who found out?

Hope paced in and out of her galley kitchen, adrenaline fueling her as she contemplated Aaron's words. He couldn't be talking about the anniversary of when they started dating. The timing didn't line up. So, what happened last December?

"Oh my God." Hope dropped the card. "No, no, no..."

DEVON

*R*oses. The scent swamped Devon as he stepped through the door, the first thing all day strong enough to distract him from the memory of her the night before. On her knees. Between his thighs. Blue-green eyes staring up at him as she—*Christ*. Roses weren't unpleasant, but Hope always smelled like lavender, except when she smelled like him. Devon paid attention, and every bottle of shampoo or lotion she owned had *Lavender this or that* emblazoned on the label in purple lettering.

Hope pressed a kiss to his lips, but it came with a disconnected sort of energy, as if she'd kissed him because she was supposed to. He caught himself frowning and wiped the expression fast. It was just roses, just a kiss. Wasn't it?

"Sorry I'm late. Nix needed a few more hours at home, and I was already at the bar," he said, studying her for clues. "Let me put your keys back and—"

"I got it," Hope blurted, snatching them from his hand, and darting toward the kitchen.

Devon followed at a distance, an overpowering floral scent invading his sinuses with every breath. Nothing seemed out of place beyond the smell and her behavior. Hope studiously avoided looking at him as she dashed to the drawer, yanked it open, and deposited the keys. Then she was out of that kitchen like it was on fire, big fake smile plastered on her pretty face.

Demon bristled.

Devon bristled too.

"Okay, ready to go," Hope said brightly, backtracking past him and pulling on a coat.

"Hope," he said, coming up short in her living room.

"Come on," she repeated with that tight smile.

Devon planted his feet and canted his head. "Where are the roses?" he asked. Because there *were* roses, and something was wrong.

She opened her mouth, then closed it, before dropping her gaze to the floor.

"Hope?" He heard his tone shift along with his temperament, her flash of submission doubling as a dinner bell. Devon watched her fiddle with the pull on her zipper, as he considered the merits of zip ties. Less fidgeting, more explaining… And he was half a second from saying that aloud when she spoke.

"In the trash," she said, not meeting his eyes.

Devon cursed under his breath, guessing where this was headed.

She didn't say another word, didn't look at him. But he could see it there— all those things she held beneath the surface. The same shit that had nagged at him, since the last time she admitted her ex dropped in unannounced. Demon made a decent case for hauling her into the playroom and asking her anything he liked once she was a quivering mess. Devon had the gear. He'd make the time.

And he'd likely ruin everything in the process.

But Devon couldn't stand this. She was afraid, upset, or anxious as often as she was warm and open. It was maddening, and there had to be a solution. At least a way to better understand all the stuff going on behind those gorgeous eyes of hers—like an interrogation. Devon could run an interrogation. This one time... Well, no, that wouldn't work. A *little* interrogation, he decided. That's what this situation called for.

"Fuck yes."

"I'm sorry?" Hope looked at him, all wide eyes and worry, and Devon realized that he'd spoken aloud.

"Are you hungry?" he asked, ignoring his slip.

When she shook her head, Devon nodded. He'd planned a walk around town and dinner—or the other way around if she'd skipped lunch. A normal date by anyone's standards, but now he needed privacy.

"Then, let's go."

HOPE

Seventy pounds of silver pit greeted them at the door. Hope smiled down at Apollo, even though she didn't feel much like smiling. She stroked a hand over his cement block head then found herself sinking to her haunches and hugging the pup. Apollo parked himself in a sit, panting over her shoulder with his signature sloppy grin.

There were things that Devon deserved to know if they continued seeing each other, but she didn't know *how* to tell him. Devon, who had virtually no experience with romantic relationships, had opened up about so very much, while Hope hadn't even told him the reason she nearly ended their relationship before it began. And she was a freaking therapist... Sort of.

As she stayed wrapped around Apollo, Devon stalked the periphery. Hope could feel the weight of his attention as he took off his shoes, stripped his coat and sweater, leaving the black t-shirt underneath. He ran Apollo out back before reaching down and taking one of her hands, tugging her to her feet.

"Time to get up," he said, in a way that required no response.

Devon took her coat, led her to the couch and gestured for her to sit. He crouched in front of her, tugging off her boots. He looked *determined*, she thought, as he pulled his phone from his back pocket and turned on the stereo. A low, rhythmic beat poured out of the speakers, nearly drowning out Apollo's whine at the door.

"Place," Devon ordered in that tone of his that made everyone in earshot pay attention. Apollo headed for the bed in the corner of the living room. "Other one, buddy," he added. Softer, gentler, but every bit the command. The dog huffed and turned down the hall toward the back of the house.

"He's such a good boy," Hope mumbled, staring after him. Devon nodded.

"Are you ready to talk to me?" he asked, leveling intense hazel eyes on her.

"Are you mad?" she asked on impulse, voice quavering. The answer flashed in his eyes plain as day—the kind of anger that leaves a metallic tang on your tongue. He wiped it away with a hand run up one side of his face and into his hair.

"Not at you," he said.

Hope swiped the heel of her palm over her eyes, before drying it on her pants. She should have told him sooner—that night she accidentally walked into the playroom. "Maybe you should be," she said.

Snatching the throw from the back of the couch, Devon folded it into a thick square. He dropped it in the middle of the living room, then turned to face her. His feet shifted farther apart on the blond wood floors. His spine stiffened; shoulders squared. Everything in Hope went deliciously still in response. When the base of her skull prickled, Hope knew exactly what it meant. *Connection.* And she needed it.

"This," Devon said, pointing from her to himself. "There's a problem with this. There's a goddamn wall in the middle of it, and I've been throwing pieces of myself over the top, but I'm not getting much back."

Hope didn't know what she'd expected him to say, but it wasn't that. *That* wasn't even in the ballpark. His tone, his expression, combined with that arrangement of words nearly knocked the breath out of her.

"Devon—"

The tingling connection exploded, fanning down her neck and shoulders like fingers grasping for purchase, leaving fear in their wake. Not because she thought he might lose his shit like her ex, but because he already didn't think this was going to work. Hope hadn't said a word yet, and Devon was throwing in the towel.

She wasn't supposed to feel this way over the idea that he might put a stop to them. Hope wanted her apartment, her own bed, locked doors so she could fall apart in peace. Why not leave her there with her stupid trashcan full of roses if he intended to stop seeing her?

"No."

Hope's head snapped up at Devon's voice. He jabbed a finger at the empty air between them.

"You stay right here in this room," he bit out. "Don't you dare go traipsing around in your head alone. I'm not blaming you for the wall you built. I can spot a defense, as surely as a conditioned response. But I am *done* standing on the other side of that fucking wall."

As he spoke, Hope's focus zeroed in on him, as if he were the only thing in the room. The spiraling in her mind ceased.

Devon pointed to the makeshift floor cushion—and waited. Hope's chest rose and fell fast, as time stuttered to a halt. It felt like an eternity, like they would stay there forever—her on the couch and him pointing mutely, expectantly to that spot on the floor. Waiting for her to yield.

She'd never been good at yielding. Hope was better at stubbornly going her own way even if it hurt because at least then you were the one in control. You made the choices. Any deviation from that approach had only brought her pain. But this time, for him, she found herself pushing to her feet, crossing the hardwoods, and dropping to her knees on the mat. A peace came over her as she tucked her feet under her butt and linked her hands tentatively in her lap.

Letting go was also a choice.

"Your safewords are *yellow* and *red*," Devon said. The unsteadiness in his voice smoothed into something practiced as he continued. "*Yellow* means you're near a limit. It tells me to slow down or change direction. *Red* is a hard stop, game over, no more. I will respect those words immediately if you use them. I won't be angry. I won't push. I won't punish. I only have as much control here as you give me, understood?"

Hope nodded, though her head swam with questions. What was he planning? Would she be able to handle it, or would she shout *Red* the moment he stirred up something he had no knowledge of? On the other side, would she feel safe enough to talk to him? That was the one thing she had to do. Probably the first thing she should do. If she didn't talk to Devon soon, he would get someone else's version of her history. He'd never look at her the same way again. Then again, he might not after Hope talked to him either.

"I can't hear you." Every inch of him settled deeper into his role.

Hope hesitated, something in her pushing back against what he wanted until an uncomfortable energy hummed through her. *Compulsion.* She ducked her head. "Yes, Sir."

A confusing sense of relief flooded her. Hope didn't look up, but she could feel his eyes on her, and she wanted so badly in that moment for him to be satisfied with what he saw.

Devon brushed a hand over her crown and sighed. "I'll be right back. I need a few things."

"Yes, Sir," she repeated, uncertainty whispering through her reply.

Devon cocked his head and looked at her. "What are your safewords?"

It was a softball question, but at least she knew the answer. "Yellow and red, Sir."

"Good girl," he murmured, before turning on his heel and heading into the hall. Hope couldn't help but think of the display of harnesses, paddles, and more. Leather cuffs. Metal ones.

Snick, snick, snick...

She shuddered, shoving down the desire to get off the floor.

"Let's have you cross-legged," Devon said, walking back in and settling in front of her. Hope didn't see anything in his hands, so if he'd brought something from the playroom, it was small enough to keep out of sight. "This might take a while. I want you comfortable."

When she complied, he held up something black and leather.

"Trust me?" he said, arching a brow. Hope nodded. "I can't hear you, darling."

"Yes, Sir," she said, quickly. "I trust you, Sir."

Devon smiled. "You are perfection," he said, carefully enunciating each word. He trailed a fingertip down her cheek. Hope blushed and glanced down until he slipped that finger under her chin and lifted. "Now, now darling," he chided. "That's what this is for." He placed the bit of leather—a blindfold—over her eyes, then folded her forward until her head sat in his lap. Devon buckled the straps in back. "See now?" he said, his smile audible as he righted her. "I made it easy. No more uncomfortable eye contact. Say, *thank you, sir.*"

"Thank you, Sir," Hope echoed, turning her head in the blackness, listening to the low thrum of music, the soft sounds of breathing.

She wet her lips, chewed the lower one, then found herself lost in the delicious sensation of a warm mouth against her own. A decadent, languorous sliding, and parting, pulling her into a dizzying swirl of deep connection and scorching desire. Hope lurched forward, meeting empty air, as Devon pulled away.

Out of the darkness, a firm hand caught both of her wrists, and something narrow passed over, under, between them with soft *swishes* and *thumps* until she was wearing what felt like— Hope panted through her nose, her ears ringing, and eyes uselessly searching.

"Ye... ye..."

She stopped herself as Devon froze. Through the contact of his hands on her wrists, Hope got the sense that his whole body had gone rigid. That awareness of his, before she got the word out, slowed her pulse and her breathing. Actions spoke louder than anything sometimes, and when she'd uttered a single syllable, Devon stopped.

"Sorry, Sir," she managed.

"No apologies. Are you okay?" he asked, voice laced with concern.

"Can you talk, please?" Hope heard herself say. "I don't care what you say. I think...I need to hear you." She felt her face flush and wondered how much the blindfold hid. It covered the tops of her cheeks, at least. But her trembling lower lip and shaking hands were on full display.

"Safewords." Devon cleared his throat. "What are your safewords?"

"Ye... yellow and red, Sir."

"There's my good girl," he said, his voice all honey and whiskey in her brain. "Do you need to use one?" Hope shook her head, and instead of saying he couldn't hear her, Devon let it slide.

"I'll take the rope off when we're done, alright?" He jostled her around as he finished tying off the cuffs. "Unless you need something off sooner."

"Yes, Sir." She twisted her wrists, experimentally.

"Too tight?" Devon asked.

Hope loved the sound of his voice. She twisted again and shuddered as heat kindled in her core. "No, Sir. They're good, Sir," she breathed.

"Good girl. Still trust me?" Hope licked her lips and nodded, leaning forward. Two fingers pressed against her chest, pushing her back into place. "Tell me a story," Devon said.

Hope stilled. "What kind of story?"

"The one I want to hear," he said.

She thought this was about sex—an intense physical connection to make them closer so she'd talk to him. He was doing the dominance thing. She was tied up and wearing a freaking blindfold. How could this not be about sex?

"What happens if I don't?" she asked obstinately, diving headlong back into the M.O. that nearly kept her on his couch.

Devon sighed. "Nothing, you stubborn, little thing," he admonished. "*Nothing* happens. I'm not going to turn you over my knee and spank you until you talk—" Hope quivered. "Though, I'm not sure you'd hate that," he added. She could almost see the way his head tilted, as he studied her response. The visual made her squirm. "I suspect it would be...*effective*."

Devon took a breath and seemed to refocus.

"Aren't you tired of being stuck in there with all your secrets? All those things that sting. I'm giving you the permission you won't give yourself. More than that, I'll give you the order you crave. The one you'll respond to because you've been waiting forever for someone to give you that. Tell the story, darling. Last time I'm asking before *nothing* happens."

Hope turned her head, lowered her chin, brought her face back to where she knew he sat. When she found nothing to look at, no eye contact to break, she settled. Hope hung in the void, the music drowning out every sound that didn't emanate from the two of them. No averting, no avoiding, and her only escape route was away from Devon—a direction that she didn't want to go.

"Aaron left roses at my apartment, today," she said, before she could change her mind. Jerking her bound hands up, Hope realized that she couldn't indulge the urge to fidget. She dropped them in her lap again. Okay, so add that to the list of sensory deprivation going on. She was in a Devon bubble, but it was kind of... *secure*.

"I figured that much," he said, his tone cautious.

"I threw them in the trash. I swear I didn't want them," she replied, in a rush.

Devon caught the rope between her wrists and pulled them forward a fraction. He held them there, solid and immovable. "I know," he said.

Rationally, Hope knew that she sat in a room flooded with natural light as he watched her blather on, wearing a *blindfold* of all things. But her head was a different story. Hope sat in the dark with all the things she couldn't say. Things she'd hidden from everyone.

But alone in the dark, Hope started to feel as if maybe she could tell Devon. God, it would feel good for someone to *know*.

"The card said *happy anniversary*, but it isn't our anniversary," she began. "It isn't. We started dating in April. And it said *What if they found out you loved it?* I didn't know what that meant. I couldn't figure it out— This is out of order," Hope said, shaking her head in frustration.

"Take a breath. Start again. We'll get it sorted out," Devon promised.

Hope focused on slowing her breathing, trying to find an order to the mess. Things got disorganized when she looked back at how it all played out with Aaron. The feelings muddled the story.

"I told you I met Aaron at my last job. He was a cop assigned to the school." She tugged against Devon to gesture out of habit. When he didn't budge, she went on. "We started dating, and the sex was good. Like even when we argued, that part was fine. God, it's weird telling you that."

"It's just sex," Devon said. Somehow, Hope felt both his shrug and his tension through the rope that bound her.

She nodded. "Okay, this one time, like maybe three or four months in, I made a joke about his..." Without the ability to finger the hem of her sweater, Hope went back to biting her lip—something she couldn't do while speaking.

"Keep going. You made a joke about what?"

Hope took another breath. "Handcuffs," she all but whispered. Once it was out, she began to panic. "Because he was a cop, you know? And it turned into a thing. Like he would get them out and—"

Snick, snick, snick... She jerked hard against Devon and shook her head against the vicious sound crawling into her ears.

"Hope—" His insistent voice cut in, and the snicking stopped.

"Right, Sir. Sorry, Sir," she murmured. "He'd...um... put me in handcuffs, like... *often*. Which was fine because... Well, it was fine. I mean, I..." She trailed off.

"You liked it," he said, triggering an undeniable urge to train her unseeing eyes on the floor. "It's okay to like it," Devon said gently. "There's nothing wrong with that, Hope."

"It's just..." Her breath came faster, her body reacting before she could get it out.

Even as she sat in Devon's living room, Hope was right back in Aaron's kitchen, face down on the tile. Knowing that it was some stupid trauma response—some flood of survival chemicals saturating her brain—didn't stop it.

"A year ago, I got the job offer for Costings." She pushed on, hoping that working from the beginning would lead to a cohesive tale, and a way through her panic. "I went to his house to tell him. He'd always had a temper. He yells, throws stuff, though. He doesn't, like, *hit you*."

Hope shook her head, trying to put it all in proper context.

"And it wasn't all the time. God, I make him sound like a monster. He can be incredibly sweet. Really thoughtful... But you never know which Aaron you're going to get. I got good at being what he wanted—or trying, anyway."

Hope's arms abruptly went slack, her bound hands settling in her lap. She could no longer hear Devon breathing. She could still feel him in front of her though, listening.

"I told him about the job, and...and he got mad. *So* mad. I'd ducked things before. Dishtowels... Clothes... Nothing dangerous. He threw a glass once, but that wasn't at me. Chucked it at the fireplace. Wine went everywhere." She shook her head again, clearing the disorganized fragments of memory. "But I could see it in his eyes, that night. I'd never seen him like that." Hope kept pouring into the void.

"I didn't tell him when I applied because I figured it would start a fight. We'd been together a year and a half, at that point, and Asheville was two hours away. I'm sorry," she blurted, shying away from what happened next. "This is—"

"I'm here," Devon said. "Don't stop."

"Okay..." Hope swallowed. "I... I thought, why fight about it when I probably wouldn't get the job, you know?" she said.

"Except, you did," Devon supplied.

Hope tilted her face toward her hands in her lap. "I shouldn't have sprung it on him. He was so angry."

She felt like a broken record, compulsively repeating an arbitrary description of a time when Aaron got mad, and she wondered how she ended up spilling this tale while blindfolded and tied up in Devon's living room. She also wondered why that made it easier.

"I told him I was going home, so he could cool off. That we'd talk about it in the morning." A sickening heat washed over her, as she forced the next words out. "And he...snapped."

Hope heard the rustle as Devon pushed to his feet, muffled steps as he walked away from her and back again. This was too much to dump on someone you'd only dated a few weeks. He wanted behind her walls, but this was—

"Still here," Devon said gruffly. "I just need to move. Finish the story, darling."

"Well, um... I grabbed my coat, and I don't know... One second, I was opening the door to leave, and the next—" Hope hesitated as the darkness engulfing her was momentarily interrupted by the close-and-getting-closer image of Aaron's kitchen door in her mind's eye. She snapped her head back, embarrassment swamping her when the image dissipated as quickly as it appeared. She pulled in a sharp breath. "My...my face was against it," she managed. "He, um, grabbed my hair and got me on the floor somehow. Got on top of me to keep me down." She listened to Devon pace away and back, away and back. Heavier footfalls each time.

"I should be able to deescalate a situation like that, but when he grabbed me, all I could do was try to get away. He's your size," Hope explained. "He's a cop. He knows how to restrain people way bigger than me."

The December cold crept through the walls, inching ever closer, as she spoke—choking out the anxious heat that flooded her. Hope focused on Devon's footsteps—away and back, away and back. But instead of distracting her, the rhythm, the increasing force, and speed, sucked her deeper.

"I thought he'd let me right back up. I thought..." Her eyes stung with the threat of tears. "He had on street clothes. I didn't expect the handcuffs. I remember being so surprised by that, which is stupid. I guess he had plans, so—"

Hope blinked in the darkness. Aaron's face stared back at her, cheek to the floor, putting them eye-to-eye. The weight of him crushed into her. Everything melded together. Even as her arms sat in her lap, they were painfully wrenched behind her, the steel of Aaron's belt buckle grinding against the cuffs—pressing them into her spine.

Hope let out a sob. "They make this sound." *Snick, snick, snick.* She tried to cover her ears, whacking herself in the face because of her bound wrists. "I keep hearing it," she cried over the sound of fast footfalls, pressing a shoulder to one ear, blocking the other with her tied hands.

Devon thumped to the ground in front of her. He pulled her hands forward, fumbled with the ropes, and cursed under his breath. Hope had an increasingly difficult time registering any of it.

"That's the fucked-up thing," she said hysterically, words tumbling over one another, between frantic breaths. Devon abandoned the knot and took her hands in his. "I don't know why that part stays with me when it was fine before. It shouldn't stay in my head like that. I was in those things fifty times before that night, and I barely remember any of them." She squeezed his fingers tighter, holding on. "He thinks I'm crazy for being upset because I liked it before, right? So it wasn't that bad. And what if he's right? I slept with him, two months after we broke up. *Stupid*," she spat. "I don't know why I did that. Who does that?"

Hope absently noted the blindfold sliding against her skin and something dripping down her face. Tears.

"He had a bottle of wine and a million apologies," she said, pulling in an unladylike breath through her nose to keep snot from joining the rest of the mess on her face. "I knew nothing good would come from it, but I didn't want him getting loud in the hallway. I downed a bottle of Pinot Grigio and fucked him on the couch, like an idiot. I don't even drink Pinot Grigio. I let him... I let him..." As Hope crumbled, Devon pulled one hand free.

"This is cold, but you are safe," he said, as cool steel wedged between the rope and her skin, the intrusion cinching her bindings tighter.

Hope barely had time to flinch before the rope fell to the floor. Devon moved to the blindfold next, unbuckling it with quick efficiency. Hope squinted against the light, wiping her face on her sleeves, as Devon scooted in close behind her. Flanking her with his legs, he wrapped his arms around her like a shield.

"That's what the flowers were for..." Hope sniffled, feeling the too-fast rise and fall of his chest at her back. "For this sick *anniversary*."

"I'm sorry." Devon ran his hands up and down her arms, over her wrists, then linked their fingers, squeezing her tighter. His voice rumbled down her spine, like a caress. "I shouldn't have done this. I don't know how—" He exhaled sharply, shook his head. "I'm so sorry."

"I needed to tell you," Hope said.

"But not like this." He pressed a kiss to her cheek. "I'm just so sorry," he repeated.

Hope bit her lip, considering. "I think this made it easier."

Devon made a sound between a grunt and a huff, behind her. Nothing about it sounded happy or relieved. Not knowing what to say next, Hope let the conversation fade to a silence that Devon didn't interrupt. For the longest time, there was only the music and the pressure of his arms around her. And then—

"Hope, darling?"

A shiver shot through her nervous system, calling her mind and body back online. "Hmm?" she managed, scooting her hips back against him.

"Can I ask you something?" he ventured.

"Sure." If she was talking to him about her sex life with her ex and the time Aaron basically held her captive, there wasn't much off the table, was there?

Devon let go of her hands and leaned forward, causing Hope to fold up on herself momentarily. He straightened back up with a piece of the rope he'd used to bind her wrists in his hand.

"If you didn't..." He trailed off, aimlessly fingering the frayed edges of the rope. Hope stared at his hands; at the way his fingers anticipated the movements of the cord. The back of her skull prickled. "If things were *different*, do you think..."

"Yes," she said.

His quick exhale tickled her ear. "I'm not sure you understand. I was trying to ask about the... uh... the dominant stuff. If you'd—"

"I know, and I would. At least to try it."

Devon stiffened behind her, his busy hands stilling.

"And…" Hope continued, staring at the rope he held. "I don't know that I wouldn't still want to try it. Probably not handcuffs, because—" Devon pulled back a fraction to give her room, as she tucked her shoulders up.

"Hey, I don't need you to be into any of that," he said, leaning close again. "It was foolish curiosity because of the handcuff thing. I'm an asshole for bringing it up." He shook his head again. "I'm an asshole for all of this. When I don't know how to fix something, I try to top my way through it," he admitted. "This wasn't the time."

"No, really, it's okay. Maybe more than okay." Hope could feel adrenaline singing in her veins again, but for a different reason than the remembered trauma of what happened with Aaron. "There are things that sound…" She swallowed hard. "There are some things that always sounded interesting, but they're kind of taboo, you know?"

Devon nodded, stubble brushing her cheek.

"The one time I hinted at that, it… Well, I just told you how it worked out. But you get it. You wouldn't judge it; you wouldn't use it to hurt me. I mean…" She chewed her lip and tugged the piece of rope from his hands, twisting it between her fingers.

"It's complicated," Devon said, over her shoulder. This time Hope nodded. "When you want something, but people think it's wrong—it feels complicated sometimes. I understand that, pretty well."

"How did you get to a place where you didn't feel… you know…" Hope trailed off, embarrassment making the words difficult.

"Dirty?" Devon chuckled. "I didn't know what that felt like until I met you. I used to wonder if I was capable of shame." He laughed, again. "I realize how fucked up that sounds. I've done some really questionable shit, but always with other people that were into really questionable shit. So, maybe that's the secret. I don't ask people for their opinion. I'm only after their consent."

DEVON

Devon moved everything in the washer to the dryer and did the whole dials and buttons thing. Hope would have clean clothes in the morning, so at least there was that. He wasn't sure the trade-off was worth it when he needed to close Cleary's tomorrow, though. Actually, it was tonight, at this point. Devon considered checking the time until he remembered he'd left his phone on the bedside charger. It didn't matter enough to go get it. Tired was tired, no matter the hour.

Lack of sleep wasn't the only drawback to this little laundry run. One also had to consider the way Hope looked in his t-shirt. The way her nipples pressed against the thin fabric. The sensation of his skin and hers separated by *only* that thin fabric. He didn't want her back in her own clothes. So yeah, insomnia was a mixed bag, but the sin...the *real sin* was that he was currently standing in his stuffy basement. Alone.

Not that Devon put any weight into the notion of sin. About seven months earlier, he'd whipped a woman who was more likely to dole out a beating than be on the receiving end of one with a Delrin cane until she safeworded loud enough that the entire club ground to a halt—a rare occurrence at Edge. As far as Devon could tell, there was no Sky Daddy out there holding any of that against him. Not the marks on her thighs, not the tears on her face, not even the crowd of aroused onlookers following his every move like he was some sort of sadistic Pied Piper.

If there was a judgmental, all-powerful prick taking notes on Devon's deviant behaviors, Devon wanted a few words with that asshole. His mom, his sister, the clients coming through R&R daily... unacceptable. *I'd like to speak to the manager...* Devon cracked his neck, rolled his shoulders, and clenched his hands.

Okay, now he was drifting.

It was a sin to be alone in the basement when a warm and soft Hope lay upstairs in his bed. Since that first, unexpected night he spent at her place, Devon had thought of little else beyond getting her there. Her absence between his sheets was a tangible thing—and not for a lack of sex. The desire bordered on insatiable, but that didn't stop them from trying. And trying, and trying, and... No, the deficiency wasn't a lack of sex. It was the other part.

Devon wanted her there when he closed his eyes. He wanted her there when he opened them again.

Talk about unsettling. He had never wanted to wake up beside anyone, but now that he did, he couldn't ignore the craving. Much like his dominant tendencies, this wouldn't go away. And now that he had her in his bed—fast asleep, after one hell of a day—Devon worried that the rage coming off him might wake her unless the racket of his screaming thoughts got the job done first. So, he'd slipped out.

Devon had watched her shift, heave a contented sigh, and snuggle into the spot he'd vacated. Sprawled across his bed, with the hem of his shirt sliding up the thigh she'd hiked over his pillow, Hope looked like everything he'd never known he needed. If he'd stayed, that leg would be across his hips, and her head would be tucked against his shoulder. Something inside him had ached at the sight of her like that, while something else had whispered that no one so full of fury should touch her. Ever. Devon knew it on every level, just as he was angry on every level. All of them.

All his pieces were finally coming together, as Nix would say. But holy fuck—the edges. Slicing. Cutting. This wasn't a fuck-ing jigsaw puzzle. One-thousand-piece sunset and a fruit bowl, or whatever. This was metal and glass. Those rusted razor blades you find under a nineteen-seventies vanity during a bathroom reno and are afraid to touch. Did all his different sides have to be sharp and seething as they converged?

Tonight, they did, and Devon needed a way to file down their edges...at least temporarily.

Looking around his unfinished basement, he weighed his op-tions. He couldn't clank around weights upstairs; he'd wake her for sure. He also wasn't going to Cleary's to knock back a bunch of whiskey and talk to Nix. He wouldn't leave Hope here alone anyway, and he didn't need to see the hour to know the bar was already closed, the staff long gone. Besides, he didn't want to talk to Nix. Not really. What Devon wanted...what he *needed* was to hit something. Repeatedly. Super healthy. So well-adjusted.

Devon eyed the heavy bag hanging from the rafters deeper in the room, only visible because of the light from the stairs skimming down one side, giving the impression of mass in the darkness. Worth a shot, he supposed.

Walking over, Devon balled up a fist and swung. The vibration of the contact traveled up his arm and echoed through his torso. The bag jerked in time, chains letting out that metal on metal grind. When it didn't feel particularly satisfying, Devon set his stance, noting the grip of his bare feet on the concrete, and hit harder.

Devon's earliest childhood memory was of his father dragging his mother by the hair. Just a snapshot in his brain, lacking context. He couldn't remember the floor under them or where his father was dragging her to or from. He couldn't remember *why*... But he could see his father's hand tangled in the dark hair at the crown of his mother's head, as she grasped at his wrist and scrambled on her knees—begging him to stop. Devon had a lot of memories of people begging his father to stop.

He shook out his hand, as pain zinged across his knuckles—sharp and stinging. *Clean*. Devon refocused.

The void that surrounded that sliver of assault was irrelevant. Pick the details from any of the hundreds of others; fill in the gaps. He knew what it looked like when a man lost his temper on someone smaller. Knew what it felt like too. So, when Hope was bleeding out her story in his living room floor, Devon *knew*.

And tonight, in the dark, it ate at him, again—that question he'd never shaken for long. Was he capable of that? Like some *sins of the father* type shit? Or even if he wasn't, was Devon any better? Sure, he took volunteers, and he'd always heeded boundaries. But that thing he needed to get out of his system, wasn't that the same?

But this wasn't the time for another trip down that rabbit hole. Consent was key. Consent made him not a monster. *Consent, consent, consent.* Accept it as truth, and move on. He didn't have time to get wrapped up in his own hang-ups when the guy who'd slammed Hope into a door over a job interview was currently spiraling because she was seeing Devon.

Slammed her into a door. Hit the bag. *Pinned her on the floor.* Hit the bag. *Trussed her up in handcuffs because she tried to leave.* Hit the bag, hit the bag, hit the *fucking* bag. Wipe the sweat out of his eyes, and hit it again. Ignore the pain in his hands, and hit it again. Again... Until his blood hummed, and his body vibrated with energy that he had to get out, or he would explode—until his ears pricked to a sound upstairs.

Devon pulled his last punch, willed his frenzied breathing calmer, and listened. Trying again to wipe the sweat out of his eyes, he cursed under his breath. He'd only bothered with a pair of pajama bottoms, but the furnace kicking in the corner and the running dryer made the space damn near a sauna when you added the physical exertion of pounding on a punching bag. It was also as loud as an airport runway. But those were footsteps above him, and Apollo was too lazy to be the source at this hour, so he took the stairs at a jog.

The blood in Devon's veins went icy when he stepped into the hallway. The playroom door stood open, light painting a bright wedge across the floor and opposite wall. A gnawing sense of déjà vu bloomed in his stomach, and he tried to remind himself that she'd already stumbled into that room once. Hope knew what was in there, and she was still here.

Hurrying to the doorway, he softly called her name. She turned to him with a soft expression, sleep-tousled hair falling past her shoulders in dark waves, and his t-shirt brushing the tops of her thighs invitingly. He suddenly wanted to play with the hem, feel the sensation of his fingertips against the soft fabric and her softer skin. Looking at her standing there, so utterly *perfect*, Devon could barely breathe.

The look that flashed on her face a split second later shattered that fantasy. It wasn't the fake smile and flinch in the hallway from the first night she'd accidentally entered his playroom. It was worse.

Hope's eyes went wide, and her hand covered her mouth as Devon, once again, found himself trying to piece together how she ended up in this room and how to navigate the fallout. Christ, did she sleepwalk? She could fall down the stairs sleepwalking through a house she barely knew, and how did she even open the... He'd unlocked the door when he came in for rope and a blindfold, but then things got intense and he... he... Damn. Devon was not qualified for this level of responsibility, especially when he really wanted to kill something.

Hope was still staring at him, and he needed to say *something*.

"I forgot to—"

"What happened to your face?" she asked, horror plain on hers. Hope walked straight to him, and reached up to touch his brow, gently probing her fingers around the orbit of his right eye.

"Let's get you in bed," he urged, catching her hands and tugging. Whatever she was going on about could be handled out of this room.

Hope snatched them back. "I need the light to see your face." She leaned sideways looking behind him, as she said it.

Devon's brow creased in confusion. "Hope, I'm fine. Come out of here."

"Were you in a fight? Oh my God. Please tell me he didn't..."

Did sleepwalkers speak this coherently? Devon had always assumed they'd mumble or babble or say nothing at all. Hope seemed lucid. Whatever the case, he couldn't have her hanging out in a dungeon, so it was back to bed for her. And Devon would lock the fucking door this time. Probably needed a lock for the basement steps too. His brain rattled off safety precautions, as his mouth started making promises.

"I'll turn on the bedside lamp," he said. "Come to bed."

Linking a hand firmly around her wrist, Devon tugged. Hope met his effort with more resistance than he was willing to override, given the circumstances, and since hauling her over a shoulder didn't seem like the safe move, it looked like they were handling whatever this was right here in the playroom—which Devon hated.

"Hope—"

"You're bleeding," she said.

"I'm— Wait, what?" Devon looked down at his bloody hand encircling her wrist and cringed. "Tape," he breathed, mentally kicking himself for another oversight. "It's nothing," he said, shoving both hands behind his back.

Wrong move.

"Why are you hiding your hands?" she demanded. But didn't she already know? She was the one who pointed out that he was bleeding.

"I'm fine," he assured her.

"Devon, show me. Now." The command in her voice had Devon blinking and Demon bristling.

"Okay. Fine. See..." He held out his knuckles for her inspection, and Hope recoiled like she hadn't even noticed they were busted before. "I should've taped them, that's all. It looks worse than it is. There's a punching bag in the basement. It was dark, so I didn't realize, and..." He thought of her reaction. *Oh.* "I tried to wipe the sweat out of my eyes." He gestured, vaguely. "I didn't realize. It's just my hands. It's nothing. I'm sorry about..."

Hope reached out and gently took his hands. "These look awful," she said, worried eyes the color of the sea finding his, after studying the damage he'd done. "Why did you do this?"

Because he put his hands on you the same way my dad put hands on my mom. Devon shook his head. That thought was for the basement.

"Devon, talk to me."

But I'm not a kid now, and I'll fucking kill him if he touches you again. Unsettlingly dark, possibly true, he realized. "I couldn't sleep," Devon said, instead, forcing a shrug. "I needed an outlet."

"It's three-thirty in the morning, and you're covered in blood." Hope wouldn't stop staring at him, unrelenting eyes peering deeper than his surface. Devon felt as if she could see down in there—see all those sharp edges slicing away. He tried to put it away, tried to swallow it down, but the words wouldn't stay in his mouth.

"He put his hands on you," he blurted. "He put you in restraints when you told him no, and no is a goddamn safeword in Aaron's world. It's supposed to be a fucking safeword." The shock of what he'd said hit him like a slap, causing Devon to take a step back from her, try to pull his bloodied hands from hers. Hope followed, holding on. "Sorry," he stammered, slamming his anger under again, and meeting her gaze. "I *am* sorry."

Hope brought one of his hands to her lips, and then the other, brushing feather-light kisses over each set of knuckles. Devon resisted the urge to stop her. "I am both flattered and concerned," she said, with a soft smile. "But we need to get you cleaned up now."

HOPE

Waking alone in an unfamiliar room, it had taken Hope a moment to get her bearings. She remembered their conversation in the living room and had a vague recollection of Devon putting her in a t-shirt and tucking her in bed when she'd crashed on his lap after pizza and a Lord of the Rings marathon. Still, Hope had struggled to wrap her brain around the idea that she was in his bed and Devon was not.

Well, now she'd found him, and he was a mess.

"Come on," she said, keeping a hold on one of his hands and turning for the door.

"It's fine," Devon protested. "I'll just—"

"You'll come with me, and we'll get you cleaned up. That's what you'll do." Hope led him back into his room and through the door that she assumed went to the master bath.

"You did this?" she asked, stopping short as she flipped on the light.

An expanse of dark slate and pale wood greeted her. A massive tub sat under a frosted window, and a glass-enclosed shower took up the entire back wall. It was like walking into a spa, except darker. Spas were all white and seafoam, but this... this was sensuous.

Devon shrugged, glaring at his knuckles as if they'd let the whole team down. "It wasn't a weekend thing. I chipped away at it for a while. Look, you head back to bed. I'll be in after I wash up." He grabbed a washcloth and scrubbed at the blood on his face.

"Are you kidding?" Hope said. "You're sweaty; you need a shower. This bathroom is gorgeous." She grinned. "So, I need one too." Hope pulled the borrowed shirt over her head and let it drop to the floor. Devon's throat bobbed.

"You go first." He put his hands under the tap, wincing at the first contact of water.

"I don't want to go first," she said, walking up behind him and wrapping her arms around his waist. Hope pressed her breasts into his back and planted a kiss on the wolf's brow between his shoulder blades. "Come with me." Devon stiffened, his eyes meeting hers in the mirror before he went back to scrubbing.

"Look," he said carefully. "It's not that I don't want to get naked with you. It's just that I know where that's going to lead, and I'm in a weird headspace."

"Like a *playroom* headspace?" She felt a shudder go through him.

"No," he bit out.

"Well..." Hope considered. "Good thing we left the playroom, then. Come on." She hooked an arm through his and pulled him toward the shower, grateful when he turned off the faucet and reluctantly followed. "You aren't the only one awake and looking for an outlet, you know," she tossed over her shoulder, as she opened the glass door and spied the controls.

Hope twisted a knob. Water shot out of the lower showerheads. Great for getting everything from her crotch down squeaky clean, but she wanted an actual shower. She reached for another dial which must have controlled the temperature because nothing else started spraying.

"You went into... you went in there looking for *an outlet*?" he said, from behind her.

"Do you need a license to operate this thing?" Hope muttered as she twisted something else. The bottom jets shifted to a pulsating massage rhythm. "Whoa... That's cool." She switched it back. "I went looking for you, silly."

"In the playroom?" he said, tone incredulous.

"The *where* didn't matter. I woke up and you weren't in bed, and..." She glanced back at him. "I needed you. Figured I'd take a peek in there before I went looking somewhere else. Then once the lights were on, I thought maybe I could look around a little." The sound of spraying water filled the silence between them. Then, Hope heard a rustling of fabric and felt Devon, warm and naked at her back.

"I've got it," he said in her ear, reaching past her.

With a few twists, the lower showerheads stopped spraying, and water began falling from above. Then, he was turning her to face him, his mouth finding hers, as he backed her into the shower. Hot water rained over them, as his hands slid down her hips, cupped her breasts, skimmed up her neck and cradled her head. He was everywhere. Soft and stroking. Her body buzzed with pleasure. Devon scooped an arm around her waist, and with a quick lift, he sat her on the edge of a floating shelf, smiling at her wickedly as he sank to his knees. No wonder he'd killed those extra shower heads, she thought absurdly. He would have drowned down there.

"Devon…" she whimpered, as he spread her thighs and dropped his head between them. "Oh God, Devon…" Water poured over her breasts, her stomach, soaking his dark hair. He stared up at her—hazel eyes locking on hers as he licked and sucked. The licking. The sucking. The world pitched, as Hope's breath caught on the edge of release.

And then, he stopped.

"I built this shelf to my own specifications," he said proudly, pressing lazy kisses up one thigh, across her pubic bone, and down the other.

Hope panted.

"I've always wanted to try it out." He sucked at her clit, swirling his tongue against her as he did. Her hands slid off the walls of the shower, his solid grip on her thighs the only thing that kept her on her perch.

"Fuck," she breathed.

"I've got you," he said, voice husky, lips brushing against her.

"What…what specifications?" she stammered, hoping like hell that this shelf was built for fucking.

Grinning, Devon stood and stepped into her, scooping his erection up against his belly as he did. "Well," he purred, sliding the shaft of his cock against her slick, wet sex in a manner that made her forget her question entirely. Oh… wait… penetration. P in V. Please, in the name of all things holy, bury your cock in me and pound repeatedly until— "If I measured correctly," he said, "this shelf should be about the same height as your bathroom counter, but with legroom underneath." He rocked his hard length against her again. "Mmm… Things are going to line up nicely, don't you think?" Hope made a sound lost somewhere between a whimper and a moan. Devon clicked his tongue, sending shivers through her. "Impatient little…" he trailed off, stopped sliding against her, froze with his mouth inches from the curve of her neck.

"Devon?" Hope said, registering the abrupt shift in him.

He backed away to look at her. "Can I have you in my bed?" he said, water dripping off his chin and the tip of his nose. "We can take another shower tomorrow, but… Can I just… Can I…"

"Take me anywhere," she whispered. And she meant it. She'd go anywhere tonight, so long as he went with her.

Devon carried her to his bed, a minute later. Laid her out as if she were something precious. Skimmed his hands, his mouth, over her still damp body. Hope arched and moaned, on the razor's edge of release, even though he wasn't touching her in the places guaranteed to bring it. Then, he was rolling on a condom and sliding into her. Slowly. Looking her in the eye for every inch of that first glorious stroke, like he wanted to savor it. Savor *her*. Hope's entire body shuddered with pleasure.

"I've never wanted anyone the way I want you," he said in a guttural voice, as he pushed into her. Another stroke, another confession. "It terrifies me."

Lost in the sensation of him deep inside her, the near desperate need in his words, Hope's only response was to whisper his name and beg him not to stop. "Please..." she breathed. "Please... Devon... Please, Sir..." Never, *never* stop.

As he found her hands, his eyes flashed to hers, pushing them gently, insistently, up, up, up above her head. The weight of him pinned her there, stretched out and open for him in every way imaginable. Only for him. And when Hope found her release, Devon tumbled over the edge with her.

HOPE

Hope didn't have to work on Sunday, but Devon needed to be at Cleary's by eleven. Okay, technically ten, but he said that eleven was close enough. It was the only thing that got them out of bed. He brought her clothes up from the basement, warm after an extra five-minute turn in the dryer, and Hope burrowed into toasty-clean goodness that smelled like him.

"I'm not trying to be domineering," he said, as they got in his car. Hope cocked a brow. "Hey, I said *trying*. I'm a Dom; it's hard." Hope snickered; Devon sighed. "He's tracked you down at home or work how many times in the last few weeks?" he asked. "You could hang out at my place until I get off. Seriously, I'll turn around, right now. It's not a problem."

Hope smiled, indulgently. She felt lighter after their conversation the day before, but it hadn't had the same cathartic effect on Devon. "What's he going to do? Try to embarrass me? It sucks, but who's he going to badmouth me to? I already told you about...everything. If Aaron wanted to find me at your house, he could get your address. He's not that level of crazy, though. Just the annoying sort that doesn't respond well to not getting his way. He drops in when he's driving past and thinks of me."

Although, if Hope were being honest with herself, the planning involved in leaving roses on her doorstep on the anniversary of the day she left him felt different from stopping by because he happened to be in her neighborhood or saw her on the street.

"What makes you think he would look for you at my house?" Devon asked. "How would he even know where I live?"

Hope shrugged. "He knows where you work, and what you look like. I'd be surprised if he doesn't know your name. If he doesn't already know where you live, he could find out. He's a cop." She reminded him, as Aaron had reminded her. "That was the thing that really got me about that card—the threat in it. He knows where to find you. I won't be surprised if he tries to talk to you, screw this up for me. He'd love that."

Realizing the tone of her babbling, Hope's cheeks burned. Once she started talking to Devon, she often said more than she intended. Regardless of what he might say during 4 a.m. sex, this was broad daylight, and she was putting a lot of pressure on this new thing they had going.

"Not that this has to be a long-term thing..." she added. "Or *not* a long-term thing..." Well, crap, she thought as she trailed off. That didn't make it any better. In for a penny, in for a pound, Hope went back to digging. "I wasn't trying to say—"

"Wait," Devon said, as if he'd missed everything after *Aaron knows who you are*. He downshifted rather aggressively, and the engine sent a *WTF are we doing?* vibrating through Hope's seat.

"You think he's going to try to talk to me? Like show up at Cleary's or *my house*, and tell me that my girlfriend liked to be handcuffed, but he fucked it up? Because that isn't going to work out how—"

Hope laughed.

"That isn't funny," Devon said. "It won't go well for him for a lot of reasons, and several of them are going to get me arrested."

Hope turned to face him. His eyes smoldered with rage, as he glared out the windshield, but in typical Devon fashion, he had it on a tight leash. That was his true dominant side, she thought. Not Demon, who wanted a playroom full of implements of pleasure and torture, and had no patience for irritation, but the other side. The side that could, and did, bring Demon to heel. Wield every skill in Demon's arsenal to get what Devon wanted, or what he knew was needed out of a situation. Power and control. When he wasn't splitting his knuckles on a bag in the basement.

"You called me your girlfriend," she said.

He kept staring straight ahead, pulled in a steadying breath. "Did I?"

"Pretty sure you did."

"How would you feel about that?" he asked. "Assuming your ears aren't playing tricks on you."

Hope noted the flutters in her tummy, her flushed cheeks and happy heart. "Good," she said simply.

"Good enough to indulge me by not staying at your place alone for a few days?" She watched him glance at her from the corner of his eye, as he put on a turn signal. Hope chuckled.

"I think we can work something out. Chloe and I were going to get together, anyway. Gotta catch her up on the drama. I'll chill across the hall with her until you get off, then I'll pack a bag and head your way for a sleepover. We still have to test out that shower shelf properly." Devon cracked a smile. "We can take it a day at a time," Hope promised.

"I can live with that plan."

"Can you, Sir?" she said playfully.

Devon shifted in his seat and reached for the stick. "Mmm... Careful, darling," he warned, sliding into third.

***

When Hope knocked on Chloe's door with Devon at her side, an overnight bag of Hope's things slung over his shoulder, Chloe didn't ask why. Devon had offered to help her get her stuff together—something Hope pegged as an effort to not have her alone in her apartment once he went to the bar. It was an easy enough request to honor when she could see the tension in him. He didn't like leaving her anywhere Aaron might look for her.

Since Cleary's closed at 2 a.m. on the weekends and Hope had her own opening shift at Silver Sassafras the next morning, Devon stuck his spare key in her purse. Hope tried telling him that wasn't necessary. Giving him a key to lock up felt different than him giving her a key to get in, when he wasn't even home. She was grateful when he insisted, though. She would be a zombie at work if she didn't get to bed before he got off.

"You look all kinds of satisfied," Chloe said, sipping her coffee, "when you aren't looking all kinds of anxious. So, what's the scoop?"

Hope sighed. "Devon is amazing, and Aaron is awful."

"Fair enough. Want to talk about it?" Chloe folded her fuzzy-sock clad feet up under her on the couch, as Hope fiddled with the mug in her hands.

"I wish I'd met Devon first, but I'm also not sure that would've kicked off if I hadn't met Aaron first. Does that make sense?"

Chloe nodded. "Totally. Experiences change us. Good or bad... We evolve, right?"

"I think he really likes me," Hope said.

"Of course, he does. He also seems pretty concerned about you," Chloe added.

Hope shrugged. "I guess."

"He waited for you to pack." Chloe pointed at the overnight bag in the corner. "And we usually hang out in your apartment. You're the homebody."

Hope looked at the bag, then back to her friend. "Can I tell you some stuff, and like... not have you judge me for it?"

"Have you met me?" Chloe said, with a smile.

They talked about everything. The way her relationship with Aaron evolved, the things about it that were so confusing or intoxicating that they kept her with him even as she fell apart as a person. Everyone found Aaron intoxicating when he wanted them to. Except for JJ, Hope's family would be thrilled if she and Aaron got back together. Probably unfair to judge them on that when they were missing vital information, but come on... Was a little parental support so much to ask?

Hope eventually told Chloe about the awful night when she'd told him her news of landing her dream-job counseling position in Asheville, only to have Aaron throw her around and handcuff her. Chloe listened silently with a pained expression, handing over a box of tissues when Hope began to cry.

Hope couldn't remember what transpired to get her out of that situation. The shock of him grabbing her and the *snicking* of the handcuffs tightening were crystal clear. Those memories still made her flinch when doors locked, or someone shifted toward her sometimes. They caused her pulse to race as she recounted the tale to Chloe. But getting off the floor? Driving home? *Nothing.* She made it home that night, but the *how* had vanished.

She hadn't mentioned that to Devon because she hadn't thought of it. But talking to him had helped her get to this place where she could talk to Chloe, and the longer she talked, the more she remembered—or realized that she couldn't remember about that night.

Hope hadn't forgotten a single detail of what happened afterward, though. It took her days to get up the nerve to report him. Maybe it would have been different if the cop taking her statement hadn't known Aaron, but he did. Some police departments are incestuous dens of good ol' boys. His disruptive chuckles stoked her unease. His blatant eye-rolling made her want to disappear. Her tale came out in an incoherent mishmash of emotional nonsense, and Hope knew the gist of what he would say the moment he put his pen down and stared at her.

Her suspicion was spot on.

I don't think you're lying intentionally...

His isn't the only reputation on the line here...

Do you think he was just upset? I mean, you did throw him one hell of a curveball. He's not a violent guy...

Men get passionate...

These little bruises aren't much to go on. You should hear my wife go on about all her little bruises and having no idea where she got them. Do you have anything more substantial?

Are you sure you aren't just mad at him?

Hope explained to Chloe how she had muttered an apology for wasting his time, gathered her things, and left. The cop made it seem like she was being irrational, overreacting, but things never felt quite safe again. Aaron kept calling, texting, showing up to Christmas... Hope moved, and he still didn't go away. Like the time he'd shown up at her apartment with wine... All the other places he'd shown up, *still* showed up.... The things he said or did to torment her... All of it found a place in the story.

And then, they made it to Devon.

Discussing Devon felt like a balm over all the invisible parts of her that Aaron left raw. Because Devon *was* kind and considerate. It wasn't a mask he took off when no one was watching. Seeing him at the nonprofit, or with his mom. Watching him try *so* hard to sell her on Apollo, who sported innumerable scars but even more love. And the sex, despite being something she needed, was the kind of rough that Hope wouldn't be able to handle if she didn't trust him down to her marrow. That felt like a balm too. Devon could sense her discomfort as surely as he could sense the edge of her release. And while he drove her wild toying with the latter, the former brought him up short with the most sincere concern she had ever felt from a partner.

Chloe hung in through the whole, convoluted mess. By the time Hope stopped talking, they had killed a pot of coffee, bag of microwave popcorn, sleeve of Oreos, pint of salted caramel ice cream, and half a box of tissues.

Hope stared at the aftermath on the coffee table. So many tissues. "Sorry," she said. "I think I needed to get that out."

Chloe took a deep breath and got to her feet. "Stand up so I can hug you." Hope stood and found herself pulled into one of Chloe's impressively strong embraces. The kind of squeeze that fused broken pieces back together. "It is not your fault that Aaron is the way he is," Chloe said, holding her close. "It's not your fault that he's treated you the way he has. And I know you've been through some shit, but if Devon is good to you, and you're happy, you *enjoy* that. You deserve to have someone treat you like you matter and worry about you and bust his knuckles on punching bags at three a.m. because someone hurt you and he can't go back and stop it."

"It turns out that I'm kind of a mess," Hope said, with a sniff.

Chloe laughed and squeezed her tighter. "Oh honey, we all are. Didn't they teach you that in school?"

Hope laughed too. "He was supposed to be for fun," she said, backing away a fraction. Both women laughed. Hope wiped away more tears.

"I'm glad you're talking..." Chloe trailed off as a loud knocking sounded out in the hall.

Hope's gut did a weird oily-liquid thing, and bile rose in the back of her throat. She quickly stepped back from Chloe and put a finger to her lips in the universal request for silence. The knocking escalated to pounding as they crept toward the apartment door. Hope desperately wanted it to be anyone else, but she knew who she was going to see before she put her eye to the peephole.

Aaron stood with his back to them. He wore street clothes and held a large yellow envelope in one hand, rapping the other fist on the door of Hope's apartment. All Hope could think was that she was so, so grateful that Devon was a little overprotective. Looking to Chloe, she mouthed *It's him,* then put her finger to her lips again. Chloe's eyes went wide.

"I know you're in there," Aaron called. He was wrong, of course, but being so close to him while he yelled and pounded chilled her to the core. "Your car is outside," he snapped.

Chloe and Hope looked at each other wordlessly as another round of banging sounded out.

"Open the damn door, Hope."

Even the air moving in and out of her lungs felt too loud. A cold sweat washed over her skin, and Hope reminded herself that Aaron couldn't hear her pounding heart.

"Fine. Have it your way, but you might want to come get these before a neighbor picks them up. Maybe they'll jog your memory."

Hope peeked back out the peephole in time to watch him throw the envelope at her apartment door. It clattered to the floor, sliding to a stop half on her welcome mat, half on the tile, as Aaron stalked down the stairs. Behind her, Chloe rushed to a front window to watch him go.

"What the fuck was that?" Chloe demanded, peeking through the blinds.

"I need to get that envelope," Hope said.

"You have to call the cops." Chloe's brown eyes were wide, worried, and insistent.

"That's why he's doing this. Last time he came to Silver Sassafras, I threatened to report him if he didn't leave me alone. He knows how it went when I spoke to the cops in Charlotte. I can't do that again," Hope said, unlocking the door with shaking hands. "Is he gone?"

Chloe looked back and forth between the window and Hope. "Yeah, but—"

"Just yell if he turns around. It'll only take a second." Hope ducked into the hallway, grabbed the envelope, and retreated to Chloe's apartment again, locking the door behind her.

"You need to report this," Chloe repeated.

Ignoring her friend, Hope flipped over the envelope with her name scrawled on the front in black marker, and unfastened the metal tab. She reached inside and pulled out a stack of... Hope put a hand over her mouth, looking back up to Chloe.

"What is it? You're white as a sheet. Hope, what is that?"

DEVON

"Uh oh..." Nix said, as Devon put his back into it.

"What the fuck is this? I've seen glossier gravel. Did you wipe this down last night or did Lucas?"

"I'm not telling," Nix said, smugly. "He closed by himself again, by the way. Didn't ask me a single question. He's more than ready. Don't you miss being able to take the same night off occasionally?" Devon gave a noncommittal grunt.

Since his last manager moved on two years into this business venture, and Devon hired Nix to fill the void, they hadn't been in the local dungeon together for more than the odd hour or two after Cleary's closed. Edge didn't serve alcohol, so no one was shutting them down in the wee hours like the bars; however, that still didn't leave a lot of time. How he and Nix had managed this long without a third closer, Devon had no idea. A combination of luck and his stubborn streak, most likely.

But Devon hadn't been to Edge in six months or more, and that wasn't likely to change if the thing with Hope didn't crash and burn. Fuck... He didn't want to think about that. Devon had a wicked bad feeling that if Hope left the equation, he'd be breaking down the dungeon doors as soon as he was sober enough to top—and he'd probably do enough damage to his bar that he'd need to refinish it.

He didn't need to go now though, he told himself. Not really.

"Did he put some weird cleaner on here?" he groused. "Did you?"

Nix rolled her eyes. "There's nothing wrong with your bar, Dev, but your knuckles look like you went a few rounds with a meat grinder. How about we chat about that?"

"Forgot to tape them. It's nothing," he said, the same broken record he'd played for Hope in the early morning hours. He tensed, as Nix rested a hand on his shoulder.

"Hey..." She sounded way too sympathetic. "You okay?"

Devon shrugged her off. "I'm fine."

"He said in a voice that was definitely not fine..." Nix narrated to no one.

Devon put the towel down and turned to face her, throwing up his hands. "I don't know how to do this, okay?"

Nix leaned an elbow against the bar and settled in.

Devon glanced around the mostly empty space. They were between the lunch and dinner crowd, with little to distract him. "You should probably—"

"Stand here until you talk," Nix said. "Now, get back to scrubbing. You're better with the touchy-feely when your hands are busy, and you don't feel like you need to look at me."

She was right, of course. Most people were that way if you paid attention. It's why he had put Hope in a blindfold the day before. Why he'd tied her wrists and given her something to tug against—take the pressure off, but with the kind of flavor that would make that darling little sub in her want to comply.

And sure, it worked, but Devon still wondered if the whole thing hadn't been a mistake. The stuff Hope said sat in his brain like acid—a fantastic addition to all the sharp edges he had going on. He'd literally restrained her to get a story about some asshole forcefully restraining her. Fucking perfect... Devon sighed, picked up the towel, and began slowly wiping the bar which maybe wasn't as neglected as he'd originally thought.

"Hope has an ex," he said.

"Most people do, by our age," Nix replied. He could hear her smirk, and it grated on his nerves.

"Yeah well, her ex won't leave her alone, and he's a cop. And he won't leave her alone," Devon said.

"You said that twice."

He flipped his gaze to Nix. "I need him to leave her alone," he bit out.

Nix nodded. "That sounds pretty normal, especially for someone like you."

"Doesn't feel normal," Devon grumbled, turning his attention back to the job in front of him. "I want to hurt something."

"Ah," Nix said knowingly.

"Not her," he added. "I just— Everything is—"

His knuckles stung as warm wetness ran between his bird and ring finger. Devon looked down at the brilliant red staining the white cloth clenched in his fist. Cursing under his breath, he threw it in the trash. "I've got to go deal with this."

"Come on, I'll help," Nix offered, pushing off the bar.

"No, you stay here."

"Boss Woman! Boss Man!" Lucas shouted in greeting, as he burst through the front door, still buttoning his black button-down.

Devon and Nix glanced sidelong toward each other.

"*Lucas* will take the bar," Nix said, parking her tongue ring in the corner of her mouth, smug as a cat with cream. "I'll help you sort out your hands before the health department shuts us down."

Devon bitched all the way to the office, even though he knew she was right. He'd slap some tape over bare skin and call it a day... then rip everything open again when he pulled it off. Nix, on the other hand, would get fancy with the ointment and gauze. While Devon appreciated good wound care as much as the next guy, he knew that once she got him alone in the office, she'd go poking at *all* his wounds. Nix was tenacious about that sort of thing, and Devon was exhausted.

When the door latched, he didn't give her a chance to initiate.

"I like her, okay?" he said, as Nix dug out the first aid kit and set it on the desk.

"Um... okay. We've established that."

"No, I *really* like her," he repeated, thinking Nix didn't get it. She couldn't.

"I'm not oblivious," she said, unzipping the case and gathering supplies. Devon paced back and forth in the small office, running his non-leaking hand through his hair.

"And her ex fucked up," he growled because it wouldn't stay in any longer.

Nix stopped organizing, and focused on him, realization washing over her face. "You think he's why she's... What did you say?"

"Flinchy," he snapped. "Yeah, he's the fucking reason. And I knew that in my gut, but now I *know* it—and that makes it a hell of a lot harder to ignore." Devon paced some more, struggling to get a handle on the agitation inching into full-blown rage territory. "I want to—" His hands contorted into claws that wanted to wrap around a throat and squeeze.

"Sit," Nix said, patting the desk. "Let me see." Devon scowled, but he flopped into the office chair and put both hands on the desktop. Nix cringed, as she started poking around the wounds. "I'd say you need stitches for some of this but..."

"I'd split them anyway. Do what you can with it."

"You know you can't actually murder her ex, right?" Nix said, leaning over for a better look. Devon rolled his eyes, an action that went unseen as she studied his hands. "For what it's worth," she said, dabbing a clean gauze pad to the fresh blood, "I don't think it's all that abnormal that you want to."

"It's just that..." He searched for a way to articulate his fears without sounding irrational, but the words didn't come easily. "She said things started out good between them, but he got controlling, and eventually violent."

"Do you worry she'll regret you someday, like she regrets him?" Nix asked.

"No," Devon shot back. "I mean... I'm not going to fuck up like he did. I just—" He hissed, as Nix spritzed his open wounds with a bottled incendiary. "Christ, what is that?"

"Ammonia," she said dryly. "It's an antiseptic, crybaby...but sorry. Last thing you need is freaking gangrene, so this is where we are. I'll warn you next time."

As Nix's hands tended his own, Devon pretended that anything he said was going into a vault. "I want to be right for her," he said. "I'm doing the best I can, but I think she needs someone... better."

He watched her body swell and contract with a breath. "You mean someone normal," she said. "Don't worry, I'll ignore the personal insult."

Devon bounced his heel under the desk. "I mean someone who could fix it."

"It's her life. You can't fix it for her. If you two want to make a go of it, your job is to support her. Give her what she needs to thrive. That's her job for you too, by the way."

"She's amazing."

"You deserve someone amazing." Nix finished taping the first set of knuckles and started on the second.

"Doesn't feel like I deserve her," he mumbled. Nix sighed and shook her head. Devon swallowed hard, wet his lips. "I don't know if I can—" He closed his mouth, opened it, and tried again. "I'm worried I'll need—" He looked at Nix, waiting for her to understand, and because she got him in ways no one else could, she pressed her mouth into a tight smile.

"I told you that would be a problem," she said, without censure.

"I know. You win." He pinched the bridge of his nose with his already bandaged hand. "I didn't expect everything to get this complicated so fast."

"It's been what, six months since you had a scene? Acid rain incoming." She sprayed, and he cursed low and hard.

"Yeah," Devon agreed when his eyes stopped watering.

"And you're under a lot of stress," Nix continued. He shrugged, refusing to acknowledge the energy crackling and arcing under his skin—begging for an adequate outlet.

"This is a hard time of year for me, anyway," Devon said. He didn't bother reminding her that it would get worse before it got better. For nearly two decades, January had been a nightmare for Devon, and it had a way of showing up right after December every freaking year. "Hope adds a new layer," he said. "A *current* layer... Her ex was emotionally and physically abusive. He's stalking her, even if she won't call it that, and I don't think I'd make it if something happened to her." He ran a hand through his hair, frowning when the tape caught. "I know that sounds ridiculous. I just... Yeah... I'm feeling a little stressed. I can't go work this out at Edge, though, and nothing else is cutting it."

"You need a night out, Dev," Nix said. "Minnie asked about you again. She misses you."

Devon looked to the ceiling. "Minnie misses having a guy to hang on that won't push for more."

Nix dropped that approach, unable to argue with the truth. "Look," she said, "you're a hairsbreadth away from a Pub Night, and you'll end up at Edge after that, anyway. Edge is the better option. Be proactive."

Devon's heel stopped bouncing, as he willed his body still. He had to find a way to do this. His magical reset button for all things bullshit used to be a trip to Edge and/or a trip to his playroom with someone who could handle what he needed to purge, but it had gotten increasingly harder to get a release out of either of those in the last year. Sure, he could get off no problem, but that *other* release? The one he really, *really* needed... That stayed out of reach.

And the only thing more frustrating than not being able to squeeze out an orgasm when you wanted was working up a sweat swinging a cane, only to feel...*nothing*. No, worse than nothing. The same bullshit you tried to beat into submission but with a side of filthy, noxious shame.

"It doesn't feel right anymore," he said. "Even before I started seeing Hope, it got...*wrong*. I'm not going to risk it when I've got this thing going with her. I *know* that works."

Nix pursed her lips, and Devon watched the gears turn. "Have you considered taking her with you?"

"To Edge?" He laughed in an incredulous burst, then, realizing she was serious, stared in horror.

"What?" Nix asked as if she hadn't just suggested he take Hope to a public dungeon. "She's subby," she said, with a shrug.

"She flinches if she thinks I'm annoyed," Devon countered. "She's seen the inside of the playroom twice, and I think *I* have mild PTSD over it. The closest I've gotten to running a scene with her was a conversation that I regret." He shook his head. "I'm not taking her to a dungeon to watch me top for someone else. You know how that goes, Nix."

"I didn't suggest topping someone else."

"Then what would be the point in taking her? She couldn't handle—" Devon slammed his mouth shut, but the truth sat leaden on the tip of his tongue. *She couldn't handle the scene I need.* All the times he'd told her he didn't need more than she could give, but there it was. "I... uh... I'm rougher at Edge than I am with her, and I don't know how she'd feel about watching me top someone else. I don't know how I'd feel about it either," he said.

Except he did. The idea of Hope watching him in his element at Edge... Seeing the perverse satisfaction he took... He pictured her sweet face, confused, then disgusted, as the image she held of him shattered into a million tiny fragments.

"You could tone down the scene," Nix said.

"No. I'll figure it out, but Edge is off the table."

"If you say so." She sounded unconvinced.

Devon's phone buzzed in his pocket, and he pulled it out. He quickly read the cryptic text from Hope about how she was heading to his place early, and to wake her up when he got home because she needed to talk to him. Then there was the *Really, everything is fine* that came on its heels.

"What's wrong?" Nix asked, reading the concern on his face.

"I don't know, but I'm not waiting until after closing to find out. Tell Lucas that he's losing the training wheels tonight. He better not burn down my bar."

"He's more than ready," Nix said.

Devon shook his head. "He better be."

HOPE

Hope relocked Devon's door, then settled on the couch with Apollo. The dog had adopted Hope in the same way his owner had adopted him—Completely—and Hope appreciated the devotion on such a miserable day. His furry affection didn't slow the maddening wheels in her brain, though. She had to tell Devon. Even though it would only increase his level of concern. Even though it made her ignore-Aaron-until-he-calms-down approach a harder sell.

Chloe heard Aaron's theatrics, and Hope told her the gist of what that envelope held, though she hadn't shown her the contents. Her friend would bite her tongue around Devon if asked, but that was a crappy position to put Chloe in and a terrible precedent to set in a relationship.

Another reason that the Cut and Run technique was a winner. If Hope didn't have those pesky tangled attachments, she could ignore Aaron until he left her in peace...in peace.

But Chloe and Devon weren't completely off base either. Red flags were flying, and Aaron didn't seem to be letting up so quickly this time. Hope's stomach rolled at the thought of the envelope shoved into the bottom of her bag. How did he have those? What if he shared them?

Tears spilling down her cheeks, Hope sank into a bone-deep weariness. She wanted a shower—wanted to scrub until her skin went pink, but she felt clean again. Then maybe catch a few hours of sleep before Devon made it home.

Leaving Apollo to his own devices, Hope stashed her overnight bag on Devon's bed, and headed for the bathroom. She stepped under the spray, imagining the water rinsing away every grimy, terrible thing. Soothing heat soaked deep, making her think of Devon.

If he were there, she'd wash it all away in another way entirely. Crash into him. Feel the strength of him, the power. Let him take her against the shower wall, hard and fast until her lungs burned, and her core ached from his relentless—

The soft knock at the bathroom door brought her head around and her heart into her throat.

"Hope?" Devon said, through the crack.

Her adrenaline spike crested and fell like a wave. "Come in," she called, sliding a hand across the glass to see him. "You're home early."

"I thought you might need me. Sorry, that's…" He trailed off, dragging a bandaged hand through his hair.

The scent of cedar and sandalwood whispered through the steam, stoking the thoughts his knock interrupted. And maybe it was selfish to use him like that, before telling him stuff he deserved to know, but it wouldn't stop her.

"I do," she admitted, a sharp edge to her voice. "I need you now. I'm so glad you're home."

Hope watched the pronounced rise and fall of his chest for two breaths before he began shucking clothes on his way toward her. Then, he was in the shower with her, wrapping his arms around her, nothing but water between them as he kissed her.

"Fuck," he said, pulling away. "I don't—"

"Please..." Hope whimpered, voice dripping desperation.

Her plea flipped a switch in him. Hope's back hit the shower wall hard, and his hand shot into her hair. With a sharp yank, Devon gained access to her throat, nipping and sucking his way from her ear to her shoulder. He sank his teeth into her flesh at the same moment he hitched one of her legs over his hip and buried his cock.

Hope cried out, a blurry mix of pleasure and pain, as an orgasm ripped through her without warning. No build up. No climb to the precipice. It blossomed and exploded, like the two-part beat of a heart. Devon kept her upright and kept pumping.

Hope shifted her position, wrapping her other leg around his waist. Desperate for more, she hooked her ankles behind his back. She wasn't even sitting on the shelf; they hadn't made it to that side of the shower. Digging her nails into his shoulders, she urged him on. *Harder. Faster. Do it again.* A second orgasm had her crying his name, and then, Devon's hand slid from the back of her head to her throat. He squeezed until her eyes watered.

"Feet on the floor," he growled in her ear. "Now."

Devon stepped back from her, slid out of her, as she complied. Keeping one hand on her throat, the other gripped his cock. His hazel gaze settled on her face, but Hope's eyes flicked hungrily over the entirety of him. That burning expression. The corded muscles of his inked forearm as he stroked himself. Tip to base, and back again. Over and over. Pleasure smoldered in his eyes. Devon's body shuddered, and the hand at her throat tightened as he neared his release. The sight nearly put Hope over the edge again. And then he came—milky-white jets shooting across her belly, before running down her sex and thighs with the rivulets of water coursing over her skin.

Devon released her and put his forearm on the wall by her head, bringing them close again. "I—" He closed his eyes tight and panted. "Are you okay?" he asked, gruffly.

"Better now," she breathed.

"Okay," he said, with audible relief. He pressed kiss after kiss to her cheeks and brow. "Okay."

***

Devon vigorously scrubbed the towel over his hair, swiped it down his body, then spent about fifteen seconds peeling off the saturated bandages on his knuckles and tossing them in the wastebasket. When nothing started bleeding, he seemed satisfied.

"I'll find you clothes, while you dry off," he said, pressing another kiss to her cheek on his way out the door.

After dealing with the near-gallon of water in her hair, Hope strolled into his bedroom in her birthday suit. Devon stood, naked to the waist, and elbow-deep in her bag. A navy sweater that she'd never seen before sat on the bed beside him, and next to that, the envelope from Aaron—the one she'd all but forgotten while fucking her lover in the shower. Heat inched up her chest and face.

"What are you doing?" she asked. Devon looked up with a smile, pulling out her yoga pants as he lifted his dark head.

"I was going to give you one of my sweaters, but I thought you might need pants. It's chilly."

Hope instinctively looked from him to the envelope, and back. And because he was Devon, he didn't miss it. She watched the light go out of his eyes and suspicion take its place.

"Wasn't there something you wanted to talk about?" he said, casually picking up the envelope, but stopping short of putting it back in her bag. "You were very distracting in the shower, but your text... You said to wake you up when I got home so—"

Hope marched across the room, snatched the envelope from his hand, and shoved it back in her bag. Digging a sweatshirt from its depths, she began yanking on clothes. Devon's brow furrowed in hurt or confusion that Hope refused to acknowledge.

"Did I do something wrong?" he asked. Then, his eyes widened, distress plain on his face. "The shower? Was that..."

Hope wanted to scream, and she didn't even know why.

"I don't like it when people dig around in my stuff," she snapped.

"Okay. Sorry," he said carefully. "I'll stay out of your bag." He paused for a breath. "If it matters, I didn't look in that envelope," he added like someone trying to defuse a bomb. It didn't make Hope feel *defused* at all.

"Good," she bit out. "It's from Aaron, since you're going to ask. He came by my apartment today. And *no*, I didn't talk to him. We let him bang on the door then leave. So that's what I would have told you if you'd given me a chance."

"What's in it?" The fact that Devon responded to what had happened with Aaron instead of her current meltdown made her blood boil for some absurd reason.

"Stuff I don't want people to see," Hope said, glaring at him. "Which is why I don't like coming in to find you digging through my stuff."

Devon's face paled, and he breathed faster, but his affect remained intentionally calm. Hope hated *intentionally calm*. It felt like coddling. Condescension because she was *so* dramatic and prone to overreaction. Everything her family said about her when she didn't come to dinner. *You know how Hope is. Poor Aaron having to put up with her tantrums... That man is a saint.* A saint who throws stuff and slings you around when he's pissed off. A saint who keeps secret pictures of your most private moments and uses them to torment you when he doesn't get to have you anymore.

Hope looked around Devon's ordered bedroom. Light wood furniture, dark grey comforter, and Apollo's bed in the corner.

Nothing out of place. Her overnight bag sat in the middle, like a container of chaos.

"Do you think it's time to file something?" Devon asked. "An order of protection or... Hope, this is getting out of hand," he said.

"No, *you* are getting out of hand." She jabbed a finger at him. "You and Chloe act like I can't figure this out. You're making it worse. I was fine before you two turned this into something it isn't. You don't even want me to stay in my own apartment. Do you realize how paranoid that sounds? He wasn't bothering me anymore before I started going out with you. Not really..."

Hope wasn't sure how she'd ended up yelling at the person that she'd been using to scour away all her worries ten minutes earlier, but she couldn't pull out of the tailspin. She wasn't even mad at Devon. He was just *there*, saying all the rational things that made her rage harder because, a year after breaking up with Aaron, she still hadn't managed to make him leave her alone.

Devon threw up his hands in exasperation, but they didn't stay there long. "No one is saying you can't handle your shit, Hope. But my fucking God... He keeps showing up where you are," he said, gesturing wildly to her—to *everything*—between dragging his hands through his hair. "And now he's leaving you flowers and cards and whatever the fuck is in that envelope that you don't want anyone to see. *Christ*, Hope. I'm about to have a fucking aneurysm because I'm worried that he'll snap and kill you. He could *kill* you. And like you said, it'll be my fault because he wasn't a problem until I came around."

"This isn't about you," she hissed.

"Then why are you trying to say that it is?" he all but shouted back at her, driving his point home by drumming a hand on his bare chest. "Is it all my fault because I took you on a date and started... Fuck. I don't even know." Devon let out a sound that would've passed for a laugh if she couldn't see him. "Or is it *not* about me, and he's just another violent ex who is still stalking you *a year* after you broke up with him?" His cheeks flushed with color. "I have to say something, Hope. You have to understand that I can't watch him do these things and keep my mouth shut like it isn't my goddamn business."

It should have been easy for Hope to back off her line, in that moment. Meet him halfway. His fear for her safety was so solid that she could have reached out and brushed her fingers against it.

But she didn't.

"You know what? Forget it," she spat. "This is pointless. I'm going home."

"Wait..." Devon took a single step toward her, hands reaching.

"I said, I'm leaving," she snarled. "Do I need to use a safeword for you to let me go?"

He froze, mouth open but mute. His surrender didn't stop her.

"I don't have room for your dominant bullshit, here." Another line delivered with the cruel efficiency of a scalpel slice. Hope watched it gut him and told herself that she didn't care that he was in pieces.

"Please," he finally managed, "don't go." His tone, the polar opposite of dominant made her feel oddly powerful, and her next response came out with all the grace of a spoiled teenager who knows no one can enforce the rules.

"Look, it's been a weird day, and I want my own space. Sorry I came over. This was a mistake."

"I can sleep on the couch," Devon offered. "I'll leave you to whatever room you want and make myself busy somewhere else."

Hope shouldered her bag and started walking. "I'll call you tomorrow," she said, as Devon trailed her through the house. "After work." Finding her shoes by the door, she slipped them on.

"Stay with Chloe," he pleaded. "Be mad at me all you want but be safe. Hate me; it's fine. But I'm begging you, please take this seriously. Please..."

Hope froze with her hand on the door. She only needed to twist the deadbolt, the lock on the knob, then go. But between one heartbeat and the next, something strange happened. She stopped being mad, and instead felt very, very...*sad*. Tears brimmed in her eyes and spilled down her cheeks in the same way that first orgasm had taken her in the shower—without hesitation. A sob came with them. She couldn't stop it. She couldn't hold it in. The bag slipped from her shoulder, and gentle hands turned her around.

"Hey, there," Devon said, softly, carefully.

Hope's unfocused gaze settled on the space between them. She felt so tired, and sad, and...*lost*. Walking away from people had never made her feel lost before, but this time—

"Is it okay if I get you now?" he asked, his words all honey and whiskey warmth. "Because I really want to get you."

Hope relented with a nod, and Devon instantly wrapped her up, holding her like he needed her touch as desperately as she needed his. He pressed a kiss atop her head, as her body shook with sobs.

"I'm sorry," she cried. "You didn't do anything. That wasn't fair."

Devon stroked a hand up and down her back. "I'm fine. We're fine."

"They're pictures," she said into his chest. "Pictures of me."

Devon tensed but kept stroking her back. "Hey, we can handle that," he assured her. "We know people who are more than capable of—"

"I don't *want* to handle it. I don't want anyone to see them," she wailed. "People always believe him."

His embrace tightened.

"I believe you."

"What if he shares them? That stuff never goes away."

If Hope did try to use her degree and license in the future, having an internet search pull up the details of her accusations against her respected cop ex-boyfriend would make it hard. If that same search netted the contents of that envelope? She wanted to crawl into a hole.

"It wouldn't be like that," Devon promised.

"Are you sure? Because it was pretty clear that it was going to go down that way, when I talked to the police before, and I didn't even know those pictures existed back then."

Every part of Devon went hard as stone.

"You didn't know he took them."

Hope sobbed harder.

"I'm going to kill him," he said.

***

Hope doubted that Devon ever crashed so early, but she was running on fumes. Between the little sleep she'd gotten the night before and the emotional rollercoaster of her day, getting horizontal was a necessity. They lay in his bed, as Devon played with her hair.

"I really am sorry," she said into the darkness. He sighed heavily, doing nothing to ease her guilt.

"You were scared. You're impatient, and greedy, and gorgeous..." He pressed kisses down her neck, between words. "And you bite when you're scared." He nipped her shoulder, gently. The bruise he'd left there in the shower whispered hello, and Hope's pussy pulsed in response. "But I'm here for all of it," he said. She snuggled closer.

"I wanted to rip that envelope open when you looked at it like you did," Devon admitted.

"I know, and I couldn't have stopped you," Hope said. So, she had skipped straight to anger. Triggered by her own vulnerability. Trained on him like a weapon. Hope would never forget the look on his face when she'd asked him if she needed a safeword to leave.

"I know," Devon said. He got quiet for a time. "I won't take something from you that you aren't willing to give. That's a hard line for me. I need you to understand that."

"Devon—"

"But I can't stand this," he went on. "I need it to change." The same emotion that strangled his words twisted her heart. "Do it alone or let me help. Or I can stand beside you and keep my mouth shut. I *can* keep my mouth shut if you need me to— If it means—"

"I don't doubt that for a second." She fibbed a little. Hope couldn't imagine Devon keeping silent if he had been there the last time she'd tried to file something against Aaron. "I appreciate the offer, but—"

"No." He shook his head beside her. "Take Chloe with you if you want. Get your brother. I need you safe, and that's not happening while Aaron is throwing fits outside your apartment door. I know you tried before, but—"

"Let me think about it," she said, hoping it would satisfy him long enough for Aaron to lose interest.

As if he knew she was full of shit, Devon pressed a rough kiss to her temple, his body tense as steel. "Get some sleep," he ordered. "It's been a hard day."

HOPE

At work the next morning, Hope replayed the last few days on repeat, as Silver repetitively rammed his head and body into her lower legs in an effort to nudge her into a better mood. Like Apollo the day before, his attempts failed.

The only thing she'd handled well—or managed to fix before it was too late, rather— was not leaving Devon's. Truthfully, Hope found Aaron's behavior unnerving, and as shortsighted as it might be when she was out of sorts, she found herself wanting to be near Devon more and more. *Craving* might be a better word, and that unnerved her too. The possibility that she was trading one problem for another flitted at the edge of her consciousness—drowned out when tattooed arms slipped around her, harder to ignore when left to her own devices.

"Yes, you're a very good boy who deserves all the scratches and head-pats," she said to the cat, in the same voice she used on Apollo. Silver meowed a response, while Sassafras sat on the counter, one leg extended obscenely over her head. Cats...

The bells on the door chimed, and a massive box with legs shuffled in. Hope bolted around the desk and hooked her fingers under the edge, looking across the top of the box into Margo's satisfied face.

"Ha!" the older woman exclaimed. "I knew I could get it in here."

"What in the world…" Hope strained under the shared weight, wondering how Margo had managed to lift it at all. "This thing weighs a ton."

"Went to a gem show this weekend." Margo grunted. "Big ass box of rocks. I knew I couldn't manage the step at the backdoor, so…*ugh*…" She heaved. "I parked up front. Let's put it behind the counter and see what we've got." They wove their way through the store and settled the box behind the checkout. "Couldn't wait to get these babies out on display. So, how was your weekend?" she asked, straightening up and rubbing her lower back. The action smooshed her shirt against her body and reminded Hope how deceptively small Everyone's Heathen Grandma was under her favored flowy attire.

Hope answered with an ambiguous noise and hopped up to grab the label gun and a roll of price stickers. "You want me to put these with the others?" she asked.

"Yeah… I'll sort by price, then you can label and make the display look pretty."

"Sounds good," Hope said.

They worked quietly for nearly an hour when the bells chimed again, and Hope looked up to see Francis coming in. Sassafras appeared out of nowhere, weaving between his feet. Francis scowled at her. They really were perfect for each other.

"Afternoon, Francis," Margo said.

"This cold has my knee acting up something awful," he groused back, as he hung his coat and hat on a rack of windchimes by the door.

Margo looked to Hope and rolled her eyes. "You go on to lunch, and I'll finish up the last of this. Should pick up in a bit," she said.

It wouldn't. Evenings and weekends were bread and butter for Silver Sassafras, and those were also the hours that Hope didn't work. Nevertheless, she was hungry, and having spent the night with Devon, she hadn't packed a lunch. She would need to venture out for nourishment. Hunter-gatherer and all that jazz.

Opting to duck out the back door to shorten the walk to her car, Hope grabbed her purse and stepped into the December chill. After a quick trip through a drive-thru, she headed for the relative comfort of Silver Sassafras's tiny break area. The entire ordeal took less than thirty-minutes, including eating and popping in the restroom to pee. Margo's tone slowed her on her way back to the front.

"Well, she isn't here," Hope heard the older woman say.

"Pretty sure someone's in the back, unless you've got a ghost stomping around and flushing toilets back there."

Fucking Aaron.

Hope stood for a moment, torn between *run out the back and drive away* and *This is my job, asshole.* Eventually, a third option, *go out there and salvage this situation,* presented itself, and because she was an adult, she chose option three. They were in a store with two witnesses. More if there were customers. She could do this.

Walking into the front room with her chin high and her heart pounding, Hope scanned the scene. More street clothes—jeans, boots, unzipped leather jacket. His casual look was barely less *cop* than his uniform. Aaron had another envelope in his hand, identical to the one he'd thrown at her apartment door. Hope's blood chilled, at the sight of it.

"Ah, see... There's our girl." He smirked.

"Do you need something?" Hope said, ignoring the creepy-crawly sensation turning her skin to spiders. Irritation flashed in his eyes because he'd wanted her visibly shaken. While Hope took pride in his disappointment, she also felt a sense of foreboding. He'd try harder until he got what he wanted; that's who Aaron *was*.

"Yeah... Actually, I was looking through some pictures from back when we dated," he said. "I came across some stuff that I knew you'd want to remember." He smiled then, warm and inviting—and *malicious*. Hope swallowed hard, her cheeks heating. "I tried to drop them off yesterday, but you didn't answer the door." Hope glanced from his face to the oversized envelope in his hand, her tongue sticky in her mouth. "So, I thought, *hey, I should drop by today...just to make sure she got it*. I don't mind leaving it for you, but it's hard to know if you really got it," he stressed, his tone implying that the *it* in question wasn't in the envelope at all. "You're so hard to find these days. This is the third place I've tried."

Hope squared her shoulders and held out her hand. Coating her tongue in enough sarcasm to respond, she said, "Well, you found me. Excellent police work." Aaron pinned her with cold blue eyes until the defiance drained out of her. He held an envelope full of *her*. Hope relented, dropping her gaze.

"Right." He chuckled. "So, here you go." He did a slight tug then release, as if he might not let go when she grabbed what he offered. Hope wanted to fade away.

"You've delivered your package, Officer Marden," Margo said in a clipped voice. "You can leave."

"Now, Margo," Francis cut in, "don't you be disrespectful—"

"Francis, you can go too," Margo said.

"Excuse me?" The old man's face reddened. "I just got—"

"YOU CAN GO TOO," Margo repeated, as if the only misunderstanding possible here was the kind remedied by an increase in volume. "Both of you, out of my shop. You've no more business here today." When neither man moved, she growled, "*Now!*"

Hope had never seen the woman look so formidable. Feathery wisps of white hair stuck out of her bun, and she vibrated with a wild energy that increased the longer they ignored her command to *GTFO*. It was like watching a mother bear threaten to disembowel the guy looking at her babies, and Hope couldn't remember a time that she'd been the cub standing behind a woman like that.

Aaron continued staring at Hope, amusement tugging at the corners of his mouth. "No more business *today*," he agreed, inclining his head and turning on his heel. "I'll see you soon, babe."

Francis grabbed his coat and grumbled along after him. "That man is a po-lice officer," he protested on his way out the door.

"That doesn't earn him the right to be an asshole in my store," Margo called. Clearly balls had nothing on aged ovaries.

As the door swung shut, Hope realized that she'd become a statue of a woman clutching an envelope to her chest. A whole tumultuous storm swirled through her, but the shell remained rigid. The moment she cracked, everything might spill out.

Margo spun to face her, her usually joyful face grave.

"I'm so sorry," Hope began. "I'll tell him—"

"You can't tell him anything, child. He won't listen to you."

Hope looked at the floor.

"What's that then?" Margo asked.

Hope chewed her lip. "It's like he said. Some pictures from when we dated," she answered. "He left the same thing at my apartment yesterday."

"Does your bartender know about all that?" Margo asked, jutting her chin toward the envelope. Hope nodded. "Do the police?" Hope sighed; Margo continued. "You know what I'm going to say, right? Probably the same thing everyone else is telling you."

Hope blinked, frustrated at her stinging eyes. "I just want him to stop. I don't want to involve anyone. I thought he'd stop again."

"He isn't going to stop until he feels like it, or until someone makes him. He has such a terrible aura," Margo said.

For once, Hope didn't roll her eyes or argue. "I know," she said, the threatened tears slipping down her cheeks. She'd had enough of bawling in front of people. "You told him to leave, and he went, though," she said.

"But that's here at the store. There's nothing keeping him from coming to your apartment again. Look, what if you took a few days off? Go get this sorted out," Margo said, as if someone had given Hope's friend, boyfriend, and boss the same script.

"I need to work," Hope said.

"Sweetheart, if it's about the money, I'll pay you. But you can't ignore this. He's stalking you, harassing you. At home and at work. This is serious."

"Thanks, but I don't need you to pay me when I'm not here." A week without her meager wages didn't matter in the scheme of things. Hope needed a different job or something supplemental soon, whether she lost a week of pay or not. The real crux was the interruption—the *allowing* of Aaron to alter her life again. "I love my shifts. I don't want to leave you short-staffed," she said.

Margo gestured to the empty store. "I'll manage. What I can't have is someone terrorizing or hurting you."

"He'll calm down. He always does."

Margo's face pinked, Hope's first indication that her boss's patience with her had reached its limit. "Get out of my shop," Margo said.

"Margo, I—"

"I said, get out of my shop and don't come back until you've taken steps to protect yourself."

Margo had that angry mother bear vibe about her again. No longer *I will eat you alive*, but instead *You will climb this mountain on your own, or with me nipping at your heels the whole damn way.* She wasn't judging Hope. She was trying to protect her. On impulse, Hope reached out and wrapped the woman in a tight embrace. Margo squeezed her back like a tiny, bony vice.

"Now, go on," Margo said, stepping away. "Get out of here. And call me. Let me know what's going on."

HOPE

By the time Hope arrived at Devon's, the winter evening had nearly tucked Asheville into darkness. Hope killed the engine and sat in her car, organizing everything in her brain before going inside.

She had driven straight from Silver Sassafras to Redact and Recover, where she'd run into Monique in the lobby. Hope had barely finished asking if Sydney Malone was in the building when the attorney clicked out of a side hallway in a tailored pantsuit and stilettos, her blond ponytail swaying from side to side like the pendulum of a clock. She took one look at Hope, clutching her pair of matching envelopes, and crooked a finger for her to follow.

Sydney was exactly what Hope expected—magnified. Direct, kind, smart as a tack. *Aggressive.* She only pushed as far as Hope would let her and took care that little of that pushing targeted Hope. Feeling bullied already, Hope appreciated the approach. Her biggest fear could still come to pass, but it wasn't a given like the cop in Charlotte had led her to believe.

It would only be public if Aaron didn't respond appropriately to the steps she and Sydney took today. A shot across the bow and a prayer for him to change course. If Aaron refused, Sydney would sink him—or maybe eat him. Castrate him? Regardless of how she decided to end him, the woman would win. At least, Hope kept telling herself that, like a security blanket for her frazzled mind. She refused to consider what would happen if Aaron successfully rebuffed Sydney's efforts.

Speaking of security blankets, with the car getting cold, she thought fondly of her favorite real-life comfort item in the house. Hope glanced at the envelope on the seat. Its twin sat in a locked filing cabinet in Sydney's office with assurances that no one would see the contents. Hope weighed again whether she should take the thing inside with her and hand it to him. They would probably be tame, compared to the things Devon had seen— things he'd *done*. But Aaron took those pictures without her permission, and sharing them felt like the very definition of vulnerability.

Still, Hope had a persistent thought that if Devon saw them, he might understand something she couldn't articulate. Or perhaps he could help her make sense of it for herself. Devon didn't seem any closer to initiating her into the darker part of his world. It crossed his mind frequently, though. Hope saw it in the way he'd snap out of his own, dominant headspace with the kind of vicious efficiency that left her wondering what Demon would get up to if Devon let go of the leash for a few minutes. The thought made her skin prickle, arousing her curiosity enough to distract her from the shit show of her day. That alone was miraculous.

The front door opened, and Devon's silhouette came into view. Hope shoved the envelope under the seat and got out. Maybe she'd run back out for the pictures; maybe she wouldn't. At least she wouldn't worry he might open them while she slept tonight.

As she climbed the steps of his small porch, Devon's face went from shadowed nothingness to visible and bleak. He was all hard lines, as he pulled her into his arms. He smelled like always. Cedar and sandalwood. Currently, with a hint of Cleary's thrown into the mix. It was like breathing in exactly where she wanted to be, and Hope knew the delay in getting that hit of him was all on her.

Devon had texted her through the day, but she'd chosen superficial responses. She could have told him, of course. Explained what happened at work and what she planned to do. And he'd have dropped everything and anything to sit beside her, even though they hadn't been together long. But Hope needed to meet with Sydney alone; she needed to prove to herself that she could.

"I was starting to worry," Devon said over her shoulder, squeezing her close like he needed the reassurance of her pressed against him.

Hope looked up at him. "I have things to tell you," she said.

"I have something to tell you too, or give you," he corrected. He sounded as tired as she felt.

"You go first. Mine's heavy."

Devon frowned. "Mine isn't great either. Not the kind of present I'd ever give you." He pressed his mouth to hers. "Sit. I'll pour wine, and then we'll talk."

Hope gave Apollo his pets before Devon sent him to his bed with the one-eared Bear. Once Hope was settled with a glass of wine, he pulled a yellow envelope from the top shelf of the coat closet and brought it to her. Her stomach sank, as she put down her glass to reach for it.

"He gave it to Nix," Devon said. "I was in the office." The set of his jaw told her he wasn't happy about that fact.

"Did she open it?" Hope asked with a cringe. *Did you?* she wondered.

Devon shook his head. "No one looked in there." He stared at her intensely for a beat, and in his hazel eyes, Hope found her footing. "He asked Nix if you were around. When she said no, he told her to have me give that to you." He gestured to the envelope in her hands. "I thought about calling you or telling you in a text, but I didn't know if that was a good idea. You were at work and...uh..."

"You didn't want me sobbing at work."

"Right."

"Aaron knows I work during the week," she said, shaking her head. "He took them to Cleary's because he wanted you to see them."

"It was addressed to you."

Devon's brow creased as he said it. Hope sighed. How could so much naivety come out of someone so far from innocent?

"He would have opened it in a heartbeat," she explained. "He assumed you would too. I'm surprised he didn't ask Nix to get you so he could watch."

Devon shrugged, even though he looked tense enough to chew through steel. "Nix said he wasn't wearing a uniform, so maybe he felt a little less untouchable. My house. My crew. We don't have bouncers that early, but I'd love to throw him out," he said.

"He came to Silver Sassafras in street clothes too," Hope said.

Rage poured out of Devon.

"Sorry..." She glanced up into the storm. "Like I said, lots to tell. I'm... I'm glad you two didn't run into each other. I don't think I could handle that on top of today." She clutched the envelope to her chest. "Thank you for not opening this," she said softly.

"They're not mine—and they aren't his to leave all over town." Devon seethed, as he sat beside her. "So, he came to the store," he prompted.

"Yeah."

"Did he leave pictures?"

Hope swallowed, wet her lips. "He, uh, gave them to me. He said it was his third attempt. If I'd thought about it, I would've wondered where stop number two had been, but I was so upset that it didn't really register. Not until you pulled these out of the closet."

"I should have called you." Anger rolled off him in waves, but it didn't unsettle her like it always had with Aaron. Devon's anger felt safe. Controlled.

"You couldn't know. He was there when I got back from lunch. I clocked out after he left." His head pivoted toward her, the math not adding up because of the missing hours. "I went to R&R," she said, glancing over at him.

"Why?"

Hope shifted in her seat. "To talk to Sydney." Visible relief washed over Devon's features, and Hope realized how badly she had needed to see that expression on his worried face. "I don't want to hash out the details because I'm so tired of it all. But Sydney's on it, working her lawyer magic." Hope dropped the envelope in her lap and wiggled her fingers in the air before grabbing it again. "As long as Aaron backs off, everything will calm down. I know you probably think I need a restraining order or something, but my gut says that might do more harm than good, and Sydney thinks I make a good point. I don't want to agitate him; I just want him to leave me alone. But I'm doing something."

"What happens if he doesn't back off?" Devon asked. "It's been a year, and he's still bothering you. Sydney's great, but how far are you willing to let her take it?"

Hope took a deep breath, meeting his stare. "As far as he makes me."

Devon brushed fingertips down her cheek, then scooped his hand around the back of her neck. When he pulled her mouth to his, the kiss was ownership and reward. Thorough, and deep. A physical *good girl* that went straight to her head, heart, and core, as his grip tightened. He backed away, leaving Hope breathlessly wishing he hadn't stopped.

"I'm glad you talked to her," he said, clearing his throat and focusing on her glass of wine on the table. "Sydney can sort this; I know she can. And you are so smart and so brave for going to see her."

"I don't feel particularly brave right now," Hope admitted. She bit her lip, her palms clammy against the envelope in her grip. The room warmed. "There's, um, something else."

Devon arched a brow and waited. She could see his unease. So, like ripping off a bandage, Hope swallowed hard and shoved the envelope at him.

Devon stared at her, unmoving.

"Take it," she said, pushing it into his hands.

"Hope..." His expression wavered between repulsion and confusion.

"Look, there's a possibility that other people will see these. People that I don't want to see me like that. But you—" She swallowed again. "Maybe it would help you understand some things. Maybe...maybe it would help me work through some things."

Everything she said sounded like a question because she wasn't entirely sure of her motivation. She knew what she needed right now, though. Hope needed to trust him—not in theory, but in that rubber-meets-the-road, money-on-the-table, trust-fall kind of way. If she were wrong, it would hurt like hell, and that made it real.

"Take some time to think about this," Devon said. "Yesterday, you almost stormed out of here because I picked up an envelope like that."

"I've been thinking about it all day, actually."

"I'm not opening this," he said, handing it back.

"Fine." Hope felt the smooth paper under her fingers, the weight of the images inside. Twenty-some-odd sheets of paper shouldn't be so heavy. "If you won't, I will."

"Hope... Don't..."

She got her nails under the metal brad, its sharp edges biting into her skin. Devon made a frustrated sound in his throat then shut up. The pictures slid free with a *swish*, as if they had no idea that they weren't supposed to be seen. Hope recognized the image on top from the other two sets—her, in some bastardization of balasana, her wrists handcuffed to her ankles, one cheek against the floor. She looked to Devon, found him staring at the dog in the corner, all but vibrating with everything he held in.

"Devon," she said. His head snapped around, but he studiously looked no lower than her eyes.

"I can't do this, okay? I can't look at those," he said, shaking his head.

"They're just *me*," she said in confusion. Truly, the content wasn't the issue. It was that Aaron hadn't asked, that she hadn't known, that he'd crafted them into a weapon.

Devon looked like he might get up and walk out of his own house. If this was a mistake, it was going to be a doozy, and Hope felt the weight of that as she second-guessed her decision. She'd flipped through the other two stacks, but she gave the new set a quick shuffle through too. She needed to be sure. Devon kept his gaze far above her hands, as she did. As expected, there wasn't a single image that wasn't focused on her. Aaron wasn't in them at all. Maybe it was because he took them stealthily, or perhaps it was simply that he didn't want his own images floating around out in the world.

"That's the problem" Devon said, as she finished thumbing through them. "It's *you*, in pictures you didn't even know existed, and situations that you have hang-ups about. And he's passing them around."

"But—"

"I'm going to guess a lot of those pictures also show situations that I *dream* of putting you in," Devon said, cutting her off. "And how fucked up is that? That your triggers are my goddamn fantasies. Probably the *tame* ones," he scoffed.

"Devon, please just—"

"Don't *please* me," he pleaded. He ran his hands through his hair, shook his head again. "I'm trying to *not* be awful here, okay? I can't—"

Hope slapped the stack onto the coffee table in front of him harder than she'd intended, rattling her glass of wine. Devon's eyes instinctively tracked her movement. Only a split-second slip, and then he was staring at her again, agitated and flushed. Mouth set in a hard line.

And... then he glanced back to the table. Straight back to Hope. She watched his jaw twitch, his nostrils flare as he fought his nature.

"Fucking hell," he bit out, as he reluctantly looked to the stack of pictures. The room became a vacuum—quiet and empty save for the two of them and the images on the table. "God, Hope..."

he breathed, resting a finger tentatively on the bottom corner of the top picture.

Hope studied his profile, as Devon leaned forward, lips parting, breath coming slow and deep as his agitation cooled to fascination...*calculation*. He glanced at her, fingering the edge of the picture in silent request because the part of himself that he didn't want her to see couldn't resist the temptation. Hope reached out and brushed her hand against his, as she pulled the top sheet from the pile. She put it on the floor between them.

"I needed to show you these," she said.

Devon looked at her with uncertainty. "Okay, but—"

"For me," she said firmly, "You aren't taking anything from me. *I* needed to show you these."

He nodded, looking back to the table. Devon's brow knitted; his head canted ever so slightly. This one showed her with her hair down. It had been in a messy bun in the first, but the positioning here was much the same. He looked to Hope, back to the pictures, and hesitantly reached out and flipped past another. Then another. And again...

"These are from different scenes—nights." He corrected himself, with a shake of his head.

"Um, yeah. Looks like." Hope twisted the hem of her shirt in her hands, chewing her lower lip.

"You, darling," Devon said, as something stirred in him, "are exquisite as always, but..." He discarded another picture; this one containing three sets of handcuffs and Hope essentially hogtied.

"But what?" she asked, fidgeting more.

"You aren't satisfied." His voice took on that husky, hungry tone that turned her core into the hollow ache of desire. The tingle at the back of her skull made a mad dash for her entire body.

Devon reached forward, grabbed a random image, and began pointing out details like a car dealer rattling off make and model. "This one... Your makeup is ruined. Your hair is a mess. This is after."

"Well, yeah," she said uncomfortably. They were probably all *after.* Aaron left her cuffed while he cleaned up and found his clothes. It would've been his best opportunity to take the pictures.

"But you aren't done," Devon said simply, putting the picture back. He began spreading the remaining pages out on the table, not in neat, orderly lines, but a disorganized, ever-moving puddle of images. "There isn't a single picture here where you're spent," he said, mostly to himself as he searched. "Some of these you haven't even—"

"How can you—" Hope cut in, but Devon cut right back.

"I pay attention," he said, without looking away from the table in front of him. "You have that little V between your eyebrows in this one," he said, motioning between his own eyes. "Same one you have right now, while you're wound tight enough to snap. And here." He pointed again. "You're stiff as a board. All tension... You aren't finished in any of these, not really." He slid a flat hand toward himself, uncovering the images beneath. Several pages fluttered to the floor. "You aren't even close. Big on denial, are you, darling?" Hope felt her face contort with confusion. Devon huffed out a breath that could have been a laugh and tried again. "Do you have a kink about not being satisfied that I'm unaware of?"

"Um..."

"No, you don't," he answered for her. "It's seductive as fuck to play around with. You'll beg before I even get started. But when it's done, you *need* to be satisfied. Challenging as it is sometimes, you insatiable, greedy, impatient little—" Devon stopped the purring list of name-calling and blinked at her in abject horror. "Sorry," he said, pushing to his feet.

"No!" Hope reached up and caught his hand, his momentum pulling her upright. "Wait... I need you to be *you* tonight, okay? I need... I need..."

Tears threatened to run down her cheeks. Hope had to blink very softly, or she'd be officially crying, and that was...*weird*. This whole day was so damn weird. She needed an off switch, and she wanted it to be him.

"I need you to make my head shut up." Her lip trembled, but she kept talking, her gaze shifting down his body toward the floor as she went. "About Aaron, and my career, and my family...all of it. And maybe most of all," she went on hesitantly, "about all the reasons that I shouldn't want the things I want from you. Things I *need* from you. Devon, I need you," she said softly, glancing up at him only long enough to see that he had stopped breathing.

DEVON

Devon's heart hammered hard behind his ribcage. At any moment, the bones would snap, and the thudding thing in his chest would come tearing through the soft tissues, dangle outside of his body, and then wrench itself free. At that point, it would either use the remnants of veins and arteries to scale his torso like a bloody spider and strangle him, or it would fall to the floor with a wet *plop*; whereupon Devon would collapse on top of it. At least, the lack of carpeting would make cleanup easy.

Those were the only two possibilities, and one would happen momentarily. Any minute now...

When seconds ticked by and nothing of the sort occurred, Devon was left with a complicated, or if you asked Nix, not so complicated problem. The problem was about 5'5, brunette, and her blue-green eyes were currently trained on the floor, after having asked something of him that was likely incredibly hard for her to ask.

I need you to make my head shut up... Devon, I need you.

He knew exactly what she needed, but for once in his life—

"I can't do that," he said.

Her eyes shot up, watery and full of shame. Devon considered punching himself in the face.

"Shit... Hope—" He reached for her, but she took a step back.

"It's fine," she said, swiping at her eyes. Devon looked on helplessly, dragging a hand through his hair as she pushed past him in her rush to gather up the pictures from the coffee table and floor. "Sorry," she said. "I thought—"

"Hope—" He tried again. This was *boyfriend territory,* and Devon was miles out of his element.

"Really, it was stupid. Fucking stupid..."

The sight of her, embarrassed, upset, wedged between his couch and coffee table, sucker-punched him square in his feelings.

"It's not stupid," he said.

I can't do this, he wanted to scream. *I've gone over six months without doing this, and you shouldn't trust me to do it now.* He said none of that as Hope kept cramming pictures into the envelope, wiping at her face between sheets.

"Stupid. Stupid." Tears fell onto the pages in fat drops as she spoke, low and harsh. Each word slicing at him—prodding at the part of him that could make her stop. "So fucking..."

"Stop it," Devon snapped. "Stop it right now and look at me." When it came out as an order, Hope froze mid-cram. "I'm not running a scene with you. Not tonight." Even as he said it, Devon could hear his conviction wavering. Like with the pictures...

"I said, it's fine." She sniffed and reached for one more sheet of paper. Devon watched yet another image of her—hands cuffed at the small of her back—disappear as she fumbled it in with the rest.

She put those pictures in front of him seeking connection—the kind built on the thin line of trust. The space between *wanting* a breath and *needing* it, between deliciously used and irreparably broken. Her reaching for Devon like that while Aaron actively shredded her sense of security was an extraordinary gift.

Devon shook his head clear. He *couldn't*. It wasn't right. An abusive ex, turned stalker, had access to at least two dozen pictures of her in the most vulnerable positions she'd ever dared let someone put her in, and he was using them to torment her. She might not even be in Devon's house tonight if her apartment felt safe. Her *stable* and *normal* were in tatters.

And that's why she needed it.

Because her day, her week, had been scary. Because she'd spent a year looking over her shoulder, while her family took Aaron's side. The people charged with making her safe convinced her she'd made a mistake in reporting him. The last time... the *only time* she'd flirted with what Devon could drown her in, Aaron rewarded her with betrayal.

And she was a *submissive*. As surely as Devon was a Dom, Hope was a sub, and she needed him.

"Drop it, darling. Now." The order rolled off his tongue in fluent *dominant*, even though he'd never *darlinged* a sub before her. And Hope's reaction? Textbook. She sat the envelope on the coffee table, left the last rogue pictures where they lay. Still as a statue before the sound of his voice faded, like she'd waited her whole life for him to say it.

"I'm going to give you what you need," Devon promised, even as he questioned every choice that brought him to this moment. Red-rimmed, blue-green eyes looked up at him, disbelieving. "You shouldn't have to beg a Dom to top," he said. "The next time you beg, it won't be for that."

He watched her lips part, heard the soft sound of her quick inhale. She had no idea that he was suffocating in his own skin, that she had swallowed every molecule of air in the room with that tiny gasp of hers.

"Thank you, Sir."

Devon held out a hand, pulled her off the floor, and started walking. Her grip tightened as they made it into the hall, whether from fear, anticipation, or both, he couldn't know. Maybe it was more of her search for connection. Well, it was coming. For better or worse, Hope was about to get all the connection she needed, and Devon hoped like hell that it didn't destroy whatever magic tied the bonds between them.

With a twist and a shove, the door swung wide. Muscle memory sent his hand straight to the controls for the lights. Not the one Hope had used—the switch that flooded the room in harsh white—but the other set that Devon had installed himself. A low glow flickered to life from behind the crown molding, turning the space into exactly what it was. A dungeon. He was going to take the girl who couldn't get the sound of handcuffs out of her head, the girl who flinched if he moved wrong, into a dungeon.

It was a terrible idea and the thing he wanted more than anything in the world. This was what insanity felt like, Devon thought. Like knowing it's wrong and right and the worst way and the only way and that he'd murdered this fantasy a million times, only to end up standing in this doorway with her now.

Because she'd all but begged.

Devon leaned against the threshold, bounced the back of his skull against the wood, and tried to ignore the growing heat in his blood at the idea of getting her where he'd always wanted her. This wasn't a thing he could undo after. If there were ever a time for focus, and control, this was it.

Devon would keep Demon leashed tight enough to strangle, as he pushed Hope exactly as far as she needed. He would play with her for a while once he got her there though, he thought wickedly. He wouldn't be able to help himself. Devon could do a lot within the confines of that last inch. He could make her whimper and squeal and— Devon refocused.

"I won't be careless with you," he told her. "I'll always give you a chance to safeword something intense before I start. If I think something might be beyond your limits, I'll discuss it with you first. But if you have any hard limits—things you *absolutely never* want to do—I need to know now. Especially if you think it's something that I might not realize is a limit for you." This part was easy, grounding even. Devon could do this in his sleep.

"I don't really know," she hedged, twisting the hem of her shirt with her free hand. Devon squeezed the hand he held, reminding her that he had her.

"I get that this is uncomfortable," he said, "but if this conversation doesn't happen, I don't take you in this room. That's nonnegotiable. This only works with communication and consent. Anything else is—" He shook his head. "Something I'm not willing to do." She looked everywhere but his face. "And it's okay if you change your mind," Devon assured her. "You don't even have to say that. You can literally say nothing right now, and I'll pull the plug for both of us."

Wanting a scene with her so much it scared him didn't negate the risk. It would be easier if she couldn't get through this part. Devon could take her to his room, the shower, the couch in the living room. Hell, he could fuck her in the hallway floor. Right here in front of the playroom door if— Hope chewed her lip while his brain rattled off all the places he could get her naked, places less complicated than the room she seemed so keen to get into. Who knew that the boundaries chat would be such an effective gatekeeper?

"I...um... wouldn't want any marks on my face," she said.

Devon pushed off the doorframe, straightening before he'd made the conscious decision to move. His brain stopped listing other parts of the house. "Do you like the marks I leave in other places?" he asked, feeling the familiar sensation of his head tilting on his spine, watching her struggle with where to look. "When I'm a little rough with you, darling?"

Her throat bobbed as she nodded. Devon found the nonverbal nature of her response *unacceptable.*

"I can't hear you, Hope," he said, stance shifting wider with the amount of thought he put into things like breathing or blinking.

She glanced up at him, cheeks blushing crimson, and Devon wondered how far he could make that blush go. So far... He wanted to push her *so very far...*

"I do, Sir," she admitted. Devon grinned.

"So, if I were to smack you on the ass with something *thuddy...*" God, getting into this was too easy when she looked at him like that. "And if I did it hard enough to leave marks..." He raised a brow, watched her shiver. His hand itched for the weight of a specific flogger. But six months without a scene reminded Devon that he'd need to watch himself if he picked that thing up. Safer to leave it on the wall tonight. "Tell me another," he said.

Good little submissive that she was, that blush got deeper, but Hope barely hesitated. Devon's jeans became remarkably less *relaxed fit* because of it. "Uh...don't come in the front door if you've already been through the back?" she said. She didn't look at him at all, and Devon had to bite back a laugh. She couldn't say the word *anal.* Fucking adorable.

"Do people switch doors on you often?" he teased, grinning when she mutely opened her mouth and looked at him pitifully.

"No," she eventually managed. "They really only use the, uh, one door." She chewed her lower lip. "It's just that... if someone were going to... you know..."

As much as he enjoyed watching her struggle, Devon chose mercy. He'd have to be an idiot to shame her out of something he'd thoroughly enjoy exploring with her, and for all his faults, Devon was rarely an idiot. Except occasionally. Usually around her.

"For tonight, maybe it's best if I come through the front. We'll check out the back another day, and I'll give you a heads-up." He winked. "Is anything else coming to mind?"

"If I can't see you, I might need to hear you," she stammered. "I don't know if that counts, Sir."

"Oh, it counts," he said, squeezing her hand again. "And no handcuffs," he added. They weren't on the playroom wall anymore, but he didn't want that fear popping into her head mid-scene. "But are you okay with other restraints? Rope? Leather?"

Hope nodded quickly. "Yes, Sir, and maybe... maybe if you could not say anything that's..." More with the fidgeting. "*Mean?*" Devon told the muscle in his jaw to stop twitching. "When you say I'm *impatient*," she went on, "that feels good. But I don't think I'd like it if you said I was stupid or..."

Aaron. Fucking Aaron. Devon was not going to lose his shit right now over goddamn fucking Aaron.

Instead, he leaned in. Grazed his nose behind her ear. Inhaled the heady, aroused, mouthwatering scent of her. "I prefer to tell you true things," he purred, reveling in the way her breath came faster. "So, I might say that you're an insatiable, impatient, little thing. That you're needy and greedy and gorgeous, or that the way you whimper *please* makes my cock twitch. But I'd never call you stupid unless you asked me to lie to you." He pressed a lingering kiss to the side of her throat. "And I'd make you say *please* first."

Devon straightened, satisfied with the way she stared at him wide-eyed and didn't utter a word. "Safewords?" he asked.

Hope blinked.

"Darling?"

"Yellow and red, Sir."

And that was it. He didn't have anything else to go over with her. His heart jumped from a jog to a sprint in his chest because this was really happening. This was *finally* happening.

"I need a few minutes," Devon heard himself say, his mind already jerking open the dresser drawer that held his cargos, stripping his clothes to yank them on. If he hurried, he could begin before reality discovered the mix up. Before it snatched this away. "Go pee then meet me in here. If you don't come back, we can do something else. Watch a movie, go grab dinner, screw in the shower. Anything you want." Promises he made to her... "But if you *do* come in here, I'm not going to stop until I'm satisfied that you're finished, or you safeword." Promises he made to himself... "Understood?"

He thought he said that, anyway. Hard to tell with his brain seven steps ahead, but given that she glanced up at him and said, "Yes, Sir," he couldn't be too far off.

HOPE

Hope stopped at the threshold. Devon stood across the room with his back to her, black cargo pants riding low on his hips and bare feet. He faced a wall of shamelessly displayed restriction, carefully organized pain.

Devon Cleary belonged there.

Hope had no idea how he'd changed and settled into this state of *waiting* so quickly. She'd barely had time to pee and rinse her tear-stained face. The wolf on his back studied her, found her amusing. *Silly little girl so deep in the woods. Didn't they warn you to stay on the path?* She could nearly hear the growl.

Devour me, she whispered to the secret confines of her mind.

As Devon took a breath, the animal in his skin shifted, sending a ripple of understanding across its features.

"Close the door," he said.

Hope did as he ordered, the latch sliding home with a *snick* that didn't unsettle her for a change. Devon slowly turned to face her. She registered relief on his face first, a shot of fear close behind. Then his expression settled into *control.* His eyes skimmed from the top of her head to the socks on her feet, and the butterflies in her stomach danced dizzy circles of anticipation.

"I've been telling myself that this wouldn't happen for so long," he admitted with a short laugh. "And now—" He gestured to her with a hand. Hope looked down at herself. She tugged at the hem of her shirt, suddenly hyper-aware that she didn't look like she belonged in this space at all. "You're such a sweet little thing, and I'm—" Devon sighed as he paced to the middle of the room. He pulled out his phone and turned on some music—a hypnotic instrumental beat, only loud enough to keep her ears from straining for the outside world.

Hope shifted her weight from foot to foot, flexed her toes against the floor. "Do you want me to take off—"

Devon looked up at her, expression unreadable. "Did you know that most questions are statements in disguise?" he said. When she opened her mouth to respond, he went on. "Why don't you show me what *you* think I want." Hope chewed her lip. "What you think would please me."

"I've never—"

"I know." A dangerous smile tugged at the corner of his mouth. "Call it an experiment. Indulge me."

"But...aren't you supposed to tell me what to do?" she asked hesitantly. Hope was pretty sure that was the entire point unless she'd missed some vital piece of information.

Devon cocked a brow. "Did I stutter? Look, I'll even turn my back so you can get ready. Surprise me. You're always surprising me." He walked to the closed door and stood with his nose nearly touching it. Hope stared at the back of his head. "Move, Hope," he snapped. "Now."

Heart tripping in her chest, she clumsily stripped out of her clothes, catching herself on the thing that looked like a short, wide ladder when she lost her balance. *Not smooth.* Her discarded clothes were an eyesore in the regimented room, so she quickly folded them and stacked them against the back wall.

"Tick tock, darling," Devon said.

Hope looked around. She wanted to show him that she belonged here, that she got it even if she wasn't certain what *it* was yet. And then her gaze landed on his wall of gear. There, hanging between what looked like a wooden frat house paddle and a row of crops and canes, something caught her attention. Hope inched closer.

Glancing over to see that Devon still faced the door, she reached out and brushed her fingers through the supple leather. A giddy fear tightened her throat, making it hard to get a breath—but only for a second. This was not a toy. This was *art*.

Slipping the braided loop free from the hook, Hope silently studied every detail, from the elegant wrapping of the leather to the dark as night hue. The solid handle was heavy enough to aid in momentum, and the...*tails*? That seemed like the right word. They were no joke, either. They spilled toward the floor like oil, the weight of them urging her hand to follow. *Physics* said that you could hit a person hard with such a thing, but it wouldn't hurt like a cane. The impact would be spread out, she imagined. Jarring, instead of a searing white-hot stripe. *Thuddy?*

Checking over her shoulder again, Hope locked eyes with the wolf on Devon's back. Her focus then expanded to its tattooed tethers and traced those over his muscular arms. She wondered how much effort Devon would put into a swing. Probably a lot. Probably more than she could handle. She should probably put the weapon... the *flogger* back on the wall. That's what a smart person would do, but she still had it in her hands when she got on her knees.

"Finish up," he said.

Gathering the tails in one hand, and the handle in the other, Hope held the flogger aloft, bowed her head, and closed her eyes.

"I'm ready, Sir."

Every nerve ending in her body called her a liar. Goosebumps erupted across her skin, and her limbs vibrated with tension, but there was no turning back now.

Please let this be right, please let it be right, she thought.

"Hope—"

Her name came off his lips tinged with an emotion other than *happy.* Admonishment, maybe? Censure? She squeezed her eyes tighter, not wanting to see what she could so easily hear.

"I don't know what I'm doing," she whispered.

Devon laughed, short and vicious. "Oh, that's obvious," he said, walking away from her. Something unpleasant twisted in her gut as she listened to him move through the room. He'd said to please him, and he wasn't pleased at all. He was so *displeased* that he was currently stalking around looking for a way to fix her mistakes.

A *thump* and the rustle of stiff fabric in front of her got her chattering again. "I'm trying," she said. "If you could tell me…"

"Eyes open, darling," he ordered.

Her lids fluttered open, and Hope stared into the slick surface of a large, framed mirror—the one that usually leaned against the playroom wall. Devon sat on his haunches, half hidden behind the glass, as her own face stared back at her.

"Do you see?" he asked.

Hope dared a quick glance at him, found him studying her reaction, waiting for her to see the problem. So, she tried, she really did. Hope drank in the details in the mirror. *What Devon saw.* She measured the distance between her knees, the soft part of her lips and limitless pleading in her eyes. She'd suspended every ounce of trust she possessed in her hands, offering it to him.

Jerking away from her reflection, she looked to Devon.

"Naked. On your knees. Offering me *that?*" His eyes flicked to the flogger, then back to her face. "And you think you didn't do it right. So, yeah. Clearly, you have no idea what you're doing to me."

The expression on his face before he pushed to his feet to return the mirror transformed Hope into a limping lamb. A wet, needy, limping—

"I bet that flogger's getting heavy," Devon said, as he sauntered back. "You can hang it up."

This was him offering her an out. It didn't surprise her. He was Devon, after all. The astonishing realization was that she didn't want it. Hope pressed her lips together, ducked her head while peeking up at him. "I got it for you, Sir," she said, unmoving.

Devon's jaw twitched. He stared down at her for a breath, then let out a not-quite-chuckle. "Funny you should say that," he said.

He trailed a fingertip up her forearm, triggering an explosion of sensation before stopping at her wrist. His hand hovered above the flogger's handle before he simply took it. With bated breath, Hope dropped her hands to her lap. She watched his knuckles go white on the grip. Leather creaked in his fist, as Devon swished it from side to side, then gathered the tails. He pulled them through his other hand until they tumbled free. Her butterflies danced disjointed tangos of fear masquerading as fascination—unless Hope had the two mixed up.

Flipping the flogger around, Devon tilted her chin up with the back end of the handle. He looked like a mountain up there, bare to the waist, with black cargo pants. Tattoos crawling up his arms and over his shoulders, restraining the beast on his back. So many metaphors inked into his skin, and Hope suspected she hadn't known him long enough to think of half of them. His head cocked to the side, something wolfish flashed in his eyes, and his chest rose with a breath.

The animal coming out to play.

"You are mine tonight. Understood?"

"Yes, Sir," she breathed, heat building in the place where her sex rested against her heels.

"Who do you belong to?"

"You, Sir," she answered, her body relaxing into the truth of it.

"Say it again." The command rolled off his tongue with all the rapacious desire of a man who intended to feast on the next thing out of her mouth.

"I belong to you, Sir," she promised. "Every inch of me is yours."

Devon looked at her like she'd made a terrible mistake, but one that he thoroughly appreciated. "Side of the bed. Grab the bar up top. Spread your legs."

Hope blinked at his abruptness.

"And don't make me repeat myself."

"Yes, Sir," she answered, ordering her body into action. When she didn't make it off the floor fast enough, Devon pulled her up, marching her to where he wanted her with a hand on the back of her neck.

"This is taking too long, and I am done waiting," he said. "You've had this coming since August, and my patience is *gone*."

Hope tried to follow his meaning but failed. She heard the raw desire in him, though. The all-consuming need, whose twin blossomed in her. Her breath came too quickly. Everything *tingled*. Her whole body was an exposed nerve, that Devon held by the scruff of the neck.

At the bedside, Hope reached up and gripped the bar like he'd ordered. She spread her legs, even though he held something that made her want to press them together. The sticky-sweet taste of submission flooded her system, shorted out her judgment. She didn't care. Judgment was his job, this time.

Devon stepped in close behind her—legs and hips grinding into her backside as he forced her against the side of the bed. The hand with the flogger found her hip, its leather tails trailing down her thigh, tickling, teasing. Reaching around her, Devon slid his other hand between her legs, before dragging it up the middle of her stomach. Hope's own juices marked a path from her groin to her collarbones. Her head went fuzzy. She was going to come apart, explode into infinite pieces. But only if he let her.

"Mmm... Such a wet little kitten," he crooned. "You should have put it back." His whispered words were an amused warning two minutes too late as he wrapped his fingers around her throat. Hope arched, letting her head fall back on his shoulder. "Remember your safewords," Devon said against her ear. "This will sting."

The temperature dropped about thirty thousand degrees when he stepped away from her. The first strike materialized out of the chill.

THWACK!

The impact drowned out the music, knocked her forward until she nearly lost her grip on the bar. Hope's breath surged out of her lungs. Pain didn't register at first, secondary to the sheer force. There was no preparation for sensation so intense. You had to live it to understand.

"I wasn't going to pick this thing up tonight," Devon said from behind her, his timbre eerily calm.

THWACK!

Another blow landed across her ass, tiny fires igniting at the termination of each leather tail. She heard him pace back and forth as he spoke and hoped he burned off some energy doing it.

"I wanted it too much, and when you're involved, that makes it…" He blew out a ragged breath. "Challenging."

THWACK!

Hope bounced on her toes, biting back the wail that clawed its way up from her gut. What made her think she could do this? How many had it been? Three? Three wasn't very many.

"But then, I turned around." *THWACK!* "And you were hold-ing *this* flogger." *THWACK! "This specific flogger."*

THWACK! THWACK! THWACK!

"*Agh!*" Hope cried out, unable to help it. Her rear was as hot as the sun, the rest of her covered in a cold sweat that made her fingers slip on the bar every time he made contact.

Devon stopped swinging and rubbed a hand over her burning flesh. It felt amazing and terrible. Her mind bounced back and forth between the two. Wanting him to keep rubbing. Wanting him to step back and swing. This was so much more intense than she'd imagined. How could she want him to keep doing it?

When he removed his hand and her entire body instinctively braced for the next impact, Hope decided that the rubbing was def-initely better. She didn't know if she could stand there for another lash of that flogger across her ass. She heard the leather-wrapped handle creak in Devon's grip, and then his voice, clear and con-trolled, in her ears.

"I bought it for you, you know."

THWACK!

Hope's teeth clapped together with the force of the impact. The flogger landed with the same wicked accuracy, the same biting connection, and something in her brain snapped in two. Her pain and pleasure held hands. They flirted, and whispered secrets about the very pretty flogger, made of inky-black leather, and how Sir bought it just for her.

"I bought it after you came into *my* bar." *THWACK!* "And drank *way* too much." *THWACK!* "And I couldn't do a fucking thing about it because *you weren't mine.*"

THWACK! THWACK! THWACK!

Hope could hear his temper beneath his control. He might call it *play,* but this was more than a game to Devon.

"So, I watched you on my dancefloor." *THWACK!* "In a sea of assholes who wanted to put their hands on you. *Did* put their hands on you."

THWACK! THWACK! THWACK!

"And I fantasized about bringing you here." *THWACK!* "Ordering you to hold that bar," *THWACK!* "And laying into you with a flogger just like this." *THWACK!* "Not a belt." *THWACK!* "Not a cane." *THWACK!* "A flogger like this because you *might* be able to take it until I got it out of my system."

THWACK! THWACK! THWACK!

"But I didn't own a flogger,' he said, breathless. "I had everything *but* a flogger. So, I bought you one, even though I was never, *ever* going to use it."

Devon threw it on the bed in front of her. *Her flogger.* The one he bought just for her. Then, he was on his knees before her, pulling her hands off the bar and strapping leather restraints on her wrists.

"I don't want to hit your hands," he explained. He reached above their heads and clipped the cuffs to a ring on the bar she'd been holding. Hope tugged against them and knew she wasn't getting out until he took them off. She should probably feel anxious about that... "You've been such a good girl, but you're going to pull your hands off that bar and try to cover your ass, because I'm going to make you," Devon said. Hope's mind tumbled over the nonsensical words. It sounded like a warning, but there was no apology in his gaze—just the same ravenous hunger that threatened to consume her. Plus, he called her a good girl. It couldn't be too bad.

Devon leaned in. "I also need you to remember that *No, Stop,* and crying aren't safewords in this room because I'm going to make you try all of those too." He kissed her cheek and disappeared behind her.

Hope stared up at her bound wrists, as if they were miles away, and possibly not even a part of her body, as a final string of biting lashes rained over her butt and thighs. She didn't say *no,* and she didn't tell him to stop, but only because she didn't see the point. She also wasn't sure why she was wailing and sobbing, but she didn't think it had anything to do with her ass. Not really. Eventually, she accepted that he would never finish, but she didn't mind.

Then Devon's hands were sliding over her—hot as her flesh—and when their skin met, every point of contact exploded in extraordinary sensation. He kissed the back of her neck as he unclipped her restraints from the bedframe. Hope's entire body quivered. Even the things that hurt felt good, and for the life of her, she couldn't figure out why he stopped.

"You have no idea how proud I am," he said in a guttural voice, breath brushing the hollow below her ear.

Proud. He was *proud* of her. *Someone should bottle this and sell it,* she thought as a vicious shivering quaked through her. Devon froze at her back.

"I'm... I'm okay." Hope managed. "You don't have to stop, Sir."

He turned her toward him. Hope studied him as he seemed to study her. A sheen of sweat covered him, and his hair stood on end, Devon having gotten his hands in it at some point. "I don't need your permission to be done, darling," he reminded her. "That's not how this works. I need you for other things now."

"Okay, Sir," she said.

Devon exhaled, sharply, through his nose. "On the bed. Ass up."

Hope scrambled up but found it harder than expected with her wrists bound, and her brain stringing thoughts together in the wrong order. Eventually, she climbed on top of the mattress, and a breath later, Devon hopped up behind her. Leaning over her, he clipped her wrist restraints to an eyebolt on the headboard, then he yanked her up to her knees and pushed her chest into the bed.

"When I say *ass up,* this is what I mean," he said, rubbing his other hand over her rump, replacing it with his mouth, then sinking his teeth brutally until she bucked and squealed. He used the hand on her back to push himself upright again. "I'm going to fuck you now, darling," he said.

And then Devon was unbuttoning, unzipping, his hands brushing against her because he was so close. Hope panted.

"Christ, you're soaked," he said, sliding the head of his cock over her slit. "You were wet before, but one little spanking and it's dripping down your thighs. Surely you didn't like it…"

Hope pushed her hips back to get him inside faster and was rewarded with a sharp smack on the ass. She shrieked and jerked but couldn't go far with her wrists clipped to the headboard and Devon between her legs.

Devon clicked his tongue, the sound crawling up her spine like a promise. "Impatient," he said, circling the tip of his cock around the opening of her pussy. Hope quivered and whimpered, but she held still. "Greedy," he growled. "So. Fucking. Greedy. You know that I'm the one who decides, right? You didn't forget that part, did you? I decide when we're done. When you come. When you get a cock shoved in this aching—"

"Sir… p-please," Hope begged. It was the only thing she had left. She *needed* him, like food and water and air… Like *air*. Hope would have traded all of it, right down to the tiny gasps she managed to pull into her lungs. Anything to sate the wanting. "God, please…"

Devon chuckled behind her. "There it is," he said. Satisfaction molded into syllables, then stitched into words. "That's what I was waiting for. Say that again." He slowly fed his cock into her cunt, setting off an orgasm that felt like a precursor to the next, rather than a satiating release. Her muscles clenched tight around him, but it wasn't enough.

And then he started to move.

Hope leaned back into him, pulling against the restraints until her wrists, elbows and shoulders were all taught. She tilted her head back to keep it from being sandwiched between her arms. "Oh, God... Please... *Ungh*... Sir... Fuck... God... Sir... *Umphh*..."

She didn't choose the string of disconnected words and sounds he pounded out of her. Her mouth had a mind of its own. Much like the rest of her body, which incessantly rocked back against his thrusts with a single focus. *Him*. She needed him. Him inside her. Come on him. Bounce and bounce and bounce until he came in her. Even as her muscles sang, and his vicious grip on her hips slid in the sweat coating her skin. Even as her ass and thighs burned anew from the flogging. Him. *Him...*

Stars danced across Hope's vision, as a hand snaked up around her throat and stole her breath. The other clamped down harder on her hip. Devon slammed into her and held on. His orgasm was an ownership that Hope had no desire to renegotiate. It felt like *full*. It felt like *done*. It felt like *fed* and *quenched* and *breathing* and *His*.

And it didn't stop there. Before she knew what was happening, he flipped her to her back, latching his mouth onto her over-sensitized clit.

"Can't..." Hope stammered; her arms twisted up above her head, her body trying uselessly to wriggle free. "I—"

"Give me another," Devon demanded.

She stared down her breasts and belly at him. Then it was his mouth on her again, sucking and swirling, and his fingers pushing into her, filling her. His eyes were a dozen shades of green and gold looking up at her as she shattered. Tiny, miniscule fragments. Nothing left of her at all.

"That's what I wanted," Devon said, as he rocked back on his knees. "I knew you had one more for me."

Whatever Hope intended to say next came out as a mewling jumble of sound. Devon sat there, staring at her like he'd never seen anything like her before. Which was silly because Devon had seen so many people like this, hadn't he?

He reached above her head and unbuckled the restraints, gently lowering each of her arms to the mattress. Grabbing a towel from the chest of drawers, he carefully wiped down all the dripping parts of her. Hope lacked the energy to feel shame about that; her body lay limp, while he tended to the mess they'd made. Shimmying the comforter out from under her, Devon tugged it over her, then pulled his pants higher on his hips, not bothering to fasten them.

"Give me two minutes," he said, pressing a kiss to her forehead. "Let me deal with this condom and clean up. You're safe, I'm here, and I'm not going anywhere." Hope tried to mumble an agreement, but her mouth declined. Devon smiled softly at her, then ducked into the hall.

It took years for him to slide back into bed. When he did, Hope shifted up against him, needing the anchor of his body pressed against hers. That was the reason for his assertions on the way out of the room, she realized. Devon knew she would start to feel like this. Like she had no right being here. Like some part of her that she couldn't even name would never be warm again. Okay...

he probably didn't know that exactly. Another vicious tremor. Another wave of worry. Devon pulled her closer.

"I'm n...not cold, Sir," she said through chattering teeth. "I don't know—"

"It's normal," he promised, kissing her temple, and finding her hand with his own. He rested them both on his chest, and Hope savored the feel of his heart thudding reliably beneath them. "It'll stop in a bit, but we'll keep you covered up anyway, okay?"

"I'm so tired," she mumbled. Her eyelids weighed five-thousand pounds, and her body was made of sand that shook for no reason.

"I've got you," he said. Those words poured into her ears with the sweetness of honey and the warmth of whiskey, as sleep pulled her under.

DEVON

"**R**ed!"

Her scream vibrated in his ears, before morphing into an unintelligible cry of agony. The moment it faded, she'd scream again, and again, and again, and... And Devon would keep swinging. This couldn't be real. There was no version of reality where he wouldn't stop if she safeworded—no version where *this* could happen. But the proof stood in front of him, beaten and broken, trussed up from the side of the bed.

Devon stared out of a body that he couldn't control, horrified by every shameful sensation that he would adore under other circumstances. The back and arms burned from exertion. Lash after callous lash laid maliciously across her skin, while the sweat of a job well-done cooled on the brow and the erection throbbed.

The hand went to the crotch, rubbing, and Devon thought he'd be sick—except he wasn't.

This isn't me. I would never hurt her like this, he thought.

The body paused, canted its head as if noticing the stowaway in its brain. The mouth stretched into an exaggerated, cheek-stinging grin. *Devon's* mouth. *Devon's* body. His cargo pants and tattoos.

He'd bought the flogger in his hand, for fuck's sake. So, why couldn't he stop?

"Red, red, red, red, red..." She whimpered, sagging against the restraints.

Drip...

Reds, purples, blues, and greens marked every inch of her. The patterns of canes, paddles, whips, and hands easily identified. How long had they been here? Why had he kept her in this room?

Drip...

Devon wanted her down more than he wanted his next breath. Carve an apology out of his chest and hand it to her before it stopped beating, so she could see how much he meant it.

Drip...

I didn't mean to. I'm sorry. I would never... Words too hollow to say aloud, even if Devon could force them past his lips.

Drip...

His blood scorched a fire through his veins. The treacherous thing controlling him wanting her in all the ways it shouldn't. Vile ways. Unforgivable ways.

Drip...

And that annoying fucking dripping... It made about as much sense as the rest of—

"No," he breathed, the first word he'd managed since this nightmare began.

Devon's gaze lowered, mechanically. Blood fell from the falls of the flogger in fat drops, landing in a puddle beside him. *Drip.* It smeared the floor beneath his feet, some like *red* and some like *rust*—his pacing marked in layered footprints. *Drip.*

Jerking his head up, he looked at Hope, his breath coming out in anguished pants. Tears blurred his vision, but not enough to shield him from what he had done. Long gashes, vicious and deep, now crisscrossed the myriad of bruising. Devon would never flay someone open like that. Sometimes he broke skin but this... He couldn't undo this.

"Red, Sir. Red..." she whined weakly.

Devon's ears rang. A welcome wave of nausea rolled through him, threatening to put him on his knees. At least that meant he'd stop. You couldn't beat the shit out of someone while puking.

Except the sensation faded into the background. His body straightened, chin inching up, and a dark chuckle rumbled out of him, making the hairs on the back of his neck stand on end. Leather creaked as his grip tightened, and her blood was sticky under his feet as he left a new set of prints toward the bed.

"Red," she whimpered again. "Devon, please..."

***

Devon surfaced in free-fall, a split second before he hit the floor. He looked around, confused by the dim lighting, the strange orientation of things. In his half-lucid state, the line between dream and reality blurred, but his sense of urgency, his racing heart remained.

Scrambling free from a tangle of black fabric, he catapulted himself to all fours, sliding his hands over the hardwoods, while fighting the urge to retch. Smooth, slick floors, he told himself. *Clean* floors. Collapsing back on his ass, he pulled his knees to his chest and squeezed.

"Not real," he whispered, rocking to-and-fro. "Not real."

The memory of her flayed back flashed in his mind, as solid as the room around him. Devon shuddered, blinking it away. He scrubbed his hands over his sweaty face and through his hair, frowning at the overpowering scent of leather.

Up on the bed, Hope mumbled something unintelligible, then shifted. Devon glanced guiltily at the comforter he'd taken to the ground on his descent. She had chills when she was coming down, and he'd ripped away her blanket during a nightmare.

With trembling hands and ragged breath, he got upright. He wanted to see, to assure himself it had all been a dream. But Hope lay face up, her bare breasts rising and falling gently in the low light. He cocooned her inside the comforter, nudging and adjusting until she made a contented sound and rolled to her stomach. Devon froze, fingertips aching to reach out and expose her fair back. But his hands were sweaty, and they smelled of leather.

He took a step back. The soles of his feet gripped the floor, making it feel tacky. Ice flooded Devon's veins, as he looked down. Clean floors, he reminded himself. He'd already checked.

He headed for the master bathroom at a steady clip, flipping on lights, ignoring his reflection in the mirror. Not waiting for the temperature to adjust, he grabbed a washcloth, stepped into the shower, and started scrubbing.

It was a nightmare.

It would never happen.

Devon scrubbed his hands, his body, the soles of his feet. Everything looked clean, but nothing *felt* clean, so he re-lathered and started again, before rinsing the last suds down the drain and killing the spray. He'd kept her in there too long and it triggered weird dreams. Nothing more to it than that. He knew better than—

"Goddamnit."

HOPE

"**H**ope?"

Devon's voice was low but insistent. In her drowsiness, she wondered why his body didn't vibrate against hers as he said her name, why she couldn't feel the heat of him.

"Hope?" he said again, his urgency cutting through the fog.

She opened her eyes a fraction. Disoriented after having woken up in two new rooms over the course of a few days, it took her several seconds to determine that they were in the playroom. Which meant— A delicious flush of heat crawled across her skin and out to the tips of her fingers and toes. She made a sound embarrassingly similar to a purr. Devon cursed under his breath, yanked back the covers, and scooped her up.

"Sorry, Sir." She yawned, snuggling in. He'd put on pants at some point, leaving her the exceptionally naked one.

"It's fine," he snapped, as he hauled her toward his room.

Hope's mind teetered in and out of coherent thought, as he slogged through his bedroom, into the master bath, and deposited her atop the frigid lid of the toilet. Her tender bum approved of this, making her wonder if she had marks back there. She glanced toward the vanity, considered going to look, but fog transformed the surface of the mirror to a flat, grey nothing. Hope frowned.

"Devon?"

"You're shivering again. I should've wrapped you up," he said, more to himself than to her.

She noted the beads of water that dotted the glass shower door, the warm, humid air.

"Quick rinse then bed. Or snacks then bed? Are you hungry? Fuck, I should have fed you."

Hope watched a drop break free from the edge of his soaking hairline, traveling down his spine as he turned on the shower with quick, efficient movements. Unease took root in her stomach.

"I'm not hungry, Sir."

Devon winced. "Okay then. Hair up, and in you go."

He handed her a hair tie, then shuffled her into the shower, standing outside in a pair of heather-grey joggers Hope had never seen him wear. Devon reached in and began soaping her up, turning her this way and that. Rogue droplets spattered his pants, as he worked.

Hope silently watched him—his focus, his hands, his intense expression. He didn't look her in the eye. He didn't even glance at her face. Occasionally, his teeth sank into his lower lip, and his brow creased, like whatever ran through his head troubled him. But otherwise, Devon remained as unreadable as the fogged mirror.

"Okay," he said, turning off the shower and guiding her out.

He herded her to the sink and handed her a toothbrush, then focused on nothing beyond which parts of her were still wet as he dried her off.

"Is it because of what we did?" she heard herself say, two seconds after rinsing her mouth.

Devon froze in a crouch, then went back to running the towel over her legs—slower, more gently. "Hmm?" he said.

"Something's wrong."

He looked up at her. "Do you need—"

"With you, Sir. Something's wrong with you," Hope said.

Devon pulled in a breath through his nose and ducked his head. He kept working. "You don't have to call me that."

Sorry sat unspoken on the tip of her tongue. If he didn't want her calling him *Sir*, he wouldn't appreciate a worthless apology either.

"Let's get you to bed," he said, without looking up. Then he was hustling her into the bedroom and folding back the covers. Hope settled cross-legged, fiddling with the edge of the sheet. "You want a t-shirt? I'll grab one." He headed for his dresser and pulled open a drawer.

"Are you mad at me?" Hope asked.

Devon closed the drawer.

"Why would you ask that?"

She took in the details of his room. Nightstand lamp glowing. Apollo sound asleep in the corner. The contrast of this space and his playroom felt especially jarring when her bridge between the two would barely look at her. "I don't know. I feel...*weird*, and you're acting weird." She shook her head at the accusation in her voice. "Sorry." *And* there came the worthless apology... Great.

"No," he said, sitting down beside her. "I'm sorry, I... It's not anything you did or didn't do. You're perfect," he breathed, brushing fingertips over her knee, before pulling away.

"You wanted me out of the playroom. You put me in the shower like—" Hope didn't want to pick that one apart. "You won't look at me, won't touch me any more than you have to," she said.

"And you were the bottom in a pretty intense scene—at least for someone who's never done that before—so you think you've done something wrong," Devon said. He looked around, uncomfortably, scrubbing his hands over his face. "I'm an idiot," he said to himself before facing her. "You have no idea how well you did in there. How much I enjoyed doing that with you."

"Then why are you—"

"I don't sleep in there—the playroom," he clarified. "No one has ever slept in there. It's not a place for that."

"Oh." So, she messed up the vibe by using his playroom for something off-limits. That made sense. One look at the gear on the walls and you could tell he took what he did in there seriously. "Sorry," Hope said. "Next time—"

"I wanted you in my bed. Can you understand?" he asked. Hope blinked at him. "I sleep in here, and I play in there, and you... You aren't a thing to be played with." He ducked his head, but his eyes stayed fixed on her. "I didn't expect to feel like this."

"Okay..." Which was *how?* she wondered.

"Every time I do something with you," he said, "I worry it's going to be the thing that's too far. I forget about that, in the heat of it, but I think about it all the time. You're so," she watched him struggle for a way to finish the sentence, then give up. "I don't want to get to the part where you change your mind."

His eyes were dark in the low light, tattoos running up his arms and spilling over his shoulders out of sight, and the tragic look on his face reminded Hope that the parts of this relationship that were old hat for her were scary and new for him. Maybe it was her realization that he was vulnerable to her in ways she took for granted; maybe it was the fact that parts of her brain were still floating above her body; but she opened her mouth, and raw truth came out.

"I don't think I could change my mind," she said. "I didn't pick you; I needed you."

"*Me?*" he said, his tone incredulous.

"You." She watched his eyes dart from side to side, as if she'd again shorted out his capacity for eye contact. "I needed you from the first time you *saw* me." Hope shrugged. "Just took me a while to admit it."

Devon stopped talking, stopped moving, as she crawled into his lap and curled up. Without a word, he reached over and switched off the light. Resting a hand gently on the back of her neck, he hooked his thumb around one side, fingers encircling the other. His warm palm nestled against the back of her skull, cradling the place the tingles began every time his dominant side whispered her name. His other hand stroked from the top of her spine to the small of her back.

When Hope was dozing in and out with the hypnotic rhythm of his movements, Devon shifted her off his lap and stretched out over her. Finding her mouth in the darkness, he kissed her, slow and deep, hands skimming reverently over her body.

"I need..." he whispered, pulling away to hover above her in the void.

"You need what?"

"Just you," he said, with a sigh. "Just you, like this. This is everything I need."

Devon pressed his forehead to hers, and Hope wrapped her arms tightly around him, feeling the tension drain out of him.

"You have all of me, Sir," she whispered.

HOPE

"Can I help?" Hope asked, leaning across the bar, as Devon returned from carrying the last of the plates and glasses to the kitchen. Everyone else was taking it easy, but it wasn't his nature to leave things for later. She'd be lucky if he didn't insist on washing the dishes before they left.

"You can keep me company while I wipe this down." He pulled one of those white towels from hiding.

"I could do…" Hope stilled under the heat of his gaze. "I'll keep you company," she agreed.

"There's my good girl," he said, his husky tone telling her that she probably wasn't going to bed anytime soon. Fine with Hope. Settling down from the excitement would take time, and nothing on earth settled her like Devon when his stance shifted and his grin turned wicked.

His yearly Christmas Eve party shut down the bar, bringing together most of his various circles of friends and acquaintances. The Cleary's staff and his mom, Maria, were there, along with everyone from R&R.

Hope had gotten to know the latter more intimately in recent weeks, having agreed to sit in on Monique's group sessions. The idea was that Hope could run groups if Monique were absent for an extended period, but Hope had gained far more than a few extra bucks from the deal.

The sessions helped her process all that had transpired over the last year. Listening to the participants of Survivor's Circle and Ladies Night helped her feel less damaged. Less alone. Which is why when Monique, Dre, and Sydney approached her about the additional counseling needs at R&R shortly after arriving at Cleary's, Hope had agreed to give it a shot on a trial basis. She had a warm and fuzzy, *stunned* feeling about the whole thing. It would take time to sink in.

After New Years, Hope would begin working Tuesdays and Thursdays at R&R. Redact and Recover needed another person; she needed another source of income and the field hours to solidify her licensure. Margo could easily schedule Hope's Silver Sassafras shifts around the new opportunity. Perhaps her personal experiences would make her a better therapist, instead of an incapable one. Hope would never know unless she tried, and with Aaron leaving her alone, now seemed as good a time as any.

There were spouses, partners, and earlier in the night, a few kids at Devon's party. JJ and Chloe also netted invitations, and they were currently... yup. Sitting *really* close together at one of the high-tops, chatting with Nix.

Food was eaten, drinks imbibed, and there had been a fair amount of dancing. But now, it was getting late. Maria and everyone towing kids had left hours ago. The R&R guests dwindled, with the Cleary's crew also filtering out. The evening had been nothing like the chilly get-together at Hope's mother's earlier in the day, and it didn't make her want to fast-forward to her father's house tomorrow—even if Devon would be able to tag along for that one.

Nothing felt rushed or forced, at Cleary's. It was just...comfortable.

"This was amazing," Hope said, looking around at the lingering happy faces, the haphazardly strung holiday lights.

Devon smiled. "Best Christmas yet."

Weird that he could be right about that, even with all Hope had been through in the past few weeks. Whether Aaron had finally seen the error of his ways, or he feared losing his career, Hope hadn't heard a peep from him since involving Sydney. With his history of fluctuating interest in her, Hope wasn't holding her breath that he was gone for good, but she would take the peace while it lasted.

"Thank you for a lovely evening," Sydney said, as she wobbled up on her signature stilettos, the latest in a string of tipsy goodbyes.

"Need a ride, Syd?" Devon asked.

Sydney put a hand over her heart. "Oh... What a love."

She sounded like someone addressing a seven-year-old who offered to help with heavy machinery. Hope snickered.

"My ride should be here any minute. I planned to have a glass or two, so I left the car at home." She shifted her focus and took both of Hope's hands. "Hope," Sydney said, "I am so glad you're here this year, and I look forward to working with you. And if Aaron fucks up, I look forward to destroying him." Sydney kissed her on the cheek and spun away in a dramatic twirl of sparkle and blond.

"*Glass or two...*" Devon chuckled. "She's had about a bottle of champagne. Oh look, next contestants..." he added as JJ and Chloe walked over together.

"Are you coming home tonight?" Chloe asked.

"She'll be tied up at my place," Devon said, flashing a devilish grin. Hope shot him a hard glare, and blushed when it changed absolutely nothing about his expression.

"Text you tomorrow?" Hope said.

Chloe nodded as JJ slipped a hand around her waist and asked if she was ready. There were hugs and kisses, and one of those hard, manly-men handshake things.

"Come on," Chloe said, tugging JJ's arm. "Walk me home."

Next up was Nix, and she was...

"Don't worry," Mark called from across the way. "Stacy and I are taking her."

"*Pshhh...*" Nix leaned in close.

She smelled like apples and a whole bottle of spiced rum, and Hope was momentarily struck by how pretty she was with those dark eyes and ruby-red glitter falling from her spiked pixie cut like bloody snow.

"Hey look, I need to talk to you about something." Nix's tongue ring made a clicking sound, as she passed it back and forth across her teeth. "You're great, really, and he's different with you," she said earnestly. "But if he doesn't—"

"Nix..." Devon cut in, all warning that made Hope tingle. Being one of the only people on earth immune to that tone of his, Nix plowed onward.

"Hush, while I'm talking," she scolded. "What was I saying? Oh! What I was trying to say is... *Am* trying to say?" She scrunched up her face, apparently trying to pull a *Grammar 101* out of her inebriated brain.

"Nix..." Devon said again.

She leaned closer and looked Hope dead in the eyes. "He's going to end up on this bar if he doesn't get it—"

"Mark!" Devon shouted over his drunken friend. "Can you—"

"OUT OF HIS SYSTEM," Nix finished, loudly, glaring at Devon like she was one interruption away from turning him over her knee. Hope giggled at the mental visual.

"Come on, cupcake," Mark said, hauling her into a fireman's hold. "Time for bed."

"I was *helping*," Nix protested, from her new location atop his shoulder.

"Sure, you were," Mark said, patting her hip.

"I've got her bag and coat," Stacy, Mark's wife, announced. "Devon, come get the door."

"I'm serious!" Nix yelled, kicking and squirming. "If he says he's fine, he's lying! Just wait until after New Year's! You'll see!"

Stacy hauled off and smacked Nix on the rear, earning a glare of her own from the now upside-down *short, dark, and dominant.* Stacy was...unaffected.

"Do not give me that look, little lady," she snapped.

"You know I'm right," Nix spat.

"I know you've had too much to drink to be running that mouth of yours. Shut it before I gag it," Stacy replied.

"You *wouldn't*," Nix said indignantly.

"Ball, spider, or something more creative..." Stacy said, counting them out on her fingers. "I keep an assortment in my purse for *rogue brats*."

Devon hustled to the door and propped it wide. Mark navigated out onto the sidewalk, without whacking Nix on anything, Stacy bringing up the rear. The last Hope heard from them was Mark assuring Nix that his wife wasn't kidding about gagging her.

"Is, uh, that going to be okay?" Hope asked, gesturing after them as Devon flipped the locks.

"Oh, yeah. They'll take her home and tuck her in the guest bed. Return her safe and sound in the morning. Someone does it every year. It's tradition," he said, peering through the wide windows at the front of the bar.

"But I mean..." Without a nicer way to say it, Hope opted for, "Nix is really drunk."

She caught his smile in profile. "That's why I gave her to Mark and Stacy. No offense to JJ, but your brother couldn't handle Nix and Chloe drunk at the same time. No telling what would happen to that boy." He shook his head. "Stacy might gag her if she gets too mouthy. That's not a joke. Safest place for her though...with people who get it. Strange little family, but we take care of each other. I promise that the only thing that's going to happen to Nix is a hangover."

An unnatural quiet fell. Hope had never experienced Cleary's without the hustle and bustle. She looked around in the stillness, took in all the details that Devon loved about the place—the wood, and brass, and glass that gave it life. You overlooked those things when people and noise got in the way.

Hope snuck her hand into the pocket of the coat hanging on the back of her barstool. Pulling out the small package she'd been waiting to give him, she held it beneath the bar. Her nerves prickled as he turned away from the windows.

It was probably a silly gift, and she didn't know if he'd gotten her anything. They'd been dating about a month, which felt like a blink *and* forever. So much had happened around them and between them. What was the gift-giving protocol for that?

"Thank you," he said, so earnestly that it surprised her.

"For what?"

"Giving a shit about the people I care about."

Hope shifted on her stool. "Everyone had a blast," she said, as he made his way back toward her.

Devon smiled. "They're certainly feeling good right now, anyway."

"What in the world was Nix going on about?" Hope asked, as he caught her by a wrist and towed her in his wake. She put the present behind her back. "Pretty specific rambling..."

Devon paused a beat too long. "I haven't a clue."

"Liar," she said to the back of his head.

He smirked over his shoulder. "You get to know me any better, and I'll have no secrets left. Then you'll be bored."

"Mmm... Will you still do the growly, dominant thing?"

He laughed. "You know I will."

"Then I won't get bored. Now, what was Nix saying?"

They navigated the step, and Hope found herself standing on the business side of the expanse of honey-colored wood. The change of perspective when first viewing Cleary's from Devon's domain disoriented her.

"She's just yammering."

"Yammering about you needing to get something out of your system."

"You never drop anything. You're as bad as she is," he said, turning to face her. "Okay... Sometimes when I'm...having a bad day, I drink whiskey...on the bar."

Laughter bubbled out of Hope.

"On your bar? No wonder you never get drunk. This thing is your baby. I used to think you'd cut anyone who scuffed it, or..." Or that he'd lay you out on it, like an all-you-can-eat buffet, she remembered.

"You went quiet," Devon noted, taking her waist and lifting her onto the edge.

"I got you a present," Hope said, pulling the silvery-blue package from behind her back, as a distraction. Her *fuck me* heels dangled in the open air. "It isn't much. It's silly." She handed it to him. "And I didn't expect you to get me anything, I... Well, you'll see."

He smiled up at her, then tore into the shiny paper.

"You bought me bag gloves." He slid one on even though it was still attached to its mate. Strapping it tight, Devon flexed and straightened his fingers.

"I know you use tape, but the sales guy recommended these. He said they would give more protection, and still let you, uh, *feel* the punches. I hate it when you hurt your hands," she added.

"They're perfect."

"If they don't fit or—"

He hooked a hand behind her neck, pulling her in for a kiss.

"Perfect," he repeated. "Thank you." He set the gloves down beside her butt, looking around nervously. "I got you something too," he said, reaching into his back pocket and producing a slender box. Cherry-red velvet. A jewelry box.

"Oh," Hope said, embarrassed. "But I—"

"Got me the perfect gift," Devon said, as he handed her the box. "This wasn't expensive. Promise." The colors from the lights sparkled in his eyes, bringing the hazel to life. "Sorry I didn't wrap it. My solution for that is a bag, and that wouldn't fit in my pocket. I wanted to find a good time to give it to you, and here you are: sitting on my bar in that dress and those shoes, and saying that you'd rather not see me trash my hands, so..." His throat bobbed. "Open it?"

Hope savored the rainbow happening in his irises for another moment, before popping the lid.

"See?" he said, rolling his lower lip between his teeth. "I told you it wasn't expensive."

Hope stared down at the short length of black rope, with silver fastenings at the ends.

"Stacy makes jewelry. It's a hobby, but she's good at it. I told her what I had in mind, and she figured it out for me. I waxed the rope," he said, gesturing. "It should hold up for you. I can do it again if it needs it. I mean, you don't have to wear it if you don't—"

"Is this from that day in your living room?" Hope asked, already knowing the answer. The line they had crossed that day had nothing to do with sex and everything to do with intimacy.

Devon nodded, a quick dip of his head. "Yeah. Yeah, it is. It's weird, isn't it? See, I'm not great at this stuff—"

Hope blinked fast. "Will you help me put it on?" Devon froze for a second, before responding.

"Yeah... Here, let me..."

He caught his lower lip between his teeth, as he reached for the bracelet, fastening it around her wrist. A circular silver clasp connected the bales at each end of the rope. Simple, so very pretty, and different from anything Hope had ever worn.

"It fits," he said, brushing a thumb against the clasp. "I second-guessed the length after she finished."

"This is..." Hope swallowed hard. "Devon, I love this."

"I love you," he said.

Hope's head snapped up. She stared at him, waiting for him to add something like *sitting on my bar* or *dressed like that*.

He didn't.

"I love you, Hope," Devon repeated.

Her whole body buzzed, and her cheeks flushed at the intensity in his expression because he meant it. Her breath came faster. Her heart pounded under her sternum like it wanted out, and Devon? He kept talking.

"I'm in love with you. I've been trying to put a name on it for a while, and that's the only one that fits." He raised his brows and shook his head, as if the entire thing had taken him by surprise. "It's okay if you aren't there, but—"

"I love you, too," she blurted. Hope watched the words go out of him as he stood there with his mouth open, eyes searching her face. "I love a million things about you, but I'm in love with you."

"Uh... Thank you," Devon stammered, blinking incessantly. Her answering giggle got him fully functional again. "Is that not the response you were looking for, darling?" he asked with a sly smile. He shifted on his feet, took a breath. "Maybe something like this would be better?"

Reaching behind himself, he flipped a switch, and the whole of Cleary's went dark except for the multi-colored glow of Christmas lights. Devon stepped between her legs, her dress sliding up her thighs as he did. Hope arched toward him on an exhale, before reality checked in. Devon frequently rendered her a quivering mess of *please,* but currently, only glass and low lighting separated them from the public sidewalk.

"Um...Devon..." Hope went to close her legs but only succeeded in pressing them against her boyfriend's hips—a sensation that almost shorted out her thought process. Almost. "I don't think—"

Devon lowered her back onto the bar.

"They can't see you," he said, in that deliciously deviant voice.

Hope shivered, looking up into strings of twinkling lights. "But what if—"

"I locked it," he said, trailing fingertips up the outsides of her thighs, inching her dress higher. "Christ, this is like unwrapping another present."

Hope let out an *unghh...* and then... "I can't—"

"You aren't," he reasoned. "I am."

For some absurd reason, she thought of that framed health department score on the wall behind the register. "Aren't there rules about—"

Devon chuckled, low and dark. "Are you going to tell on me, darling?"

"Well, no," she squeaked. "But you said—"

"That I would tie you up at home, and I will." He nipped his way up her thigh, as she shuddered.

"Devon," she breathed. "This is—"

"My bar," he said. "And I intend to have you on it." He raised his head and looked at her. "Unless you want me to stop. You do remember how to get me to stop, right, darling?"

His tone, that deep, dominant tone that was whiskey and honey in her brain made everything go a little fuzzy. Hope opened her legs wider and reached for his belt. "Yes, Sir," she whimpered.

Dear Readers,

I cannot adequately express my gratitude for your taking a chance on Hope and Devon—on *me*. The Edge Series is a labor of love—one that I desperately wanted to share with you from the start. I set out to capture the magic of an evolving, romantic, power exchange dynamic, but Hope and Devon's pasts, their traumas, inevitably colored every line of text.

And isn't that how it is for all of us? Our experiences write upon the pages of our lives, but they do not define us. Others judge us based on any number of social constructs; they don't define us either.

I am besotted with the way these characters care about each other. The sex is hot and getting hotter with each installment, but the part that steals my breath over and over is their connection. We all deserve partners who accept us completely. We all deserve the kind of love that means safety.

So, thank you for coming along on this journey. I can only hope that some tiny piece of Hope or Devon burrowed its way into your heart. See you at the Edge of Ruin.

All my love,
Lennan